J

FERTILE
GROUND

Other Books by Rochelle Krich

Where's Mommy Now?
Till Death Do Us Part
Nowhere to Run
Fair Game
Angel of Death
Speak No Evil

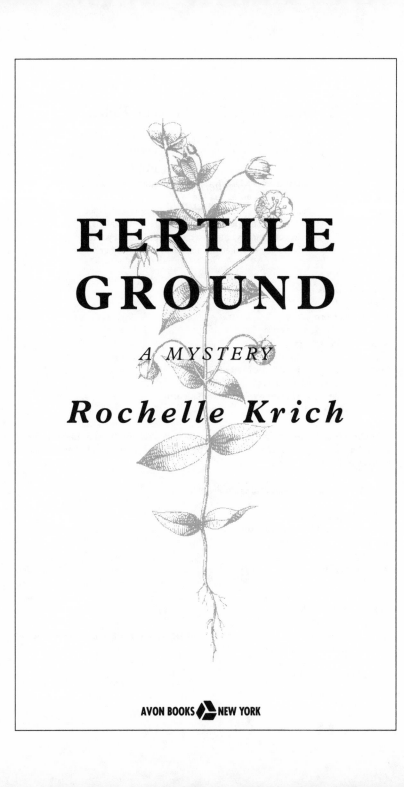

FERTILE GROUND

A MYSTERY

Rochelle Krich

AVON BOOKS ◆ NEW YORK

AVON BOOKS
A division of
The Hearst Corporation
1350 Avenue of the Americas
New York, New York 10019

Copyright © 1998 by Rochelle Majer Krich
Interior design by Kellan Peck
Visit our website at **http://www.AvonBooks.com**
ISBN: 0-380-97378-2

Library of Congress Cataloging in Publication Data:

Krich, Rochelle Majer.
  Fertile ground : a mystery / Rochelle Krich.—1st ed.
    p. cm.
  I. Title.
PS3561.R477F47   1998   97-28608
813'.54—dc21   CIP

First Avon Books Printing: February 1998

AVON TRADEMARK REG. U.S. PAT. OFF. AND IN OTHER COUNTRIES, MARCA REGIS-
TRADA, HECHO EN U.S.A.

Printed in the U.S.A.

FIRST EDITION

QPM   10   9   8   7   6   5   4   3   2   1

For the new young couples:

Marcy and Eli
Michelle and David
Sabrina and Joshua

With much love and with thanks for the joy
you continually bring us.

acknowledgments

My thanks to those who generously shared their knowledge and assisted me in my research for this novel: Margaret Svoboda, Patient Care Coordinator, and Lisa Rice, lab technician, Century City Hospital, Center for Reproductive Medicine; Dr. Edward Liu, OB-GYN; Laura Locander, office nurse; Jennifer Sanders; the staff of Dr. Eric Surrey; and attorney Michael Moroko. Any mistakes in the novel are mine.

I'm indebted to my agent, Sandra Dijkstra, and to my editor, Carrie Feron, for their enthusiasm, support, and "fertile" suggestions.

author's note

While the infertility techniques and procedures and fee schedules described in this novel are real, the fertility clinic, the doctors, administrators, and support staff who work there, as well
as all other characters in the book, are products of my
imagination.

prologue

The young woman lay motionless on the bed, her arms on top of the light blanket. She didn't hear the nurse approach, didn't know she was at her side until she felt her hand being lifted.

"How are you doing, Felicia?"

The nurse's voice sounded far away and muffled, as if it were coming through a tunnel. Felicia's eyes fluttered open, then shut. "Okay. Tired, and a little groggy. How many did they get?" She'd been asleep, not unconscious, during the egg harvesting. She vaguely remembered the doctor speaking to her afterward, but found it difficult now to recall what he'd said.

"I don't know, dear. You'll have to ask the doctor."

She felt the nurse press two fingers on the inside of her arm, just above her wrist. The woman's nails dug lightly into her skin, but not so that they hurt.

Felicia tried again, and this time was able to keep her eyes open. "Is my pulse okay?" she asked when the nurse released her hand.

"It's a little fast, but fine." She wrapped a blood-pressure cuff

around Felicia's upper arm and pumped. "Blood pressure's fine, too," she said a moment later.

The vein where the IV tube was inserted throbbed. "That's good." Her speech sounded slurred and thick to her ears. She mentioned this to the nurse.

"That's the sedation. It should wear off within the hour. Don't worry, dear. We'll keep you in Recovery till it does, then send you to Outpatient. Then you can go home."

"Home" sounded good, but she didn't know how she would move off the bed and get dressed, let alone get into her car and drive all the way to her apartment.

"You've been crying," the nurse said, surprise and worry in her voice. "Are you in pain, dear?"

"Not really. I'm just a little . . . sad," she whispered.

"That's from the sedation, too. There's nothing to be sad about, Felicia. The egg retrieval was successful, and you're fine." She smiled. "Just rest now."

"Hagar, the handmaiden of Abraham, abandoned her child," she whispered.

"What, dear?" The nurse bent down to hear.

"That's what the man in my dream said. 'Hagar, the handmaiden of Abraham, left her child to die alone because she didn't want to hear him cry. But in the end Hagar didn't abandon him. Why are you abandoning your babies?'" Tears welled in the corners of her eyes. "I don't even know who Hagar is, but it's so sad, isn't it?"

"It was just a dream, Felicia."

"I know. But he seemed so real." His voice—quiet, stern—had been so clear. She'd tried to open her eyes to see him, but her eyelids had felt heavy, so impossibly heavy, and when she'd finally opened them, she realized that he'd never been there at all, that she'd been dreaming.

"Try to relax." The nurse patted her arm.

"It isn't the same, is it?" she asked urgently. "Giving away my eggs and giving up babies?"

"Of course it isn't. Try to rest."

"That's what I told him. In my dream, I mean. But he said it was the same. He said . . . he said he was the voice of my babies, that my babies are crying. He said I would be punished." Tears were now streaming down her face.

"You did a very lovely thing." The nurse's voice was soft, reassuring. "You're helping other couples have children, aren't you?"

"Yes."

"Well, then. It was just a dream. Don't let it upset you."

"And everything's fine? The eggs are fine?"

The nurse patted her arm again. *"Everything's fine. You just rest now,"* she repeated.

Felicia nodded. She breathed deeply and let herself drift off into sleep.

chapter one

They'd been making her self-conscious all night, the two men at the corner table—watching her, calling her over to repeat the specials, smiling to catch her attention whenever she passed their way. So Chelsea wasn't surprised when the older of the two, both of whom were wearing almost identical navy wool blazers, said, "You're very pretty," as she refilled his cappuccino. "I'll bet people tell you all the time that you look like Julia Roberts."

It was hardly an original come-on, she thought, thanking him. The funny thing was, she *did* look like Julia Roberts. Dennis said so all the time. She had the same wide, Cupid's-bow mouth and slender, sloping nose; the same long, wavy, warm brown hair Julia used to have. Sun-kissed hair, Dennis called it.

She might have looked like a famous movie star, but she didn't feel like one, not tonight. The veins at the backs of her knees were throbbing in protest at the many hours she'd been standing, and the balls of her feet were aching and tender. As soon as she got home she would take a long bath with water so hot it would steam the mirror and the windows. She still had a few of the jasmine-scented amber bath-gel balls Dennis had given her for her eighteenth birthday, along with a small diamond pendant. She was wearing it now under the white shirt she'd pressed before coming to work.

"I'm James and this is Roy," the man said. "We're producers. Always looking for new talent." He smiled at her, revealing capped front teeth. "What's your name?"

"Chelsea," she said, returning the smile. "Chelsea Wright." Judging from the gray at their temples, she guessed they were in their forties. Good-looking, well groomed, the snowy monogrammed cuffs of their shirts peeking beyond the sleeves of their blazers. Gold, chunky rings with inset diamonds sat like miniature hotels on their pinkies, and they were wearing too much cologne. She didn't know if they *were* producers—L.A. was filled with people who claimed to be in The Business. She *did* know they had to be a little high from the cocktails and wine she'd served them, and hoped they would leave her a generous tip.

"Chelsea Wright. *Chel*sea." The man called James repeated the name slowly, letting the *l* roll off his tongue, as if he were tasting it. He nodded. "I like it." He glanced at his companion, who looked bored but nodded, too. "Matter of fact, Chelsea, we're casting a small feature. If you're interested, you can audition for a minor role."

She planned to teach Special Ed, not act, but she could use the extra cash, especially now that she was transferring from Santa Monica City College to USC. Her parents had paid for the fall quarter ("Dad and I are so proud of you," her mother had said when the acceptance letter arrived, "all your dreams come true"), but Chelsea regarded the money as a loan. The tuition was steep for her parents, who had refinanced their small house in Culver City several years ago to help pay the bills.

There were always so many bills, never enough money. Things would be different now if she hadn't been so strapped for funds. She felt a wave of sadness and forced the thoughts from her mind. "What kind of role?" she asked, shifting her weight to her right hip.

"Exotic dancer." His eyes moved to her chest. "I think you'd be perfect. Don't you, Roy?" he asked, turning to his companion and receiving another nod.

A stripper. She felt a flash of disappointment, then almost laughed, he was so transparent. She thought about the tip and smiled again instead and said, "Thanks, but I don't think so," in a voice that conveyed a hint of regret. She doubted that he was legit, and she wasn't interested in stripping. And if she ever did something like that, her parents would kill her.

She moved away and made a circuit of the room, pausing at each of her tables to make sure everything was fine. Thirty-five minutes later she'd collected the checks and was ready to leave, her black apron folded and stored in her metal locker.

"See you tomorrow night, Ramón," she said to the short, muscular bartender.

"*Vaya con Dios*, baby." He smiled. "How'd you make out?"

"Ninety-eight. Not bad for a Sunday night." The producers had left a twenty and a card—"In case you change your mind, Chelsea," one had scrawled underneath the raised lettering of their company's name, First Star Productions. Maybe he *was* legit, or maybe he'd gone to a Kinko's and had a thousand cards printed for twenty-some dollars.

She told Ramón about the producers, laughed about it.

"See the type of people you meet? How can you leave this gold mine?" Ramón shook his head, drying the inside of a champagne goblet with deft swipes. "Just two more days, huh? Bet you'll be begging for your job back within a week."

"Betcha I won't." She stuck her tongue out at him playfully, then waved good-bye. She would miss Ramón and the others and the easy camaraderie she shared with them, but she was looking forward to her new job, to USC, to everything that was suddenly within easy reach.

Don't expect too much, she warned herself, but she couldn't repress the excitement that surged through her. She found it hard to believe that two weeks ago she'd been despondent, isolated by fears that had occupied her every waking moment. She was glad that she hadn't told Dennis or her parents—there was no undoing what she'd done, so how could they have helped, after all, except worry with her?—and though she had every hope that things would be all right now, and she hated keeping secrets from them, hated not sharing what had happened, she'd promised.

She said good night to Yvonne, the waitress who was balancing the night's receipts, slung her brown canvas backpack over her shoulder, and left the restaurant. It was cold outside and she'd forgotten to bring a sweater or jacket. She hugged her arms across her chest and walked quickly, wishing her car weren't two blocks away. It was dark outside, too, but this was a quiet, residential neighborhood, as safe as any neighborhood in L.A., and she'd walked this route without incident countless times after work.

Approaching her Honda Civic, she groped inside her purse for her keys and touched the edge of the card the producer had given her. She shook her head, smiling, and bent down to insert her key into the car lock. Dennis would laugh when she told him about the Julia Roberts comment. "You're *my* pretty woman," he'd say. Then he'd lean over and kiss her. God, she loved him.

The sharp blow at the back of her neck—swift, sudden— slammed her forehead into the metal of the car. She moaned and slid like a rag doll to the ground, her knees thudding against the concrete. Fear knifed through her.

Dazed, her hands trembling, she jerked her backpack off her shoulder and thrust it away from her. "Take whatever you want!" she whispered, keeping her eyes tightly sealed. She didn't want to see her assailant, didn't want to be able to identify anyone.

She heard a popping sound, felt a stinging sensation in the hollow of her neck, then searing, exploding pain.

---

chapter two

"These are the arm buds. This is the spine." Dr. Lisa Brock-man barely moved the ultrasound transducer over the lower ab-domen of the thirty-eight-year-old woman lying on the table to her right. "And over here, Diane, is your baby's heart." She pointed to the tiny, pulsating embryonic organ at the upper center of the funnel-shaped image on the small gray ultrasound monitor. "Can you see it?"

The woman squinted. "I don't—Oh, my God!" She was beam-ing now. "Oh, my God!" she whispered, turning toward her hus-band and grasping his hand. "Hank, can you see it? *Can* you?" Her voice was breathless, hushed.

He nodded and tightened his grip on his wife's hand; they stared at the slowly shifting peanut-shaped image on the gray screen. He was a large, burly man with a brusque manner, but his eyes were moist, just as they were the day Lisa had informed the anxious couple that after six years of treatments, including one un-successful in vitro fertilization, Diane had conceived.

"Can you tell if it's a boy or a girl?" Hank asked, his fingers still linked with his wife's. "We've decided we want to know."

"Not yet. The internal sex organs are defined at twelve to fourteen weeks, but the genitalia aren't visible until the middle of the fourth month. So we'll *all* be in suspense for some time."

She smiled and waited a moment, giving the couple time to study the monitor. Then she wiped the conductive gel off Diane's bared middle and pulled down her pale mauve examining gown. "After you're dressed, Diane, come into my office."

She pressed a button on the monitor. Seconds later she handed Diane two gray, three-by-four-inch prints of the ultrasound images. "Here you are—your baby's first portrait." Lisa smiled again, but the Clermans had turned their attention to the prints. They didn't even notice when she opened the door to leave.

She wanted to stay—she loved witnessing the awe, the intense joy, knowing she'd helped bring it about. The excitement never staled. But Diane and Hank were entitled to enjoy the moment in private, especially since for them, the complex process of conceiving had been anything *but* private.

Exiting the darkened room, Lisa blinked at the bright hallway light and walked to her office. At her oak desk she adjusted her tortoise banana clip to recapture several strands of shoulder-length, streaked honey-blond hair that were always escaping, and began writing on Diane's chart. When her intercom buzzed, she picked up the receiver and continued writing.

"I know, Selena," she said quickly. "I'm running late." The forty-five-year-old office manager took pride in running the clinic with promptness and efficiency, and Lisa's life with a maternal concern that was endearing and sometimes amusing. Lisa was usually prompt, too, but her nurse, Ava, had just left on a two-week vacation. Lisa was counting the days until her return. "Tell the Hoffmans I'll be there shortly."

"It's not the Hoffmans," Selena whispered. "It's a detective. He wants to talk to Dr. Gordon. I explained he's doing a procedure. So are Dr. Davidson and Dr. Cantrell. So I thought you should talk to him."

Five times over the past two months the billing department had reported large sums of cash missing from the clinic safe. "Is this about the stolen money?" Lisa asked, putting down her pen.

"He wouldn't say. He looks grim, though."

"Okay. Give me five minutes." She wanted to talk with the

Clermans before they left. "And please tell Naomi Hoffman I'll be there as soon as I can."

The Clermans, still euphoric, had many questions (they were entitled, Lisa thought defensively as she noted the minute hand on her desk clock moving inexorably forward), and more than ten minutes elapsed before she asked Selena to usher in the detective, who introduced himself as John Barone.

Barone was over six feet tall and movie-star handsome: burnished, caramel-colored skin; a chiseled nose and strong chin; high cheekbones. He had broad shoulders, a lean physique, and close-cropped, dark brown hair, all of which gave him a military air, Lisa thought. She had stood when he entered her office. Now she shook his large, firm hand across the multicolored folders stacked on her desk.

"How can I help you?" she asked when they were both seated. Selena was right—his eyes were pleasant, but his lips, tented by a trim brown mustache with more than a hint of gray, formed a serious line. She smiled and hoped this wouldn't take long; she hated keeping patients waiting.

"Do you know a Chelsea Wright?" He spoke in a low, melodic voice with an exotic cadence.

So it wasn't about the stolen cash. Lisa considered, then shook her head. "Is she a patient here?" She tried to place the detective's accent. Jamaican?

"I was hoping you could tell me." From an inside pocket of his camel jacket, he removed a three-by-five color photo and handed it to Lisa.

It was a high school graduation picture with a swirly blue background. The chestnut-brown-haired, brown-eyed girl in the photo was pretty and had an engaging, ingenuous smile. She'd positioned her burgundy cap low over her forehead—the way you're supposed to, Lisa thought, remembering with nostalgia her own graduation thirteen years ago from an all-girls' Orthodox Jewish high school in Brooklyn; she and her classmates had set their hunter-green caps at the backs of their heads and secured them with tens of bobby pins, so as not to disturb their teased, lacquered, ladder-high bangs.

She shook her head again and was about to return the photo to the detective, who was watching her intently. Something about the girl's heart-shaped face caught her eye. "I may have seen her in the waiting room a few weeks ago. The young woman I saw looked older, though."

Barone nodded. "This photo was taken a year ago, so she may have looked different. Did you speak with her?" He leaned closer.

She heard the heightened interest in his voice, saw disappointment in his deep brown eyes when she said, "No." She concentrated, picturing the young woman in the waiting room. "I noticed her because she looked about twenty—that's younger than most of our patients. And she was fidgety, pacing back and forth. Then again, many of the women who come here are tense. Is Miss Wright in trouble?" she asked, wondering how much longer the detective would stay and whether she should have someone else see Naomi Hoffman, who was eight months pregnant with twins.

"She was murdered two days ago."

Lisa flinched. "My God!" she whispered. She glanced at the photo again—the girl was so young!—then at the detective, who was slouching in his chair, as if he'd been deflated by the news he'd imparted. The small, square room, warmed by the afternoon May sunlight streaming through the partially opened gray miniblinds, was heavy with silence. She gazed at the swirling dust motes caught by the light's diagonal rays and wondered what she could possibly say.

"The clinic's name was written in Miss Wright's daily planner," Barone said. "Next to it was 'Dr. G.' Would that be Dr. Matthew Gordon? I understand he's the head director of the clinic and one of the founders."

And my fiancé, Lisa added silently. "It *could* be Dr. Gordon." Suddenly she was wary, though she wasn't sure why.

"Any other doctors here whose last names start with G? Or first names?"

Wondering whether he used the same pleasant, unhurried tone in his interrogations to catch suspects off guard, she did a mental check of the clinic staff, then said, "No," and picked up the receiver, surprised to note that her hand was shaking. "I'll see if Dr. Gordon's available now."

"Thank you." He rose from his chair and crossed the room to the wall where her framed diplomas hung.

Lisa punched Matthew's extension and spoke to his nurse. "Yes, Grace, it's urgent," she said, trying not to sound impatient. While she waited for Matthew to come on the line, she watched the detective, who had moved from the diplomas and was studying a multicolored fertility treatment chart on an adjacent wall. He spent only a second in front of another chart detailing the female anatomy, then returned to his seat. Most men, Lisa had found, took pleasure in observing unclothed women but were uncomfortable seeing what lay beneath their skin.

A moment later she was relieved to hear Matthew's voice. She spoke in an undertone, explaining quickly why Detective Barone, whose eyes were again on her, had come. She felt ill at ease having to deal with this by herself, because she had nothing to tell the detective, who probably assumed from her nervousness that she was withholding information.

In medical school she'd dissected countless cadavers, and during her emergency room rotation she'd seen patients die of gunshots and stabbings and heart attacks and drug overdoses. But this was a prestigious fertility clinic in Westwood, not a morgue or an emergency room where mortality was a frequent, violent intruder. She stole another glance at Chelsea Wright's photo and thought about the ultrasound prints and the tiny life she'd watched minutes ago, beating insistently on the screen. She didn't know Chelsea but felt like crying.

She buzzed Selena and reluctantly asked her to have someone check on Naomi Hoffman. Then she replaced the receiver. She was anxious about how she would fill the silence until Matthew arrived, but in another minute he was there, striding into the room with the confidence and energy that had attracted Lisa to him during her first interview fourteen months ago. From the pained expression in his marine-blue eyes and the hard set of his jaw, she could see his agitation.

Barone stood, and the two men shook hands. At five feet eleven inches, Matthew was almost as tall as the detective, who had a more solid build. Lisa moved from behind her desk and handed the photo to Matthew. He glanced at it quickly.

"That's her." He sounded angry. "God, how could this have happened?" He tossed the photo on Lisa's desk and slumped down onto a chair, stuffing his hands in the pockets of his pale gray medical jacket.

Lisa wanted to put a comforting hand on his arm. Instead, she leaned against her desk and returned her attention to the detective, who had taken the seat next to Matthew and was opening a small black notebook that he'd removed from his jacket pocket.

"Was she your patient, Dr. Gordon?" he asked.

"I can't believe Chelsea's *dead*." Matthew shook his head, then sighed and looked up. "Sorry. What did you say?"

Barone patiently repeated the question.

"Chelsea was an egg donor. Which reminds me—" He got up

suddenly, said, "Excuse me a minute, please," and picked up Lisa's phone receiver.

"What's an egg donor?" the detective asked, turning his attention to Lisa as Matthew spoke quietly into the phone.

She could hear Matthew talking to Grace, giving instructions. "For one of the assisted-reproduction procedures we do here, IVF—in vitro fertilization—a woman's eggs are harvested—retrieved," she explained when she saw Barone's quizzical expression. "Then they're fertilized in vitro with the partner's sperm. The fertilized embryo is then transferred into the woman's uterus. Sometimes—"

"What does 'in vitro' mean?" Barone interrupted.

"Literally, it means 'in a glass.' We use petri dishes." She supposed he was trying to put her at ease or fill the time until Matthew finished his call. "Sometimes we aren't successful in harvesting eggs from the patient, so donor eggs are necessary. Also, with women in their late thirties or forties whose eggs aren't as viable as we'd like, we use younger eggs to increase the chances of conception."

"Like Chelsea Wright's." Barone nodded. "But why would she do it? What's in it for the donor?"

"Often she's a friend or family member. Other women donate anonymously to help infertile couples."

"Really?" He sounded impressed.

"Yes." Lisa hesitated, then added, "The anonymous donors are paid. I don't know which type of donor Chelsea was."

Barone said, "It's nice that nobility gets rewarded, isn't it?" and Lisa couldn't tell from his tone whether or not he was being sarcastic. She assumed he was. She watched as he wrote Chelsea's name on his pad, followed by a dollar sign, then a question mark.

"So who pays the egg donor fee?" he asked.

"The recipient. The clinic issues the check. She also pays the donor's medical expenses." Lisa inched to her right to make room for Matthew, who had hung up the phone and was frowning.

"Sorry about that, Detective," he said, moving next to Lisa. "Last minute post-op instructions for a patient who's receiving donor eggs." He ran both hands through his thick, sandy brown hair. "I'm still reeling. You're sure it's Chelsea? Could there be some mistake?"

"Unfortunately, no. Her parents made a positive identification. She was their only child, too."

Lisa shut her eyes. She couldn't begin to imagine their anguish, their horror. She heard Matthew whisper, "Christ, how awful!" and tried not to picture Chelsea's blank-faced parents standing in a morgue, watching a stranger peel back the white sheet that covered their lifeless daughter. Lisa had spoken to her own parents yesterday; she would phone them again tonight.

"Do you have any idea who killed her?" Matthew leaned against the desk. "Any leads?"

"Nothing definite. Was Miss Wright a paid donor?"

"Yes, she was." There was curiosity in his voice.

"How much does an egg donor receive?" Barone asked, crossing out the question mark.

Matthew tilted his head and squinted in puzzlement. "Does this have anything to do with her murder?"

"Probably not. But I like to be thorough—it prevents duplication of effort and embarrassing questions from my lieutenant." Barone smiled.

"Of course." Matthew put his hands in his pockets. "Well, the current rate for donors is around twenty-five hundred dollars per retrieval."

The detective whistled and wrote down the figure. "A fellow at the station donated sperm several times. But he got only fifty dollars each time."

"Donating eggs is far more involved. The donor devotes about fifty-six hours to the retrieval process." Matthew was frowning and had taken on a lecturing tone. "She has to take fertility drugs to increase ovulation. That means daily injections for ten or more days, blood tests, ultrasound screenings." He'd ticked off the details on his fingers.

Barone nodded. "Not so simple, then."

"Hardly." Matthew folded his arms across his chest. "There are possible side effects to the drugs—abdominal pain, rash or swelling at the injection site, headaches, mood swings, weight gain. The harvesting itself involves anesthesia, which can have complications, and there may be discomfort from the procedure, possibly infection."

"You've convinced me, Doctor. I don't think I'll volunteer."

Barone was smiling good-naturedly, but Lisa could see curiosity in the way he was studying Matthew, whose frown had frozen in place. She knew he was sensitive to criticism about the clinic. Edging closer, she pressed his arm lightly—a gentle warning not to overreact with the detective, who was just doing his job—and wondered again why he was so tense lately, why he couldn't confide in her. Not that she confided her every concern to him, either. It goes two ways, she told herself.

"So how do you find donors?" Barone asked.

"We work with several donor agencies." Matthew unfolded his arms and half sat on the desk.

"Which agency referred Chelsea?"

Matthew creased his brow in thought. "Actually, if I remember correctly, Chelsea responded to an ad we placed in one of the local colleges."

"Right under the 'Looking for a roommate' card on the bulletin board, is that it?" Barone smiled again.

Lisa resumed her pressure on Matthew's arm. He smiled woodenly and said, "Not exactly, but yes, we do place ads on bulletin boards. There's nothing wrong with that."

"I'm sure you're right." Barone scribbled something indecipherable on his notepad. "Dr. Brockman says she saw Chelsea at the clinic a few weeks ago. Is that when Chelsea donated the eggs?"

Matthew shook his head. "Chelsea donated the eggs long before that. I'd have to check her file to find out exactly when. She came here two weeks ago because she wanted to donate again. I reviewed her records then and noted that the first time, her ovaries had become hyperstimulated from the fertility drugs."

"Is that a dangerous side effect?"

"It's a *possible* side effect," Matthew corrected. "And yes, if it isn't controlled, it can be dangerous. Obviously, we monitor our patients carefully. In Chelsea's case, we controlled the hyperstimulation and successfully retrieved her eggs, but I told her donating again was medically inadvisable."

"How did she react?"

Matthew sighed. "She was very upset. She *begged* me to let her do it." He hesitated. "She told me she needed the money. I told her that wasn't a good reason to donate."

"Did she tell you *why* she needed money?" Again, heightened interest tinged Barone's voice.

"She didn't volunteer, and I didn't press her. It wasn't exactly my business."

Poor Matthew. Lisa could tell from his defensiveness that he was feeling guilty, though he had no reason to be. He'd probably be agonizing over Chelsea for a long time.

"Is that why she donated the first time?" Barone asked. "For money?"

"When I first interviewed her, she said she wanted to help in-

fertile couples. I thought she was sincere. Now I'm not so sure."
He sounded troubled.

"Why would a young woman like her be desperate for money?"
The detective's tone was speculative; his eyes had narrowed. "Was
she on drugs, do you think?"

"She definitely wasn't when we harvested her eggs." A muscle
twitched in his cheek. "We do extensive screenings—physical and
psychological—on all egg donors and monitor them throughout the
cycle."

"I didn't mean to suggest otherwise." The detective's smile
and tone were conciliatory. "I'm just reaching. Sorry."

"No, *I'm* sorry. It's just—" Matthew expelled a breath. "Chelsea was so damn nice, Detective. So damn young! I'm shocked and
saddened by what happened. If you want to know the truth, I'm
pissed." His hands gripped the rounded edge of the desk.

"So am I," Barone said in a quiet, sad voice that indicated he
hadn't become inured to the brutality he witnessed almost daily.
"So who received Chelsea's eggs?"

Matthew shook his head. "Sorry. Medical ethics prevent me
from revealing that information."

"But you told Chelsea?"

Another shake of the head. "No. The recipient has a right to
keep her identity secret. Chelsea understood that. She never
asked."

"I see." Barone jotted more notes. "Anything else you can tell
me about Ms. Wright?"

Matthew locked his hands behind his head. "I can tell you she
was a terrific young woman, Detective. She never complained once
during the entire treatment cycle, even with the discomfort of the
hyperstimulation. She wanted to be a teacher, did you know that?
She was bright, full of life . . ." He dropped his hands to his sides.
"Not exactly information that will help you find her killer, is it?"

Barone didn't answer.

"Maybe I should have spent more time with her, found out
what was troubling her," Matthew said, as if he were speaking to
himself.

Lisa covered his hand with hers. "You couldn't have known
what would happen, Matt. You couldn't have changed anything."
She looked to the detective for confirmation.

"Everything points to a mugging," Barone said. "Her watch
and a small diamond pendant her boyfriend gave her were lifted—
her parents told us both were missing. We found her wallet a few

blocks away from where she was killed. The credit cards were there, but the cash was gone. The bartender at the restaurant where she worked said she'd made over ninety dollars in tips that night."

"You see?" Lisa turned back to Matthew. "Nothing you could have told Chelsea would've changed that."

"I guess. How . . . how was she killed?"

Barone slipped his notepad into his pocket. "She was bludgeoned at the back of her head, then shot in the neck."

Lisa winced, then swallowed hard.

Matthew winced, too. His face looked pasty. "No one heard anything, saw anything?" His voice was shaking and resonated with impatience and anger at an indifferent world.

"It happened late at night, when she was going home from work. More often than not, you know, people hear things they don't want to hear and never come forward. Too afraid." Barone shrugged. "And if it wasn't a mugging, if it was a planned hit, the killer could have used a silencer."

"You just told us it was a mugging," Lisa said more sharply than she'd intended. She knew she was being silly, but she was annoyed with the detective for bringing back the haunted look to Matthew's face.

"Either that, or someone was careful to make it *look* like a mugging. Why bludgeon her, then shoot her? Why shoot her at all, for that matter?"

They were good questions. She realized the detective wouldn't be here if he thought Chelsea's murder was the aftermath of a mugging.

Barone reached into his inside jacket pocket, took out two cards, handed one to Matthew, the other to Lisa. "In case you think of anything else."

chapter three

"Why can't you tell me what's wrong, Matt?"

They were sitting on the taupe-colored leather sleeper sofa in her living room. Matthew had turned on the television but wasn't watching—he was using the remote control like an electronic toy, switching impatiently from channel to channel.

They'd just returned from their favorite restaurant in Santa Monica, near the pier. She'd offered to cook dinner, but he'd insisted they go out. "We need a break," he'd said, but she knew the real reason: in a restaurant, he could avoid her questions.

He'd been quiet there, had poked at his salad Niçoise—almost angrily, Lisa thought—taken a few bites, then pushed his plate away. "I'm not really hungry," he'd said, though she hadn't asked. "You go ahead." Lisa hadn't been all that hungry, either, and when she'd suggested that they leave, Matthew had protested halfheartedly, then agreed.

"Some date, huh?" He'd smiled ruefully. "I'm sorry." The waitress had hurried over when they rose from their chairs. "Nothing's wrong, just a change of plans," he'd assured her, pulling out two twenties from his Gucci wallet and placing them on the table.

He'd slipped his arm around Lisa as they'd left the restaurant, but he'd been silent when they walked to his black BMW. In the car he'd sat for a moment before turning on the ignition, staring at the windshield, his hands gripping the gray-leather-wrapped steering wheel.

It wasn't just Chelsea Wright, she sensed. He'd been upset about the murder all day, long after Barone had left. That hadn't surprised her. Matthew was caring, committed to his patients, to his friends, to her. But he'd been preoccupied for weeks. On Saturday night they had seen a Mel Gibson movie in Century City. Afterward, when she'd asked him something about one of the scenes, he'd looked blank, then admitted sheepishly that he hadn't really watched the film. "What's on your mind?" she'd asked. "Things," he'd said. "I'm sure they'll work themselves out."

Obviously they hadn't. "Is it the missing money, Matt?" she asked softly now, ignoring the flush that was tinting his neck. She reached for his hand and linked her fingers through his. When he didn't answer, she asked, "Is it something to do with us?" and held her breath, partly because she'd been here before, partly because she didn't know what answer she wanted to hear.

He turned and looked at her, puzzled. "With *us?*"

Her face felt uncomfortably warm. "You've been different lately, a little distant. I thought, maybe . . ."

"That I was having second thoughts about marrying you?" He cupped her face in his hands. "I love you, Lisa. You know that, don't you?" His gaze was intense.

Asher had gazed into her green eyes and told her he loved her, too.

Lisa nodded. Matthew kissed her and pulled her close. She rested her head on his shoulder and told herself she was incredibly lucky to have found him and wondered why she couldn't let things be.

"I *have* been preoccupied," he said, stroking her hair. "The stolen money's part of it. Another fifteen hundred was taken last week, five hundred yesterday, and I have no idea who the hell did it. All cash, of course, so it's hard to trace."

Many of their patients, especially those who traveled to the clinic from South America, made cash payments. Each bill was supposedly photocopied, and the money was deposited in the bank only twice a week. "How much is missing in total, Matt?"

"Over twenty thousand. Not exactly pocket change."

She was stunned by the amount. Lifting her head, she stared

at him. "Matt, don't you think you should reconsider and call the police?"

"You know I don't want the publicity. I'm changing the safe combination again. This time only Selena will know it. She's the *only* one who'll put cash in the safe, and I know she's careful about photocopying the money. And I'll make sure Victor understands that *anyone* who comes in before or after regular hours has to sign in and out. He's lax sometimes." Matthew switched the channel, and canned laughter filled the room.

"And if there's another theft, you'll call the police?"

"Persistent, aren't you?" He laughed lightly. "Probably." He switched channels again, finally settling on CNN. "The money's not the only problem. We need to find a better anesthetic for the retrievals—I'm not happy patients are waking up agitated. And I'm still trying to figure out what went wrong with the protocols. The results looked so promising!"

Aside from treating patients, Matthew was doing research on freezing unfertilized eggs. Two weeks ago he'd told her excitedly that he was on the verge of a breakthrough. Days later he'd been dejected—the data were disheartening.

She squeezed his hand. "The fact that you were so close means that next time you'll find the answer." No response. She kicked off her black suede flats, tucked her legs beneath her, and studied him. "What *else* is bothering you?"

He grunted. "It's obvious, huh?" He hesitated. "I may have to fire someone—this has nothing to do with the stolen cash."

Her eyes widened. "Who?"

"I'd rather not say until I'm sure. If I'm wrong, it wouldn't be fair."

"Wrong about *what*?" When he didn't answer, she rose to her knees and massaged the back of his neck, then his shoulders. "You're so tense, Matt."

"No kidding." He was silent for a moment, then swiveled to face her. "You can't tell anyone, but the clinic could be facing a serious lawsuit."

His tone was grudging. The clinic was his passion—he'd spent years and endless hours, he'd told her on their second date, convincing investors to share his dream and build one of the most prestigious fertility clinics in the world.

"Have you talked to Edmond about this?" Edmond Fisk was the chairman of the clinic's board of directors.

"Definitely not!" Color tinged his cheeks. "I haven't told him that someone's been stealing cash, either. Edmond doesn't like to hear about problems—he likes solutions. Promise you won't say anything to him, Lisa."

"I promise," she said, troubled by his vehemence. "Does Sam know?"

"No. You can't tell him, either."

"Sam isn't only on staff, Matthew. He's your friend." He was Lisa's friend, too; they'd met in Downstate Medical School in New York. It was Sam Davidson who had encouraged Lisa to interview for a position at the clinic, Sam who'd put in a good word with Matthew, Sam who'd found her this one-bedroom apartment on Keystone in Palms, not far from Westwood and the clinic.

"You know how easily rumors start, Lisa. A slip of the tongue . . ." He shook his head. "I'll tell you everything once I've verified what's going on. Until then, let's drop it, okay?"

"Is that why you were defensive with Barone?"

"You noticed, huh?" He grimaced. "Chelsea really was sweet. I can't believe she was *murdered*." He shuddered. "Yeah, I was defensive, *and* nervous. Here I am, trying to find out who's stealing us blind, about to fire someone I think is responsible for serious garbage at the clinic. The last thing I need is police questioning the staff. Also—" He stopped abruptly.

"Also what?"

"Also nothing." He clicked off the television, tossed the remote onto the coffee table, and settled back against the leather sofa cushion. "How's the search for the dream wedding gown?" He played with the oval two-carat diamond on her finger.

"Changing the subject?" she teased.

"Very astute, Dr. Brockman." He smiled lightly.

She knew better than to press. He was always careful to separate their professional and personal lives. That was the difficulty with co-workers becoming involved, he'd told her at the end of what had begun as a dinner meeting to review her first two months at the clinic but had quickly become more intimate. She'd felt attracted to him for some time—he was handsome, bright, dynamic, caring—but she'd said with feigned nonchalance, Well, maybe becoming involved *wasn't* a good idea. Partly meaning it. And he'd stared at her and said, Probably not. And then he'd kissed her.

"So what's with the dress?" he asked again.

It was her turn to equivocate. "I haven't found one I love."

She hadn't tried on a single gown, even though the wedding was set for August, only three months away. From the time they'd become engaged, five months ago, she'd had the feeling—irrational, she knew—that if she bought a dress, something would go wrong, the engagement would be broken, just like last time.

And now she had doubts about marrying him. She didn't know whether to tell him or wait. If she told him and resolved her uncertainties, she'd have hurt him unnecessarily.

But if not . . .

She wondered again, as she did occasionally, what her mother had done with the gown they'd chosen together at Kleinfeld's eleven years ago. It was a beautiful gown—a beaded lace bodice with a voluminous tulle skirt sprinkled with tiny pearls; trying it on in the store and later at home, she'd felt like Cinderella.

When the Rossners broke off the engagement, two weeks before the wedding, her mother had secreted the gown out of Lisa's closet. Maybe she'd given it to charity. Lisa had often helped her mother bake for the teas held by a Jewish organization that raised funds to assist needy brides to marry and outfit their homes. ("Our sages tell us," her mother had explained, "that one of the first questions posed to a person in the next life is, 'Did you help the needy brides enter the wedding canopy?' " Her mother, she knew, would be able to answer that question easily.)

Or maybe her mother, nurturing hope, had given the dress to be preserved for a future date. Lisa was still a size six and could fit into it. Not that she wanted to wear it.

Matthew put his arm around her. "Did I mention they delivered the new armoire? Plenty of room for all your sweaters, and my condo is five minutes from the clinic. So how about it? 'Come live with me and be my love'?"

" 'And we will all the pleasures prove.' " She smiled and said, "After the wedding." He asked her this every few weeks. Every few weeks she gave the same answer, though now the reasons had subtly changed.

"Come on, Lisa. This is silly, living apart. I'm sure your parents figure we're sleeping together." An edge of irritation had replaced his bantering tone.

She'd explained her reasoning before and tried not to be annoyed now by his persistence, which she knew was normal. "I'm sure they do. But I don't want to upset them more than I have."

Her parents were devout Orthodox Jews and were grievously disappointed that their only child was marrying a man whose Jewishness was merely a fact of his birth. She respected her parents and loved them dearly and had felt terrible announcing her engagement over the phone. They'd responded with silence. Then her father, his voice heavy with sadness, had said, "Can we talk about this?" and she'd said, "Please don't, Daddy. This is what I want."

She'd spoken with conviction, though something nameless had been nagging at her even then. Lately she'd started contemplating what kind of life she envisioned for herself and Matthew and their children; and she'd also been thinking, more and more, about her patient Naomi Hoffman, who was Orthodox. After every appointment with Naomi, Lisa had felt unsettled, vaguely dissatisfied, almost irritated with the woman for being so serenely content with her observant lifestyle. Several weeks ago she'd admitted to herself that her irritation was a form of masking envy, that what she'd dismissed for years as nostalgia was a yearning to return to the religious observance of her adolescence.

She'd been putting off telling Matthew what she was thinking, waiting for the right time, but there *was* no right time. "What would you say if I wanted us to be Orthodox?" she asked now and saw surprise flash across his handsome face.

"If I said yes, would you move in with me tomorrow?" He laughed, then assumed a sober expression and sat up straight, resting his arm on top of the couch's high back. "I thought you were done with all that years ago."

"I thought so, too. But I've felt for some time that something's missing in my life, Matt, and I've been thinking about taking some outreach classes." From a local synagogue she'd learned that there were several programs for *ba'alei teshuvah*, those who returned to the faith; there was one in the Pico area, near her. The phone number and address were on a pad on her nightstand.

"You didn't tell me." His voice held a hint of accusation.

"I wasn't sure how I felt. I'm still not." She didn't add that she'd been nervous about telling him. "We've talked about having kids, Matt, but we haven't talked about what kind of religious upbringing we want to give them."

He frowned. "I'm not sure they *need* religion."

"I think they do, Matt." She rested her hand on his arm.

He was silent for a while, still frowning. "My parents never took me to a synagogue—you know that. I never had a bar mitzvah. I don't think I'm deprived."

She didn't answer.

"All I know about Orthodoxy is the little you've told me, Lisa, and you've said yourself it's complicated, with hundreds of rules and restrictions that sound outdated to me." He paused. "There are other, less restrictive types of Judaism."

"I've been to Conservative and Reform services, mainly for Rosh Hashanah and Yom Kippur." She'd avoided visiting her parents on the High Holidays—she'd had no desire to return to the synagogue she'd attended almost weekly for over eighteen years, to pretend she didn't see the curiosity and criticism in the veiled looks of her former friends and her parents' friends. Her parents must have understood her discomfort, because they'd never pressed her to come. Or maybe her presence at services would have made them uncomfortable, too. "The services were beautiful and inspiring, and the people were great—warm, welcoming." She hesitated. "But I didn't feel as though I was home. I want to feel that I'm *home*, Matt." She gazed at him, willing him to understand.

"Maybe you need to give them another chance."

"Maybe." She realized she might be seeking something that didn't exist, that what worked for her parents and Naomi Hoffman—and for Sam Davidson, who was Orthodox, too—might not work for her.

He ran his hand back and forth on the leather cushion. "I have to think about this, okay?"

"Of course," she said quickly. "It's taken me a long time to come to this point. You're entitled to take a while." She smiled, hoping to lighten the mood, but was met with another silence.

"You'd want to keep the Sabbath and keep kosher, right? The works?" he finally asked.

"My kitchen is kosher anyway, in case my parents visit." It took so little effort and made them so happy. "And Sam says there are lots of good kosher restaurants in L.A."

"But they don't serve lobster or oysters, do they?"

She smiled again. "Not quite." She'd never developed a fondness for shellfish or ham or cheeseburgers—she'd tasted guilt with every bite—and she didn't think she'd mind giving up the convenience of eating in nonkosher restaurants. Then again, she hadn't tried. "Keeping kosher isn't all that difficult, Matt. Neither is keeping the Sabbath, once you're used to it." Was she trying to convince him or herself?

"Maybe not for you, because you did it for so many years. Imagine if I said I wanted us to be Buddhist or Mormon." His eyes narrowed. "You think your parents will dislike me less if you go back to the fold—is that it? Or has Sam been doing a number on you because he's Orthodox?"

"Sam and I never discuss religion." She pressed closer to him. "My parents don't dislike you, Matt. Once they meet you, they'll love you." She nuzzled his cheek. "And they don't know I'm thinking about becoming Orthodox again. I won't tell them until I'm sure." It would be cruel to raise their hopes. She hesitated, then told him about Naomi Hoffman. "I envy what she and her husband have, Matt. I can't help wondering whether we could have the same thing."

"So I have *her* to thank for this, huh?" he said lightly.

"I know I'm not being fair, throwing this at you."

"No, you're not. But this isn't about 'fair,' is it?" He looked at her thoughtfully. "I can't make any commitments, but I guess if it means a lot to you, I can go to a couple of these classes with you, see how I feel."

She should have been pleased with his response—it was a surprisingly promising beginning—but she wasn't. The possibility that she wanted him to back out so she wouldn't have to, that there was more to her mixed emotions than religion, startled her.

He took her hand. "The most important thing is that we love each other, Lisa. Everything else will resolve itself."

That's what Asher had said, too.

Matthew kissed her. "Let's go to bed," he whispered.

She wondered wryly how he would react if she told him Orthodoxy prohibited intimacy between unmarried people. She followed him to her bedroom, miserable because she was being less than honest about her doubts, and tried to lose herself in his love-making, which was tender and passionate, if a little more intense than usual.

Afterward, he lay staring into the darkness, his interlaced fingers cupping his head.

"Are you brooding about us or about the clinic?" she asked softly, smoothing his hair.

He was silent for so long that she thought he wasn't going to answer. Then he said, "In a matter of days the clinic could be ruined."

She felt a flutter of alarm. "The clinic has a spotless reputation, Matt, and an unbelievably terrific success rate. That's why patients come to us from all over the world."

"One whiff of suspicion of wrongdoing, and they'll stop coming and we can close the doors. And the board will blame me."

"Matt—"

"I'm the head director. The buck stops with me." He swung his legs off the bed and bent down to pick up his clothing.

He was right, of course. She watched in silence as he dressed. "I wish I could help."

He sat down next to her. "You help just by being with me, Lisa. You're the best thing in my life, don't you know that?" He leaned over and kissed her. His lips lingered on hers.

"So what are you going to do, Matt?"

"I'm going to play detective. I don't have much time." He buttoned his shirt. "Maybe I'll find out that things aren't so bad. You know me—morose Matthew." He forced a smile. "Try not to worry, okay?"

chapter four

Lisa watched intently as Charlie McCallister, his eyes fixed on the lenses of a heated microscope, guided the needle containing a single sperm into the ovum in the petri dish. The clinic used this relatively new procedure when the sperm count was low or the sperm had low motility. ("Lazy swimmers," Matthew called them.) Typically, doctors didn't oversee lab technicians, but Lisa had promised the husband and wife, a particularly anxious couple, that she would observe the micromanipulation.

"Bull's eye." The red-haired lab director covered the petri dish, already labeled with the patient's name, and took the dish to one of the dull gray, boxlike incubators at the far end of the lab.

"What's next?" Lisa asked when he returned a moment later carrying test tubes.

"The Chapman eggs."

Early this morning Lisa had aspirated thirteen eggs from Susan Chapman. Of the eggs that would be fertilized and developed into viable embryos, a maximum of four would be implanted to increase

Susan's chance of sustaining a clinical pregnancy. The others would be cryopreserved—frozen—and stored for a later date.

"Let's make some babies," the lab director said.

Lisa smiled. She'd witnessed in vitro fertilization hundreds of times; though the process was simple, the concept never failed to amaze and excite her. She watched as Charlie transferred the first egg from the sterile test tube into a petri dish labeled with Susan's name. Then he added Jason Chapman's "washed" sperm and affixed another label with Jason's name.

"Any bets on how many will take, Charlie?"

"I only bet at the track, Doc. And thirteen isn't exactly anyone's favorite number." He grinned, then turned to the tall, blond-haired man who had just entered the lab. "What about you, Norman? Any bets on how many of these little critters will be sending Mother's Day cards?"

"I think you know I'm not a betting man." A brief smile flitted across the man's serious, angular face. "But I'm reasonably certain every one of these will develop into embryos. If I may say so, Dr. McCallister, you have a gift."

"A paid political announcement." Charlie's face had turned red, disguising the freckles splashed across his nose and cheeks.

"Hardly. Norman's right, you know." Lisa smiled warmly. "Your track record's pretty damn good." She caught Norman Weld's darting look of disapproval and remembered that Charlie had told her the lab assistant was a little straitlaced.

Charlie was transferring an egg from another test tube into a new petri dish when Lisa's pager beeped. It was Selena.

"You'd better come up here quick, *mi hija*," the office manager said urgently when Lisa contacted her. "There are so many hysterical women demanding to see Dr. Gordon, I barely made it to my desk."

Lisa frowned. "What do you mean, 'hysterical women'?"

"They're not making sense. Reporters are here, too. With cameras. I don't know what's going on."

Tossing her green, sterile paper gown, cap, and booties into a cardboard box at the entrance to the lab, Lisa raced up the wide flight of stairs to the ground floor. Though Selena had warned her, she was startled to see the long, narrow hall crowded with people who seemed to be talking at once.

"Dr. Brockman? Is it true what they're saying?"

Turning, she saw Diane Clerman. "Is *what* true?"

Yesterday Diane had been euphoric, effusive in her gratitude. Now Lisa heard anger and panic in her unnaturally high-pitched voice. Within seconds she was surrounded by more than two dozen men and women, several of whom were her patients and their husbands, and by two men and a woman who elbowed their way around the others and snapped her picture.

The media photographers. "What's going on?" Lisa demanded, blinking at the barrage of flashes. Pinpoints of light danced in her eyes.

"That's what *I* want to know!" yelled a woman Lisa didn't recognize. "Where's Dr. Gordon? Why isn't he here to answer our questions?"

A chorus of "Yeah, where *is* he?" assaulted Lisa.

"Would you care to comment on the allegations made against the clinic?" another woman asked.

A reporter, not a patient. Behind her, a jeans-clad, ponytailed man was balancing a minicam on his shoulder. Wonderful, Lisa thought. I'll be on the eleven o'clock news, and I don't even know why. "I can't comment about an allegation I know nothing about," she said, forcing herself to sound calm.

The people around her weren't calm. Their voices were a rising cacophony of agitation and hysteria. Lisa scanned the hall for help, but neither Matthew nor any of the other doctors or staff were in sight.

"This *is* my baby, isn't it, Dr. Brockman?" demanded another patient. Her hands rested on her swollen midriff.

What had Matthew said? *One whiff of suspicion . . . and we can close the doors.* Was this what he'd feared? Lisa felt her stomach muscles knotting but made her voice sound reassuring. "Of *course* the baby you're carrying is yours, Cheryl."

"Can you be certain, Dr. Brockman?" a male reporter asked. "According to reliable sources, this clinic has been switching embryos and committing other related violations."

"That's ridiculous!" It *was* ridiculous. There were too many safeguards. She craned her neck and looked around. Where was Matthew? He should be here to deal with the patients, with the media. Where was Sam Davidson? Or Ted Cantrell? And where was Selena?

"*Is* it ridiculous, Dr. Brockman? Then where is Dr. Gordon? Somewhere south of the border?"

Lisa glared at the reporter. "That's an insulting and totally unwarranted insinuation."

He was referring to two doctors who had left the country when their Irvine, California, fertility clinic had come under investigation. The clinic had ultimately been shut, and the scandal had reverberated, placing the entire community of infertility specialists under scrutiny.

"I *knew* they gave my eggs to someone else!" another woman cried. "I *knew* it!" She grabbed Lisa's arm.

"Mrs. Allen, calm down," Lisa said firmly yet gently, loosening the woman's tourniquetlike grip. She spotted the tall, black-haired office manager at the far end of the hall and had to yell, "Selena!" several times before the woman heard her and hurried to her side.

Selena was breathless. Her chest was heaving beneath her pale blue cotton sweater, and her round face was flushed. "Dr. Gordon phoned Grace early this morning and told her he'd be late," she whispered to Lisa. "She's paged him several times, but he hasn't phoned back. Dr. Cantrell was here earlier, but he's doing surgery at another hospital. And Dr. Davidson—"

"I want my babies!" Cora Allen pulled at Lisa's arm.

"Someone stole your babies?" the same reporter asked the woman. Behind him, the minicam motor whirred.

Putting her arm around the woman, Lisa piloted her away from the reporter and the cameraman. "Cora, I don't blame you for being upset. Selena will take you to a room where you can relax. I'll be in to talk to you soon."

The woman jerked away from Lisa. "I don't need to *relax*. I need my *babies*! I want to know who has them!" Her face was streaked with tears and mascara tracks.

Selena put her arm around the woman. "Please come with me, Mrs. Allen," she said in her softly accented voice. "Everything will be fine." Murmuring soothingly, she led her away.

"We want to speak to Dr. Gordon!" Hank Clerman yelled. "We have a right to know what's going on!" Angry red blotches had mottled his face, which was beaded with perspiration.

The clinic's air-conditioning couldn't accommodate the crush of people in the narrow hall, now stuffy and uncomfortably warm. Lisa was perspiring, too, and her head was beginning to throb.

"Ladies and gentlemen, can I have your attention, please? Ladies and gentlemen?" Making herself heard was difficult, but after a moment the crowd quieted. "First, I want to assure you that nothing irregular has been going on at the clinic. You—"

"If nothing's wrong, where's Dr. Gordon?" Clerman demanded. "Why isn't he here to answer our questions?"

"Dr. Gordon will be here soon," Lisa said, hoping she was telling the truth. Matthew hadn't mentioned that he'd be late, but he *had* said he needed answers soon. Was he searching for them right now? "False rumors have obviously been spread about the clinic," she continued, careful to make eye contact with the reporters. "We intend to find and expose their source."

"How do we know they're false?" a woman asked. "They switched embryos before, at that other clinic."

A murmur of agreement rippled through the crowd.

"But not here." Lisa cleared her throat. "These rumors are unfounded. In the meantime, we need your cooperation. If you're here for a scheduled appointment, please wait in Reception. If not, there's really no reason for you to stay." A polite way of saying, Go home.

"I'm not leaving until I have answers!" Clerman yelled.

Lisa continued to speak, to reassure. She was interrupted several more times by women and men shrill with anger and fear, but after a while the accusations stopped, and though only a few people took her advice and went home, she felt she'd achieved a relative calm. With help from Selena and Grace and the other nurses, she dispatched the more agitated patients and their spouses to examining rooms.

On the other side of the still-packed hall, she saw a familiar face topped with a thatch of wavy, dark brown hair. At six feet two inches, Sam Davidson towered above the crowd, and she could easily read his mouthed "What the hell's going on?" God, she was happy to see him! A moment later he was at her side.

"Nice of you to show up!" she whispered, her relief tempered with irritation. "It's almost ten o'clock." She felt as if a day had passed, not a little over an hour.

"Flat tire. Sorry—I tried phoning in, but the lines were jammed or something." He scanned the crowd. "What'd we do? Advertise a Wednesday half-off special on in vitros?"

"I wish. Rumor is we've been switching embryos."

Sam pushed his wire-rimmed eyeglasses back against his nose. "Bull!" he exclaimed, but concern flickered in his gray eyes. He looked around again. "They all seem pretty calm."

"You should've seen them twenty minutes ago." She adjusted her banana clip and wiped her brow. Her throat ached from speaking so loudly and she was desperate for a cup of coffee.

"Why are you handling this?" Frowning, he centered his black suede yarmulke on his head. "Where's Matt? And where's Ted?"

She shrugged. "Grace said Matt phoned and told her he'd be late. Ted was in earlier, but left to do a procedure at another hospital. How's your schedule today?"

"Tight, and that's without the nine o'clock I missed. But I'm all yours if you want me. Professionally, of course." He winked, then smiled reassuringly.

"I need Ava, but she's somewhere up the coast, lucky woman." Lisa sighed. "I tried to persuade everyone without an appointment to go home, but most of them won't budge. You can help with that. If they insist on staying, have them wait in Reception. I figure we can see our regular patients and divide today's emergencies among you, me, and Ted when he gets back."

"Sounds like you've got everything under control. Not that I'm surprised." He smiled again. "Matt's lucky to have you—personally *and* professionally."

"Thanks." Sam always made her feel good. For the first time since she'd left the lab, her spirits rose. "I'm going to check on Cora Allen. She's had two failed IVFs, poor woman, and thinks someone stole her eggs and gave them to someone else. One more thing—if you can, get rid of the media." The reporters were still there, approaching patient after patient in search of a story.

"Easier to find a cure for cancer."

Three hours later she was exhausted. Selena had sent her from examining room to examining room, providing her with updates, folders, encouraging smiles, Dixie cups with water, a granola bar, and two rest-room breaks. Lisa had passed Sam and Ted Cantrell several times in the hall—they'd looked equally tired. Sam had managed to retain his good humor. Ted hadn't.

"Where the hell is your fiancé?" Cantrell barked at her now. "At the racetrack?"

They were in the middle of the hall, and patients were within earshot. Lisa clenched her hands. "I don't know." She didn't like the handsome, divorced forty-four-year-old doctor—she found him arrogant and difficult—but told herself he had a right to be annoyed. She was annoyed, too, and worried. Matthew was always punctual. She was surprised he hadn't called in.

"Nice of him to leave us to deal with this crap. I'm sick of fending off the press and trying to calm hysterical women." His black eyes were smoldering coals.

Sam rested his hand on Cantrell's shoulder. "Hey, we're all tired, Ted. Lighten up. You'll live longer."

Cantrell scowled and shrugged off the hand. He faced Lisa. "I've seen twenty patients in the past three hours. How many have *you* seen? Or are you just *administrating*?"

"Get off her case, Ted," Sam said quietly.

"What are you, her white knight?" Cantrell glared at him, then stomped down the hall, the coattails of his gray medical coat flapping behind him.

"Nice guy," Sam said, watching Cantrell. "He's been awfully tense lately, have you noticed?" He turned to Lisa. "Any word from Matt?"

She shook her head. "He told Grace something important came up." *I'm going to play detective.* Had he discovered something? Even so, why hadn't he phoned?

"It's not *like* him to be late," the petite, blond nurse had told Lisa. "He phoned at seven and said he'd be home for about half an hour, that he had to take care of something important. I've been paging him all morning, and he still hasn't called back. I hope nothing's wrong, Dr. Brockman." Grace had been clutching a stack of folders against her chest. The skin around her pale blue eyes had been creased with worry, and she'd seemed on the verge of tears.

"He'll probably phone soon," Sam said. He kneaded the back of his neck, then rotated his head several times. "I wonder what's number three."

Lisa frowned. "Number three?"

"You know—bad things come in threes? That's what my sister says. First this clinic patient is murdered. Now some nut's accusing us of egg switching. What's next? They'll find out we're doing illegal human cloning?"

"Didn't your sister also tell you not to borrow trouble?" Lisa said lightly, but she was a little uneasy, and annoyed with Sam for making her feel that way.

From her office she phoned Matthew's home and left a message on his machine. She left a message on his pager, too, and tried reaching him on his cellular phone.

On an impulse she punched her own number and waited for her answering machine to go on. She heard a message from a company trying to interest her in winning a trip to Hawaii, then Matthew's voice against a background of static and street noise.

"It's six forty-five. . . . thought I might catch you at home . . . didn't want to phone you at the clinic in case . . . listening in on the line . . . may be onto something . . . not to worry. I'm stopping at my condo, then checking out some things. Don't say anything to anyone. Talk to you later. Love you."

He sounded excited, pumped up. That had been early this morning.

She wondered where he was now.

She wondered, too, who he thought might be listening in on the line, and suddenly felt uncomfortable in her own office.

chapter five

"Absolutely unfounded, I can tell you that," Edmond Fisk said calmly into his receiver as he waved Lisa to a seat and swiveled back and forth in his burgundy leather armchair.

The chairman of the board of directors was an imposing, large-framed man in his early sixties with thick, silvery, Phil Donahue hair and a handsome, square face dominated by deep-set steel-blue eyes. According to Matthew, Fisk had overcome his impoverished childhood and made his first million in real estate even before he met his beautiful, stately wife, Georgia, who had brought her own family money to the marriage.

The Fisks were childless. Lisa suspected that was one of the reasons Edmond had been so enthusiastic when Matthew approached him five years ago about building a fertility clinic that would provide hope for thousands of couples yearning for children; and, of course, Matthew's prospectus outlining the potential financial success had been compelling. Fisk had invested significant sums of his own money and convinced several business associates to do the same.

Lisa had seen Fisk only three times since their initial meeting the day after her two-hour interview with Matthew: on her first day at work; at the kosher champagne-and-pizza fete Sam had arranged to celebrate her engagement to Matthew; and at the lavish, black-tie dinner-dance engagement party Edmond and Georgia had hosted in the tented gardens of their Holmby Hills estate. Matthew had insisted on buying Lisa a royal blue Valentino gown at Neiman Marcus to wear to the party. He'd looked so happy and proud, introducing her to everyone, that her misgivings about the extravagant expense had evaporated. She'd wished her parents had been there—Matthew had offered to send them tickets—but her father had claimed that he couldn't leave the business, and her mother hadn't wanted to come alone. Lisa hadn't really believed either excuse, but hadn't pressed.

"Absolutely," Fisk was saying. "I have no problem with that. Tomorrow is fine." He replaced the receiver and faced Lisa. "That was a reporter from *Minute by Minute*. I've had calls at my other office all morning from the media." He paused, as if to let that sink in. "Tell me what the hell is going on."

Feeling as though she'd been called into the principal's office, she told him what had happened, what she'd done to control the situation. He was tapping a Mont Blanc ballpoint pen on his black leather desk mat while he listened. When she was done, he nodded and carefully set the pen on the mat.

"Sounds like you did everything right, Lisa. I'm impressed, and grateful." A half smile softened his face. He clasped his hands and leaned forward. "Still, the situation is extremely damaging. According to media sources—unnamed, of course"—he grunted dismissively—"we're switching embryos, taking eggs from women and giving them, without knowledge or consent, to other patients. Et cetera, et cetera."

"But the charges are unfounded, Mr. Fisk."

"Edmond. Please." This time the smile was wider. "*You* know that, Lisa, and *I* know that. But the public doesn't. Neither do our patients. And following on the heels of the Irvine scandal . . ." He pursed his lips. "The D.A.'s office called. The state medical board advised me that they're going to investigate the clinic's procedures." Slipping on bifocals, he bent his head and read from a lined pad. " 'Pursuant to our investigation, the licenses of all the clinic doctors may be suspended indefinitely.' " He removed his glasses and looked up at Lisa.

Her license suspended. She stared at Fisk, openmouthed. Her palms were clammy.

Fisk walked around his desk and sat in the gray tweed chair next to Lisa. "Where's Matthew?" he asked quietly.

"I have no idea. He phoned his secretary to tell her he'd be late, but didn't tell her why."

Fisk shook his head. "Lisa, you know that doesn't make sense. Matthew must have heard what's happened. He must know that the media have stormed the citadel. Why the hell isn't he here? Why the hell hasn't he called?"

"I don't know." Edmond was right. Matthew had left her a message, but that had been early in the morning. Again she asked herself where he was now. For the first time, she felt a stab of fear.

"He's been preoccupied lately, have you noticed?" Fisk said. "Something's been bothering him. Do you know what?"

She heard concern in his voice and considered telling him. But Matthew hadn't confided in Fisk. He'd said not to tell anyone. Not even Sam. "No. I'm sorry." She met his eyes but flushed under his intense gaze. Her cheeks were warm.

"You're keeping something from me, Lisa. Why? You know how much I care about Matthew. He's like a son to me, and to Georgia."

She believed him. "Edmond, I wish I could help you." That much was true.

He reached over and clasped her hand in both of his. "They're saying Matthew knew that the charges against the clinic were about to be exposed. That he's responsible for the wrongdoings and fled to escape arrest."

"That's insane!" She tried yanking her hand away, but he held on tightly. "You don't believe that, do you, Edmond?"

"I don't *want* to believe it, Lisa. But where is he?"

"I don't *know!*" His eyes were like drills, she thought, boring into her.

Finally he nodded. "Matthew may be unable to come forward because something terrible has happened to him. Or else he's run away, leaving us to deal with a disaster he's created." Fisk paused. "First and foremost, I pray to God he's safe. I think you believe that."

"Yes, of course."

"If he's done something wrong, if he's acted out of desperation,

I'm not saying I wouldn't be disappointed, even angry. I'd feel betrayed. But I'd try to understand, Lisa," he said gently. "I'd try to help him. I can't help him if he's run away."

She almost told him, he sounded so forlorn. But she'd promised. "Matthew hasn't done anything wrong, Edmond. And he hasn't run away. I'd stake my life on that." Which meant something terrible had happened to him. Her chest felt hollow; her eyes smarted. She blinked back tears.

"I hope you're right." Fisk sighed and released her hand. His gait seemed heavier as he returned to his desk and resumed his seat. "Tomorrow a reporter from *Minute by Minute* is coming. If Matthew hasn't appeared by then—and I pray that isn't so—I want you to take her around. Show her that we have nothing to hide, that what these 'unnamed sources' suggest is impossible."

The last thing Lisa wanted was to deal with the media. "What about Sam Davidson? Or Ted Cantrell? They've been with the clinic far longer than I have."

"If I'd wanted Davidson or Cantrell, I would have asked them." Fisk sighed again. "I know that sounded testy, but to tell you the truth, I'm disappointed in you, Lisa, and hurt. I thought you could trust me."

"Believe me, Edmond—"

He held up his hand. "Don't make it worse." He swiveled back and forth, then stopped the chair. "You have patients waiting, don't you?"

She had never been a good liar. She would be married to Asher if she'd been willing to live a lie, as her mother and father had urged her, *begged* her. The same lie they'd lived with for twenty years. The lie her mother had confessed to her, in tears, two weeks before the wedding.

Lisa—she was Aliza then—knew something was wrong. She overheard her parents, who never raised their voices to her or to each other, arguing behind the door to their bedroom. She saw them sneaking glances at her when they thought she wasn't looking. "Tell her!" she overheard her father say one night. "Tell her, or I will!"

And that night her mother told her.

"This is so hard," Esther Brockman began when she was seated next to Lisa on the white-canopied bed. Her face was pallid, her eyes red-rimmed from crying.

"Is it money, *Ima*?" Lisa asked softly. "Because if the wedding is too expensive, if you can't afford it . . ."

Her mother placed her hands on Lisa's head and began to weep so bitterly that Lisa knew this wasn't about money, that her father was gravely ill. Her heart felt pinched, and she tried to banish the thought from her mind, because it was bad luck to contemplate misfortune. "Don't put words in the mouth of Satan," her father had often warned her.

"Don't cry, *Ima*," Lisa whispered, "please don't cry." And that was when her mother told her she was adopted.

At first she was sure she hadn't heard right, but her mother was saying something about "only three days old . . . the happiest day of our life, after so many years of trying." So she sat on the white eyelet comforter and stared at her mother, who was looking down at her hands.

They had searched for a child for years, her mother said. And when the lawyer phoned them and told them about Aliza, they rushed to the hospital and picked her up that same day.

"You were the most beautiful baby," her mother said, glancing up. "Like an angel, with wisps of blond hair for a halo." She reached her hand toward Lisa and touched her hair. "We named you Aliza for your father's grandmother."

"Why didn't you tell me?" Lisa asked, feeling as though this were happening to someone else, as though this were a dream.

"Your father said it was wrong not to tell you. But I wanted you to feel secure, loved. I didn't want you to think, Why didn't my birth mother love me enough to keep me? How can those thoughts be good for a child?"

A lie, Lisa thought. My entire life has been a lie.

"I worried that if you knew, one day you would search for her and love me less." Esther wiped her eyes. "I worried that if people knew, your chances of making a good marriage would be limited. I've seen it happen," she said softly. "It's not right, but it happens. So I convinced your father."

They had been living in Detroit at the time. But Esther had worried even then about keeping the adoption a secret, and she'd persuaded her husband, Nathan, to move to New York and open a new retail clothing store. Not even the family had known the truth. Esther later explained that after trying for so many years to conceive, she hadn't wanted to tell anyone about the pregnancy until after the baby was born. She'd worried about an *ayin hara*, she'd told them—the evil eye. And they'd believed her. Only Esther's parents had known, and they had gone to the grave with the secret.

"But all those pictures you showed me." Her mother in a denim skirt and a royal blue-and-black plaid shirt ballooning over her huge midriff, her father's arm around her. Her mother in a gray flannel jumper and a white blouse. Lisa at five had crayoned a red "Me!" in the center of the jumper.

"I used a pillow." Her eyes were focused over Lisa's head.

"Very clever," Lisa said and saw her mother flush. She felt a thrill of satisfaction, then went hot with stinging shame. "Why are you telling me now?" she asked, surprised by her calm.

Her mother twisted the simple gold band on her wedding finger. "Your father gave me no choice. He's angry I waited till now." She sighed. "You're getting married in two weeks. Under the *chuppah*, a rabbi will perform the ceremony, and another rabbi will read the *ketubah*, the marriage contract with your Hebrew name and Daddy's. But he won't be reading the complete truth."

"I don't understand," Lisa said, but suddenly she knew. "My birth mother isn't Jewish, is she?" she asked and saw from her mother's face that she was right.

"It's not a problem," Esther said quickly. "When you were six weeks old, we took you to the *mikvah*, and three rabbis witnessed your immersion. You had a kosher conversion."

She was converted. How odd that she had no memory of such a momentous event, of being dipped in the rainwaters of the ritual bath, the same kind of ritual bath she would be going to on the night before her wedding.

Had she cried? Had the water been cold? Hot? Had her mother cradled her against her chest and soothed her? Who was her birth mother? Who had fathered her? Why had they given her up?

"The thing is—" Esther cleared her throat. "Since you were a child when you were converted, you were supposed to affirm when you became bat mitzvah that you wanted to be Jewish." Again her mother studied her hands. "We should have told you then."

Lisa stared at her. "So if *Aba* hadn't forced you, you would have let me go through with a sham wedding?"

"It's not a sham! In my eyes you're Jewish! In God's eyes you're Jewish! I believe that with all my heart!"

It wasn't a big deal, her moother said. Aliza didn't even have to go to the *mikvah* again. All she had to do was affirm her acceptance of Judaism by continuing to keep all the Torah laws. "And no one has to know." She grabbed Lisa's hands. "Your children will be one hundred percent Jewish, and their children, and their children."

"I have to tell Asher. He has a right to know."

Her mother looked stricken. "What *difference* would it make to him if you were born Jewish or became Jewish? Does it change your face? Your heart? Your soul? You're *Jewish*, Aliza."

"It's *unethical* not to tell him!"

"Don't be stupid! Don't throw your life away for nothing! I'm *begging* you, Aliza!"

Her father begged her, too.

In the end, she decided to tell Asher. He listened quietly and told her it didn't matter who her parents were. "You're the one I love," he said. "Nothing changes that."

"You see?" she told her parents, her voice ringing with triumphant vindication. "You were wrong."

Two days later Asher's father called Aliza's father. She picked up the extension in her room when she learned her future father-in-law was on the line and heard him talk about "misrepresentations" and "deceit" and "dishonor."

"We would never have allowed the match if we'd known," Jacob Rossner said just before she hung up the phone, unwilling to hear more.

Asher phoned her and told her not to worry. His parents were understandably upset—more shocked than upset, really—but they would come around. It was just a question of time.

And Aliza had been hopeful.

But the next morning a messenger returned the gold Ebel watch and the twenty-volume, gilt-edged set of the Talmud that Aliza's father had given Asher as an engagement gift. And Aliza returned the one-and-a-half-carat, pear-shaped diamond ring Asher's parents had bought her, along with the gold bracelet and two sterling silver Sabbath candlesticks.

Within the year Asher was married. By then Aliza had moved out of her parents' home into an apartment she shared with two other young women she'd met at Brooklyn College. She'd distanced herself from the close friends she'd known since her childhood—she never knew for certain how the Rossners had explained the broken engagement, but she'd sensed stares, imagined whispers. "Did you know . . . ?" And she'd changed her name to Lisa.

She stopped keeping kosher and honoring the Sabbath out of bitterness and anger—at her parents for keeping the truth from her; at Asher and the Rossners for rejecting her so cruelly; at a community she decided was filled with others like them, others who would always regard her as second best; at a religion that condoned their behavior.

She quickly forgave her parents, who had acted with the best of intentions, and she made her kitchen kosher so that they could eat in her home. Later she began to understand the pain of their childlessness, the pain of their choice to keep her adoption a secret; ultimately, she chose a career that would allow her to help couples like them conceive children, to help only children have the siblings for whom she had always yearned.

She found it harder to forgive the Rossners. But at some point she began to wonder whether she was being fair in condemning an entire community because of the actions of one family. Pride and cowardice kept her from trying to find out, just as confusion kept her from returning to the ritual and traditions she missed, traditions that had shaped and colored her life. (They weren't, after all, *her* traditions, were they? she'd argued with herself; why should she follow a religion she hadn't voluntarily chosen, particularly such a demanding one?)

Somewhere along the way, confusion was cemented by convenience, so when she met Matthew, she told herself there was no reason not to date him, no reason not to allow herself to fall in love with him.

Now she didn't know how she felt.

And she didn't know where he was.

She had stopped praying a long time ago, but after being dismissed by Edmond, she closed the door to her office and, in the Hebrew that came back haltingly from memory, recited a psalm and asked God to keep Matthew safe.

chapter six

"I hope I'm not disturbing you," Selena said, entering Lisa's office. "You looked so upset when you came back from seeing Mr. Fisk. I wanted to make sure you're all right."

"He said people think Matthew ran away to avoid being arrested for wrongdoings at the clinic." Her lips trembled. She pressed them tightly together.

"Dr. Gordon? Never!" Selena approached Lisa, who was standing in front of the office window. "You haven't heard from him?"

She'd tried him at home and in his car again; again there had been no answer. She turned around and shook her head. "Where *is* he, Selena?" She started crying quietly.

Selena put her arms around Lisa and rubbed her back in slow, small circles. "You'll see, *mi hija*," she whispered. "Everything will be all right. Trust in God."

Lisa rested against Selena's pillow chest, which smelled faintly of roses. It was so comforting. For a brief moment she closed her eyes and imagined she was with her mother; reluctantly she drew away. "Do me a favor?" She wiped her eyes. "Phone the highway patrol and find out if Dr. Gordon was involved in an accident. He drives a black BMW, but I don't know the license-plate number."

"Right away."

"Phone the area hospitals, too. And the police." Lisa adjusted the clip on her hair. "I must look a mess. How many more patients today?" For the hundredth time she wished Ava were here.

"Six scheduled, five unscheduled. You can do it. And you look fine—just a few mascara streaks." Selena handed Lisa a tissue from the pocket of her skirt and nodded approvingly as Lisa dabbed at her cheeks and under her eyes. "The Hoffmans are here, by the way. I put them in a room."

Lisa frowned. "Naomi was here just yesterday. Is she having contractions?" Naomi was almost thirty-six weeks pregnant. It wasn't unusual for someone carrying twins to go into premature labor, but Lisa wanted to delay delivery until Naomi had finished thirty-seven weeks and the babies' lungs were well developed.

"She didn't say she was. Actually, she left yesterday without being examined. I saw her in Reception, and I *know* she went to one of the examining rooms. But Dr. Cantrell said that when he went in to see her—you were with the detective, remember?—she wasn't there. He was very annoyed." Selena was rolling her eyes.

Lisa smiled in sympathy. "I'll bet he let you know it, huh?"

"He threw Mrs. Hoffman's file at me and yelled about my wasting his time." She shrugged to indicate she didn't care, but her face had reddened.

Lisa pursed her lips. "Do you want me to talk to him?"

"No, thanks. I can handle *el doctor* Cantrell." She smiled grimly.

Not everyone could. Lisa had heard stories about the doctor's tantrums. One of the two operating nurses refused to work with him. His nurse had quit a week ago, without notice, joining a long line of predecessors. Lisa had already seen her replacement in tears; she doubted that the young woman would last the month.

"Do you have any idea why Naomi left, Selena?"

"No. I should have been more on top of things. Sorry." The color in her cheeks had deepened.

Lisa squeezed Selena's shoulder. "Don't be silly. You know how emotional pregnant women are. And they *do* fixate on one doctor." Especially women who have gone through a great deal to become pregnant. "Maybe she was tired of waiting. What room is she in?"

"Seven."

That was another thing about Ted, Lisa thought as she walked down the hall to the examining room. He often kept patients waiting. Really, she didn't know why Matthew tolerated him.

The thought made her stop short. Was that whom Matthew was contemplating firing? *Ted Cantrell?* Matthew always defended him. "Ted's a genius at what he does, Lisa," he'd respond whenever she related Cantrell horror stories. "And you know how high-strung geniuses can be."

Had Matthew tired of the complaints?

Or had a staff member targeted by Cantrell threatened to sue the clinic for workmen's compensation? Fisk would be annoyed, to say the least.

But Matthew had told her that if what he suspected were true, the clinic could be destroyed. Workmen's comp suits were expensive, but they wouldn't ruin the clinic. Unless there was an *epidemic* of suits. . . .

But what about the media allegations about embryo switching? Had Matthew known beforehand about the charges?

And where *was* Matthew?

Naomi Hoffman, wearing a pale mauve cotton clinic gown, was lying on the examining table, her face hidden from view by the huge mound that was her swollen midriff. Her husband was standing in front of the large window that faced the velvety green clinic grounds, opening and shutting the slats of the gray mini-blinds. At Lisa's entrance, he turned and walked over to his wife.

They could have been brother and sister. They had the same dark brown hair, hazel eyes, fair complexions. Baruch Hoffman was pleasant-looking, slender, and a little under six feet; Naomi was petite and fine-boned, with a delicate beauty Lisa found arresting.

She approached the examining table, Naomi's file under her arm. "I'm sorry if you've been waiting. How are you feeling, Naomi? Any contractions?"

"No. Other than huge and ungainly, I'm fine." She propped herself up on her elbows.

"You look beautiful," her husband said, helping her to a sitting position.

"If you like Humpty-Dumpty." Smiling, Naomi tugged on the

bangs of her dark brown wig until they reached just above her eyebrows.

Many married Orthodox Jewish women covered their hair, some with wigs, some with hats or berets or scarves. When Lisa had met the Hoffmans, she'd known from the husband's black velvet yarmulke that he was Orthodox, but she hadn't realized at first that Naomi was wearing a wig. Out of practice, she'd thought wryly. Growing up in Brooklyn, she and her friends had been experts at detecting wigs and rating them according to how natural they looked.

As a child, Lisa had delighted in trying on her mother's light brown wigs and parading in front of her parents. For her marriage she'd ordered two wigs that had exactly matched her own honey-blond hair. Asher's parents had paid for the custom-made one; she'd returned it along with the other gifts. She assumed her mother had passed the other wig on to a needy blond bride.

"We heard the news, Dr. Brockman," Baruch said. "It was on all the networks and radio stations. Frankly, I don't understand how something like this could have happened."

He sounded calm but disapproving, and he was frowning. Lisa braced herself for anger, recriminations. "Mr. Hoffman, nothing *has* happened. No embryos have been switched. We take precautions with every step of the fertility process to prevent something like that from happening." She'd repeated the same information so many times today to so many patients and their spouses. She knew she sounded tired. She hoped she didn't sound rehearsed.

"If there's no truth, why would the media publicize these charges?" Baruch's voice, like his jaw, had taken on a hard edge.

"Baruch, *please*. We agreed we wouldn't dwell on this, okay? It doesn't concern us." Naomi lay down on the table and placed her hands on her rounded abdomen. "We *know* these babies are ours. Thank God we had a *shomer* all the time, so of course nothing could have been switched."

The *shomer*. The word meant a "guard." Lisa had momentarily forgotten about the tall, reedlike, blond young man the Hoffmans had hired to supervise every step of the IVF process and verify that Naomi's eggs had been joined with her husband's sperm.

Lisa had sensed the Hoffmans' initial awkwardness at having the dark-suited *shomer*, a man they didn't even know, join them in the operating room during the harvesting of Naomi's eggs. She herself had been acutely aware of his presence. But the *shomer* had been discreet and careful not to violate Naomi's modesty. Naomi, anesthetized, had been oblivious to what was going on around her, and Lisa had quickly forgotten about him as she concentrated on the ultrasound images that guided her in aspirating the eggs from Naomi's follicles into test tubes.

The *shomer*, Lisa recalled, had overseen the lab technician in the operating room as she'd transferred the eggs into labeled petri dishes, checked their viability under a microscope, and transferred them again into sterile test tubes—labeled with Naomi Hoffman's name—which the *shomer* had initialed in Hebrew. He'd observed the removal, by microsurgery, of Baruch's semen and the mingling of his washed sperm with Naomi's eggs.

For three days the *shomer* had kept vigil in the lab, hovering over the Hoffman petri dishes every morning as a lab technician checked the fertilization progress. Finally, he'd been present while Lisa had implanted the fertilized embryos in Naomi.

Given the clinic's precautions, Lisa had been annoyed by what she'd deemed unnecessary complications. (Annoyed, too, she wondered now, by the intrusion of Orthodox rules into her world?) Yet she'd been defensive when Charlie had questioned the *shomer*'s presence in the lab. "Is he blessing the eggs, or what?" Charlie had asked. Lisa had explained. Charlie had shrugged and said, "It takes all kinds, huh?" and she'd wondered what he'd say if she told him that she and the *shomer* were the same kind, that they came from the same world.

Baruch was scowling. "That's not the point, Naomi. What if we *hadn't* hired a *shomer*? Can you imagine the disaster we'd be facing now?"

"But we *did* have a *shomer*. Can we stop talking about this? *Please*?" She turned her head. Her face was flushed from exasperation or embarrassment at her husband's outburst, or both. Her lips were trembling.

There was an uncomfortable silence in the room. Then Baruch quietly said, "I'm sorry, you're right. Please don't get upset. It's not good for the babies. Or for me." His smile was strained.

So was Naomi's. She faced Lisa. "By the way, Dr. Brockman, I'm sorry about leaving yesterday without telling anyone. I don't know what got into me." She laughed self-consciously.

"Must have been hormones." This time Baruch's smile was more relaxed. "She's been moody lately, Doctor. I'm contemplating turning her in for a new model. What do you think?" he asked Lisa while gazing affectionately at his wife.

Lisa was relieved that the tempest was over. "I'd hold on a little longer," she said, gratified to see the return of the tenderness in the way they looked at each other.

When Lisa first met the Hoffmans, they'd been trying to conceive for nine years. Naomi had undergone surgery to deal with endometriosis, then another surgery to open a blocked Fallopian tube. She'd taken Clomid, an oral fertility drug. When that failed to produce a pregnancy, the couple had tried artificial insemination using Baruch's sperm, then IVF. Both procedures had failed, too. Finally, a friend had recommended the Westwood clinic.

During the first few appointments with the Hoffmans, Lisa had sadly noted anxiety, depression, self-recrimination, tension, and desperate, tenacious hope—all so typical of couples frustrated and heartbroken and often financially strangled by their failed attempts to conceive a child. Adding to the Hoffmans' pressure was the fact that Baruch was the only son of Sender Hoffman, a Torah scholar descended from a small rabbinic dynasty in Poland that spanned five generations. Baruch's married sisters had children, Naomi had told Lisa, but he was expected to produce an heir who would continue the line.

The pressure had taken its toll. Though Naomi and Baruch had often expressed their unwavering faith in God and acceptance of His will, they weren't stoic. Naomi had cried bitterly when the first cycle of fertility drugs failed to produce enough follicles to harvest her eggs.

Lisa was frustrated and heartbroken, too, each time she had to relay negative news. "Don't identify so intensely with your patients," Sam had warned her several times. "It takes a toll." Matthew had said the same thing. Good advice, but she suspected that behind Sam's jocularity and Matthew's carefully maintained equanimity lay emotional involvement equal to hers. (In her mind she heard again the pain in Matthew's voice when he had learned of Chelsea Wright's murder. She wondered suddenly whether Detective Barone was making any progress in finding her killer.)

There was ego involved, too. A negative pregnancy test spelled failure not only for the couple, but for the doctor. And a positive result presented its own dangers. Lisa tried to keep fresh in her mind her mother's soft-spoken comment: "It's a wonderful thing you're doing, Aliza. Just remember, only God creates babies. Doctors are there to help carry out His plans."

It was an important reminder in the exciting world of assisted reproduction, where grateful patients were all too eager to deify their physicians. One wall in her office was filled with snapshots of her successes—many of them twins—here at the Westwood clinic, and earlier at the Manhattan clinic where she'd previously worked. On the snapshots were handwritten messages from the infants' parents: "Thank you for our baby." "You changed our lives!" "You're an angel!"

Naomi Hoffman had cried when she'd learned she was pregnant with twins. Then she'd thanked Lisa. "A double blessing," she'd said, clutching Lisa's hands. "God works miracles, doesn't He?" And when Baruch had stepped out of the room, she'd whispered, half joking, "You saved my marriage!"

It was an awesome responsibility, one Lisa didn't feel comfortable shouldering.

Now Naomi was just weeks away from giving birth. Lisa examined her and listened to the two distinct fetal heartbeats. "They both sound great." She let Naomi and Baruch hear the heartbeats, then coiled her stethoscope. "Remember to let me know the instant you have a contraction, Naomi, no matter how small."

"I will."

She slipped Naomi's chart back inside the green folder. "I'll see you next week. Until then, continue to stay in bed as much as possible. No lifting, no housework, no—"

"No sex. I know." Naomi flashed a quick, playful smile at her husband, whose face had turned pink. "Thanks again for seeing me today, Dr. Brockman. I know you're swamped with patients because of the news reports. I hope you find out who's behind all these horrible rumors."

Lisa hoped so, too.

She saw two more patients, then checked with Grace, who still hadn't heard from Matthew. And he'd left no new messages on Lisa's home answering machine. Over the nurse's halfhearted protest Lisa entered his office and thumbed through the pages of his black leather-bound desk calendar.

Nothing.

The drawers revealed nothing. Neither did the neatly stacked folders on his rosewood desk. The message pad was blank. There was a lone ball of crumpled white paper in the antique brass trash basket. She picked it up and smoothed it open. He'd written "data lies?!" and "forget sig!"

She studied the cryptic writing. "Forget sig" was probably "forget signature." Whose signature had he forgotten? And what data was he referring to? She stuffed the paper into her jacket pocket. She would puzzle it out later.

"Mrs. Martin is waiting in five," Selena told her when she returned to Reception. "The highway patrol has no report of an accident involving Dr. Gordon's car, *gracias a Dios*. There's no police report on him, and he hasn't been admitted to any of the local hospitals. Why are you frowning? No news is good news, *mi hija*."

"Sorry. That *is* good news. I was thinking about something else." What was the paper doing in the trash basket? The custodians emptied the baskets every evening when they cleaned the building. Lisa's basket had been empty this morning.

She made sure not to rush through the examination with Linda Martin and spent time answering her many questions. Then, telling Selena she'd be right back, she hurried downstairs to the lab.

Charlie McCallister told her he'd arrived at the clinic at seven in the morning as usual, but he hadn't seen Matthew all day. Neither had Norman Weld, the soft-spoken lab assistant, or any of the other lab technicians.

"Wish I could help," Charlie said, putting his arm around Lisa. "He'll show up, you'll see. And you can give him hell for pulling this Houdini act, right?"

"Right." She forced herself to smile.

"It's all bull, by the way—this stuff about embryo switching." His voice, normally jovial, was hard with anger. "Not on my watch. Not in my lab. That's what I told the Hoffmans."

"The Hoffmans were here?" She squinted at him, puzzled.

"They came to check their frozen embryos. I took them next door, lifted the vials from the vats, showed them that their embryos were properly labeled. They seemed relieved."

She felt sorry for the Hoffmans, who shouldn't have to worry about the safety of their frozen embryos, and was grateful that Charlie had been able to calm their fears.

Back on the ground floor, she headed for her office, then changed her mind and walked to the main entrance. The uniformed guard was outside, his back to the wide glass double doors; his arms were folded across his chest. When she opened the door, he turned quickly to see who had exited the building.

"Hey, Doc." A gun protruded from the pocket of his black uniform trousers.

"Hey, Victor."

At six feet five inches and two hundred and twenty pounds, the dark blond former boxer was an imposing figure. He was mean-looking when he scowled, but he was always nice to Lisa. Too many poundings to the head had taken their toll, but he was excellent at obeying orders, and his eyesight and hearing were keen.

He clacked the gum he was chewing. "Look at 'em."

He inclined his chin toward his trunklike, muscular neck and nodded in the direction of the two men standing in front of a white van in the clinic's large, crowded parking lot. Lisa had already noticed them. They'd been leaning against the van. At her appearance they'd jumped, as if electrified, and bent their heads together in conference. Now they were staring at her.

"They don't know, is something going down or not?" Victor said. "Are you important or not? Drives 'em crazy." Another satisfied smack of the gum.

"Victor, have you seen Dr. Gordon?"

"Today, you mean?"

"Yes." She tried not to sound impatient.

"Most of the media have gone, you know. These are the scouts. Mr. Fisk said, 'Keep 'em out, Victor.' "

She thought she would scream. "Victor, about Dr. Gordon?"

"You haven't talked to him?" He narrowed his eyes in bewilderment.

"No. Not since last night. I'm worried about him, Victor. If you know something about where he is—"

"I don't know where he is. How would I know that, Doc?" He sounded aggrieved. He chewed for a moment, then said, "He made me promise not to tell, but of course he didn't mean you, 'cause you're his fiancée."

Her heart skipped a beat. "You saw him?"

He nodded. "Early this morning. Around six."

Why hadn't she thought to ask Victor earlier? "Did he say why he was here so early?"

"Nope. He didn't sign in, neither. I said, 'Hey, Dr. Gordon, you got to sign in, 'cause it's before seven o'clock. It's the rule.' And he said, 'C'mon, Victor. I'm the one that *made* the rule.' " Victor shot a quick glance at Lisa to make sure she understood, then faced forward again. "See, they're huddling again, wondering what you and I are talkin' about."

"How long was Dr. Gordon here?" And why had he gone in so early? Whom had he hoped to avoid?

"About half an hour. When he was leaving, he said, 'Victor, don't tell anyone I was here.' So I didn't. Not even Mr. Fisk."

"Do you know where he was—where in the building, I mean?"

Victor shook his head. "He has keys to everything, so he could have been anywhere." He frowned. "You won't tell Mr. Fisk that I lied to him, will you? 'Cause he might fire me."

"I won't tell."

"You think I did right, not telling?"

"You did right, Victor."

The guard turned toward the lot. "You don't think Doc Gordon's in real trouble, do you? 'Cause I like him a lot."

"I like him a lot, too, Victor," Lisa said softly.

chapter seven

Matthew's BMW wasn't in his assigned space in the condominium's underground lot. Lisa parked her white Altima in his slot and took the mahogany-paneled elevator to the twelfth floor. She unlocked the door to his apartment, using the set of keys he'd given her only last week. "Just in case you want to surprise me one night," he'd joked.

Standing in front of his door, she felt dizzy with fear. Matthew had said he was stopping at his condo. What if someone had followed him here, robbed him, stolen his car? What if Matthew was inside, unconscious, or . . . She didn't allow herself to finish the thought. She opened the door and stepped onto the beige marble tile of the rectangular entryway.

"Matthew?"

She edged into the large living room, hugging her arms in protest against the frigid temperature. The central air-conditioning must have been running all day. Fear had led her to expect a room in shambles—upturned furniture, tilted artwork, shredded pillows.

But everything seemed in order. Nothing, as far as she could tell, was missing. Still, her heart was pounding. Holding her breath, her eyes darting right and left, she walked quickly past the brass-and-glass sofa table into the dining area, then past the compact, state-of-the-art kitchen and down a short hall. Finally, she pushed open the door to the master bedroom.

He wasn't there. Not on the king-size bed, neatly made up with a geometric-patterned tan-and-hunter-green comforter and matching shams. Not on the cream-colored Berber carpet.

She checked the master bath. A plush hunter-green bath sheet hung over the brass-framed door to the large beige-marbled stall shower. The room was empty. So were the other bedroom and the powder room and the office where Matthew often worked late into the night. His laptop was shut. The notepad on his mahogany desk was blank.

She returned to the bedroom and, approaching the large walk-in closet with trepidation that she told herself was the product of too many suspense films, yanked open the door.

She saw immediately that some of his suits were missing. So were his Louis Vuitton garment bag and satchel, part of a set he'd recently bought for their honeymoon.

There were shirts missing, too. And shoes. And ties. And underwear from his dresser drawers. And his electric shaver.

They're saying Matthew knew that the charges against the clinic were about to be exposed, Edmond had said.

"He didn't run away!" Lisa said defiantly to the walls.

She sank onto the bed where they'd made love many times and, hugging her knees, rocked back and forth, willing herself not to panic. But there was no escaping the fact that if Matthew hadn't fled, something sinister had happened to him. She got off the bed and stared again into the closet, into his dresser drawers, into his medicine cabinet. Then she walked into the kitchen and phoned the police.

"I want to report someone missing," she said quickly when a male dispatcher answered the call. "Dr. Matthew Gordon." She gave the condominium's Brentwood address. "I'm Dr. Lisa Brockman. I'm his fiancée."

"How long has Dr. Gordon been missing?"

A lone coffee mug lay upside down on the white drainboard on the black granite counter, next to Wednesday's *Los Angeles Times* and a printed listing of California fertility clinics. Those in the L.A. area had been highlighted in yellow. "He left a message on my answering machine this morning, but—"

"Ma'am, we can't declare someone missing until twenty-four hours have elapsed."

"But I *know* he's missing! Something is terribly wrong!"

"Is there any sign of foul play, ma'am? Anything to suggest he's been kidnapped?"

Hearing someone verbalize her fear chilled her. "No."

"Ma'am, I'm sorry. You can call back in the morning if you still haven't heard from Dr. Gordon."

Lisa listened to the dial tone blaring in her ear, then replaced the receiver and sat down on a black leather bar stool. She could call Edmond, but Matthew's missing clothing and luggage would confirm the director's unwilling suspicion that Matthew had fled. She could call Sam, but what could he do, other than provide comfort? He was a doctor, not a detective.

She thought of Barone. Her purse was in front of her, on the counter. She rummaged through its sections and found the detective's card. She punched the numbers. When a voice answered, she asked for Barone and heard he'd left for the day.

"Is this urgent?" the woman on the line asked Lisa.

"Yes, it is."

The buzzing of the intercom startled her. She jumped up from Matthew's bed, where she'd been lying, and hurried to the entry. When she heard Barone's accented voice through the intercom, she pressed the button to admit him into the lobby.

Minutes later the doorbell rang. She was jittery from worrying and waiting and pacing around the apartment, and though she'd just heard his voice, she made sure to look through the security window before she opened the door.

"My wife and I were at a movie when the dispatcher reached me," he said, following Lisa into the living room and sitting down next to her on one of the plush beige chenille sofas. "She said it was urgent. You've remembered something about Chelsea Wright?"

His brown eyes were intense with excitement; his whole body exuded energy. She felt guilty, knowing she was about to disappoint him, and nervous, because he would be angry. "This isn't about Chelsea. Dr. Gordon is missing. Something's happened to him.

This is his place, by the way. He's my fiancé," she added before Barone could ask why she was here.

"I see."

She met his eyes defiantly, marveling at the control he exercised over his face, which revealed nothing, wishing she could do the same.

"You didn't mention this to the dispatcher," he said, his voice more questioning than accusing.

"I was afraid you wouldn't come. I didn't know where else to turn." She saw a hint of a nod; encouraged, she continued. "I phoned the West L.A. police and told them I hadn't heard from Matthew—Dr. Gordon—since this morning. They told me he won't be considered missing until tomorrow."

"I'm afraid that's department policy. You'd be amazed at how many 'missing' people show up within that time period." He paused. "Dr. Gordon may have been involved in a car accident."

"Not according to the highway patrol and the area hospitals. And there's no police report involving him." She'd checked again before leaving the clinic. "Matthew *is* missing. He's being held against his will, or . . ." *Don't put words in the mouth of Satan.* She started crying and took the tissue Barone handed her.

"When did he contact you?" he asked after she'd composed herself.

"He left a message on my home machine at six forty-five this morning. I haven't heard from him since. Neither has anyone else at the clinic. That's *totally* out of character."

"Especially today, with everything else going on. I can imagine the tension you must be feeling, Dr. Brockman. And you can imagine my surprise when I heard your clinic mentioned in the news today. Quite a coincidence, don't you think?" His voice and eyes were still noncommittal. His mustache camouflaged his mouth.

"Yes, it is." Of *course* Barone had heard the allegations. Was that why he was here? Was he inferring a connection between Chelsea's murder and the uproar at the clinic? And how would he view Matthew's disappearance? She picked up a fringed beige damask pillow and hugged it to her chest.

"What did Dr. Gordon say in his message?"

"Last night he told me he suspected something was wrong at the clinic. He refused to be specific, but he was determined to find out who was responsible. In his message he said he might be onto something."

"He didn't say what?"

Lisa shook her head. "He was at the clinic at six this morning." She repeated what Victor had told her. "And I found this in his trash basket at the clinic." Laying the pillow aside, she picked up the piece of paper on the marble-based glass coffee table in front of the sofa and handed it to Barone. " 'Sig' is probably 'signature.' I don't know whose. And I don't know which data he's referring to—unless it's for the research he's been doing."

Barone looked at the paper. "What kind of research?"

"Freezing patients' eggs. There's been limited success at turning frozen eggs into healthy infants. The process is still too costly and inefficient. But I don't know what he meant by 'lies.' " She'd barely had time to think about it. "His laptop is here. It might explain the 'data' reference, but I didn't turn it on. I didn't want to ruin any fingerprints."

"I don't think you need to worry about that." Barone put the paper on the table. "Dr. Gordon tells you he's onto something. Hours later you think he's met with foul play because he hasn't called you?"

She hesitated before telling him—she knew what he'd think. "Some of his clothes are missing, and some luggage. But he didn't run away." Her eyes welled with tears. "He said he was stopping at his condo before checking out some things. Someone followed him here. Someone took his things and his car to make it *appear* that he ran away because of the charges against the clinic."

"Do you have any idea who that could be?"

"No." She hadn't come to terms with the idea that someone she worked with every day, talked with, joked with, had engineered Matthew's disappearance. The thought was preposterous, obscene. "He said he hadn't phoned me at the clinic because someone could be listening in. He didn't say who. And last night he said he might have to fire someone because of problems at the clinic."

"But he wasn't specific as to that, either?"

She searched his voice for sarcasm but found none. "No."

Barone pulled at his mustache. "Maybe his investigation made it necessary for him to leave town immediately. Or maybe he learned of a family emergency."

"His parents are dead, and he's an only child. He's never mentioned any close family. In either case, he would have called by now. I keep checking my machines at home and at the clinic. He hasn't called. Someone took his things," she repeated.

"What makes you believe that?"

She'd thought about this while waiting for Barone. "I know

which suits are missing. Matthew was planning to give them away—they're outdated. And they took his electric shaver, but he wasn't using it anymore. About a month ago he started using a razor."

Unbidden images—intimate, sensual—flashed through her mind. Matthew standing in his shorts in front of her medicine cabinet, stripping away the thick white mounds of lather in neat, parallel rows that exposed the contours of his cheekbones, his chin, his jaw. Matthew shaving her legs. Though she was plagued with uncertainty about marrying him, the possibility that she would never see him again was a physical ache.

"Anything else?" Barone asked.

It took her a second to focus on his question. "The air-conditioning was running all day. Matthew would never have left it on if he'd gone away of his own will—he's frugal about things like that."

"He may have left in a hurry."

"Even so," she said. "And someone searched through his dresser and armoire. His shirts and underwear and socks—everything is a little messy. Matthew likes everything perfectly folded, in its spot." His obsessive neatness, usually somewhat annoying, seemed suddenly endearing.

"My wife would be envious. With me, neatness is, to borrow from Shakespeare, 'a custom more honored in the breach than the observance.' I'm afraid our two sons follow in my footsteps." Barone smiled.

"I know this sounds silly."

"Not silly at all," he said soberly. "It's the details that are often key." He glanced around for the first time since he'd arrived, his eyes lighting on the black baby grand piano in front of the uncurtained French doors at the far end of the room; the ecru silk moiré padded walls; the lithographs and sculptures that accented the serene beauty of the room. "This is very beautiful, very elegant. Your design?" he asked, turning back to Lisa.

He hadn't asked, "Very expensive?" but she heard it in his voice. "Matthew hired a decorator." He was unabashedly proud of this spacious, three-bedroom condominium and his BMW. Growing up in Minneapolis, he'd lived in a one-bedroom apartment and slept in the living room. Lisa often thought how sad it was that his parents weren't alive to see their only child's success.

"I'll take a look," Barone said and left the room.

She sat for a moment, then walked to the French doors and stared past the balcony at the twinkling lights of Century City. Was Matthew nearby, being held against his will? Was he alive?

"Dr. Brockman?"

She turned and walked toward the detective. She saw immediately from his face that he had nothing to tell her. What had she expected? A dramatic, Sherlock Holmes solution?

Barone was frowning. "I know this is painful, but you have to consider the possibility that Dr. Gordon left voluntarily."

"No." Lisa shook her head and sank onto the sofa.

He sat down next to her. "His car is gone. There's no evidence to support that it's been stolen. There's no evidence of foul play here, no evidence of a break-in."

"Someone got hold of his keys," she said impatiently. "Someone took the wrong things." Hadn't Barone been listening? Her fingers dug into the sofa cushions.

"Dr. Brockman, try to think as a scientist, not as a fiancée. Dr. Gordon heads a clinic charged with misconduct. If he's responsible, he had good reason to flee."

"If you knew Matthew, you'd also know that he didn't do anything wrong. He was trying to find out who *was* doing something wrong!" Why didn't Barone understand that Matthew was in danger?

"Perhaps. Even if he's not responsible, he may have decided he had to leave town for a while. So he doesn't take his best suit. So he takes his electric shaver. He's not careful about being neat when he's packing. He's in a rush. He's not thinking clearly, you understand?"

"But he didn't call."

"He may not want to place you in danger. Or he may be worrying that any call he makes to you can be traced."

There was a nugget of comfort in what he was suggesting. "Is that what you think? That Matthew is lying low until he finds out who's behind the problems at the clinic?"

"As you pointed out, I don't know Dr. Gordon."

Which meant that Barone believed Matthew was guilty. "What if he didn't leave voluntarily? Can you make some inquiries, try to find him?"

"I'm a homicide detective, Dr. Brockman."

"I see. So someone has to be *dead* to get your help, is that right? I'm sorry," she added quickly. "I'm frightened and tired. I shouldn't be taking my frustrations out on you." She pushed herself up from the cocoon of the sofa. "Thanks for coming. I'm sorry I wasted your time." And mine, she said silently.

Barone stood, too. "I'm investigating Chelsea Wright's murder. If Dr. Gordon's disappearance is connected to that, then of course I'd do my best to locate him."

Was he offering to help her? All she had to do was say yes, there was a connection. "Matthew told you everything he knew."

"What if the 'something' he learned tied the clinic problems in with her? Think about it, Dr. Brockman," he said when she didn't answer. He walked to the entry.

Lisa followed him. "You really think there's a connection?"

"Two weeks ago Chelsea Wright visited your clinic. Three days ago she was murdered. Today the clinic is in the news and the director has disappeared. I'm a detective, Dr. Brockman. I don't believe in coincidence. As a scientist, do you?"

"So you'll look for him?" She was light-headed with relief.

"Chelsea Wright's murder is my first priority. Get me something concrete, and I'll check into it."

"You're the detective." Anger stirred within her. Was he playing games with her?

"You're at the clinic every day. You know the people. You have access to the files."

"What about Chelsea's boyfriend? You said he gave her a diamond pendant, so they must have been serious. Maybe she confided something to him that could be significant."

"Dennis Hearly." Barone sighed. "I spoke to him at the Century City Brentano's, where he works. He knew Chelsea donated eggs, but was surprised to learn she was at the clinic two weeks ago. A nice young man—bright, sensitive. He cried when he told me he and Chelsea were planning to marry." Barone opened the door. "Find me the connection, Dr. Brockman."

She locked the door behind him and walked through the condominium again. At the door to Matthew's office she stopped, then crossed the room to his desk. She turned on the laptop computer and viewed the directory for the main drive.

There were countless files. Judging by their names, most of them were patient files, probably duplicates of the ones Matthew kept at the clinic. She had no idea where to start, what to look for. None of the files was named "forget sig" or "data lies."

She scrolled again through the directory. The latest entry— Matthew had named it "Notes"—had been made at 12:08 this morning. He'd worked on it after coming home from her place.

She accessed the software program and tried calling up the file. The prompt asked for USER'S PASSWORD. She typed MATTHEW. The prompt blinked: "Access denied."

The ringing of the phone jarred her, and she jumped in her seat, then picked up the receiver, unsure whether to say hello. When she finally did, there was silence at the other end, then the sound of a receiver being hung up.

She pressed STAR 69, a feature that would connect her with the last incoming number. She listened to the ringing of the phone for over a minute before she hung up.

It occurred to her that the caller had wanted to see if anyone was in the condo. She was jittery and had difficulty focusing on the "Notes" file. She typed Matthew's birthday. Again access was denied. She tried her own name, his mother's name, his father's name. With each rejection she was increasingly frustrated. Finally, she admitted defeat for the night. She was anxious to read the file and find out why Matthew had protected it, but she was too tired to think, and the call had made her feel vulnerable. She decided to take the laptop with her.

On the way home she thought again about the "Notes" file. She also contemplated Barone's offer and wondered whether he was sincere in wanting to help, or whether he thought Matthew had run away out of guilt, and was hoping, through Lisa, to trap him.

She was normally a cautious driver and always checked her rearview mirror every thirty seconds or so, a habit her father had ingrained in her when he taught her to drive. Several minutes after leaving Brentwood, she started paying careful attention to the car behind her. She'd noticed it when she was driving west on San Vicente; it had turned right when she had turned right onto Barrington, then left onto National. It was possible that, given the day's events, she was paranoid.

It was also possible that she was being followed.

By Barone?

By Edmond Fisk, who hoped Lisa would lead him to Matthew? He hadn't believed that she didn't know where Matthew was.

By the someone who had engineered Matthew's disappearance?

Her heart beating faster, she drove under the San Diego Freeway overpass and turned right onto Sepulveda. The car pulled back but was still behind her, its headlights glaring at her. At Palms she made a sharp left and accelerated.

She'd already decided that if the car stayed on her tail, she wouldn't go home. She dialed 911 on her cellular phone and asked for the address of the nearest police station, which she learned was about one mile away, in Culver City.

"Is there a problem, ma'am?" the dispatcher asked.

She was two blocks from Keystone and her apartment building. She looked in the rearview mirror again.

The car was gone.

"No, no problem. Thanks anyway." Her hands were shaking. Her thighs and underarms were drenched with perspiration.

Get a grip, she told herself.

chapter eight

The *Minute by Minute* reporter, Gina Franco, was tall and thin and strikingly pretty, with creamy skin set off by short, thick black hair that sat like a glossy helmet on her head. She was wearing tan slacks and a navy blazer. A lace-edged, ivory cotton camisole peeked out from the V of the jacket.

"Thanks for seeing me, Dr. Brockman," she said after they shook hands. "I'm sure your schedule is hectic enough without having to make time for the media." Her smile softened her angular face and the intensity of her gray-blue eyes.

"That's quite all right." The smile seemed genuine, Lisa thought as she led the way from Reception, but she knew that the reporter would be assessing her and the clinic throughout the interview, looking for a dramatic story. The morning *Times* had devoted three pieces to the allegations; the one on the front page had shown a photo of Matthew beneath the bold headline: INFERTILITY SPECIALIST DISAPPEARS—FUGITIVE OR FOUL PLAY?

Inside her office, Lisa motioned to one of the upholstered visitors' chairs. "Can I get you coffee or tea?"

"No, thanks. My bladder's a sieve. But you go ahead." Dropping her woven hemp-colored bag near one of the chairs, Gina Franco approached the wall with the charts detailing assisted reproduction and the female anatomy.

Lisa walked over to the credenza behind her desk. With one eye on the reporter, she poured boiling water from the electric coffeemaker into a porcelain Wedgwood cup and selected a packet of amaretto-flavored coffee. She'd been trying to cut down on coffee and ice cream, but her willpower had disappeared along with Matthew.

"Interesting," Gina said. She'd crossed to the left side of the room and was standing in front of a framed gray poster board filled with snapshots of children. "Your success stories?" she asked, turning to face Lisa.

"Yes." Lisa added two packets of sweetener and a packet of creamer and stirred. "I don't know if you noticed, Ms. Franco, but along the walls of the hall you'll find many more snapshots of babies conceived in this clinic."

"Please call me Gina. And yes, I noticed. Very touching, and very impressive." She moved to one of the armchairs and sat down. From her bag she removed a pen and a burgundy spiral notebook. "You're younger than I expected. Thirty?" she asked, making no attempt to disguise the fact that she was studying Lisa.

"Thirty-one." Lisa placed her cup on a dark brown coaster and sat down at her desk.

"I'm thirty-four. You must be very smart to have come this far in such a short time."

"I worked very hard."

Gina smiled. "All work and no play?"

"Basically." After leaving her parents' home, Lisa had been driven to succeed quickly. She'd overloaded on courses, finishing college in three years. During medical school and her internship and residency and her stint at the Manhattan clinic, she'd sacrificed her social life to excel, to make her mark.

There had been few men in her life. She could barely remember the college senior to whom she'd given her virginity (this was soon after Asher; she'd been rebellious, hurt, angry, desperate for affection). She dated more and more sporadically and became increasingly reluctant to become physical. She enjoyed sex, but found that sex without love left her dissatisfied and uneasy (she'd moved out of her parents' Orthodox world, she realized now, but hadn't rid herself of its values). And until Matthew, she hadn't had time for love. Lately she wondered whether it hadn't been the other way around—whether her single-minded focus on her career had been an excuse to prevent her from entering the risky world of relationships.

"Was it worth it?" the reporter asked. "All that hard work?"

"I love what I do." Lisa lifted the porcelain cup and, inhaling the fragrant steam, realized she hadn't really answered the question. She took a tentative sip.

"Me, too." Gina smiled again. "I don't know if Mr. Fisk explained, but we've been planning a piece on fertility clinics for a while. I'm not here to do a hatchet job. I want to get background for an in-depth piece. And I'd like to come back with a film crew." She cocked her head. "I *will* be asking some tough questions about your clinic in light of yesterday's allegation. Fair enough?"

"Fair enough." If the woman was telling the truth.

"Okay." She flipped open her pad. "Percentagewise, how many couples who come here to the clinic achieve a live birth?"

"I don't have our latest statistics, but I'd say between twenty-five to thirty-two percent. There are many variables—the age of the woman, any physiological abnormalities or diseases, the sperm quality and quantity."

"Good rates." Gina looked at her with interest. "*Newsweek* did an explosive piece on fertility clinics a while back. Based on data submitted to the American Society for Reproductive Medicine, the national success rate is twenty-one-point-two percent. How do you account for this clinic's superior rates?"

Lisa was familiar with the *Newsweek* piece. So was everyone in the field of assisted reproduction. Edmond should be handling this, she thought with a flash of irritation, but he hadn't come in, wasn't expected to be in.

She put the cup on the coaster. "We have a superior staff of physicians and lab technicians who have perfected the assisted-reproduction techniques we use. We also have unique methods of dealing with male infertility and problems related to the woman's immune system."

"That's what your brochure says. Mr. Fisk messengered all the literature to me yesterday." Gina paused. "It doesn't really explain all that much, though. You mentioned you don't have the latest statistics. Are they forthcoming?"

"The new brochures are at the printers'."

"As the clinic's founder and one of its directors, Dr. Gordon would know the statistics. But he's *not* available?"

There was no mistaking the innuendo in the reporter's tone. Lisa hoped her own face was impassive. "That's correct."

She'd barely slept last night. She'd phoned Sam as soon as she'd stepped inside her apartment, still shaking, even though she'd realized that no one had been following her, that her imagination had invented menace. She hadn't mentioned the car or the "Notes" file, but she'd told him that Matthew was missing, that Barone thought his disappearance might be linked to Chelsea Wright's murder. She'd heard Sam's shock when he finally spoke. "I'm coming over," he'd told her. "You shouldn't be alone." She'd turned down his offer—it was late, and she hadn't wanted to take advantage of his friendship—but they'd talked for a while, and she'd taken solace in the warmth and caring his voice offered.

Edmond had phoned, too. She'd repeated what she'd told Sam but hadn't mentioned the missing luggage and clothes; she'd told him she'd tried to file a missing-persons report and would try again in the morning. She'd done so on the way to work and had been pestering Selena, who was too kind to show annoyance, asking her every half hour for news.

"You have no idea where Dr. Gordon is?" the reporter pressed.

"No." Lisa made a point of looking at her watch, as if time were her problem. Normally, it was—the clinic saw over five hundred patients a year, and the pace was grueling. But today she had too much free time. She'd been busy till now with patient procedures, all of which were scheduled for the early morning. Interviews with prospective patients took place later in the morning or in the afternoon. Many of today's appointments had canceled. She was certain the reporter had noticed the relatively empty waiting room.

"Since you're interested in assisted reproduction, Gina, I thought we'd start with the retrieval of the patient's eggs. This is after the patient has taken fertility drugs, like Pergonal."

"The retrieval's done here, in the clinic?"

Lisa nodded. "In an operating room, under what we call conscious sedation. The patient is in a light state of sleep and needs no assisted breathing, just an oxygen mask."

Gina wrote on her pad. "How do you remove the eggs?"

This was the kind of question Lisa felt comfortable answering. "Using an ultrasound screen as a guide, I insert a needle attached to a transvaginal probe into the ovaries and puncture each of the mature follicles. The needle has a suction tip that aspirates the egg from the follicle into a tube attached to the needle."

"Just a sec." The reporter was scribbling quickly. "How do you activate the suction apparatus?"

"With a foot pedal. On the ultrasound screen you can see the follicle collapse when it's empty."

"Neat." Gina nodded. "It would be great if we could get that on film. Do you always find an egg?"

"We don't do a retrieval unless there are at least four follicles, sixteen millimeters or larger. The ultrasound shows the size and quantity of the follicles. Blood tests show the hormone levels that indicate the probability of eggs being present." Lisa drank more coffee and watched Gina write.

"So each egg is aspirated into a separate test tube?"

"Usually. Sometimes the needle punctures two follicles at once. In that case, both eggs will be aspirated into one tube."

Gina nodded again and flipped a page of her pad. "How many eggs do you typically aspirate during a retrieval process?"

Lisa shrugged. "There is no 'typical.' Harvesting can yield from one to thirty eggs."

Gina raised her brows. "Thirty eggs! That's a tribe. Imagine Thanksgiving dinner." She shuddered.

"Thirty eggs *is* a lot." Lisa smiled. "We're pleased with twelve to fourteen."

"What happens next?"

"A lab technician checks the contents of each test tube through a microscope. The tech tells me whether an egg is present or not and rates the egg as mature or immature."

"I guess it's true what they say, that society labels its young early, huh?" The reporter's laugh was low and throaty.

Lisa laughed, too. "I guess." She lifted her cup and drained its contents. "The lab tech labels each test tube, of course. We're scrupulous about proper labeling. It's imperative that the records are complete and accurate."

"But mistakes are possible, aren't they?"

Here it comes. Lisa felt her stomach muscles tensing. "I don't see how. The labels for each patient are typed the night before the egg retrieval. The lab tech makes sure the labels correspond with the patient's name."

"Okay. So the test tubes are labeled. Then what?"

Lisa relaxed in her chair. "They're stored in a lab incubator at womb temperature. Meanwhile, the partner's sperm has been collected, prepared, and labeled. The ratio is one egg to about two hundred thousand sperm, by the way."

"Talk about overkill." Gina smiled and shook her head.

"Uh-huh. Sometimes, if the sperm is sluggish, a caffeinelike booster is added."

Another lift of the finely arched brows. "No kidding! A little espresso to get them going?" She inclined her head toward Lisa's cup.

"Something like that." Lisa was beginning to like Gina Franco. She reminded herself not to mistake charm and humor for sincerity. "Two to three hours after the retrieval, the eggs are fertilized with the sperm in labeled petri dishes and incubated."

"How many eggs are successfully fertilized?"

"The national statistic is eighty-six percent. We do somewhat better. Three days later the fertilized eggs are transferred into a catheter, which is inserted into the patient. The eggs float into the uterus. This time there's no anesthesia."

Gina crossed her legs. "How many eggs?"

"We do a maximum of four. Some clinics implant five or six, sometimes more. That's because the chances for conception increase with the number of implanted embryos."

Gina frowned. "So why does your clinic do only four?"

"More embryos *can* result in multiple gestations. Multiples are more difficult to sustain than singletons, especially when you're talking triplets and higher. Prenatal and postnatal care is far more expensive. The mother faces greater risks, and there are often serious birth defects and complications—blindness, brain damage, learning disorders. There's also a high incidence of cerebral palsy. Sometimes the complications are fatal."

She hoped the reporter would include that in her piece; she'd seen heartbreaking examples of permanently handicapped newborns. The images still haunted her. "Some specialists prefer to increase the chance of conception by using more eggs. Then, if there are three or more embryos, they encourage selective reduction." That was what Ted wanted to do. "We have to be competitive," he'd insisted angrily at the last staff meeting. Lisa and Sam had voted him down.

"That's a euphemism for abortion, isn't it?" Gina tapped her pen against her pad. "I'll bet the pro-lifers aren't happy."

"They aren't. And many patients refuse to do it. It's a complicated, controversial issue." The Hoffmans, Lisa recalled, had discussed the possibility of multiples before Naomi conceived. A rabbinic authority had advised them that to save the remaining fetuses and protect the health of the mother, selective reduction was permissible, but should be done as early in the pregnancy as possible, preferably before the fetus was forty days old. The Hoffmans had decided against selective reduction and were thrilled when Lisa told them Naomi was carrying twins.

"What happens to the fertilized eggs that aren't implanted?"

"They're labeled and frozen in liquid nitrogen for later use, just as sperm are. Approximately seventy-five percent of thawed embryos survive intact."

"And the unfertilized eggs?" Gina asked, hunching forward. "The ones from donors, for instance? Are they frozen, too?"

"They're too fragile to withstand the freezing and thawing. Researchers are working on finding a solution." Including Matthew. She thought again about the "data lies!?" he'd scribbled yesterday morning, and the "Notes" file.

"Well." Gina looked as if she'd swallowed sour milk. "I thought I'd have my eggs frozen now, while I'm relatively young. I read that a woman's chances of conceiving drop significantly after she's thirty-five. I guess that gives me one more year, huh? And all the good men are taken."

Lisa smiled reassuringly. "Those are just statistics, Gina. I wouldn't panic."

"Off the record? You're three years younger, and I assume from your engagement ring that you don't need a sperm donor. But are you at all worried that you'll have trouble getting pregnant?"

Lisa glanced automatically at her ring and felt her chest tighten as she thought about Matthew. "I think every woman worries until she *is* pregnant. Off the record? Yes, I worry. But I know assisted reproduction provides me with numerous options."

"And if none of them work, that would make some ironic story, huh? 'Fertility eludes infertility specialist.' "

"Highly ironic." The possibility had crossed her mind more than once. She and Matthew had talked about starting a family as soon as possible—at least three children, they'd agreed. As an only child himself, he'd understood the loneliness she'd felt growing up. *Why can't I have a brother or sister like everyone else?* she'd often pleaded when she was a little girl, not realizing the pain her questions must have caused her parents.

"Back to the eggs," Gina said, turning another page of her

notepad. "What happens if the patient decides she no longer wants them?"

Lisa was relieved to switch to a less personal discussion. "It depends on what arrangements are made."

"And if there *are* no arrangements? If patients move and lose contact with the clinic? What happens then?"

Lisa hesitated. "Generally, we dispose of them. That's standard procedure in fertility clinics around the world."

"And the pro-lifers are unhappy about that, too, right? Another controversy?" Gina's eyes gleamed with interest.

Lisa wondered if the reporter was going to make these issues the focus of her piece. "There are numerous ethical questions regarding assisted reproduction. It's a new field, and we're encountering different issues as we discover new techniques. We don't have all the answers yet."

"Why can't you give the donor eggs to other patients? I mean, why chuck them when they could benefit someone else?"

Was this a trick question? "Not without the donor's written consent. That would be unethical, *and* illegal. California made it a felony to steal eggs." Punishable by up to five years in prison and a fifty-thousand-dollar fine.

"But it *could* happen accidentally?"

From a desk drawer Lisa pulled out a blank form, then walked around the desk and sat next to the reporter. "This is a lab form. Across the top we list the surgery date, the names of the patient, partner, retrieval physician, and lab tech. Underneath that we list the number of follicles and eggs retrieved."

She pointed to the middle section. "In these columns we grade the eggs and note the date and time of the insemination and embryo transfer." Her finger moved to the bottom of the page. "The sperm specimen is dated and graded and purified—the partner's or donor's name is listed, as is the tech's. Below that is information regarding the transfer. Again, the tech's name is listed.

"Now look here." Lisa indicated a box at the bottom right-hand corner of the page. "We check whether the embryos were frozen or not. If they were, we indicate the date and time, the number frozen, the number of vials frozen, the stage at which they were frozen. As always, the tech's name. We keep accurate cryologs on all frozen embryos, and we use a separate form for the embryo transfer. There's a clear line of accountability and origin all the way through."

Gina scanned the form again. "Where are these kept?"

"After the embryo transfer, it's added to the patient's file in our central filing system. During the course of the IVF, this form stays in the lab. The attending physician also keeps a copy for patients currently undergoing IVF." She tapped the blue loose-leaf folder in front of her.

" 'IVF—DO NOT REMOVE FROM OFFICE.' " Gina read aloud the words handwritten in thick black ink on the binding. "What happens if this is removed from the office? It self-destructs?"

"Actually, there's a tiny transmitter embedded in the folder's metal rings for tracking purposes."

The reporter stared at Lisa. "You're pulling my leg, right?" When Lisa nodded, Gina chuckled and shook her head. "Not bad. I thought doctors were humor-challenged."

Lisa smiled. "I guess you haven't met the right doctors. You can keep the form if you like."

"Thanks." Gina folded it and slipped it into her bag. "Can I take a look around the clinic?"

"What would you like to see?"

"Anything that will look good on camera and give our audience an insider's view of what you do. Down the line, I'd love to film an egg retrieval with the ultrasound, a fertilization, an embryo transfer. The works." Her voice and eyes were animated.

"I'd have to check with the board and staff. And you'd need formal, written consent from the patients." Most patients, Lisa guessed, would be reluctant to give up their privacy.

"Of course."

Lisa pushed her chair away from her desk. "Ready for the tour?"

chapter nine

They stopped first at one of the ground-floor rooms where the embryo transfers were performed. The reporter glanced at the muted mauve walls, decorated with framed pastel watercolors; at the upholstered armchair in the corner; at the bleached oak dresser.

"It looks like a bedroom." Gina sounded surprised.

"That's the idea. We want this to be a pleasant experience. The partners can be present during the transfer, by the way."

"Are the delivery rooms on this floor, too?"

"Second floor. The delivery rooms are the operating rooms. Many patients use their own obstetricians to manage their pregnancies outside the clinic. Some want us to manage pregnancy and delivery."

She showed Gina a delivery room, then led her downstairs to the lab. "The scene of the crime," Lisa said and was rewarded with a quick smile from the reporter. "The door's always kept locked—obviously, security is very important."

"Who has keys?"

"All staff physicians and lab techs. Everyone has to sign in and out." Lisa knocked on the door. A moment later Norman Weld's pale face appeared in the door's small, rectangular window.

The lab assistant opened the door. "Hello, Dr. Brockman." He gazed at Gina curiously.

Lisa performed introductions. "I'd like to show Ms. Franco around, Norman, but I don't want to interrupt any sensitive procedures."

"Actually, everything's quiet right now." His voice was cotton-ball-soft. He pulled the door open wider and stepped aside.

Lisa ushered Gina into the short, narrow anteroom and was wondering how to ask Norman diplomatically to leave, when he said, "Excuse me," and disappeared into the lab.

From a carton on the floor she handed Gina a green gown, cap, and pair of booties and took a set for herself. "Standard procedure before entering the actual lab," she explained. "The techs work with eggs and sperm, and the environment has to be sterile. And warm. You probably noticed it's hotter here. We try to simulate the womb temperature."

"Thank God you told me! I thought I was having premature hot flashes." Gina grinned.

Lisa laughed. "I worked in a clinic where the lab director kept the temperature at ninety-six degrees. Talk about hot."

After both women put on the paper clothing, Lisa pointed to the cabinets against the opposite wall. "Storage for needles, probes, petri dishes, et cetera." She placed her hand on a microscope sitting on top of a cart. "This is what the tech uses to examine the eggs in the operating room. And this part is a portable incubator."

"What's that?" Gina pointed to a black volume resting on one of the counters.

"A record book. It follows the Julian calendar—how many days into the year, not which month. It lists the patients seen each day, in the order in which they were seen, and mentions what procedures were performed."

She took Gina inside the actual lab and introduced her to Charlie and the two other lab techs—Margaret Cho, a slim, tiny brunette, and John Sukami, short and barrel-chested, with shiny black hair and a matching mustache.

Charlie was eager to show Gina the apparatus in his kingdom: the incubators—gray for the eggs, white for the sperm; the "sterile hoods" where work with sperm and eggs was done; a stage heater microscope that maintained an embryo-friendly environment; a microscope with a teaching arm that enabled two people to view the same specimen simultaneously.

"This TV is connected to the microscopes," Charlie explained, pointing to a monitor on a high shelf. "And we use that VCR to tape actual procedures."

"What's that?" Gina pointed to two large metal canisters in the corner of the L-shaped room.

"Carbon dioxide. The yellow one is five percent. The gray one, a hundred percent. All the incubators have a constant flow of carbon dioxide to simulate the womb's environment, plus almost one hundred percent humidity."

"Like Miami?" Gina quipped, but she was clearly impressed.

Charlie showed her the round vats where the frozen embryos and sperm were stored in liquid nitrogen. She asked more questions, then talked to him about the logistics of bringing in a film crew, camera angles, lighting.

Norman Weld, Lisa noted, had been looking dour throughout their dialogue. He probably didn't appreciate Hollywood. When he approached Lisa while Gina and Charlie were talking and leaned in close, she tensed, prepared for a complaint.

"I know how worried you must be about Dr. Gordon," he whispered. "I want you to know he's in my prayers."

"Thank you, Norman." She was touched by his concern and rested her hand lightly on his arm. His cheeks and high forehead turned pink, and she wondered if she'd made a faux pas, but then he smiled and bobbed his head.

"I can see why you're proud of your clinic," Gina told Lisa a while later as they took the elevator to the ground floor. When they were back in Lisa's office, the reporter bent over her notebook, flipping pages, inserting words.

Finally, she looked up. "I wanted to make sure I could read everything I wrote. Ready to continue?"

Lisa sighed. "I thought we were done."

"Just a few more questions." She smiled. "The clinic literature mentions egg donors. Whose name goes on the eggs' labels if the eggs were donated anonymously?"

"Some clinics use the names of the patient and the donor. To protect the donor's anonymity, we use only the patient's name. Or patients' names, if the eggs are going to different women." Who had received Chelsea Wright's eggs? One woman? Two?

Gina flipped to the beginning of her notebook and ran her finger down the page. "Right. A 'shared donor program,' the brochure calls it." She looked up. "A little weird, isn't it? Two women giving birth to babies who are genetic siblings."

"No weirder than two women adopting children from the same birth mother." Lisa had often wondered whether she had siblings or half siblings, whether they looked like her. She'd wondered what it would be like to meet them. "The recipients share the eggs and the donor-related costs. It makes the process more affordable."

"But hardly inexpensive."

"Unfortunately, no." She wished there were some way to make fertility treatments affordable for more couples. Matthew shared her concerns. Thinking about him brought another stab of pain to her chest. She eyed the phone, but told herself that if Selena had heard something, she would have buzzed Lisa immediately.

Gina referred to her notes again. "Ten thousand dollars per IVF cycle at some clinics, if the couple pays up front. Twelve thousand at others. Fifteen thousand if they try to go through their insurance company. But few companies insure for IVF, right?" Her voice had taken on a harder edge.

"Again, unfortunately, you're right."

Gina shut her notebook. "My best friend and her husband had four IVF cycles. Sperm analysis, blood tests, fertility drug shots, and all the crap, if you'll excuse me, that goes with it. No baby. They refinanced their house, spent sixty thousand. They're willing to adopt, but now they can't afford to."

Lisa linked her fingers and leaned forward. "I won't apologize for the costs of assisted reproduction, Gina. They *are* high, but justifiably so. We make no guarantees. We're up front about our statistics for live births. We *always* mention adoption as an excellent option. But the couples we see are desperate to have their own biological child. They're willing to take their chances, and pay the price."

Adoption *was* a wonderful option—for the adoptive parents, for the child they adopted. Though she'd been shocked and upset to learn she'd been adopted, she'd soon realized how lucky she was. She wondered sometimes where she would be now if her parents hadn't adopted her and raised her with unconditional love, wondered what direction her life would have taken.

"And they pay that price two and three and four times, right?" Gina said with pointed criticism. She paused. "At least you offer a money-back guarantee. I guess that helps some couples if they qualify."

"Definitely." The guarantee had been Edmond's idea, a response to the bleak prognosis reported in the *Newsweek* piece and the subsequent drop in patients. Lisa had reservations about the refund policy—it seemed to her to be more about business than medicine. But Matthew had loved the idea, and it had brought in many new patients. "The patient pays a set amount, depending on her age, which has to be under forty. If she doesn't achieve a twelve-week gestation after one retrieval cycle and embryo transfer, including the transfer of all thawed embryos, she receives a ninety percent refund of the base cost of the cycle."

"Why a twelve-week gestation?"

"The miscarriage rate is higher with IVF. Of course, the refund doesn't apply to medications, medical screenings, anesthesia, or pregnancy management."

"Of course. 'Beware of fine print,' " Gina said dryly. "Still, it's a better deal than most. And the statistics here are better than those at other clinics. One out of three or four, as opposed to one out of five. Maybe my friend should've come here. Then again, maybe not, given the recent allegations."

"Unfounded allegations. Allegations made by 'unnamed sources.' " Lisa pronounced the two words with sarcasm.

"Sometimes people are afraid of retaliation."

"*Sometimes* they're lying."

"*Why*, Dr. Brockman?" The reporter sat forward and rested her elbows on her knees. "Why would someone spread false rumors about embryo switching? It makes no sense."

Lying in bed last night, wondering whether she'd ever see Matthew again, Lisa had thought about this, too. "Our clinic has an enviable reputation. Patients come here from all over the world because of our success rates. And as you said, they spend a lot of money. It's possible that another clinic, hoping to attract patients, did this to damage our reputation. All it takes is rumor. In your line of work, I'm sure you know that's true."

"Is that a dig, Doctor?" Gina cocked her head.

"Just a fact. Well, maybe it *is* a dig." She smiled.

"Okay." Gina smiled, too. "Are you referring to a specific rival clinic?"

"Just speculating." She was tired and thirsty. She glanced longingly at her empty coffee cup but decided against having a refill. "There's another possibility. Some patients leave our doors childless, in spite of our best efforts. They're disheartened, upset. Sometimes they're angry at us and at those women who *have* become pregnant, and they need to lash out at someone, anyone." She thought about Cora Allen, who was certain someone had stolen her embryos. Maybe Cora needed to believe that; it was easier than facing the reality of several failed IVF cycles.

"Why would that person spread rumors about the clinic?"

"To punish the clinic that failed her. To punish other patients who were successful, by filling them with fear about the status of their children, born or unborn." Lisa shrugged. "Here's a better question: Why would a clinic like ours jeopardize its reputation by switching embryos? That would be so *stupid*!"

"Maybe a patient who doesn't have viable eggs pays a staff member—a doctor, nurse, tech—to get her some."

"Come on, Gina," she said impatiently. "You saw the documentation. You saw the procedure."

"I saw *paper*, Doctor. Paper can be manipulated. Procedures can be circumvented. Labels can be switched, and doctors and techs have keys to locked labs." She leaned against the chair back. "Maybe money *isn't* involved. Maybe the doctor or nurse feels torn for this woman so desperate for children. So he takes viable eggs from patient A and gives them to patient B."

"How does he account for the missing eggs?"

"He tells patient A he harvested fewer eggs than he actually did. He only does it with patients who have yielded a lot of eggs. Most of them will be fertilized and frozen anyway."

Lisa thought for a moment—she wanted to be fair—then shook her head. "Maybe before the law was passed. It's too risky now."

"There are ways," Gina insisted.

"Maybe. But it didn't happen here."

"Where's Dr. Gordon? Rumor has it your fiancé's flown. Doesn't that make you wonder about him? Doesn't that make you think the allegations could be true?"

Lisa blinked, unprepared for the attack. "Did you read about our relationship in the clinic brochure, too?" She felt betrayed by the question, foolish for having let down her guard, for thinking the reporter hadn't done her homework and learned that she and Matthew were engaged.

"I warned you there'd be some tough questions. I had to ask."

"If you knew Matthew, you'd know that the clinic is his passion, his life," she said urgently, realizing as she spoke that she was probably wasting her time trying to convince this woman with anything but facts. "I've filed a missing-persons report with the police. I *know* he met with foul play."

"I'm sorry to hear that. Really, I am." Gina sounded sincere. "Do you think he's dead?" she asked softly.

"I suppose you had to ask that, too?" Lisa said and saw a hint of discomfort flash across the reporter's face. "Actually, I try not to think about the possibilities."

Her intercom buzzed. She yanked the receiver off the cradle and pulled it to her ear. "Did you hear anything?" she asked Selena in an undertone.

"No, sorry. Are you almost finished with the reporter?"

She relaxed her grip on the receiver. "Just about. Am I late for my next appointment?" Dealing with patients would at least provide her with a temporary reprieve from her tortured thoughts and Gina Franco's incisive questions.

"No. But Mr. and Mrs. Wright are here. They insist on speaking to you right away."

Chelsea's parents.

Hardly a reprieve.

chapter ten

The Wrights looked worn and pale and nondescript, like an old sepia-toned photo that had faded, its once-glossy surface crackled. The mother was short and plump, with a puffy face and light brown hair. The father, whose hair was the same brown, was stout and had broad, sloping shoulders and wide, large-knuckled hands. Lisa looked hard but could find no hint of the animated, lovely young woman whose photo she'd studied two days ago.

"I'm so sorry for your loss," she said. "I wish there were something I could do to lessen your pain." She was embarrassed for offering platitudes but didn't know what else to say.

"Thank you. That's very kind." Enid Wright smiled bravely. "Everybody's been so wonderful, so caring. But it doesn't bring her back." Tears trembled on her lashes, then fell onto her face. She made no move to wipe them.

"We wanted to speak to Dr. Gordon," her husband said, "but we understand he's not available."

"Not at this time. Is there something I can do for you?" Had they come to speak to Matthew because he'd seen Chelsea just a few weeks ago? Did they hope to find comfort in their daughter's last conversations?

"It's about her eggs," he said. "The detective told us Chelsea donated eggs. We'd like to know who has them."

"We never even knew." His wife sniffled. "Her boyfriend knew, but we didn't. I guess Chelsea thought Walter and I would disapprove," she added in a tone that said she was troubled her daughter hadn't confided in her.

"I'm so sorry." Lisa shook her head in sympathy and leaned forward. "I don't know who has your daughter's eggs, or whether any of them were fertilized and frozen."

Walter Wright exchanged a look with his wife. "I'm sure the information's in her file."

"Yes, but I can't share it with you." God, she didn't want to be in this position! She'd almost prefer answering Gina Franco's questions. Lisa had cut the interview short, telling the reporter she had to see a patient. Now she was intensely relieved that the Wrights hadn't come earlier, when Gina was in Reception.

"But they're Chelsea's *babies!*" the mother whispered. "Our grandchildren! They're the only thing Walter and I have left." She was sobbing now, her shoulders heaving.

"I'm sorry," Lisa repeated. Her face was ashen.

Walter clasped his wife's hand. "If you're sorry, help us."

"I wish I could. Please believe me."

"We understand she received money for the eggs," Enid said in a voice barely above a whisper. "Twenty-five hundred dollars. She was always so worried about expenses." She sighed. "If we have to, we'll pay it back, every cent."

Lisa felt physically ill. "It's not about money, Mr. and Mrs. Wright. It's against the law for me to release that information. Please try to understand."

"They're her eggs," Walter said. A note of stubbornness had stiffened his voice and his shoulders.

"She signed a contract giving up her rights to the eggs." Lisa hated the fact that she was using the cold shield of the law to deflect their heartrending pleas, that she was the enemy.

"Chelsea didn't know she was going to be killed, did she? She probably wasn't even eighteen years old when she signed that paper. I don't think you can hold her to that."

"Mr. Wright—"

"At least if we could see the babies when they're born, visit with them once in a while," Enid said. "It's not enough, but it's something."

He whirled toward his wife. "They're Chelsea's babies, Enid! We have rights!" His voice was a whiplash. "A lawyer could have that contract tossed out," he said, facing Lisa again.

"Mr. Wright, there must be some mistake. We don't accept egg donors who are under eighteen."

"Well, she turned eighteen nine months ago. When did she donate the eggs?" he said, challenging Lisa now.

"I don't know." Matthew had told Barone that Chelsea had donated the eggs long ago, Lisa recalled. What was "long"? "Even though your daughter's eggs were implanted in someone else, it's possible no pregnancies resulted from any of those eggs."

"You mean they could be gone?" Enid wailed. "All of them? All *gone*?"

All my pretty ones? Did you say all? Lisa hesitated. What was the point of offering hope, only to snatch it away in the next moment? "Not necessarily. But even if one or more of your daughter's eggs resulted in a pregnancy, those embryos belong to someone else now."

"No." Walter shook his head. "Those women can have other children. They can get someone else to donate eggs for them. My wife and I, we just have this one chance." He tightened his grip on his wife's hand. "We're not stupid, Dr. Brockman. We know we can't bring Chelsea back. But we can hold on to the part of her she left behind."

He rose so quickly that he almost upended the chair. "Come on, Enid. We're not going to get any help here." He turned to Lisa. "I know you're just doing your job, but you ought to be ashamed of yourself."

Lisa didn't answer. She watched them walk out of her office, two people broken by their daughter's death. She lay her head on her arms and cried for Chelsea Wright and the babies she would never carry, cried for Matthew, cried for herself.

chapter eleven

The restaurant where Chelsea had worked was on the corner of Beverly and Formosa. Lisa had found the name in a one-inch newspaper report about the murder, buried in the *Times*' "Metro" section that she'd dug out of the trash.

She parked her Altima in the closest spot she could find, on La Brea between Oakwood and Beverly. It was eight o'clock, and though the yellow-gray light from the streetlamps interrupted the darkness, and she'd almost convinced herself that the car hadn't been following her last night, she looked around warily as she headed toward the restaurant, conscious that Chelsea might have walked these same blocks on the way to her death.

She turned the corner. Across the street were a car-rental place and a new building that, according to Sam, had replaced a camera shop torched years ago in the Rodney King riots. To her right was a mini-mall with a pharmacy, a dry cleaner, a Domino's Pizza, and a kosher restaurant where Sam had taken her when she'd first moved to Los Angeles over a year ago.

The neighborhood, Sam had told her, was heavily populated with Orthodox families, and there were synagogues, schools, and markets to meet their needs. The same was true of the Pico-Robertson area where Sam lived. He'd chosen his apartment because it was closer to the clinic.

On an impulse she detoured into the mall, crowded with cars and two Suburbans, and stared inside the window of the kosher restaurant. A lone diner was sitting at one of the front tables, reading a folded newspaper as he ate his sandwich. All the other tables were occupied with families, or two or more women, or men.

A little boy waddled down the aisle. His mother jumped up and chased after him, then stopped at another table and, with her son anchored to her hip, talked with the people sitting around it. Crowded around another table in the middle of the long, narrow room was a group of high school girls. Lisa watched the pantomime of animated mouths and exaggerated gestures and felt a pang of longing.

This was what she missed so dearly, along with the ritual and the cocoon of faith—this sense of community, of belonging. This was what she'd thrown away.

Maybe she was feeling this way because of Matthew's disappearance. Maybe it was because of her parents' phone call. They'd reached her just before she left her apartment tonight. They'd heard a news item about the clinic and were concerned. Why hadn't she phoned them?

She was fine, she'd reassured them. She hadn't wanted to worry them. And Matthew? her father had asked—was it true he'd disappeared under suspicious circumstances? In her father's quiet voice she'd heard the awkwardness that was present whenever he mentioned his future son-in-law, but there had been no criticism, no intimation that life would have been better for all of them if Lisa had never met him. And when she told them she feared something terrible had happened to him, her mother had offered to fly out to be with her, or to send her a ticket to come home.

She longed to see her parents, but having her mother visit would complicate her life right now. And though going home was tempting, she couldn't leave her job or the city, not with Matthew missing, possibly dead. So she'd declined both offers and told them she loved them.

"Your father and I will pray for Matthew's safety," her mother had said. "If you change your mind, Aliza . . ."

A short, stocky man passed her and opened the restaurant door. "Going in?" he asked, holding it open for her.

She hesitated. "No, not tonight. Thank you."

She left the mini-mall, crossed Detroit Street, and walked two more blocks to the restaurant where Chelsea had worked. On either side of the brick-faced corner exterior were square café tables and simple hardwood slatted chairs; a stack of teal umbrellas, obviously used to protect patrons from sunlight, lay against one of the walls. The windows were topped with narrow teal-and-white-striped canopies. The air was chilly, but all the tables were occupied.

There were many restaurants like this in L.A., she'd noticed one Sunday afternoon, driving around to familiarize herself with the city. There was one just a block away. According to Matthew, they were all busy, all day. Who were the midday patrons? she'd asked him. How could so many people afford to spend their days talking and eating instead of going to work? Jealous? he'd asked, smiling, and she'd laughed and said of course she was.

She entered the restaurant and asked to see the manager. A waitress showed her to a table near the rear, and Lisa wondered which station had been Chelsea's. The lighting was dim. The room was redolent with the pungent aroma of fried onions and seared beef and coffee, and she was reminded how hungry she was. Aside from a tuna sandwich at lunch, she hadn't eaten anything all day. She scanned the menu and signaled to the waitress, intending to order a steak sandwich, then changed her mind. She'd asked Matthew to think about keeping kosher, but hadn't tried doing it herself. Hardly fair. She considered making a bargain with God—she'd keep kosher, she'd keep the Sabbath, keep all the laws, if He would keep Matthew safe. A pretty good bargain, she thought, wishing it were that simple. The waitress arrived. Lisa ordered a lemon Coke.

She was sipping the Coke minutes later when a tall, dark-haired man in chinos and a black knit shirt approached her table. "I'm Cal, the manager. How can I help you?" He had large sable-brown eyes with lashes that reached his thick brows.

She took a business card from her wallet and handed it to him. "I need to talk to people who knew Chelsea."

He studied the card, then slipped it into his pants pocket and folded his arms. "Why?"

Lisa couldn't blame him for being wary. She explained about Matthew's disappearance, then said, "The detective thinks it may be connected to Chelsea's murder, so the more I learn about Chelsea, the better chance I have of finding my fiancé." She might have twisted to some degree what Barone had said, but she didn't care.

"The police were here right after the murder. Anything my staff could tell you, they already told the detectives."

She nodded. "I'm know I'm probably wasting my time, going over the same ground. But I have to try to find him."

His hands moved to his pockets. He rocked back and forth on his heels, looking as if he were going into a trance. "She was close with my bartender, Ramón." He tilted his head toward the bar. "And she was friendly with Yvonne and Melissa. Both of them are here tonight. That's Melissa." He pointed to a thin, ponytailed brunette in a black miniskirt and white silk T-shirt. "Yvonne's not on the floor. She's got red hair."

"When can I talk to them?"

"You can try to catch them between orders. We're busy, so it might take a while. Tell 'em I said it was okay," he said, friendlier now.

"Thank you."

"Chelsea was real nice. I hope you find your fiancé."

If she had to wait, she could use the time trying to figure out how to access Matthew's "Notes" file. After work she'd played with the laptop but still hadn't found the password.

The bartender first. Taking her Coke to the bar, she sat on a dark teal leather-covered stool and watched him. He was short and well-built, with trim hips and well-defined muscles that stretched his white knit shirt. When he finished serving a drink to a woman at the end of the bar, she said, "Excuse me?" and waited for him to come over, noting the bounce in his step.

"What can I get you, miss?" He smiled at her.

She told him why she was here and saw sadness, then anger, replace the smile. She gave him her card. He slipped it into his pocket without glancing at it.

"Can you believe something like that happened, just two blocks from here?" He shook his head. "A while back, a guy was killed in the parking lot of the art store down the block. They said it was a carjacking. You heard about it?"

Lisa shook her head, too. "I don't live around here."

"It was on the news. Anyway, Chelsea and I, we talked about it. She was scared, you know? I told her, 'Hey, baby, I'm scared, too, but you gotta live your life, you know?' But I never thought something would happen to her. Man, she was sweet." He sighed. "So your boyfriend's disappeared, huh? You must be scared."

Lisa nodded.

"You gotta have hope, you know?" He picked up a tumbler and dried it. "I don't know what I can tell you that'll help. I was the last one Chelsea talked to that night, but I guess you know that if you talked to the police."

She hadn't known that, but she nodded again. "Did she say anything unusual that night?"

He put the tumbler down. "Nope. She was in a good mood, happier than she'd been in a long time. Oh, and these two producers? They were hitting on her, offered her a part as a stripper in a movie. She thought it was funny." Ramón sounded wistful. He wiped an imaginary spot on the counter.

"Were they regulars?"

"Nope." He leaned forward, pressing his palms against the counter. "I told the detective about them, but Cal—he's the manager?—he said he knows them. Strictly small-time, but legit. He gave the detective their names and stuff." Ramón scooped a handful of peanuts into his palm and dropped them into his mouth.

It was unlikely that the producers, who had made themselves visible and were known to the restaurant manager, had followed Chelsea and killed her. "You said Chelsea was in a better mood. Was she upset before?"

"*Oh*, yeah. She was always cheerful with the customers, but she'd get that look in her eyes, like the world was going to end soon. Yeah, she was depressed in a big way." He was silent for a moment, lost in thought. "She wouldn't tell me why, though."

Chelsea had refused to tell Matthew, too. "Why do you think she was more cheerful that night?"

"The new job. The police didn't tell you?" He rolled his eyes in disbelief. "See, she was tired of waiting tables, tired of the late hours, tired of men hitting on her. And I think that murder back of the art store shook her up bad, you know? So she got herself a job as a live-in baby-sitter. I said, 'Hey, Chelsea, you gonna watch *The Hand That Rocked the Cradle* to get some pointers?' We laughed about it. Did you see that movie?"

Lisa said no, she hadn't.

"Creepy. Anyway, she had two more days here, then she was supposed to start her new job. Man, she was *excited* to be getting out, you know?" His face clouded. "I teased her about it that night. I told her she'd be begging for her job back. But she isn't coming back, is she?"

"Whiskey, please," a man at the end of the bar called. "Neat."

Ramón excused himself. Lisa nursed her Coke while he filled a shot glass and slid it in front of the man, who handed him a folded bill. The bartender thanked him and slipped the bill into his shirt pocket.

"Do you know who Chelsea was going to work for?" she asked when Ramón was standing in front of her again. Maybe she'd mentioned something in passing to her new employer, something that would provide a clue to her murder.

"She didn't say. And I didn't ask, you know? Maybe she told Melissa or Yvonne." He shrugged.

"Did she say anything about Dr. Gordon?"

"Who?" His brows creased.

"My fiancé," she said and saw him turn pink.

"Oh, yeah. Sorry." He grinned, obviously embarrassed. "No, she never mentioned him. I didn't know she had medical problems."

Lisa thanked him for his time. "You have my card. If you remember anything else, please call me?" She was beginning to sound and act like Barone, she thought as she slid off the stool.

"Sure. Hey, good luck, okay?"

Melissa didn't know who'd hired Chelsea. She'd felt terrible when she heard Chelsea was killed; she'd never heard of Matthew and looked surprised when she read Lisa's business card.

"Why'd she go to a fertility clinic?" she asked, turning the card over as if the answer lay on the other side.

Lisa explained about the egg donation.

"Really? Did she get paid for this?" Her amber-flecked eyes widened when Lisa told her the fee. "So can anyone do this?"

Her eyes were calculators, Lisa thought, mildly disgusted with the waitress, who seemed more interested in making money than in the fact that a co-worker had been killed. "You have to qualify," she said and briefly explained what was involved.

"Fertility shots, huh? They make you bloated, don't they?" Melissa frowned. "I'll think about it." She looked at the card again before she tucked it inside the pocket of her apron and walked away, her dark brown ponytail swinging with every step.

Yvonne hadn't heard of Matthew or the clinic, either. She didn't know who had hired Chelsea as a mother's helper, but she remembered Chelsea saying it was someone wealthy.

"High society, that's all she'd say," the redheaded waitress told Lisa. She was wearing a miniskirt and silk T-shirt identical to Melissa's. Her face was chalk white except for maroon lipstick and black kohl smudged on her eyelids. "A Beverly Hills home with a pool and a great library. Chelsea kept talking about the library. She was really into reading and school."

"I think she wanted to be a teacher," Lisa said, recalling what Barone had told her. Or was it Matthew?

"She loved kids. That's why she took the job. She wanted to have a dozen of her own." Yvonne nodded, as if remembering. "The job had the perfect setup, too. She'd be living in this great house and have time off for college." She sighed. "God, it's so sad. I come here and keep expecting to see her."

"Chelsea never mentioned her new employer's name?"

Yvonne shook her head, making her shoulder-length auburn curls dance. "That's what the detective asked. Chelsea was so hyped up about her new job, I think she was afraid if she talked about it, something would happen to spoil it. Or someone would snatch it away. There was something about her new boss . . ." She frowned, concentrating, then shook her head again. "Sorry."

"That's okay. If you remember, call me at the clinic. And thanks for talking to me." Lisa walked over to the cashier and was paying for her Coke when Yvonne came running up to her.

"I remembered! Chelsea said this woman was the head of a group that raised money for kids who had some illness. I thought of it just now because you're a doctor and all. But I can't remember what the illness was." She inserted a burgundy-lacquered fingernail between her teeth, then turned and scanned the room. "Hey, Melissa?" she called. "Come here a minute, will you?"

A moment later Melissa was standing in front of them, looking annoyed. "I hope this is important," she said, cinching her tiny waist with her hands.

"Remember Chelsea said this woman she was going to work for was involved with some group that raised money for a kid's disease? What disease was that?"

"Sorry. I don't remember." Melissa started to walk away.

Yvonne grabbed her arm. "Yes, you do! You said you had a cousin with the same thing."

"Oh, that. Juvenile diabetes."

Oh, that. Lisa was taken aback by the woman's blasé attitude toward a serious medical condition. She stared at Melissa, who said, "Okay, that's *it*, then?" and returned to her station.

"That's all I remember," Yvonne said. "I hope it helps."

Lisa was still thinking about the other waitress. She said, "It's a place to start," and thanked Yvonne again. On her way out she passed the bar.

Ramón smiled and waved his towel at her. "You gotta have hope, you know?"

She was trying.

chapter twelve

Edmond had called. So had Sam, several times, and Selena. Lisa tensed as she punched the office manager's home number, but Selena had no news about Matthew. She'd phoned to see how Lisa was doing and to fill her in on clinic business.

"The *Minute by Minute* reporter phoned," Selena told her. "She's calling again tomorrow. Also, there's something I think you should know." She sounded uncomfortable. "Rumors are going around that the clinic will be closed down. A lot of the staff are worried. Ava called from Carmel—she wants to know if she'll have a job when she gets back from vacation." Selena laughed uneasily.

Ava was a divorced mother of two teenage boys. Selena and her husband had a mortgage to pay and two sons and a daughter in parochial schools. Of course the staff was worried.

"I haven't heard anything, Selena. You know I'd tell you if I did." Was that why Edmond had phoned? To give her the bad news?

"I know. But some of the staff are looking around for other

positions. And Grace is really depressed. She always looks like she's been crying. Maybe you can talk to her tomorrow."

Grace was devoted to Matthew. She'd been on staff from the day the clinic had opened, and he'd helped her and her husband conceive their daughter. "I *will* talk to her. Thanks for telling me about it, Selena." Not that she had encouragement to impart.

"One more thing." She sounded hesitant. "Two of Dr. Gordon's patients want to transfer their frozen embryos to other facilities. I'm sorry to bother you with this."

"No problem." Lisa supposed it was natural that Selena was turning to her—she was, after all, the missing director's fiancé. "I'll contact them tomorrow. I'm sure we'll be getting more of those requests. All we can do is try to reassure the patients about their embryos. If they insist on removing them, we can't stop them."

She thanked Selena again, making a mental note to contact her patients personally. Then she phoned the police. No, they hadn't heard anything. They knew where to reach her, the woman detective handling the case said pointedly.

In her bedroom she changed from the navy skirt and pale gray blouse she'd worn all day into a pair of jeans and a black cotton sweater. A white basket piled high with clothes she'd washed three days ago in the basement laundry room sat accusingly in the corner. Her radio was set to the oldies station she listened to while she did her fifteen-minute morning exercise routine. She turned it on— they were playing "Be My Baby"—and dumped the basket's contents onto her ecru woven jacquard comforter. She called Sam.

"I've been trying you all night," he said with a note of urgency. "I looked for you earlier at the clinic, but Selena said you'd left and were really upset. I tried Matthew's place, too."

She felt suddenly less lonely, knowing he was worried about her. Tucking the cordless receiver between her ear and shoulder, she sat cross-legged on the bed and told him about Selena's concerns, about her interview with Ramón and the waitresses, about being questioned by the reporter, about Chelsea's parents. "I felt like such an ogre, Sam. I don't blame those poor people for hating me."

"Not your best day, huh?" He sighed. "I feel for the Wrights. First they lose their daughter, now their grandchild. But you don't make the rules. And they don't hate you, Lisa. They're heartbroken, and they have to direct their anger somewhere. You were the most convenient target."

"I suppose you're right." Still, she felt at fault. *You should be ashamed of yourself*, Walter Wright had said.

"I wonder why they came to you, instead of to me or Ted. You shouldn't have had to deal with this, Lisa."

She placed a pale yellow, long-sleeved cotton shirt on the bed and smoothed away its wrinkles, taking pleasure in the simplicity of the act. "Barone must've mentioned my name and Matthew's when he told them Chelsea had donated eggs."

"And thanks to Fisk, you had to deal with the reporter, too. And then you played detective at the restaurant. Why didn't you call me? I would've gone with you." He sounded hurt.

"I didn't want to bother you, Sam." She folded the shirt, then picked up another. The singer on the radio was asking someone to be his little baby. It would be nice, she thought, to have someone else assume all her worries.

"It's no bother. Isn't that what friends are for? Tell you what— I'll come over. We'll watch a video, play gin, do something to take your mind off all this, at least for a while."

The thought was tempting, but she knew he was as tired as she was. "Thanks, but I'll be okay." She heard a click—someone else was trying to call. Thinking it might be the police, she hurriedly said good night to Sam, then pressed the FLASH button on her phone and said hello.

"Did you get my message, Lisa?" Edmond asked.

No "Hello." She detected a hint of annoyance in the board of director's voice, which in turn annoyed her. "I was about to phone you, Edmond. I just came home."

"I'm sorry to disturb you, but Georgia and I are anxious about Matthew. Have you heard anything?"

"No. Nothing." She pulled a white sport sock out of the pile of clothes and hunted for its mate, wondering whether Edmond was sitting on a throne-size chair. *It's good to be the king*, Mel Brooks had said in one of his comedies. The thought made her smile.

Edmond's sigh was audible. "I suppose that's good news, isn't it? How did your meeting go with the reporter?"

Was that why he was calling? She located the other sock and folded both together. "Actually, she's nice." She gave him a summary of the interview. "She wants to film an egg retrieval and transfer. I told her I'd tell you."

"The publicity would be terrific, but I don't think patients would consent, do you? Especially now."

"No." Why was he asking her opinion? To make her feel involved? It had occurred to her that by having her meet with Gina Franco, he'd distanced himself from the clinic and its problems.

"If she asks again, tell her I'm taking it up with the board. So all in all, it went well, do you think?"

"She was fascinated with what we do, but she's not convinced that switching embryos is impossible, even though I showed her how careful our documentation is. And she *did* focus on the high cost of assisted reproduction and the low success rates."

"I hope you mentioned our refund policy."

He sounded annoyed again. Lisa could picture his patrician frown. "She read about it in the material you sent her. I explained how it worked."

"Well, let's hope she includes that in the piece she does and that it doesn't end up on the cutting-room floor. How were things in general today? More cancellations?"

"Unfortunately, yes. And there are other problems." She repeated what Selena had told her. "I think a talk from you would bolster the staff's morale, Edmond. And you might want to send a reassuring letter to all our patients."

"Good thinking, Lisa. I'll talk to the staff tomorrow. And I'd like you to draft a letter tonight, if you can, so that we can send it out immediately to the patients."

She was tempted to tell him to write it himself but lost her nerve. "There's something else. The Wrights—the parents of the egg donor who was killed—came to the clinic. They demanded to know who received their daughter's eggs. I told them—gently, of course—that I couldn't reveal that information."

"How did they react?"

It was impossible to miss the taut wariness in his voice. "Not well." She summarized the conversation. "I did my best to explain, but they feel they're entitled to their daughter's eggs—or children, if any of the eggs resulted in a pregnancy." In her mind's ear she could hear Enid Wright's plaintive wail.

"Did you tell them their daughter signed a waiver giving up all rights to her eggs?"

"Yes, I did." She was irritated with Fisk—did he think she was an idiot? "Mr. Wright said the contract might not be valid, since his daughter probably wasn't eighteen when she signed it."

"That's not possible," he said firmly. "Did you tell him we don't accept donors under eighteen years of age?"

She gritted her teeth. "Yes. But I haven't seen her file, and I didn't want to argue with him. He and his wife are devastated."

"My heart goes out to those people, too, Lisa. But we have to protect the confidentiality of our patients. Did they mention consulting an attorney?"

"Yes."

"Terrific." Fisk grunted. "I think they'll find they don't have any rights, but I'll check with our attorney."

Was he angry with her? Bristling, she said coolly, "I tried my best to calm them, Edmond."

"I'm sure you did." Suddenly his tone was conciliatory. "We'll have to see what develops. I'll say good night now, Lisa, and I'll get Georgia. Hold on."

She didn't know why Georgia wanted to talk to her, but she couldn't very well hang up. Her stomach rumbled—she wasn't sure whether it was hunger or anxiety. She padded barefoot into the kitchen and was inspecting the refrigerator when Edmond's wife came on the line.

"Lisa, dear? This must be awful for you, just awful. How are you managing?"

"Trying to keep busy." The radio was playing "It's My Party and I'll Cry If I Want To." Isn't that the truth, she thought, and told herself to stop feeling sorry for herself.

"That was a silly question, wasn't it? It's hard to know what to say in a situation like this."

"It isn't silly at all," Lisa said, taking pity on Georgia, who sounded terribly uncomfortable. "It's sweet of you to ask."

"Edmond's left the room," his wife said, her voice lower. "You have no idea how agitated he is. He hasn't been sleeping well. He's lost his appetite. He paces around the house."

"I know he cares for Matthew." And no doubt he was worried about his legal and financial liabilities regarding the clinic.

"He loves him as if he were his son. We both do. If anything happened to Matthew . . ." She sighed. "I wanted to comfort you, but I'm not doing a very good job of it. If there's anything you need, anything at all, call us. We both want to help."

"Thank you. That's so kind." Lisa was about to hang up when she had a thought. "Georgia, you're involved in a lot of charities and organizations. Do you know who chairs the Juvenile Diabetes Foundation in Los Angeles?"

"They do such important work. Quite a few of my friends are involved in it, and Edmond and I contribute generously, but I've concentrated my efforts during the last few years on raising money for pediatric AIDS research. Can you be more specific, dear?"

"All I know is that the woman has a young child." Yvonne hadn't said how young. Chelsea probably hadn't told her. "And she lives in Beverly Hills." Along with a thousand other women.

"There's no point in guessing. They sent me an invitation for an upcoming event. The invitation should list the officers' names. Hold on while I check."

If Georgia couldn't help her, Lisa would phone the diabetes foundation, she decided as she put up a pot of spaghetti.

"Well, we're in luck," Georgia said when she came back on the line. "The woman you want is Paula Rhodes, and the dessert reception will be at her home in July."

"The name sounds familiar."

"That's not surprising. The Rhodes family has been a major benefactor for decades. I don't think there's a museum in the city that they haven't supported or a hospital that doesn't have a wing named after them. In fact, Paula's husband, Andrew, invested in Matthew's clinic. He and Edmond were business associates and friends." Georgia paused. "Five months ago he had a massive heart attack and died. Paula was pregnant at the time. It was tragic," she said, her voice filled with sadness.

"She must have been devastated." Years ago Lisa had paid a condolence call to a former high school classmate who had been four months pregnant and had been "sitting shivah"—seven days of mourning—for her twenty-seven-year-old husband. His sudden, fatal heart failure had left her with a two-year-old daughter and a three-year-old son and no means of support. Lisa could still remember how dazed the young widow had looked, how lost. She'd been happy to learn recently from her mother that the woman had remarried.

"Do you know Mrs. Rhodes?" she asked Georgia.

"Not well. She and Andrew belonged to a younger circle. But whenever our paths crossed, she was very friendly. I'd heard she wasn't going anywhere after Andrew died, so I was pleased to find out that she's becoming active again. I invited her to the party we hosted for you and Matthew, but of course, she didn't come. Are you thinking of getting involved with the diabetes organization, dear? Because our foundation could use someone like you, young and bright and energetic."

"Actually, I don't have time for volunteer work now. Someone made a reference to this woman, and I was curious to know who she was." It was a half-truth, not a lie. Lisa was too tired—and reluctant—to explain why she wanted the information. "She *does* live in Beverly Hills, doesn't she?" She had no idea how else to obtain the woman's address; she doubted that it was listed.

"Yes. On Linden." Georgia told her the address. "That's in the Flats," she added, referring to the four blocks running north and south between Santa Monica Boulevard and Sunset.

Lisa knew where the Flats were. Matthew had driven her around the exclusive neighborhood several times, pointing out his favorites among the palatial homes.

"Someday soon," he'd told her, "we'll be living here."

chapter thirteen

"I thought we agreed you wouldn't come over," Lisa said.

Sam was leaning against the doorjamb, his denim jacket slung over his shoulder. She was startled to find how pleased she was to see him.

He straightened up and adjusted his yarmulke. "*We* didn't agree. You said it wasn't necessary. I decided you were being a martyr. So do I get to come in?" He smiled.

"Sorry." She stepped aside to let him enter, then shut and locked the door. "I *am* glad you came. Thanks, Sam."

They walked into the living room and sat on the sofa. She pulled her knees up to her chest, conscious of the fact that she was barefoot, and told him about Fisk's call. "I had the feeling he thought I'd mishandled things with the Wrights." She shrugged.

"Nothing you or anyone else said would've calmed them down. Fisk knows that." He leaned back against the sofa and crossed his ankles. "It's a mistake letting young, childless women donate eggs. I'm not sure they're donating for the right reasons."

She nodded. "Twenty-five hundred dollars is tempting."

"Especially for an eighteen-year-old. Other clinics don't use childless donors. We shouldn't, either. And we should raise the qualifying age to twenty-one." He moved against the back cushion, and the leather sighed in protest. "I told that to Matt. He said he'd take it up with the board, but Ted will campaign against it. Ted's view is if childless, college-age men can donate sperm, then childless, college-age women can donate eggs. As if it's the same thing." He shook his head in annoyance.

"Ted's a jerk." They exchanged smiles. "Matt hasn't mentioned this to me. Then again, he's been preoccupied, and he doesn't like to discuss the clinic."

"Really?" Sam linked his hands behind his head. "I thought you and he talk shop, discuss patients, tear apart the staff—present company excepted, of course." He grinned.

"Matt doesn't talk about the staff—he told me it's unprofessional. About the egg donors, I agree. And I've read the literature. There are some real concerns."

There was a risk, carefully explained to every donor, that the fertility drugs used to stimulate the production of multiple eggs could result in infertility problems later on. That would be a tragic irony. Lisa had wondered how many young, childless donors seriously considered the possible risks before signing the ovum donation contract. There was also a suspicion, as yet unproved clinically, of a link between certain fertility drugs and subsequent ovarian cancer. And extreme ovarian hyperstimulation could end in serious complications, including lung failure, coma. Even death.

But young people, Lisa knew, didn't respect the reality of death. They drove recklessly and engaged in unsafe, unprotected sex and smoked cigarettes and took drugs, believing that death happened to someone else, to someone older. From all accounts Chelsea had been a bright young woman; still, two weeks ago she'd begged Matthew to let her donate eggs again, even though her ovaries had been hyperstimulated the first time.

Then she was killed. And there was no escaping the irony that because she'd donated eggs, a part of her still lived. Lisa wondered aloud who had received Chelsea's eggs.

"If her parents hire a lawyer to subpoena the records, we may know more details—and soon," Sam said. "How about you? Are you going to hunt down the person who hired Chelsea to be a nanny?"

"I found her. Her name is Paula Rhodes." She told him what she'd learned from Georgia.

"You're really playing detective, aren't you?" He looked at her curiously.

"It's an interesting coincidence, isn't it? Chelsea donates eggs to the clinic and ends up being hired by a family who helped build it. Maybe she said something about Matthew, or about the clinic, or about her problems."

"Or maybe you're reaching," he said gently. "Don't set yourself up for disappointment, Lisa."

"I know you're right." She smiled, touched by his concern. "But I have to try, Sam. The police aren't making any progress. All they can tell me is that there's been no activity on Matthew's credit cards and still no sighting of his car. They're annoyed with me for calling so often."

"That's their problem. You're his fiancée. You're entitled."

"Am I?" She plucked at the fabric of her jeans.

"Hey!" He stared at her, puzzled. "Did I miss something?"

Her eyes teared. It was ridiculous and embarrassing, the way she cried lately at the drop of a hat. She buried her face between her knees and felt his hand hovering over her head.

"Tell me what's going on, Lisa." He stroked her hair tentatively, then withdrew his hand.

She appreciated his gesture, understood his discomfiture. He'd never touched her before, and she'd assumed that in following strict Jewish law, he avoided physical contact with women, aside from his immediate family. Asher had never touched her, either . . .

She studied the damp splotches on her jeans. "I was having doubts about the wedding before all this happened. Matthew didn't know. Now he's disappeared, and I'm *terrified.* I want to see him walk in here, alive and well—" She stopped.

"Go on," he urged softly.

"I still have doubts. When I realized something happened to him, I thought, *Now* all my doubts will disappear. But they haven't." She faced Sam. "Matt's wonderful. He's caring and generous and bright, but I don't know if I want to marry him."

Sam's gaze was thoughtful. "Why not? Sounds like everything's right."

"I know." Lisa sighed. "Little things bother me. He's compulsively neat. He doesn't have the best sense of humor. I wish he'd learn to relax more, not be so driven, so private. Sometimes I think I'm looking for problems. I mean, these are hardly reasons not to marry someone, are they?"

"You tell me," Sam said quietly. When she didn't answer, he asked, "So Matthew has no idea how you feel?"

"No." She hesitated, not sure she wanted to get into this. "The night before he disappeared, I told him I was thinking about being *frum* again." Sam knew she'd stopped being observant. She'd never explained why, and he'd never pressed.

"No kidding?" He studied her, drumming the sofa cushion with his long fingers. "So what was Matthew's reaction?"

"He said he'd think about it seriously and attend classes with me. That should've made everything okay, but it didn't. I don't know what's wrong with me."

"You're asking him to change his whole life around and follow a belief system he doesn't buy." Sam shook his head. "That's not realistic, Lisa. Maybe that's why you're troubled, because you know it's not going to work."

"Maybe."

He was silent for a moment, still tapping the cushion. "So Matthew said he's willing to consider changing his life around, but you still had doubts about marrying him and didn't tell him. Is that why you feel guilty?" His voice was so soft, so gentle.

"Yes." Making the admission brought her a measure of relief. "And every time I tell people he's my fiancé—like Detective Barone, or the people in the restaurant tonight—I feel like an impostor, as though I'm asking for information and sympathy under false pretenses."

The timer buzzed. She jumped up from the couch and hurried into the kitchen, aware that Sam was behind her. She turned off the buzzer.

He leaned against the counter and watched as she transferred the pasta into a colander. "So when did you start thinking about becoming *frum* again?"

"When Matthew and I were first engaged, and I started thinking about having a family. Maybe even before then." She rinsed the pasta under cold water. "I'm not exactly sure *what* I want. I miss Friday night kiddush and challah and the singing. I miss the peacefulness of Shabbos and the beauty of the holidays—the special foods, the special smells, the blessings."

"When did you start missing everything?"

"On some level, I never really stopped." Out of the corner of her eye she saw the sudden lift to his brows, the "whys" forming in his eyes. "Sometimes I even miss all the everyday rules telling me what to eat, what to wear, what to say. Weird, isn't it?" She turned to him and smiled awkwardly, feeling a little uncomfortable baring her soul.

"It's not weird at all. Tradition is very comforting. Belief is uplifting." His smile softened the earnestness in his voice. "So what's the problem?"

She drizzled olive oil onto the spaghetti, then added dried basil and fresh garlic. "The truth? I'm a little scared about making the commitment. What if I find out this isn't for me? I miss all the rituals, but maybe that's nostalgia, not belief." She shrugged. "That's why I'm thinking of going to a few outreach classes to see how I feel."

"Why *think*? Why not just do it?"

"I was planning to call this week. Now that Matthew's disappeared . . ."

"You're just procrastinating, Lisa," he chided gently. "What are you afraid of?"

"Nothing. I *will* go to the classes, soon. You want some pasta?" she asked, taking down a green-and-beige stoneware plate from a cabinet shelf that held her dairy dishes. "I've always kept a kosher kitchen for my parents."

"No, thanks. I just had pizza. I'll have a snack, though."

He was probably unsure of how careful she was about keeping kosher. She felt a flicker of hurt, then told herself he was entitled to be cautious. "Look in the pantry and take whatever you like." She pointed to a tall, narrow cabinet at the end of the small kitchen.

While he rummaged through the pantry and the refrigerator, she took her plate and a fork to the table. Matthew's laptop was open, its blinking prompt teasing her. She shut the computer and set it on the floor.

A minute later Sam came to the table holding a package of Pepperidge Farm Sausalito cookies, a carton of nonfat milk, and a paper cup.

"So when *did* you decide not to be *frum*?" he asked, sitting down across from her. When she didn't answer, he said, "Hey, if you don't want to talk about it, tell me to mind my own business. My sister does, all the time." He poured milk into the cup and opened the package of cookies.

"It's okay. I've just never discussed this with anyone other than my parents and Matthew." She twirled several strands of spaghetti around her fork and saw Sam mouth a blessing over the cookie.

"My birth mother isn't Jewish. According to Jewish law, neither am I." She was watching him carefully—his reaction was extremely important to her—and saw his gray eyes widen with surprise. "My parents adopted me and had me converted as a baby, but they didn't tell me until two weeks before I was supposed to get married." The passage of all those years allowed her to speak without anger, as though she were narrating someone else's story.

He'd been chewing slowly, his jaw working hard as he digested the cookie and the information. Now he made another blessing over the milk and took a sip. "Why not?"

She told him what her mother had said, told him what happened when she'd informed Asher. "So that was it," she finished. "It's kind of ironic, isn't it? Matthew isn't interested in Judaism and knows almost nothing about it, but he's more Jewish than I am." She shrugged to make light of the situation. Lifting a forkful of spaghetti, she hesitated, then made a silent blessing before eating, unsure whether she was doing it to impress Sam or to take a first baby step.

Sam had taken another cookie and was playing with it. "Matt knows all about this?"

"He knows that I'm adopted, that my birth mother isn't Jewish. I glossed over the reasons for the broken engagement. I didn't want to prejudice him against Orthodoxy."

Sam nodded. "But you had no problem telling *me*, because I'm Orthodox."

She was pleased that she didn't have to explain. "Right."

"Well, that's some story." He sifted the pile of crumbs he'd made of the cookie. "So if Asher hadn't dumped you, your entire life would've been different."

"His parents did, really."

Sam grunted. "He went along with it, didn't he?"

"He was twenty-two, Sam. He was living at home, studying the Talmud at the yeshiva, being an obedient son." She readied another forkful of pasta.

"He was old enough to know not to behave like a jerk. Damn them! How could they do that to you?" With an abrupt motion, he flattened the empty paper cup with his palm.

She was startled by his anger, yet oddly pleased. "What are you saying, Sam? That their behavior was insensitive or unexpected? You think another family would have reacted differently?"

"Of course I do!"

"You're lying. Or you're unwilling to see the truth." She put her fork down. "Face it, Sam. Orthodox families embrace the convert, but don't want him to embrace their sons or daughters. It would taint the line."

"That's not true." His eyes narrowed. "Who told you that?"

"No one had to tell me. I learned it firsthand."

"You had a devastating experience with one stupid, narrow-minded family, and from that you decide everyone is like them?" He shook his head impatiently. "How is that fair, Lisa? You're a scientist. Where's your proof?"

"You know, I don't blame the Rossners anymore. They were looking out for their son. They wanted the best for him."

Sam scowled. "What does 'best' have to do with this? Once a person converts, he's considered equal to someone born Jewish. Higher, even."

"Theoretically, maybe." She'd learned that long ago, in one of her high school Torah classes. "Be honest, Sam. Would your parents approve if you married a convert?"

"Hell, yes! If she converted because she was sincerely committed to Judaism, not just because she wanted to marry a Jew. If she was willing to keep all of *Halacha*." The laws of Judaism.

"Do you know that for a fact, or are you assuming?"

"I've never asked them. But I know what they'd say."

"Then they're the exception." She shook her head. "You are *so* idealistic."

He leaned toward her, his hands almost touching hers. "Look, I'm not saying families like the Rossners don't exist. But they don't represent the Orthodox Jews I know."

She sighed. "What's the difference? It's in my past. I've come to terms with it."

"How? By running away from your community and religion? By getting engaged to a Jew who's totally uninterested in Judaism so you won't have to risk being rejected again?"

She glared at him. "That's low, Sam. And it's not true." She shoved her chair away from the table and took her still-filled plate and fork to the sink.

"Isn't it? Isn't that why you're putting off going to these outreach classes?"

She scraped the pasta into a trash bag under the sink, then rinsed the plate and fork, grateful that the noise of the running water was filling the silence. Out of the corner of her eye she could see that he was still sitting at the table. She listened to the thrumming of the refrigerator and the clicking of the wooden slats slapping against the window frame in front of her and thought about what he'd said.

"I was very attracted to you when we were in med school," Sam said. "I never knew if you picked up on it."

She turned to face him, flustered but not unpleased by his comment. "I wasn't sure. You were around a lot, but you never asked me out. Out of curiosity, why didn't you?" She wondered if this was wise, treading onto new, more intimate territory, but it was too late to retract the question.

"I don't date women who aren't Orthodox." He gazed at her. "Out of curiosity, would you have gone?"

"I didn't date men who *are*." She smiled lightly. "But I would've been tempted." She'd fantasized once or twice about him, but had no intention of saying so. She wondered, not for the first time, why he'd never married.

He nodded. "Funny, huh? Who knows what might've been?"

"Funny," she agreed, unable to read his voice or the silence that followed, but she knew something unspoken had passed between them. When he stood and made a point of looking at his watch, she wasn't surprised.

"I'd better go." He returned the milk to the refrigerator and the package of cookies to the pantry. "I have a seven A.M. tuboplasty—unless my patient doesn't show. I've had quite a few cancellations, mostly new patients or first interviews. Ditto for Ted. What about you?"

This was safer ground. "The same. I wonder if we'll have a clinic by the end of the month." She walked him to the door. "Thanks for coming over, and for listening. It really helped."

"Any time. I mean that." He smiled.

"Sam, do you think he's alive?" It was the one question they'd both been avoiding all night.

He sighed. "If someone told me a doctor disappeared the same day a scandal came down on his clinic, and his luggage was gone, I'd say the guy is sitting on a beach somewhere in Mexico, sipping a margarita. But Matthew's one of the most honest people I know. Plus, I can't believe he'd do anything to harm the clinic. It's his dream come true. Why would he throw it away?"

"He's dead, isn't he?" She bit her lip to keep from crying.

"Why hasn't he called you, Lisa?" Sam asked gently.

"Barone said that Matthew may be hiding because he's trying to find out who's behind the problems at the clinic, that he can't contact me because he's afraid he'll put me at risk, or because someone will find him through me."

Sam thought for a moment, then shook his head. "But that would mean Matthew knew about the problems before."

You can't tell Sam. "He did," she said, her face tingling with awkwardness at the surprise in Sam's eyes. Before he could say anything, she told him about Matthew's vaguely phrased concerns, about the "Notes" file, about the paper she'd found in his trash basket. " 'Sig' is probably 'signature.' 'Data' may refer to his research on freezing eggs. I have no idea what 'lies' means or 'forget sig.' Do you?"

"Nope. It's pretty obvious Matt didn't confide in me, isn't it?" More hurt than sarcastic. "I didn't even know he was doing research on freezing eggs. He must've left written data."

"I have his laptop here. I'll try to access the file again tonight." She hesitated. "Last night I thought a car was following me home from Matthew's condo. It was probably my imagination, but what if it wasn't?"

He stared at her. "Did you tell the police?"

"No. I told you, it was probably my imagination."

Sam scowled. "A young woman is murdered, Matthew disappears, and you don't treat this *seriously*?" He raised his hands in exasperation.

"I'm very careful. And why would anyone want to harm me? I don't know anything."

"People don't know that! You're Matthew's fiancée. People assume he tells you just about everything. *I* did. Tell the police about the car." He glanced past her into the living room. "Maybe you shouldn't stay here by yourself."

"I'm fine. And where would I go? Matthew's condo?"

"If you want, I can sleep on the living room couch."

"An unmarried man and an unmarried woman, alone? It wouldn't *pas.*" It wouldn't be appropriate. How many times had she heard that Yiddish phrase in conversations with her parents, her teachers, her friends? "Then again, I'm not Jewish, so it would be okay, wouldn't it?" Her smile was brittle.

"This isn't funny," he said impatiently. His eyes were dark, brooding.

"Go home, Sam. I'll be okay." She opened the door.

He hesitated, then stepped into the hallway. "Promise to call if you need me?"

"Promise." She shut the door and slid the dead bolt and was sorry, for a moment, that she'd let him leave.

She changed into a white cotton nightshirt, slipped a Simon and Garfunkel disc into her CD player, and sat at her table, trying to access the file. A half hour later she felt like slamming her fist into the computer to force it to yield its secrets.

With a wave of annoyance, she remembered the letter she'd promised to write for Edmond. She worked on a draft until she was satisfied, then checked her watch. It was almost eleven. Walking into the living room to shut off the lights, she spotted Sam's denim jacket on the sofa. She put it on top of her purse so that she'd remember to take it with her in the morning. Then, carrying a bowl of coffee ice cream (she could satisfy two cravings at once), she went to her bedroom to watch the evening news.

Ten minutes into the program, an enlarged snapshot of Matthew appeared on the screen, underneath a graphic of a syringe superimposed over the universal symbol for females.

". . . still no word about Dr. Matthew Gordon, renowned infertility specialist and founder of the prestigious Westwood clinic currently under investigation for what some are calling biomedical rape," the male anchor reported. "Police have no comment as to whether Dr. Gordon left the area voluntarily or has met with foul play."

She saw the same exterior shots of the clinic that she'd seen the night before (she hoped Victor was watching; the guard made an impressively menacing figure), the same rapid shots of herself and Ted and Sam and dozens of patients, some angry, some bewildered. Then the graduation snapshot of Chelsea.

"In a related story," the anchor continued, "police are hunting the killer of eighteen-year-old Chelsea Wright, a college student who, in a bizarre coincidence, anonymously donated eggs at the Westwood fertility clinic under investigation. Chelsea, an only child who had planned a career in education, never met the women who would benefit from her generous gift. Tonight, her parents are wondering whether they will ever meet their grandchildren. Brad?"

The camera panned to a reporter standing in front of a small house. "Walter and Enid Wright are heartbroken. . . ."

The phone rang. Probably Sam, calling about his jacket. She shut off the television and picked up the receiver. "Hey," she said, her lips curving into a smile. "Did you forget something?"

"Dr. Brockman? Detective Barone. The California Highway Patrol has your fiancé's car."

For two days she'd been anticipating this call. Now that it had finally arrived, she felt strangely disembodied, though her heart was thudding. She inhaled sharply, steeling herself. "Is Matthew . . . ?"

"There's no sign of Dr. Gordon." There was sympathy in his voice, and something else. "They picked up two teenage boys driving the BMW near Palm Springs. The boys admit they stole it Wednesday night from Lot C at LAX. They insist it was unoccupied and claim they don't know anything about Dr. Gordon. If they're telling the truth, it looks like he left the country. I'm sorry."

"They could be lying. They could have hijacked the car." She squeezed her eyes shut to block out gruesome images of Matthew with a gun held to his head, being dragged out of the car.

"They could have." Barone was clearly placating her. "Neither one has a record. Of course, that may mean they just haven't been caught till now. The CHP is taking them to West L.A., where they'll be questioned separately."

"How did they drive the car out without a ticket?" She realized she was picking on the details to tear apart the whole.

"They stole an old Chevy and drove it into the lot to get a ticket. They parked the Chevy, hot-wired the BMW, and drove it right out, using the ticket from the Chevy. The exit kiosks have cameras that photograph the rear plates of exiting cars, so we'll be able to find out exactly when the BMW was driven out."

"Matthew always sets the BMW's alarm. Wouldn't someone have heard it go off?"

"There are hundreds of cars parked in Lot C every day, all day. Car alarms are always going off. Dr. Gordon probably took a tram from Lot C to one of the terminals. It's smarter than taking a cab to the airport—taxi drivers keep records." The detective's tone revealed grudging admiration. "He was lucky, too. If the boys hadn't stolen the car, we would have found it earlier. Not that it matters. By the time you phoned West L.A., Dr. Gordon was gone. Again, I'm sorry. I know this is a shock."

She shook her head vehemently, even though Barone wasn't there to see her denial. "But why would Matthew flee the country, Detective? He hasn't done anything wrong."

"You can't ignore the allegations against the clinic," he said gently. "Have you checked the clinic files yet?"

"It's hard to know where to start, and things have been chaotic." And she had never for a moment believed that Matthew was responsible for any wrongdoings at the clinic. "Matthew *does* have a protected file in his laptop. He worked on it the night before he disappeared, after he left my apartment. I haven't been able to access it yet."

"Keep trying. I'll call you if I learn anything else."

She wasn't sure now that she *wanted* to access the "Notes" file, to read what Matthew had taken pains to keep private. She wasn't ready to learn that Barone might be right.

chapter fourteen

The house on Linden was a Spanish two-story with sand-colored stucco walls, white trim on the large, mullioned windows and front balconies, and a red tile roof. Hot-pink bougainvillea cascaded low over the porte cochere to the right, almost kissing the black Jaguar that crouched, low and sleek, in the driveway. Aside from the buzzing of several lawn mowers down the block and the passing of an occasional car, the street was quiet.

Inhaling the perfume of freshly-clipped grass, Lisa walked up a wide herringbone-patterned brick path and three steps to the white double doors and rang the bell. She heard the sound of approaching footsteps. A woman's voice said, "Yes?"

"May I speak to Mrs. Rhodes?" She held up her card to the peephole, then slid it under the door. "Please tell her I want to talk to her about Chelsea Wright."

"*Como?*"

"Chelsea Wright," Lisa repeated slowly. "*Por favor, diga a la señora que quiero hablar con ella acerca de una muchacha que se llama*

Chelsea." She had picked up passable Spanish while working with Hispanic and Puerto Rican patients during her internship and residency and in the Manhattan clinic. She'd been using it extensively to communicate with patients who came from Mexico and South American countries and whose English was nominal.

"Ah! *La muchacha. Momento.*"

While she waited, Lisa glanced around her. To her left, a high wall of trimmed shrubbery provided privacy from the house next door. On either side of the entrance, in front of what she supposed were the living and dining rooms, tall, graceful birch trees threw lacy shadows on the windows and walls. Hugging the base of the house were lush clusters of impatiens, lobelia, and other multicolored spring flowers she couldn't identify.

The door opened. A short, brown-haired woman in a knee-length black skirt and black, short-sleeved, crew-neck sweater said, "Please," and beckoned to Lisa, who followed her through a two-story foyer with beige marble floor tiles and a marble center staircase to the doorway of an enormous wood-floor rectangular kitchen.

Sitting on a black stool at a center island was a strikingly pretty woman with chestnut-brown hair pulled into a ponytail. She was wearing an olive-green cotton sweater and khaki slacks. In her arms lay an infant with its eyes closed, sucking contentedly on the nipple of a milk-filled bottle.

She smiled politely. "I'm Paula Rhodes. Berta says you're here about Chelsea?" When Lisa nodded, the woman sighed. "I'll finish feeding Andy, and then we can talk." Her voice was soft and husky with a hint of a drawl.

"Of course. I can wait in another room. I don't want to disturb you." Lisa had planned on coming after work, but two new patients had canceled, leaving her morning free.

"Oh, that's all right. Andy likes company, don't you, sweetheart?" she crooned to the baby, who had opened his eyes. She bent down and delicately smoothed his forehead with her index finger. "We're almost done, anyway. Please come in and make yourself comfortable."

Still feeling awkward, Lisa approached the island and sat on a stool. "Thank you for seeing me, Mrs. Rhodes. I would have phoned first, but your number's unlisted."

"I know. If I ever forgot my own number, I'd be in real trouble." She laughed lightly. "Please call me Paula. 'Mrs. Rhodes' reminds me of the Colossus, and I hate to think of myself as a giant statue with huge legs."

Up close, Lisa saw fine lines around the woman's eyes and across her forehead; she was probably in her mid-to-late thirties. She wore almost no makeup, just a blusher and a pale mauve lipstick. Her nails were short and lacquered with clear polish, and on her wedding finger she had only a simple wide gold band.

"How old is your baby?"

"Three months next week. He doesn't look it, I know, because he was born five weeks premature. But he's catching up. Aren't you, Andy?" She adjusted the tilt of the bottle, which was quickly emptying, leaving a filmy coating on the bottle's sides.

"He's beautiful." He had a light layer of his mother's dark hair; pink, translucent skin; wispy eyelashes. Babies' eyes often stayed blue for the first year. Andy's were navy. Lisa wondered if they would turn a dark, velvety brown, like his mother's.

"He *is* beautiful, isn't he?" Paula looked pleased. "He's such a good baby, too."

She sounded wistful. Or maybe Lisa was reading sadness into Paula's tone because she knew her husband had died recently, or because, since Barone's phone call, she hadn't been able to shake the gloom that had settled around her like a shroud.

Paula removed the bottle from the baby's mouth, set it on the island's black granite counter, and carefully positioned her son's face against her shoulder, which was draped with a diaper. She nuzzled his neck. "I love the smell of babies, don't you?" She patted his back lightly, then rubbed it in small circles until she was rewarded with a delicate burp. "There we are."

Supporting the baby's head and neck with one hand, she slipped carefully off the stool. She was much taller than Lisa had thought, about five feet ten inches, and judging from her slim figure, she'd lost the weight she'd gained during pregnancy.

"I'm going to change his diaper and put him in for a nap. I won't be long." She left the room, still cradling the baby against her chest.

Lisa looked around and sighed. She would love a kitchen like this. The cabinets—there were so many—were made of knotty pine, as were the veneers on the Sub-Zero refrigerator and freezer and the dishwasher. Many of the upper cabinets had paned windows. Behind them, she could see an uncluttered arrangement of glassware and interesting-looking crockery probably chosen by a decorator.

A pile of magazines lay on the island counter, next to a simple glass vase of daffodils, a teak bowl filled with fruit, and a small black monitor, a little larger than a phone pager, from which Paula's murmurs emerged against a background of static. Lisa picked up a copy of *Parenting* and was flipping through it when Paula returned.

"I hope I didn't keep you long." She raised the volume on the monitor and tapped the box. "Thank goodness for this. The house is huge, and I worry about not hearing Andy. The best thing is, I can clip the monitor on me and wear it around the house and in the yard. Can I offer you something to drink? Coffee? Tea? Something carbonated?"

"Water would be nice." Lisa had downed three cups of coffee this morning and refused to have another.

Paula brought two bottles of Perrier from the refrigerator and perched on the stool she'd occupied before. "Your card says you're with the Westwood fertility clinic that's been in the news the last few days." She filled Lisa's glass, then her own. "You probably don't know this, but my husband helped found it."

"Actually, someone mentioned it." As far as Lisa could tell, there was only normal curiosity in the woman's tone. "You may have heard that Dr. Matthew Gordon, the head director, is missing. He's my fiancé, and I'm terribly worried about him." At nine-fifteen this morning, just before she left the clinic, she'd spoken to Barone. The two teenage car thieves were sticking to their story. He tended to believe them. Lisa wasn't prepared to do that.

"I *did* hear. I can imagine your anguish," Paula said quietly. "My husband, Andrew, died five months ago of a heart attack. I'm sorry," she added quickly. "I didn't mean to suggest that your fiancé . . ." Her voice trailed off.

"I realize the odds aren't good. It's hard to give up hope, though." Lisa wasn't sure what to hope for. She'd lain awake for hours trying to decide which was worse—that Matthew had been killed by hijackers, or that he'd fooled her and everyone else. She took a sip of water to dissolve the lump in her throat.

"I know," Paula said, her words conveying remembered pain.

"The detective investigating Chelsea's murder thinks her death and my fiancé's disappearance may be connected. Chelsea donated eggs to the clinic, and Matthew was her doctor." Lisa noted that Paula didn't seem surprised. "Did she tell you about the egg donation?"

"No, but why would she? It was on the news last night. They

called it a bizarre coincidence." Paula drew a circle in the conden-
sation on the side of the cut crystal tumbler. "Was she paid a fee?"

"Twenty-five hundred dollars."

Paula nodded. "She told me her parents had limited means
and she was eager to earn enough money to attend private college.
To be honest, I'm not sure I approve of young women without
children donating eggs. Not that it's my business. And I'm not in
Chelsea's circumstances. My parents were able to provide me with
everything I needed. And Andrew was the most generous, giving
husband." She seemed lost for a moment in a private memory. "I
don't know what I can tell you about Chelsea that would be helpful.
I met her only a week and a half ago."

After Chelsea had come to see Matthew. "How did you meet
her?"

"I placed an ad for a mother's helper on several college bulletin
boards. She called for an interview, and I liked her right away. Of
course, I checked the references she gave me—several teachers and
some people whose children she baby-sat. They all spoke about her
in glowing terms." Paula reached for the fruit bowl and plucked a
green grape. "I suppose you could call this another bizarre coincidence—the fact that a young woman who donated eggs at a fertility clinic gets a job as a mother's helper for the widow of a man
who helped build the same clinic. Do you believe in coincidence,
Dr. Brockman?"

Where was this leading? "Sometimes."

Paula bit delicately on the grape. "I don't. Not really."

Lisa's stomach muscles tightened. "Are you saying that when
Chelsea applied for the job, she knew you were connected with the
clinic? That she sought you out?"

Paula looked startled. "Heavens, no. Why on earth would she
do that? No, I mean God or fate or whatever you believe in has
plans for us, and we don't always know the reasons. Chelsea and
I were meant to cross paths, though briefly, just as she and your
fiancé crossed paths, just as you and I are sitting here now. Did
you ever talk to Chelsea?"

Lisa shook her head.

"There was something charming about her and refreshing, very
genuine. I liked the fact that she planned to be a teacher because
she loved kids. That came through—the love, I mean—when she
played with Andy. He took to her immediately." Paula smiled. A
second later her face clouded. "I can't believe she's dead."

"When did you find out?"

"She was supposed to move in two days ago, on Wednesday morning. At three I phoned her at home. To be honest, I was annoyed more than worried, and I wondered if I'd made the right choice. You know—if she's late the first day, will she be responsible? Someone answered—a neighbor, I guess—and told me that Chelsea was dead. That she'd been *murdered*." Paula shuddered. "I didn't know what to say, I was so shaken. So I hung up."

Lisa nodded in sympathy. "Chelsea's parents didn't mind that she was going to move into your house?"

"She said they were fine with it. She *was* concerned about having time with her boyfriend. I told her she could invite him over to use the pool or the tennis court, but only if Andy was asleep and I was home. And she couldn't take him up to her room." Paula smiled lightly. "I guess I'm a little old-fashioned and overprotective, but Andy's all I have, now that his father's gone." Her dark brown eyes glistened. "I'm sorry. I'm usually in control. I guess Chelsea's death brought everything back."

"That must have been a nightmare for you, being pregnant and losing your husband," Lisa said softly.

"Some days I didn't know how I'd get through it. Andrew was an only child. I'm not close with his cousins—they still regard me as the Southern interloper, even though Andrew and I were married for over three years." She had exaggerated her drawl. Now she flashed a brief, wry smile. "My parents live in Alabama. They're elderly and can't travel. When Andrew died, I was angry and terrified and alone. For weeks I stayed in bed. I barely ate. I wouldn't see anyone except the doctor. He told me I was jeopardizing the baby's health, and that brought me to my senses. Do you believe in God?"

Lisa was surprised by the question. "Yes."

"I stopped believing when my husband died. But when I witnessed Andy's birth—" She inhaled audibly and closed her eyes for a second, and when she spoke again, her voice was a reverential whisper. "He was perfect, and I knew with absolute certainty that God existed." She laughed self-consciously. "I sound like a typical first-time mother, don't I? With all the births you see, I suppose they become routine."

"Actually, every time I deliver a baby I'm awed by the miracle of birth, and my faith in a divine being is reaffirmed. It's one of the rewards of my profession. Don't tell my colleagues. Faith isn't very scientific." Lisa smiled.

"Maybe not, but it's nice to hear it's still alive. In young adults, too. Chelsea believed in God. She mentioned it during our interview. At first I thought maybe she was trying to make a good impression, but she seemed sincere." Paula frowned, then began to roll her water glass between her slender fingers. "She *did* say something about fanatics . . . something about not liking zealots who pushed their religion and opinion on others. She said she'd had an unpleasant experience a while ago with someone like that." Paula shrugged. "I guess we all have."

"She wasn't more specific?"

"No. In general, she was upbeat, cheerful."

"The bartender at the restaurant where she worked said Chelsea had been very unhappy until just recently."

"Really?" Paula cocked her head. "I didn't see any evidence of that. Well, except for a few days before she was killed. She called to tell me when she'd be moving in, and she sounded tense. She said someone had been phoning her for the past few days and hanging up when she answered. She figured it was kids playing pranks, but it annoyed her."

"I don't blame her." What if it hadn't been kids? What if the caller had been someone sinister, trying to track Chelsea's movements? What if that same someone had decided that Matthew posed a threat, too?

"Maybe the police should know about the calls." Paula sounded troubled. "To tell you the truth, I'm surprised they haven't contacted me. Do you think I should call them?"

"Definitely. Talk to Detective John Barone." Lisa took his card from her wallet and wrote the precinct's phone number on a slip of paper Paula handed her. "Thanks for your time," she said, moving off the stool. "And good luck with your son. He's lucky to have a loving, caring mother like you."

"Thank you for that." A smile lit Paula's face. "I'm trying. I'm becoming active again with organization work, because it's important, and because I don't want to smother Andy. That's why I need a mother's helper. And I'm thinking of taking a few clients. I'm an interior designer. That's how Andrew and I met—I decorated this house."

She walked Lisa to the door. "I know that Chelsea's parents have financial problems. I'd like to help pay for her funeral."

"That's a lovely gesture." Lisa said, touched by the woman's thoughtfulness.

"Who knows? Maybe that's why Chelsea and I were brought together, so that I'd have an opportunity to help." Paula looked pensive. "I've never met her parents. They may be proud, and I don't want to come across as Lady Bountiful. I assume they've been in contact with the clinic, since Chelsea donated eggs there. I wonder if you could extend my help anonymously."

The Wrights were unlikely to accept an offer Lisa brought them. And they'd probably view an anonymous offer as an attempt to pay them off. "Your best option is to have Detective Barone talk to them."

"You're right. I can't even begin to imagine what those poor people are going through, losing a child. If anything happened to Andy . . ." She hugged her arms and shivered. "When I first brought him home from the hospital, I checked him constantly when he was sleeping. I'd put a mirror under his nose to make sure he was breathing." She looked at Lisa anxiously to see her reaction.

"You're not the first mother who's done that." Lisa smiled to show she understood.

Paula nodded. "I don't do that anymore—well, not often." She laughed shyly, as if embarrassed by the admission, then sighed. "I hope you hear good news about your fiancé."

chapter fifteen

Ted Cantrell was striding past Reception to his office when Selena called out, "Dr. Cantrell? May I see you a moment, please?" in a falsely sweet voice that set his teeth on edge. There were several patients in the waiting room, so of course he had to stop and smile as he waited for the office manager to get out of her chair and come over to him.

She moved with him out of earshot of the patients. "Your nurse, Brenda, has been frantically looking for you. She says you were scheduled to do a retrieval forty minutes ago and disappeared. I've been paging you for over half an hour. Where were you?"

He glared at her. "You may not be aware of this, Selena, but I don't report to you."

"Your patient was sedated, Dr. Cantrell." Her voice was cool, unruffled. "Luckily, Dr. Davidson was available."

"Luckily for *Brenda*, you mean. For your information, I wasn't told about the retrieval. This isn't the first time she's screwed up, by the way." He scowled.

"Brenda says she reminded you about it yesterday."

"Brenda is lying to cover her butt," he hissed. "I don't need to defend myself against a stupid, incompetent woman who no doubt got her nursing degree because of affirmative action. You can tell Brenda she's fired." His face was mottled with anger.

"You can tell her yourself, Doctor."

He stared at her. "You've been rude since Dr. Gordon's absence. I intend to report your insubordination to Mr. Fisk." He had an urge to put his hands around her thick neck and squeeze.

"Why don't you do that, Dr. Cantrell? I intend to talk to him about several things as well."

Their eyes locked. He glanced away first and, swiveling sharply, stomped off to his office. Once inside, he slammed the door and switched on the small television on top of his credenza. Hanging up his navy sport jacket on the coat tree in the corner of the room, he listened to the stock report and grimaced.

He paced around the room, then sat at his desk and drummed his fingers on the leather mat. With an abrupt motion he stood and walked out of the room to Matthew's office. He glanced around him, then opened the door and entered.

He checked the file cabinet first, thumbing through the folders quickly. Then he moved to Matthew's large desk. He was shutting the bottom right-hand drawer when the door opened.

"You shouldn't be in here!" Grace exclaimed softly from the doorway. She stared at him.

He smiled, thinking again what a mousy little thing she was. He walked around the desk toward her and saw her cower. "It's all right. I was just looking for some notes I lent Dr. Gordon."

She stepped inside. "You should have asked me to look for them." Her arms were folded across her chest.

"You weren't around. Sorry." He paused, then shook his head. "This must be a terrible time for you, Grace," he said softly.

She bit her lip and nodded.

"I know how close you feel to Dr. Gordon, especially since he helped you conceive your little girl. So it must be that much harder to accept that he's betrayed you."

Her blue eyes widened and she blinked rapidly. "Betrayed?"

"The police found his car at the airport. It's pretty clear he left the country." He sighed. "I'm so sorry, Grace. I thought you knew. It's been on the radio all morning."

"No, I—" She stopped. "No, I didn't know." Her eyes teared. She wiped them with her fingers.

He sat on the corner of the desk. "That's why I need my notes. With everything going on lately—Dr. Gordon's disappearance, all these crazy allegations—I don't know what's going to happen, which files the police may seize."

No response from Grace.

"I know you've heard horror stories about me. I'm a monster. I'm difficult. I have a terrible temper." He was pleased to see her blushing. "Don't be embarrassed. Some of it's true, Grace—I won't deny it. I'm a perfectionist. I have a low tolerance for stupidity and inefficiency. Sometimes I yell before I think. I'm not proud of that." He lowered his head, then looked up at her. "I'll bet Dr. Gordon never yelled at you."

"No, he didn't." Her eyes were tearing again. She sniffled.

"Well, why would he? If I had someone like you working with me, I wouldn't yell, either. You're a terrific nurse, Grace. Dr. Gordon raved about you." Ted smiled warmly.

"Thank you." Her tone was sober.

"When things settle down, maybe you'd consider working for me. We'd make a great team, Grace."

"I don't think I want to work here anymore," she whispered.

He slipped off the desk and approached her. "You're upset, Grace, and confused. I am, too." He rested his hand on her shoulder.

She licked her lips. "I'm scared."

He waited for her to continue. When she didn't, he said, "Maybe it would help if you talked about it, Grace. I'm a good listener." He smiled gently.

She shook her head.

"Is it the legal problems? Dr. Gordon's disappearance? That girl's murder?" Grace flinched, and he knew he'd touched a chord. "Is Dr. Gordon's disappearance connected with the murder? Did he tell you something before he left?"

"He didn't tell me anything." She backed away. "I have to go." She was avoiding looking at him.

"You're holding something back, Grace." His voice was almost a whisper. He was careful not to step closer. "I can tell. You'd feel so much better if you told me."

"Leave me alone!" she cried. "I don't know anything! I don't want to talk about this anymore!"

She walked to the door and held it open wide and waited until he left Matthew's office.

chapter sixteen

The guard stopped Lisa before she entered the clinic. "Mr. Fisk's looking for you, Dr. Brockman. Selena said if I saw you, to tell you to go right to his office."

She tensed. "Thank you, Victor."

Obviously Edmond had heard about Matthew's car. She hadn't phoned him about it last night; she hadn't been in the mood to deal with his anger at Matthew. She wasn't in the mood to deal with it now, either, but she had no choice.

Fisk was behind his desk. Seated facing him were Walter and Enid Wright, looking more washed out than yesterday, if that were possible, and a gray-suited woman in her forties with chin-length blond hair and red-framed glasses.

So this wasn't about Matthew. The suddenness and acuteness of her relief made her head throb.

"This is Dr. Lisa Brockman," Fisk said to the woman in the suit, who swiveled and nodded at Lisa. "Dr. Brockman, you've met the Wrights. This is their attorney, Jean Elliott."

Lisa had heard of her—she was a high-priced attorney who specialized in headline-making cases dealing with the rights of birth parents versus adoptive parents. Lisa sat on a folding chair to the left of the Wrights, who avoided looking at her, and wondered how they could afford the attorney's services. Maybe she was doing it pro bono. Maybe she saw another headline.

Fisk addressed Lisa. "According to Chelsea Wright's birth certificate, which her parents have brought with them, Chelsea turned eighteen nine months ago, on August fourteenth of last year. They would like to see the waiver she signed when she entered the donor program. I've asked Grace to bring it in the hope of clearing up this unfortunate matter."

If Edmond was worried, he was hiding his feelings well. Lisa's stomach was churning, and she had no idea why he wanted her here. No one made an attempt to break the silence, which seemed to last forever until Grace timidly entered the office and handed Edmond a manila folder.

Fisk made a ceremony of putting on his bifocals before he opened the folder and thumbed through its papers. "Here we are. Ms. Wright signed her waiver on August twenty-eighth of last year." He flipped a page. "And here, on the medical and history profile she filled out, she wrote that she was eighteen, and that her birthday was August fourteenth. She signed this document, too. So as you can see, the waiver is legal and valid." He passed both documents to the attorney, who handed them to Walter Wright.

Walter stared grimly at the papers, then gave them to his wife. "You're saying that just because she was eighteen and two weeks, she knew what she was doing?"

Jean Elliott put a comforting hand on his arm.

Fisk leaned forward. "It gives me no pleasure, Ms. Elliott, to upset your clients. They've suffered a tragic, insurmountable loss, and all of us here feel for them." He paused. "As to the legal disposition of Ms. Wright's harvested eggs, she gave them up voluntarily and permanently."

"Doesn't it matter that she's dead?" Walter demanded softly.

Fisk sighed. "This is a waiver identical to the one your daughter signed." He bent his head and read: " 'I understand that I do *forever hereafter* relinquish any claim to or jurisdiction over my donated ovum and any embryos or offspring that might result from my donated ovum.' " He looked up. "I wish there were something I could do, but I can't, not without compromising the welfare of the patients who have placed their trust in our hands."

There was another silence. Then Enid said, "This isn't Chelsea's signature," and everyone stared at her. "This isn't the way she makes her capital C or W or her s's. And she doesn't loop her t. I know her handwriting. I practiced with her since she was in kindergarten. This isn't hers."

Walter Wright turned to Lisa. "Well, *you* didn't waste any time trying to cover up, did you?" His look was withering.

The suspicion flashed through her mind that this was why Edmond had wanted her here—if something *was* wrong, blame would lie at her feet. Her palms were clammy. She took a deep breath, mustering up indignation. "Mr. Wright—"

"Dr. Brockman has done nothing wrong." Edmond's voice was iron. "I would be careful, sir, before I accused anyone."

"Walter, let me handle this." The attorney took the papers from Enid and examined them again, flipping back and forth several times between the first and third pages. "What about this, Enid?" she asked, pointing to the back of the eight-page medical history questionnaire. "Is that Chelsea's signature?"

Enid studied the paper, then said, "No, it isn't," with newborn confidence that left no room for argument. She was angry now. Her face was flushed.

The attorney faced Edmond. "If you look carefully, you'll note additional staple holes on the inside pages of this document. And the writing on pages one, two, seven, and eight doesn't seem to have been done by the person who filled in pages three, four, five, and six. Even the numbers have a different slant. Whoever tampered with the documents wanted to save time and redid only those pages—or the backs of pages—that asked for the date of the application or the applicant's birth date."

"May I see those, please?" Fisk took the papers.

His voice was still calm, but he was frowning, and Lisa knew what he was thinking: Matthew was responsible for these forgeries. He'd realized Chelsea's parents would demand an investigation and discover that their daughter was underage when she donated her eggs. He knew they'd sue the clinic, and Matthew. So he'd altered the documents and fled.

Fisk was poring over the papers. "I don't see additional staple holes. And the writing on all the pages appears to be the same." He glanced up at the attorney.

"Perhaps you need new bifocals. Obviously, these aren't the original papers Chelsea filled out and signed. Given the recent allegations regarding your clinic, I'm not surprised by this blatant evidence of document tampering." The attorney's tone was sweetly snide.

Fisk placed the papers inside the folder. "I don't know that there's been any tampering. We have only Mrs. Wright's opinion that the signature was forged, and only yours—hardly expert—that these aren't the original pages one, two, seven, and eight. None of what I've heard or seen constitutes legal proof."

Fisk was so good; he must be a wonderful poker player. Lisa was grateful that the Wrights and Jean Elliott weren't looking at her. She was thinking about the forged signatures—of *course* they were forged; everybody in the room knew it—feeling as though she'd slammed into a wall.

"I intend to provide proof," the attorney said. "I also intend to subpoena Chelsea's file and any other relevant files. My clients have a right to know who has their murdered daughter's eggs. They have a right to their grandchildren." She rose. "I'd like a photocopy of the signed waiver page and the medical and history profile."

Fisk nodded. "I have no problem with that."

"I also want to ensure that no other tampering takes place with this file. I suggest that it be placed in an envelope in my presence and that you and I sign it."

"I have no problem with that, either. Before we do that, however, I want the file photocopied in case my staff needs to access the information."

"As long as I witness the photocopying."

It was like watching a tennis match, Lisa thought, though she knew that Fisk and the clinic had already lost. She flashed to the cryptic writing on the paper in Matthew's trash: he'd written "*forged*" signature, she realized, not "forget" signature. This was the potential lawsuit he'd feared. Did that mean he'd committed the forgery or discovered it?

Ten minutes later Chelsea's file was in a sealed envelope. Across the flap, Fisk, Jean Elliott, Lisa, and Walter Wright had signed their names and the date.

After the Wrights and their attorney left, Edmond removed his bifocals and rubbed his eyes. "You realize it looks highly suspicious that the day after the Wrights inform you they're hiring an attorney, questions arise as to the authenticity of the signatures in the file and several of the document's pages."

She was stung by his innuendo. "I didn't make any changes."

"I didn't think you did." He sounded terribly tired suddenly, and the skin under his eyes was puffy. "Of course, it's possible Mrs.

Wright lied to invalidate the waiver. But I don't think she could do it convincingly, do you?"

Lisa shook her head.

"It would be nice if Matthew were here to explain what happened. Although now that they've found his car at the airport, you and I *both* know, don't we?" His expression was grim. "How could he do this to me, Lisa?" he asked softly. "I built this clinic for him. How could he betray my trust?"

She felt sorry for him. Beneath the anger she heard genuine pain. "Those boys could be lying. They could have hijacked the car and invented the story about the airport."

Edmond grunted in reply.

"The night before Matthew disappeared, he told me he suspected something was going on here. He said he might have to fire someone. Two weeks ago, when Chelsea came to see him, he checked her file. Maybe he discovered the changes. Maybe that's what he was referring to." That would explain why he'd been nervous with Barone. But why hadn't he told Lisa the truth?

"How interesting that you just remembered this now." Fisk's smile was closer to a sneer.

Her face was sunburn-hot. "Matthew made me promise not to tell anyone, including you. He didn't want you to worry."

"Is that why he didn't tell me someone stole twenty thousand dollars from the clinic safe? Ted Cantrell told me. I checked with Selena—she was reluctant to admit that since Matthew's disappearance, the thefts have stopped. Interesting, isn't it?"

Lisa stared at him, speechless.

"How do you explain that and the fact that he left his car at the airport and disappeared?"

"Maybe someone set him up," she said when she found her voice. She didn't know why she was fighting so hard to deny what everyone else believed. Maybe because she couldn't admit to herself that her loyalty was misplaced, that Matthew had made a fool of her. The taste in her mouth was bitter.

Edmond shook his head. "Obviously, you're having a hard time dealing with the truth. Either that, or . . ." He eyed her for a moment. "If he called anyone, it would be you. If you know where he is, now's the time to tell me."

In a cold, flat voice, she said, "He hasn't called me. And I deeply resent your calling me a liar." She was shaking with anger and didn't care what he did. Let him fire her. The clinic would probably be shut down soon anyway.

"If I'm wrong, I apologize." Which wasn't an apology at all. "I'd like you to look at this file and try to make sense of what happened." There was no indication in his voice that he'd just accused her of complicity. Right now it was business as usual.

She stepped forward and took the photocopied file.

"The legal status of donor eggs is relatively uncharted territory." He tented his hands. "The question is, do we assume that Jean Elliott will have her legal way, and do we therefore prepare the recipients of Chelsea Wright's eggs? Or do we hope that the courts will rule against the attorney?"

He lifted his phone receiver. "In the meantime, I have the unpleasant task of questioning everyone here to find out who was involved with the tampering of Chelsea Wright's file and the forging of her signature."

Bastard, she thought as she left Fisk's office. She wasn't referring to Edmond.

chapter seventeen

"You okay?" Sam asked, entering her office. "Selena said the Wrights were here and Edmond was looking for you."

"You could knock." She was changing from her navy blazer into her gray medical coat, fumbling with the snaps because she was so angry her hands shook.

"Next time I'll try to remember." He perched himself on the edge of her desk. "So what happened? Selena said Edmond came tearing into the building like he had to put out a fire."

"Well, he couldn't put it out." She prepared a cup of coffee and told him what had transpired in Fisk's office. "So now he's interrogating everyone to find out who's responsible—aside from Matthew, of course. Fisk knows they found the car." She carried the cup to her desk, stopping to take a sip.

"You can't blame him for suspecting Matthew, Lisa." Sam knew about the car, too. Lisa had phoned him after Barone's call.

She realized he was being careful not to say he agreed with Edmond, just as he'd been careful not to commit himself last night.

She set the cup down and slumped into her chair. "You think Matthew skipped, don't you? Why don't you just say so!"

"Don't *you*? Isn't that why you're angry—because you feel betrayed?" He was silent for a moment. "Matt's a good friend, and he gave my career a boost when he hired me. I owe him, and I care about him. But yeah, I think he skipped. How else do you explain the fact that his car was at the airport?"

She told him what she'd told Edmond, but her recital lacked conviction. She didn't believe it herself, and Sam was avoiding looking at her. "I just find it hard to believe that he'd change the files," she said.

"Maybe you're right." He picked up a stapler from her desk and opened it. "Obviously one of the nurses goofed. When Matthew discovered the problem after Chelsea's visit, he asked questions. Then Chelsea was murdered. The nurse was scared and changed the papers in case they'd be examined."

"That would explain the 'forget sig' note." She took a sip of coffee. "So why did he run away, Sam?"

The pitying look in his eyes said she already knew why. "Because he harvested her eggs. Because he knew he'd be named in a lawsuit, as the attending physician and as the chief director. Because he knew his dream clinic would go down with him. He couldn't face it."

"So where do you think he is?" It was the closest she'd come to admitting Matthew's duplicity.

Sam shrugged. "Somewhere in South America, sipping that margarita. Some place where he can start over. Did the police check his bank account?"

"I don't know. Fisk thinks Matthew stole the cash from the clinic safe. Selena told Fisk the thefts stopped when Matthew disappeared."

"Bingo."

She shook her head, annoyed. "You sound so calm, Sam. Why aren't you angry?"

"Hell, I'm *angry*, Lisa." He snapped the stapler shut and dropped it onto her desk. "But Matthew's gone, and I'm not going to waste energy brooding about him. We have bigger problems. If the Wrights subpoena their daughter's records, all our other patients will be screaming to see their records, too. Of course, the authorities may get there first. Any way you look at it, it's 'Good-bye, clinic.' "

"Damn it, Sam, how could he *do* this—let us think he's been kidnapped or murdered, place the clinic in jeopardy? How could he put me in this awful position with Edmond!" She wrenched the diamond off her finger and flung it across the room, where it fell silently onto the carpet.

Sam retrieved the ring. "I wouldn't chuck this. If the clinic shuts down, you may want to sell it to pay the rent." He handed her the ring. She took it reluctantly and slipped it back on her finger. "Matthew acted out of desperation, Lisa," he said quietly. "I'm sure he hated leaving you, putting you in this position."

"Then why didn't he leave me a note? Just two lines—'Dear Lisa, Sorry about everything. I'm not dead. Love, Matthew.' "

"We may never find out all the whys. I know that's hard to accept. But you're not alone—people care about you. *I* do." He was looking at her intently.

She thought about last night and wondered if he was offering more than friendship. "I need to sort out my feelings—and buy a punching bag with Matthew's face on it."

"Buy a dozen, one for everyone here." He smiled and resumed his seat on her desk. "While you're at it, get one with Ted's face on it."

"Why are you angry at him?" she asked, happy to change the subject.

"I had to cover for him this morning. He left a patient sedated, can you believe it?" He grimaced. "In the last two months I've covered for him about half a dozen times."

"You never mentioned it."

"Matthew knew. I don't like to rat on colleagues." He shrugged. "Sometimes Ted's late. Sometimes—like today—he doesn't show at all. He usually blames his secretary—whoever she is that month—and says she messed up the scheduling. A couple of times he claimed car trouble, which is strange since he has a new Porsche. Another time he said he had to do an emergency C-section at Cedars. When I asked him details, he told me to eff off, said he didn't have to effing explain himself to me." Sam rolled his eyes. "The guy has a limited vocabulary. You know how his nurses keep quitting? My theory is he makes them quit so he won't have someone around, keeping tabs on him."

She laughed. "Interesting theory."

"Yeah." He smiled. "By the way, how'd it go with the Beverly Hills mom? Did you learn anything?"

"Basically, that money doesn't solve everything. Paula Rhodes's wealth doesn't make her any less lonely, and she's still a single mom raising an infant." Lisa held the coffee cup in both hands, taking comfort in the warmth radiating through the porcelain.

Sam nodded. "It's sad, but at least she can afford to hire mother's helpers and all the other staff she needs to help fill the void. Did Chelsea say anything revealing to her?"

"If you mean, did she say anything about Matthew or the clinic, no. But she *did* tell Paula someone was phoning her and hanging up when she answered. It made Chelsea nervous."

Sam frowned. "Probably kids fooling around," he said, but sounded unsure. "Do the police know about these calls?"

"Paula's going to tell Detective Barone. Sam, do you think a judge will grant the Wrights' attorney a subpoena?"

He looked pensive. "That's a tough call. Even with adoption cases, there are no hard and fast rules. Sometimes the courts take the kids away from the adoptive parents and give them to the birth parents. Sometimes the adoptive parents win. The same thing goes with surrogacy cases. It depends on the judge."

"I guess egg donation is the modern spin on adoption. What would you do if you were judging Chelsea's case?"

"Hell, *I* don't know. What constitutes 'motherhood'? Providing the eggs that contribute half the genetic material of a fertilized embryo? Providing the fetus with a womb and nourishment? Providing a child with love and food and clothing and shelter and education?" He picked up a seashell paperweight holding down a stack of papers and spun it on her desk. "You were adopted. Who do you consider to be *your* mother?"

"That's different, Sam. Until I was twenty, I didn't know I *was* adopted." She took the seashell from him. "Stop fidgeting."

"My sister's always telling me that. Sorry." He smiled abashedly. "Did you ever try to locate your birth mother?"

"No. I thought about it, though. A lot. I fantasized about finding her and showing up on her doorstep. Sometimes I still do." She shrugged. "I had so many questions—about her nationality, her appearance, her personality, her education, her likes and dislikes. Her medical history."

Sam nodded. "So why didn't you look for her?"

"I knew my mom would feel threatened. And I decided it wasn't fair to intrude on my birth mother's life. She gave me up for a reason. What if my appearing caused her pain or embarrassment?" *What if she rejected me again?* "Or what if I located her and found that we had nothing in common, no connection? That would be worse than never finding her at all."

"Reality is rarely as satisfying as fantasy," he observed. He was silent for a moment. "But what about your medical history? You have a right to know. That's why we have donors fill out health questionnaires. That's why they have to take blood tests for HIV and other diseases." His leg was swinging back and forth.

"According to my mom, my birth mother was eighteen when she had me. My mom says she saw all my birth mother's health records and spoke with her OB. Everything was fine."

"And as a doctor, that *satisfied* you?" He sounded skeptical.

"I had a genetic screening. I got a clean bill of health, except for my propensity for worrying and feeling guilty." She smiled, trying to make light of what had been an extremely tense time. She could still remember sitting in the reception area, her hands clammy with anxiety, waiting for the doctor to call her in.

"So you don't regret not looking up your birth mother?"

She considered for a moment. "Not really. I know the trend is for open adoption, and that's fine if all the parties are comfortable. I read an article about a birth mother who baby-sits the two children she gave up for adoption. Talk about an extended family!" She smiled. "The bottom line is, Esther Brockman *is* my mother. Nathan Brockman *is* my father. She didn't provide the egg, and my dad didn't provide the sperm, but I'm their child."

Sam's leg was finally at rest. "Is that why you specialized in infertility? Because your mother couldn't have kids?"

"Yes." She looked at him with interest. "It took me a while to figure that out. I wanted to help people like her. What about you?"

"Ditto. Plus, I always liked playing doctor." His gray eyes twinkled behind his wire-rimmed glasses. "Speaking of which, my next appointment should be here any minute." He slipped off the desk and smoothed his jacket.

"If I don't see you before the end of the day, have a good Shabbos." It was the first time she'd wished him a good Sabbath— the first time in years she'd used the phrase to anyone besides her parents. It felt odd, but pleasant.

"You, too." He didn't seem surprised. "Have you been to any of the Orthodox shuls near you?"

"Not yet." She'd been putting that off, along with the outreach classes. Maybe Sam was right—maybe she *was* afraid of being rejected again. "I know there's one less than a mile away. Where do you go?"

"Shaarei Emunah." He told her the address on Pico, east of Doheny. "It's about two miles from your place—a long walk, which is too bad. The people are great, the rabbi's terrific—dynamic, caring. And, of course, there's me." He looked at her archly.

She couldn't help smiling. "Of course." Most of the people she knew worked at the clinic. She wanted to expand her circle of friends. And she needed to find a rabbi to advise her, guide her.

Sam headed for the door, then turned back. "I forgot to ask. Did you tell the police about the car that followed you?"

"Not yet. If Matthew *did* run away, there's no reason to think I'm in danger, right?"

"Right." He was frowning. "Still . . . be careful, okay?"

"Okay." She was warmed by his concern.

After he left her office, she read the message slips Selena had placed on her desk. Most were from patients. One was from Gina Franco; she'd probably heard about Matthew's car. The folder with Chelsea's photocopied documents was on her desk. Lisa opened it and scanned the papers.

According to the lab form, sixteen eggs had been harvested from Chelsea on September twenty-first. There had been two egg recipients, each named "Jane Doe" with a numerical suffix code. Each Jane Doe had received eight eggs.

Her computer was on. She accessed the confidential file that listed the egg recipients, typed in the numerical code for the first Jane Doe, and waited for the name to come up.

Cora Allen.

Lisa felt intense relief. Cora, thank goodness, wouldn't be affected by the legal decision on the subpoena. The embryo transfer hadn't produced a pregnancy.

She typed in the numerical code for the second Jane Doe and stared at the name on the screen:

Naomi Hoffman.

chapter eighteen

The Hoffmans lived in a small white stucco house in the Beverly-Fairfax neighborhood on Curson between Rosewood and Clinton. The street was narrow and crowded with similar one-story houses and duplexes and the parked cars that belonged to their residents. There were few trees, and the lawns ended abruptly, landscaped for the most part with obediently shaped shrubs rather than flowers.

Walking up the block from her parking spot, Lisa saw several toddlers careening up and down their driveways on tricycles and made way for two helmeted boys racing by on Rollerblades. At the Hoffmans' door, she rang the bell and wondered whether she was doing the right thing, coming here.

Baruch was obviously startled to see her. His face was pale and pinched as he opened the door and invited her in. "Is everything all right?" he asked, his voice tight with alarm.

"Everything's fine," she assured him, feeling guilty that she'd given him even a moment's concern. "There's something I wanted to discuss with you. How's Naomi? Resting?"

He looked at her questioningly. "Yes, in the bedroom."

They were standing in the living room, unfurnished except for light oak bookcases that occupied two adjacent walls and were filled with the gilt-bound tomes Lisa recognized from her parents' home—tall, dark burgundy volumes of the Talmud, shorter volumes of the Bible, numerous commentaries. Baruch, she knew from Naomi, was being groomed to step into his father's rabbinic shoes.

They passed through the dining room, where two tall silver candlesticks were sitting on top of a white-cloth-covered oval table, then entered a long, narrow hall. All the floors had the same low-pile dark beige carpet that looked freshly shampooed but showed signs of wear.

"Something smells good," Lisa said to fill the silence. She inhaled the blended aroma of roast chicken, of dill, of sweet noodle pudding, of challahs warming in the oven. It was like stepping into her mother's home, into her past.

"My mother and Naomi's take turns sending over Shabbos meals, and during the week I cook or stop at a restaurant just a few blocks from here that has great takeout stuff. We're following your instructions about bed rest."

Wondering if it was the same restaurant she'd almost walked into the other night, she followed Baruch down the hall and stopped when he did in front of an open door.

"This will be the babies' room," he said.

Lisa peeked inside. The room had been painted a soft yellow. The linoleum had a yellow-and-white square pattern, and white miniblinds covered the two windows. There were no cribs, no dresser, no changing table.

"It's a good-size room." She was about to ask whether they'd ordered furniture but remembered that buying anything before a baby was born was considered to be inviting an *ayin hara*—bad luck. So was having a baby shower.

The door to the next room was open, too. From the hall, Lisa could see Naomi reclining on a twin-size bed covered with a taupe-and-navy plaid comforter. She was leaning against a navy corduroy backrest with arms. A pillow sham that matched the comforter propped up her knees.

"Who was at the door?" she asked when Baruch stood in the doorway.

"Dr. Brockman's here. She stopped by to tell us something. Everything's fine." He stepped aside to let Lisa enter.

"I thought I recognized your voice." Naomi's eyes and tone revealed curiosity and a little anxiety. From the nightstand between the two beds, she picked up a black crocheted snood with tiny gold spangles and slipped it on her head.

"Why don't you sit here, Dr. Brockman?" Baruch pointed to the other bed.

"Thanks." Lisa felt awkward, sitting on his bed, but there were no chairs in the small room. "I'm sorry to come unannounced, especially right before Shabbos."

Naomi smiled. "That's okay. Baruch's taking care of everything. That's one advantage of having a teacher for a husband—he's home by three every day." She took his hand as he sat down at the edge of her bed.

Baruch, Lisa knew, received no pay for leading a daily early-morning Talmud class in his father's small shul; he earned a modest income teaching Judaic studies at a local private Orthodox elementary school and tutoring students at night. Naomi had worked for over ten years as a paralegal. Lisa couldn't imagine how the Hoffmans were managing with one salary now that Naomi had quit her job—she knew they'd depleted their savings and refinanced their home to pay for years of fertility treatments. They'd also borrowed money from Naomi's parents, who owned a fabric store downtown, and a smaller sum from Baruch's parents.

Realizing that she was stalling, Lisa said, "I told Baruch how wonderful everything smells. It reminds me of my mom's cooking."

"He's become an expert food warmer." Naomi smiled at him. "He's even learned how to scramble eggs and boil pasta. Why not stay and have Shabbos dinner with us? We have plenty, and we'd enjoy the company."

Lisa hadn't had a traditional Sabbath meal since she'd visited her parents half a year ago, but she doubted that the Hoffmans would enjoy her company after she told them why she was here. "Thanks, maybe another time." They were looking at her expectantly. "I wasn't sure I should bother you with this," she began. "There's been a development that concerns you in a way, but I don't think it's a problem."

"What development?" Baruch asked warily.

"This is a little complicated. A young woman, Chelsea Wright, was murdered a few days ago."

"I heard about that on the radio," Naomi said softly. "It's heartbreaking."

"Yes, it is." Lisa cleared her throat. "Apparently, Chelsea donated eggs at the clinic in October, and her parents have hired an attorney to find out who received them."

"I don't see what that has to do with us." Baruch was frowning now. He removed his hand from his wife's.

"For some reason, our computer codes indicate that Naomi received eight of Chelsea's eggs. Obviously—"

"Oh, my God!" Naomi's eyes widened. "But that's impossible!"

"Of *course* it's impossible," Lisa said firmly. "Especially since you had the *shomer*." Thank God, she added silently. "But I felt I had to tell you, because if they subpoena Chelsea's records, they may contact you. I wanted you to be prepared." She found it hard to face the betrayal and accusation in their eyes.

Baruch said, "I thought you ran a reputable clinic. I don't understand how this could have happened." His voice was like chips of ice. His hands had formed fists.

She didn't blame him for being angry. "Frankly, I don't, either. I can assure you I'm going to get to the bottom of this."

She couldn't tell them about the alleged forgery, or that the person who had altered Chelsea's documents might have altered the recipient code to correlate with the date of the donation. That he—or she—had chosen Cora and Naomi at random.

"To be frank, Dr. Brockman, your assurance isn't enough." Baruch was struggling for control. "Since we all know that Naomi never received any donor eggs, I want your guarantee that these people won't learn her name."

Lisa clasped her hands. "I can't guarantee that. If the Wrights get a subpoena—"

Baruch was gripping his thighs, and the veins in his hands were pronounced. "You said there's been a terrible mistake. Why let them think they know who has their dead daughter's eggs, only to find out they don't?"

"I agree with you. But if they subpoena the files, there's nothing I can do. I can't tamper with the files."

"But it isn't even true!" Naomi slumped back against the pillow and covered her eyes with her hands.

"You stood at our front door and told us we have nothing to worry about." His voice was bitter.

"You don't, because of the *shomer*. You can get a notarized affidavit that he was present during every step of the retrieval, the fertilization, and the implantation."

"The *shomer* isn't in L.A.," Baruch snapped. "When I heard

about the allegations against the clinic, I called the rabbi who hired him, just in case. The *shomer* is in Israel on a year's retreat."

Lisa had a sinking feeling. "There's no way to contact him?"

"The rabbi's trying, but he says it could take weeks." Baruch pressed his hands against his temples. "We shouldn't have to be doing this. This is outrageously unfair."

"What about my lab forms?" Naomi sat up abruptly. "Wouldn't they indicate whether I received donor eggs?"

Lisa felt herself blushing. "I can't find your file. I checked everywhere." In the central filing system, where it should have been returned after Naomi's appointment. On Selena's desk. In the billing office. In her own office. "I'm sure it'll show up soon." Unless someone had deliberately removed it.

"I don't believe this is happening." Baruch stood and crossed the room. Placing his palms on top of the long, narrow dresser, he rested his weight on his arms and stared at the wall.

"I'm so sorry, Naomi," Lisa said. "I'm especially sorry to be telling you this now. I hate ruining your Shabbos." She'd contemplated waiting until Saturday night or Sunday, but had worried that by then the Wrights might have contacted Naomi.

"You had to tell us," she said dully, not looking at Lisa.

Lisa wrote her home number on her card. "Please call if you need me—no matter what time it is." She put the card on the nightstand and crouched at Naomi's side. "Promise me you won't let this agitate you," she said quietly. "I don't want you going into labor. And I *know* everything will be straightened out."

Naomi nodded and covered her mouth with her knuckles. Her eyes were bright with tears.

"Have a good Shabbos," Lisa said lamely, standing up. "I'll let myself out."

No protest from Naomi, who responded with a softly uttered "Good Shabbos," or from Baruch, who didn't respond at all.

Maybe it was the familiar smells from the Hoffman kitchen that teased her on her way out and made her feel homesick and lonely. Maybe it was that and the fact that Matthew was gone, and Sam's gentle chiding: *Don't think, just do it.* She decided she would try keeping the Sabbath. She drove to the restaurant near La Brea, stopping on the way at the corner of Oakwood and La Brea to buy irises and lilies from a woman with a scarf wrapped around her hair who was selling flowers for the Sabbath.

The restaurant owner, a short, portly man with a beard and a large velvet skullcap, told her he was closing but took pity on her and let her inside. A thin, short, Hispanic-looking man in his twenties was mopping the white ceramic-tiled floor; another, taller man was putting away the different meats and salads displayed in the L-shaped glass case at the front of the restaurant. Lisa bought too much of everything and wished the owner "Good Shabbos."

At home, she put the bags in the kitchen and arranged the flowers in a crystal vase, then listened to her messages. Her parents had phoned to wish her a good Shabbos; she was sorry she'd missed their call. Selena had left two messages: Gina had called again. Paula Rhodes had phoned and left her home number.

She had no intention of contacting the reporter until Monday, but she was curious about Paula. The housekeeper answered the phone. Lisa identified herself and began unloading her purchases while she waited for Paula.

"Thanks for calling back," Paula said when she came on the line several minutes later. "I'm sorry I kept you waiting—I was checking on Andy." She sounded tense under the soft drawl.

"Is he all right?"

"He gave me a scare. I checked on him when he was napping— I guess because of what we talked about. He was on his stomach, and I put my finger under his nose and couldn't feel any vapor. I thought I'd die." She said this simply, without histrionics. "But a second later he was breathing. I just panicked—because of Chelsea, and everything."

"You may not know this, but it's better if Andy sleeps on his back." Lisa emptied the plastic tub of pea soup into a pot and wondered if Paula had called because she'd heard that the director of the clinic funded in part by her late husband had fled the country.

"My mother told me it was better to let him sleep on his stomach, in case he spits up, but the pediatrician said the back. I phoned him right away and described what happened. He said he's not concerned, but he wants me to bring Andy in on Monday, just to be sure. So now, of course, I'm *more* worried, and I've been checking him every half hour." Paula laughed self-consciously.

"You're wise to be cautious, but if the pediatrician was worried, he would have had you bring Andy in sooner." Lisa set the pot on the stove and turned on a low flame.

"I guess you're right." She paused. "Anyway, that's not why I called you. About an hour after you left, a man who said he was Detective Barone phoned. He said he was in charge of Chelsea's murder investigation, that he understood you'd been to see me and he'd appreciate my telling him about our conversation so he could include it in Chelsea's file. You'd mentioned Barone's name, so I felt comfortable telling him what we discussed. In fact, at first I thought that you'd called him and told him to contact me."

"No, I didn't." Barone had probably obtained Paula's number from the Wrights. But why was he interested in her conversation with Lisa? And how had he known she'd been at Paula's?

"I know that now. After Barone hung up, I realized I'd forgotten to ask him to arrange things so I could pay for Chelsea's funeral. So I called Hollywood Division and asked to speak to him. When he came on the line, I realized immediately from his accent that he wasn't the person I'd talked to before. And he had no idea who I was. I thought you should know."

Lisa had already stopped stirring the soup, which was thick and bubbly and looked like lava, and was holding the wooden spoon in the air, wondering furiously who had impersonated Barone and why. When she heard Paula say, "Dr. Brockman? Are you there?" she replied, "I'm sorry. I'm just stunned by what you've told me. What did Barone say?"

"He has no idea who this other person could be. He asked me to repeat everything the man said, everything I told him. He sounded concerned. Frankly, I'm scared. I contacted my security company to make sure my system is operating properly, and I instructed Berta not to let anyone into the house, not even someone in a police uniform. I also told the gardener to keep an eye out. I think you should be careful, too."

"Yes, of course." Her front door had a dead bolt, but her building had no security system, and it wouldn't be too difficult for someone to climb onto the small balcony and break the sliding glass door to the bedroom of her second-floor apartment. The balcony faced the alley; no one would see, no one would hear.

"What I don't understand," Paula said, "is how this person knew you were here, unless he was following you. And why would he be following you unless he's involved with Chelsea's murder?"

chapter nineteen

Barone wasn't in the station, a female detective informed Lisa. She'd let him know Lisa had called.

She'd already checked the dead bolt, which had been slid shut, and the safety bar that prevented someone from opening the sliding door was securely in place. She contemplated blockading the door with her dresser, but knew that even if she took out the drawers, it would be too heavy for her to move.

The acrid smell of something burning made her run into the kitchen, where she barely salvaged the soup. The spoonful she tasted had a smoky flavor and seared the tip of her tongue. Tears stung her eyes because her tongue was smarting, and because she was determined to make this first Shabbos meal in her own apartment special, serene, and didn't want it ruined by the fear that had settled, leadlike, in her stomach.

She placed the rotisserie-grilled chicken and a square, disposable aluminum pan with grated potato kugel into the oven. She covered the table with a pale peach cloth and lay a place setting of the Dansk stoneware and cutlery she used for meat dishes. She centered the flowers on the table. The acts of preparation gave her a measure of calm. She'd forgotten to buy the short, thick white Shabbos candles her mother used; she set two long, cream-colored tapers in the crystal candlesticks she'd bought for the first dinner she cooked for Matthew.

Before she took her shower, she checked the sliding door again. She usually enjoyed showering, letting the water cascade down her back, on her face. Now she felt vulnerable. She was rinsing the lather from her hair when she thought she heard the phone ring. She hurriedly finished and ran to the phone, but the ringing had stopped. She played back the message; instead of Barone's musical voice, she heard Sam wishing her a good Shabbos. She phoned him back, but now he didn't answer.

When she finished blow-drying her hair, it was six-fifteen, and she had an hour left before the Sabbath. Matthew's laptop was where she'd left it last night, in the dining nook. She took it into her bedroom and, sitting at her small hutch-topped desk, switched it on. Before, she'd hoped the "Notes" file would reveal what had happened to him. Now she was sorting through myriad emotions—anger, hurt, anxiety, lingering disbelief—and she wanted to find out if the file would explain what had made her fiancé betray her and the others and run away. Focusing on Matthew, she hoped, would also prevent her from thinking about the man who'd impersonated Barone.

She was free-associating, typing anything she could think of related to Matthew and the clinic. Ten minutes later she typed still another name, fully expecting to see the prompt's indifferent, blinking rejection, but this time there was no rejection. The password, upon reflection, was so ridiculously obvious that she was annoyed for not having figured it out sooner.

LOUISE BROWN.

The world's first test-tube baby, born in Britain. Matthew had often said her conception had inspired his career; several days ago he'd joked about naming their first daughter Louise. And he'd talked about getting a personalized license plate: Louise B.

She was flushed with her success. Tensing her stomach muscles, she waited for the file to come up. When it did, she resisted the temptation to skip to the end of the document and scrolled through page after page of what was basically an electronic journal.

The headings were the dates of each entry. Matthew had made the first entry four months ago. The entries contained comments on procedures he'd performed on various patients; plans he had to improve the operation of the clinic; statistics of success rates at other fertility clinics; comments on articles regarding the latest infertility treatments.

Several entries discussed his ongoing experimentation with freezing unfertilized eggs. "Could this be big breakthrough?! Must make sure data is secure," Matthew had written.

There was scientific discussion of the particulars of the experiments, but Lisa was too impatient to read them now. She scrolled forward more quickly and was almost at the end of the long document when she spotted a reference to Chelsea Wright.

Her breath quickened when she saw the dead girl's initials in an entry dated two and a half weeks ago, and she stared at the writing on the white screen:

"C. W. was here today. Agitated, needs money. Wouldn't say why. Checked her file, told her hyperstimulation during previous drug cycle contraindicates repeat donation. Told me she tried another clinic, but they wouldn't take her because she's only eighteen. She let slip she wasn't eighteen when she donated!! Cried, then admitted she wrote false birth date on papers!

"Must find out who's responsible. Do I tell Edmond, or not?

"Question: do we stop accepting young, childless donors? Hard to convince others, especially E, to screw the bottom line.

"Screw them all, then."

Lisa was chewing on her bottom lip, mulling over what she'd read. At least he'd been honest about Chelsea's visit to the clinic. She wondered why he hadn't told Barone that Chelsea had attempted to donate at another clinic, then quickly answered her own question: he hadn't wanted to discuss Chelsea's age.

But why hadn't he told her about Chelsea's lie and the predicament he faced because of it? Why hadn't he confided in her, asked for her advice, her moral support? She remembered suddenly that he'd been about to tell her something about Chelsea, then had changed the subject. Would everything be different now if she had prodded him?

"E" was clearly Edmond. Who were the others? The board of directors? Or did he mean Ted? He couldn't mean Sam—Sam had expressed similar concerns about young donors.

She read the next entry, dated the following day:

"Grace swears she didn't take C's application. Cried, said another nurse did initial interview. Who? If it was one of Ted's nurses, she's long gone. I asked Ted—he was angry, defensive. Lisa's right—he's a pain in the ass. Wish I didn't need him.

"Asked all the secretaries, nurses—no one admits anything.

"Someone is lying. But who?

"Question: what are the odds anyone will find out Chelsea was underage when she donated? Should I drop the whole thing? Wish I could ask Lisa, but I don't want to worry her, and she's preoccupied lately. Why?

"Question: does Lisa know Sam is wild about her? Sometimes I feel he's jealous of me. Can't blame him."

She felt like a voyeur, reading Matthew's personal comments. Though she told herself she didn't care, she was gratified to learn that his love for her was sincere. She was surprised he'd been aware over two weeks ago that something was troubling her; even more surprised, and discomfited, to discover that he suspected Sam had feelings for her.

She moved through the next two pages, which discussed the latest experiment results. Skimming the paragraphs, she read of Matthew's disappointment—what had seemed promising weeks ago proved to be a dead end. She felt a renewed flash of sympathy, then steeled herself. Matthew wasn't entitled to sympathy at all.

She read his latest entry, the one he'd written on Tuesday night, after leaving her apartment:

"C was murdered! Shocking, senseless.

"Barone saw I was nervous—why wouldn't I be? Still don't know what to do about Chelsea's papers. Lisa saw I was nervous, too. I'm not sorry I didn't tell her—I love her too much to get her involved with this ugly mess.

"Barone said it could be a mugging, but I know he doesn't believe it.

"Question: why was she killed?

"Did someone see C at clinic two weeks ago, talking to me? Even if answer is yes, so what?

"To fire or not to fire—still no clear evidence. Even if I find proof, it's too late to avoid disaster: C's parents will want to know who has her eggs, will learn she was underage when she signed waiver. Will sue me, clinic.

"Question: when do I tell Edmond?

"Note: ask Grace to find out about C's funeral and send flowers. Attend, if schedule permits.

"Question: does the captain always go down with his ship?"

Lisa scrolled backward and reread the last entry. She found it hard to analyze emotions from words on a screen, but Matthew had obviously been stunned by Chelsea's murder, then anxious about what would happen to him and the clinic. Still, she was left with more questions than before.

He hadn't admitted he'd forged the papers. Then again, why would he? There was nothing to suggest that he'd planned to run away, either, although the last line had a desperate, morbid tone. Again she felt a twinge of pity for him, then reminded herself that he'd let her think he'd been kidnapped or killed.

But if he'd planned to run away, why had he contemplated attending Chelsea's funeral? Or had he reached the decision to run away after having spent a restless night?

And why had he gone to the clinic so early in the morning? To get proof about who was responsible for altering Chelsea's documents? Or to alter the documents himself?

She inserted a blank diskette into the laptop's drive and copied the file. Then she inserted the diskette into her own computer and printed out a copy for herself. After shutting off the computer, she phoned the station one more time. Barone hadn't called in.

By now the food was warmed, and her kitchen smelled like her mother's. She shut off the oven, unscrewed the refrigerator bulb in preparation for the Sabbath, then walked over to the dinette table. Like most of the girls with whom she'd grown up, she'd never lit her own Sabbath candles while living with her parents. Tonight would be a first in many ways.

Feeling a flutter of quiet excitement, she struck a match and lit one candle, then the other, watching the flames leap to life. Maybe it was her imagination, but the lighting in the room seemed more mellow now, the room itself more still. She encircled the flames three times with her hands before she covered her eyes and recited the simple Hebrew prayer she knew by heart and had watched her mother mouth on so many Friday nights. Her mother silently recited additional prayers each Friday night—"May it be God's will . . ." Her father blessed her each week upon his return from synagogue. It was after ten-thirty in New York, and her parents were no doubt sound asleep. She wished suddenly that she'd taken them up on their offer and flown home.

Without the radio or television to keep her company, the apartment was eerily silent, and she was unaccustomed to being alone with her thoughts. Last week—it seemed like an eternity ago—she'd worried about how Matthew would react when she told him she was thinking about taking some outreach classes. Now, though she'd promised herself she wouldn't think about him, she couldn't help wondering where he was, what he was thinking.

Anger bubbled within her again. She didn't like the feeling—she wanted to experience the uninterrupted tranquility of the Sabbath. From the pine bookcase in the living room, she took the prayer book she'd bought a few weeks ago at a Jewish bookstore on Pico, then sat on the sofa. She leaned over to switch on the ecru stone-based lamp on the table, but pulled back her hand just in time. She couldn't do it, not on the Sabbath. She couldn't turn on the radio or the television, couldn't answer the phone, couldn't cook, couldn't tear, couldn't do any of the hundred little things she'd been doing on Friday evenings and Saturdays for over ten years.

Technically, of course, she could do whatever she wanted. She hadn't officially accepted Judaism—that was what she'd told herself eleven years ago. *I'm not even Jewish.* But she'd always considered herself Jewish, always identified herself to others as Jewish, and tonight she'd taken the first step in making a commitment to herself, and to God. For weeks she'd been filled with qualms, with apprehensions; suddenly everything seemed right. (*Don't think, just do it.*) Six months ago she'd viewed all the "don'ts" as unnecessary restrictions. Now she welcomed them as reminders that this day was separate from the rest of the week. Special, holy.

Everything was familiar, everything was new.

In the dining nook she recited the prayers—partly in Hebrew, partly in English—and when she sang *L'choh Dodi,* "Come, My Beloved," and bowed during the final refrain to welcome the Sabbath bride, she felt the Sabbath enter her home.

She didn't have a silver wine cup, so she poured a semidry pink wine into a crystal goblet and recited the kiddush aloud, using her father's melody, which she could hear in her memory. She poured water from a glass over her hands—the right hand first, then the left, then the right and left again—and said the blessing. With her hands dried, she recited the blessing over the two small braided challahs she'd wrapped in tin foil and warmed in the oven. Her mother usually baked her own challahs. As a child Lisa had loved standing next to her on a step stool at the flour-covered kitchen counter, kneading her own small mound of dough, punching it down, braiding it with chubby, clumsy fingers. Her mother's long, slender fingers had seemed to fly over the dough, weaving the thick strands with impossible grace and speed.

She wondered whether Sam was with friends tonight or

whether, like her, he was eating alone, making his own kiddush, blessing his own challahs; whether he was eating store-bought food or food he'd prepared himself. She pictured him in the kitchen she'd never seen, his hands in mitts, an apron tied around his waist. The image made her smile.

She was eating a chicken wing when the phone rang. She rose from the table and reached for the kitchen wall receiver, then quickly drew back her hand. If it was the clinic calling about an emergency, she'd answer; and if necessary, she'd drive to the clinic to attend to a patient. That was the *Halacha*, the law.

She went into the bedroom and sat on the bed, waiting for the fourth ring, then for the click and whir that indicated her outgoing message was being played and rewound. Another click, and she heard Barone's voice. She clutched the edge of the bed.

"Dr. Brockman, I assume you're phoning about Paula Rhodes. We're doing everything we can to find out who impersonated me."

She'd figured out that the impostor had learned Barone's name by calling the station and asking who was in charge of Chelsea's murder investigation. She was eager to talk to Barone, but this wasn't an emergency.

"The other reason I'm calling, Dr. Brockman, is that there's been a major development. The two boys haven't changed their story, but in checking the car for evidence, the lab technicians found what could be human blood in the trunk."

She felt as though the breath had been sucked out of her lungs. Her ribs were pressing against her chest wall, and she could feel the beating of her heart. Her hand hovered over the phone on her nightstand, shaking.

"If you know Dr. Gordon's blood type, please call me."

She didn't know whether this qualified as an emergency—if Matthew was dead, telling Barone his blood type wouldn't bring him back to life—but she picked up the phone.

"His blood type is O positive. I'm sorry, but unless you have something else urgent to tell or ask me, I can't talk now. It's my Sabbath." It *was* her Sabbath, she decided.

"The lab is running tests on the substance we found. I'll phone you with the results as soon as I get them. Good night."

If God was testing her, she'd failed, she thought as she returned the receiver to its cradle.

She lay down on her bed and told herself she'd had every reason to believe that Matthew had fled, but she was overwhelmed with guilt for having doubted him, for having lost faith.

The wind whistled through a sliver of space between the stationary door and the slider, rattling the glass. She closed her eyes and tried to decide which was worse—Matthew sitting on a beach somewhere, sipping a margarita, or Matthew lying dead somewhere, the blood in the trunk of his car a silent testimony to his innocence.

chapter twenty

The muted sounds of a raspy male voice reading the week's Torah portion greeted Lisa as she entered the synagogue's air-
conditioned foyer. The frigid air was a wonderful relief. She'd
walked two miles this morning in humid, eighty-five-degree
weather to come here. She was wearing low-heeled navy shoes, but
her toes and the soles of her feet burned, and her navy silk suit
clung to her back, and her heartbeat was accelerated because of the
brisk pace she'd maintained and the apprehension, only partly di-
minished by occasional reassuring glances around her, that someone might be following her.

She opened the door and peeked into the sanctuary, which was
almost filled. The women's seats, occupying the left half of the
high-ceilinged, rectangular room, were separated from the men's
section by a four-foot wall of wood panels topped with a two-foot
lattice border. Taking a prayer book and a Bible from a bookcase
in the foyer, she entered the sanctuary and chose a seat near the
front, hoping to catch sight of Sam.

She exchanged "Good Shabbos" greetings with her neighbors, who returned their attention to the open Bibles in front of them. Lisa had missed the morning service. She recited the major prayers, surprised at how easily her tongue formed words she hadn't used for years. When she was done, she glanced at the neighbor to her right to see what chapter and verse they were up to in the Torah reading.

The portion was *Kedoshim*—"You shall be holy." She was listening to the reader, following the Hebrew words from right to left on the page, glancing every few seconds at the English translation on the adjoining left page. She read about the importance of giving gifts to the poor, of being honest in dealing with others, of judging righteously, and she was startled when she came to the sentence "You shall not stand aside while your fellow's blood is shed."

She told herself this was just coincidence, but she'd been consumed with guilt and despair ever since Barone called. She'd fallen asleep trying to resign herself to Matthew's death; it was her first thought upon waking. The Biblical injunction seemed directed at her, and though she knew that no one was looking at her, she was powerless to stop the flush that was tinting her face and neck.

She bent her head, forcing herself to concentrate on the text and explication, but she was thinking about Matthew, and she didn't look up until more than ten minutes later, when the raspy-voiced young man had finished reading the last section.

When she *did* lift her head, she looked through the lattice and saw Sam. He towered over the panels, but he wasn't looking in her direction. With his arms spread wide apart, he lifted the tall, heavy Torah scroll and held it high above his head, turning to each section of the room so that everyone could see it.

Now he was sitting down, holding the Torah steady as another man rewound the parchment onto the two spindles, turning them inward, toward each other. The man bound the spindles together and slipped an embroidered navy velvet sleeve over the scroll. Twenty minutes later, after a reading from Prophets and the beginning of the additional Mussaf service, the Torah scroll was returned to the velvet-draped ark against the wall.

Sam had put on a white-and-black-striped fringed *tallit* to conduct this honorary ritual. He looked so fine, Lisa thought, and felt a flutter of something she couldn't define. She watched as he removed the prayer shawl and returned it to its owner, and it was at this moment that he turned and their eyes met. She saw surprise in the slight widening of his eyes, then pleasure. He was smiling broadly, and she realized with a pang that he thought she'd come here to signal a change in their relationship. *And, of course, there's me.* She realized, too, that if Barone hadn't phoned, that might have been true.

It wasn't loneliness—she'd always been attracted to him, and the other night something had definitely passed between them. As a betrayed fiancée, she'd owed no allegiance to Matthew. Now she feared he was dead, and everything was different, skewed. The fact that she was grieving for a man she wasn't sure she would have married only compounded her guilt and confusion.

The rabbi gave a short sermon, touching on some of the topics in the weekly portion. Lisa couldn't see him behind the partition, but he had a pleasant, dynamic voice. After he spoke, the service continued. She stood and said her prayers silently and, along with the congregation, sang the final hymns led by two young boys. But she was anxious to speak to Sam, to clarify why she was here before they were both embarrassed. When the service was over, she followed the women and children into the long, narrow social hall adjacent to the sanctuary, where refreshments were being served. She was surrounded by women, all of whom were friendly and welcoming and asked her whether she was new in L.A. She'd just turned down a second lunch invitation when Sam came over. She was used to seeing him in his clinic gray and thought how handsome he looked in his single-breasted, dark-olive-green suit.

"Good Shabbos. This is a nice surprise. You look terrific," he added.

"Good Shabbos. And thank you." He was smiling with a boyish shyness that tugged at her, and she hated to ruin his buoyant mood. "I need to speak to you, Sam." She spoke in a whisper, though there was no need. The room was filled with the noise of multiple conversations and children squealing.

His smile disappeared, and he nodded. "Let's go outside."

She followed him out of the building to the sidewalk. He leaned against a lamppost, his hands in the pockets of his jacket. The sun was hot and bright, glistening on the silica in the concrete, and she squinted when she looked up at him.

"Barone phoned last night. They found blood in the trunk of Matthew's car, and he needed to know Matthew's blood type. He said he'd call me as soon as he gets the lab results." Would that be sometime today? Was there a message on her machine even now?

Sam looked stricken. His face was pale, his gray eyes dark and brooding again. He was silent for a moment, then said softly, "And here I was, getting used to being angry as hell at him."

She nodded.

"That's why you came here, to tell me?"

She heard disappointment in his voice. "I thought you'd want to know. And I had to talk to someone about it. I feel so . . ." She left the sentence unfinished. "There's something else." She told him about Paula's phone call, saw him scowl.

"So you weren't imagining that a car was following you from Matthew's condo. Did you tell Barone?"

"No. I promise I'll tell him when I talk to him again. But why would someone follow me to Paula's? Why would he pump her to find out what we talked about?"

Sam thought for a moment. "Matt's disappearance must be connected with Chelsea's murder, not just with the forgery. Whoever followed you is afraid you'll figure out the connection."

"But I don't *know* anything!"

"He doesn't know that. You're Matthew's fiancée."

She jumped as a nearby car came to a shrieking stop, its horn honking angrily. Sam's hand steadied her. The driver leaned out his window and yelled obscenities at the two elderly pedestrians crossing on a red light.

"Did you figure out what's in that 'Notes' file?" Sam asked.

"I found the password yesterday. It was so obvious—Louise Brown." She smiled briefly, then gave him a summary of what she'd read. "So we still don't know who admitted Chelsea."

"Even if we did, I can't see someone killing Matthew to keep that information secret, can you?"

Lisa shook her head. "That's why I have to find out why Chelsea was killed. She's the key."

Sam was frowning. "You were followed twice, maybe more. It's dangerous. Leave it to the police, Lisa."

" 'You shall not stand aside while your fellow's blood is shed.' That's in today's *parsha*," she said, referring to the Torah portion.

"It doesn't mean you're supposed to risk your life." He sounded almost angry. "It means that if you can save someone's life *without* risking yours, you're obligated to do so."

"What if he's still alive, Sam? I know the odds are against it, but what if he is? What if I can find information that will lead to his abductor?"

He sighed. "How can I argue with that, Lisa?" he said quietly.

"I don't think it's a coincidence, my coming to shul this Shabbos and hearing that commandment." What had Paula Rhodes said—something about not believing in coincidence?

"There's another commandment in this week's *parsha* that you probably found coincidental." When Lisa looked blank, he said, " 'You shall love the proselyte as yourself.' "

"Really? I didn't notice that." She must have been preoccupied, thinking about Matthew.

"What would Freud say, do you suppose?" He looked at her intently. "I'm having lunch with Rabbi Pressler and his wife—I know they'd love to have you. And you'd like them."

"I don't want to impose."

"You won't be imposing—they always have company. And you can't do any detecting today. Why eat alone in your apartment if you can have a pleasant lunch with new friends?"

She wasn't up to sustaining hours of conversation, but the idea of being alone in her apartment dismayed her. She debated, then said, "Okay."

The Presslers, without any prompting from Sam, invited Lisa for lunch. The rabbi—short, thin, and beardless—looked to be in his forties. His wife, Elana, a petite blond, looked younger— maybe, Lisa decided, because of her ponytail wig and her impish smile.

Lisa and Sam walked with the Presslers and their five children, ages four to twelve, to their one-story, pale-apricot house on Glenville south of Pico, a few blocks from the shul. Inside, she followed the others through a small, adobe-tiled entry into a spacious, airy dining room painted a soft peach. She sat next to Sam and counted two extra place settings.

"Are you expecting someone else?" she asked Elana. She hoped she wasn't taking anyone's place.

"Not really. Benjie and I never really know how many we're going to be for lunch. I'm glad you're here," she added, and smiled warmly.

Lisa's father always brought home unexpected Shabbos guests—travelers who happened to be at shul; young men learning in nearby *yeshivot*, eager for a home-cooked meal. Her mother always received them warmly. *Hachnasat orchim*—welcoming guests—was an important commandment, her parents had taught her.

Lunch was delicious: a poached salmon appetizer, cold tongue and roast beef, assorted salads. The Pressler children helped serve.

Even the youngest, a four-year-old boy, removed the silver wine cups from the table. During dessert, after singing several Sabbath *zemirot*, the children asked to be excused. Elana smiled and nodded permission. Lisa smiled, too, at the eager exit they made from the room.

"I've often told Sam I think he's doing a real mitzvah, helping couples with infertility problems," the rabbi told Lisa. "Elana and I were distressed to read about the problems your clinic has been facing."

"The uncertainty must be unbearable." Elana shook her head. "For the doctors *and* the patients."

"One of Lisa's Orthodox patients hired a *shomer* to supervise the in vitro process," Sam said, taking a piece of apple strudel. "It's a good thing they did, and not just for *Halachic* reasons."

She hadn't told Sam about the computer records. With a pang she thought about the Hoffmans and how they were doing. Should she should phone them tonight or wait until she had something to tell them?

The rabbi nodded. "At least this couple has peace of mind. And they must be reassured, knowing that their doctor is *frum* and understands their concerns."

Lisa wondered wryly what the rabbi would think if he knew that after a hiatus of eleven years, she'd been observant for less than a day.

"It's amazing, all the new procedures researchers are coming up with." Elana took a sip of water. "As a family therapist, I've seen the pressure infertile couples face. It's especially difficult in Orthodox communities like ours, where everyone seems to be fulfilling the commandment to have children."

Lisa thought about her own parents, about the years of anxiety and desperation they must have felt. "We recommend counseling, and we have a staff psychologist patients can talk to." Not that counseling relieved the desperation.

"Barrenness isn't a modern problem," the rabbi said. "Sarah, Rebecca, Leah, and Rachel—the wives of our revered forefathers— were childless for years. They didn't have in vitro, but they had intense prayer. It worked miracles." He smiled.

Sam said, "Didn't Rachel use something to induce fertility?"

"*Dudaim*. The word means jasmine, violets, mandrakes, or figs. Rachel asked her sister, Leah, for the *dudaim* Leah's son had gathered in the field. Leah refused, but gave in when Rachel offered to give up her designated night with Jacob."

"I've always felt so sorry for Rachel," Lisa said. "First her father tricks Jacob into marrying Leah. Then she sees Leah having one child after another, hoping to win Jacob's love, while she herself has none."

" 'Give me children—otherwise I am dead,' " Rabbi Pressler said softly. "That's what Rachel told Jacob."

"And he was angry at her." Elana sighed. "He told her it wasn't his fault that she didn't have children—he'd sired children with Leah and his concubines. Rachel was afraid he'd divorce her." She turned to her husband. "Benjie, tell them about that woman who came to you a while ago."

The rabbi looked pained. "She and her husband have been trying unsuccessfully to have children for nine years. Apparently the problem lies with her. She wanted to know if it was true that he could divorce her if she was childless after ten years of marriage."

Lisa frowned. "Can he?"

"According to *Halacha*, yes. Men have done it. Often after the couple divorced, they had children with their new spouses. But we're talking about the exception, not the rule. Abraham didn't divorce Sarah, though he never expected that she'd bear him a child. I know of highly revered rabbis who never had children— they didn't divorce their wives. And nowadays there's so much medical hope, and there's adoption. Not that adoption is always simple."

It was the perfect opportunity for Lisa to ask the questions she'd never asked, but Sam glanced at her and quickly said, "Yeah, Benjie, but Abraham had Ishmael, through Hagar, so he wasn't childless. And from Ishmael came the Arabs. Talk about sibling rivalry." He smiled and shook his head. Though she knew he'd changed the subject so that she wouldn't feel awkward, she was disappointed.

The conversation turned to a discussion of the Middle East conflict, of the future of Jerusalem. The children returned to the table, and the rabbi led the after-meals grace. Lisa was surprised to find that it was past three-thirty. Over Elana's protests, she helped to clear the plates and stack them on the white-tiled kitchen counter.

"Thanks again, Elana. I had a wonderful time." She was reluctant to leave—there was an almost palpable sense of serenity and harmony in this home, in the interaction among the rabbi and his wife and their well-behaved, friendly children.

"We did, too. I hope you'll come again with Sam, or by yourself." She smiled. "Benjie and I adore him. So do the kids. He's very special, isn't he?"

"Yes, he is."

There was nothing conspiratorial in the woman's voice, nothing to suggest she was matchmaking. Still, Lisa felt awkward because she hadn't mentioned that she was engaged, that her fiancé was probably dead. Yesterday afternoon, feeling betrayed by Matthew, she'd taken off her engagement ring and hidden it, in its original black velvet box, under a stack of sweaters in her dresser. Though Barone's phone call had turned her anger into grief, she'd decided not to wear the ring this morning. She wasn't sure why.

She didn't want to end what had been a wonderful, normal few hours on a morbid note, but she felt guilty, as though now *she* was betraying *Matthew*. She hesitated, then said, "I don't know if Sam told you the director of the clinic, the one who's missing, is my fiancé."

"Yes, he did." Elana's words were a sigh. "He's so concerned about you, and about your fiancé, of course."

"The police found blood in the trunk of his car."

"I'm so sorry," she said softly. She rested her hand on Lisa's arm. "If Benjie or I can help, if you want to talk, promise you'll call."

Lisa wasn't sure anyone could help.

chapter twenty-one

Sam walked her home. "I know I don't have to," he said when she protested. "I can use the exercise, and I don't like the idea of your walking alone. Not that I think you're in danger in broad daylight."

She'd forgotten for a few precious hours that someone was following her, that she was in danger. She was a little annoyed with Sam for reminding her and told him so, half serious.

"It isn't something you should forget," he said sternly.

They took Glenville to Cashio, Cashio to Beverly Drive, then strolled through Beverlywood. The weather was pleasantly warm now, and she was in no rush to get home. They talked for a while—about the Presslers and the other people she'd met today; about Sam's family (his younger sister lived in Pittsburgh with her husband and three children; his mother, a retired schoolteacher, and his accountant father lived in Brooklyn); about movies they'd seen, books they'd read. They didn't discuss the clinic or Matthew or why Sam had never married, though she was curious. His legs were much longer than hers, and once in a while she had to remind him to slow down. Every few blocks they walked in a companionable silence she didn't feel compelled to fill.

Since carrying anything when outside the home on the Sabbath was forbidden, she'd left her key on top of the doorway molding. She panicked now—it wasn't where she'd put it; she was sure someone had taken it—but when she ran her hand along the molding, of course it was there. Fear was making her paranoid.

Sam insisted on entering first—just in case, he told her. "My hero," she said, smiling, but she was tense as she followed him inside and looked through all the rooms. Nothing seemed disturbed. The sliding glass door in her bedroom was barred and locked, just as she'd left it.

There were no messages on her answering machine. Barone probably hadn't received any lab results. Sam had taken a can of Diet Coke to the dinette table, and she was filling a blue-and-white ceramic bowl with fruit when he asked to see the printout of Matthew's "Notes" file.

"It's on the desk in my bedroom," she told him, not remembering until he returned, the papers in his hand, that the file contained Matthew's comments about him. There was nothing she could do about it now. She watched him anxiously out of the corner of her eye. At one point he glanced in her direction, then quickly looked back down again at the pages in front of him.

She brought the fruit and two glass plates to the table. He'd finished reading and had placed the papers in the middle of the table, as if he wanted to distance himself from them.

"This doesn't tell us much, does it?" she said, aware that he wasn't looking at her. "I can't see a connection between Chelsea's murder and Matthew's disappearance."

"Me, either." He sounded distracted. "Matthew's right, you know." He snapped off the tab on the can. "About me, I mean. I could pretend to be shocked or annoyed, but what's the point? I don't think this comes as a great surprise to you." He was looking at her now, his gray eyes locked on her.

She felt her face becoming warm. "Sam—"

"It's disconcerting, reading about myself in his journal, finding out that he knew how I felt, that it was so *obvious*." He shook his head and rolled his eyes in mock despair. "I'm also embarrassed knowing you've read this, too."

"Don't be. I'm flattered, Sam," she said softly.

"Flattered, huh? In my experience, that's always followed by a 'but.' " He smiled wryly, recited a blessing, and took a long sip of soda. "I had the impression that something was happening between us. Am I wrong?"

She hesitated. "No, you're not wrong. I like you a lot, Sam. I'm very attracted to you. But—"

"But it's not the best timing, is it?"

"Not the best timing," she agreed.

"Yeah." He nodded. "This has a certain Cyrano de Bergerac parallel, doesn't it? Just before Christian dies, he writes to his wife, Roxanne, telling her his good friend Cyrano is her true love. Just before Matthew disappears, he writes that your good friend Sam is in love with you." He took another sip. "Of course, Cyrano kept the truth from Roxanne for years. Then again, Christian didn't have a laptop." He laughed lightly.

"And Roxanne didn't have a printer." Lisa was smiling, trying to keep things light, just as he was, but her face was tingling. "I'm sorry, Sam. If I'd remembered Matthew's comments, I wouldn't have let you read the printout." What did psychologists say—that there were no accidents?

"In a way, I'm relieved that you know." He took an apple from the bowl. "Listen, I was never jealous of Matthew—I thought you were out of bounds, religiously speaking. I was happy for you when you got engaged. I felt terrible when he disappeared."

"I know that, Sam." She had an urge to reach across the table and take his hand.

"Good." He nodded. "Also, while I think you're incredibly beautiful and sexy and funny and bright, and I'd like to pursue a closer relationship, I realize that's impossible right now, and I'm willing to settle for friendship. Okay?"

"Okay." She felt acutely relieved.

"Whoa." He expelled a deep breath and nodded again. "Okay, then. How about some Scrabble?"

"Prepare to lose."

She brought out the set, and they started playing. While she was waiting for her second turn, she got up and scanned the printout pages, which she'd moved to the kitchen counter.

"Done." He looked up. "Why are you reading that again?"

"I don't know." Shrugging, she put them down and returned to the table. "Don't you find it interesting that Chelsea went to another clinic? I didn't know that."

"I noticed that, but what does it have to do with Matthew?"

"I don't know. Also, Ted was defensive when Matthew questioned him about his nurse's having admitted Chelsea to the program."

"Ted's *always* defensive. That's hardly news." Sam placed his tiles on his rack. "Actually, I found the research reference upsetting. Why didn't he tell me he was working on some incredible breakthrough? He discussed it with you, right?"

"Only in general terms. He was secretive about it." She felt suddenly disloyal, criticizing Matthew. She wondered whether Barone had heard from the lab yet and felt her stomach knot. "You can't blame him for being cautious, Sam. Hundreds of researchers are working on this."

"I know, but I don't understand why he didn't trust me. Did he think I'd sell the information to some other clinic? And what about you? You're his fiancée."

"I'm also on staff. I guess he didn't want to treat me differently than he treated you or Ted or anyone else."

"You're more forgiving than I am." He grunted and rearranged his tiles. "Anyway, I don't see a connection between the research and Chelsea's murder or Matt's disappearance."

She didn't, either. A half hour later she was concentrating, trying to spell a forty-six-point word that would put her in the lead, when the phone rang. She glanced quickly at Sam, then left the table and went into her bedroom to hear the message.

It was Barone. "Dr. Brockman, I have the lab results."

Sam had followed her into the bedroom. She wasn't sure what he'd think, but she picked up the phone and said, "Yes?" She knew from the mournful way the detective said her name that the news wasn't good. She thought she was prepared, but when he said the blood found in Matthew's car was O positive, she stiffened and her eyes welled with tears.

"I don't have anything else to tell you, except that we're doing everything we can to find Dr. Gordon. I'm sorry, Dr. Brockman. I'll call you if I have any information."

She hung up and turned to Sam. "It's Matthew's blood type."

He put his arm around her and drew her close.

After sundown Sam recited the *havdalah*, the blessing that separated the Sabbath from the rest of the week. Lisa didn't own a braided *havdalah* candle. She angled the two tapers she'd lit, holding them close together until their flames became one.

There was a moment of awkwardness when Sam was done—"So what are you doing tonight?" he asked. She sensed he wanted to spend the evening with her but was hesitant to ask and was waiting for her to suggest it.

But she didn't. She wanted to be with him, yet she wanted to be alone with her sorrow. She told Sam she'd talk to him in the morning and drove him to his apartment. On the way back she stopped at Blockbuster Video and rented the Audrey Hepburn version of *Sabrina*, which she'd seen countless times because she loved romantic comedies, loved feeling tingly and teary-eyed when the guy got the girl.

Tonight the movie worked its magic, and she was able to forget her problems, if only for a short while. But when she went to bed, she cried quietly for Matthew and tried not to picture the attack that had left his blood in the trunk of his car.

Who could have killed him, and why? The thought frightened her, angered her. She turned on her lamp and read the "Notes" file slowly several times. On the last reading, something struck her, but she wasn't sure. She turned off the light and closed her eyes but couldn't sleep. She switched on the lamp again and looked at her clock. Twelve-ten. She hesitated, then phoned Sam.

"I hope I didn't wake you," she said when he answered. "Can I run something by you?"

"Like I have a choice." His words were swallowed by a yawn. "Just kidding. Go ahead."

She propped herself against the wall. "We know Matthew was making significant progress with his research. He's on the verge of a breakthrough. All of a sudden, everything falls apart."

"So? Researchers often hit dead ends, Lisa. It goes with the territory." He yawned again.

"Yes, but Matt wrote 'data lies'—question mark. What if he suspected that someone had fudged his data to make it look like his procedures weren't successful? What if someone was planning to sell Matt's techniques as his own to another clinic?"

"Come on, Lisa. What gave you that idea?"

She pictured his scowl, saw the furrow between his brows. "*You* did. You said something about Matthew being afraid you'd sell his data to another clinic. Remember?"

"I was being *facetious*. News like that would be written up in every medical journal in the world. Matt would have figured out pretty quickly that someone had stolen his data."

"Everyone's working on this. How could Matt prove he came up with the solution first? And maybe this person always planned to kill Matt *before* he sold the research." It was getting easier, she thought sadly, to say that Matthew had been killed.

There was no immediate reaction from Sam. Finally he said, "So where does Chelsea fit in?"

"I don't know. That's my problem. Matt didn't discuss his research with her." She rested her chin on her bent knees and thought. From the silence she knew Sam was doing the same thing.

"I give up," he said after a minute. "Maybe I'll have a brilliant idea in the morning. Try to get some sleep, Lisa."

"I will. I'm sorry I woke you for nothing."

She said good night, hung up, and scanned the "Notes" file one more time, trying to determine if she'd overlooked something, refusing to give up. The phone rang. She knew it was Sam and smiled as she picked up the receiver. "It's not morning yet, so this had better be brilliant."

"Chelsea saw the research thief at the other clinic when she went there to donate eggs!" Sam's voice was taut with excitement.

"I don't understand." Lisa pulled herself up.

"She went there to donate eggs, right? This person—let's call him X—went there about his research. So when he saw her over two weeks ago at our clinic, talking with Matt, he panicked—he was afraid she'd mentioned seeing him at the other clinic. *That's* why he had to kill her! *That's* why he killed Matthew!"

Lisa pondered what Sam had said. "I don't know."

"It makes sense, Lisa. Think about it."

She was trying. "Do you think Matthew figured this out?"

"He suspected that someone had tampered with his data. When he started asking questions, he could've put two and two together." Sam paused. "Or maybe he didn't figure it out. In any case, X thought he was dangerous. Get it?"

"I guess so." She needed to sort this out. Right now she was too tired.

"You know what this means?" Sam's tone was urgent. "The killer doesn't know how much Matthew told you about the research, about Chelsea, about his suspicions. That's why he asked Paula Rhodes to tell him what you and she talked about. That's why he's following you."

Lisa shivered with fear. "Who do you think it is?" she asked, whispering into the phone as if the walls had ears.

chapter twenty-two

Barone sat hunched forward on Lisa's sofa on Sunday morning, wearing a beige polo shirt and brown slacks and looking more casual than she'd ever seen him, but there was nothing casual about the expression in his eyes or the intent way he was listening to her.

"That's very interesting," he said when she had finished explaining her theory. His face was expressionless, as usual. He leaned back against the cushions. "Tell me more about the research."

"We know eggs are more likely to survive freezing if they're cooled rapidly, or treated with chemicals like DMSO, which protect cellular membranes." She crossed her legs and waited for his nod, then continued. "We also know that placing thawed eggs in tissue from Fallopian tubes seems to help the eggs develop properly. But we haven't figured out an efficient way to freeze eggs that isn't prohibitively expensive. So Matthew's work was very important." She remembered with a sharp pang how excited he'd been just weeks ago about the progress he'd been making.

"How much would a breakthrough like that be worth?" Barone pulled gently at his mustache.

"*Millions.* Countless women would want to freeze their eggs now and use them later, when they want to get pregnant." Women like Gina Franco, Lisa thought. *Women like me.* "Statistically, younger eggs are more viable than older ones. There are also many women who would want to freeze their eggs for medical reasons—someone facing chemotherapy and ovarian failure, for example. A breakthrough like this would give these women the chance to have children. You can't put a price on that."

"If an egg is successfully frozen, how long can it last?"

"From what I've read, if it survives the freezing process, it should last four hundred years." She'd been amazed herself to learn that, had speculated about the children who could be born centuries after their donor mothers no longer lived.

Barone whistled. "Very impressive. Assuming that your theory is correct, Dr. Brockman, do you have any idea who could have stolen this research data?"

"No." After hanging up with Sam, she'd spent half the night thinking before she finally fell asleep. "I can't see any of the nurses or secretaries being involved. They don't have the biomedical knowledge to present the data to another clinic."

"A nurse or secretary could have stolen the data for someone *outside* the clinic, someone who offered considerable money."

"You're right. That didn't occur to me." The field was suddenly larger. Lisa took a sip of coffee—it was her third cup this morning—then put the cup back on the coffee table, next to Barone's coffee cup, still untouched, and the "Notes" printout, which he'd already read.

"Tell me about the clerical staff."

"You met the office manager, Selena Velasquez. She books all appointments and schedules all procedures and surgeries. I've never seen her take a lunch break." She smiled, but Barone remained straight-faced. "We have two secretaries and three women who do billing."

"How many nurses are there?"

"Four general nurses, one for each of the doctors, although they fill in for each other if needed. They take patient histories, draw blood, monitor ultrasound screenings, administer fertility injections. There are also two surgical nurses and one recovery room nurse."

"Who was Dr. Gordon's nurse?"

"Grace Fenton. She's very close to Dr. Gordon—he helped her conceive her daughter. She's been a wreck since he disappeared." Lisa remembered guiltily that she'd promised Selena to talk to Grace, and made a mental note to do it tomorrow. "My nurse is Ava Shemansky. She's on vacation, so Dr. Davidson's nurse, Carol Minh, has been helping me whenever she can. I don't recall Dr. Cantrell's nurse's last name—she's new. Her first name is Brenda." She considered telling him Ted's nurses quit every few weeks but decided it wasn't relevant.

Barone was scribbling on his pad. "How many people are employed in the lab?"

"Four. Three technicians—Margaret Cho, Norman Weld, John Sukami. And the lab director, Charles McAllister. Charlie's great at what he does, and the techs love him." And he's not a killer, she wanted to add.

She spelled the techs' names. Waiting for Barone to write them down, she stared at the open living room window that faced the street and listened enviously to the carefree laughter of children having fun on a Sunday morning.

Barone had finished writing. "Has anyone seemed nervous lately? Secretaries, nurses, lab staff? Take your time."

She found it difficult to think—he was looking at her so intently. She shook her head. "Everyone's tense, of course, because of the allegations and Matthew's disappearance. Selena told me lab techs and nurses are talking about quitting before they lose their jobs. I can't blame them."

"No odd behavior? Nothing unusual?"

She hesitated. "Well, there's Norman Weld. He's a little odd."

Barone's eyes narrowed. "Odd in what way?"

She was sorry she'd said anything. "More reserved than normal. A little intense in the way he looks at people. Charlie told me Norman is very devout." She finished her coffee and looked longingly at Barone's cup. "I have to tell you, Detective, I'm extremely uncomfortable talking about these people as if they're suspects."

"But they *are* suspects," he said somberly. "If your theory is right, that is. If so, someone at the clinic engineered the murders of Ms. Wright and Dr. Gordon."

Though she'd resigned herself to the inevitability of Matthew's death, she was jolted to hear the detective state it as fact. "You feel certain he's dead?" Her voice sounded hoarse to her ears.

"We won't be certain until we have a body, but with the blood in his car and the fact that there's no record of his having taken a flight or train or bus out of the L.A. area, it looks that way. I'm sorry. This must be terribly painful for you."

The gentleness of his tone made her want to cry. She nodded, unable to speak.

Barone shifted on the sofa. "You said the clinic has four doctors. Does that include Dr. Gordon?" He was all business now.

Lisa cleared her throat. "Yes. He's chief of staff as well as director. The other doctors are Dr. Davidson, Dr. Cantrell, and me."

"Tell me about Dr. Davidson."

"Actually, he's the one who figured out that Chelsea may have seen the killer at the other clinic."

"Really?" Barone arched his brows. "That's interesting."

She wasn't sure she understood his tone, or liked it. "He's a good friend. In fact, he got me this job. I *know* he's not involved with any of this."

"I've learned from my experience as a detective that friends can deceive," Barone said quietly. "The knowledge, and the cynicism that comes with it, give me no pleasure."

The thought was ridiculous. She would have smiled if this weren't so serious. "Not Dr. Davidson. First of all, he and Matthew are close friends. And he'd never kill anyone. He's a very kind, very moral person. And he's a devout Orthodox Jew."

"So was the assassin of Israeli Prime Minister Yitzhak Rabin, correct?"

She shook her head impatiently. "Yigal Amir acted out of an irrational, misguided belief that he was following a biblical mandate."

"Money—or the pursuit of it—can make people irrational, Dr. Brockman. Greed is a potent incentive. So are jealousy and vengeance and lust and a number of other human emotions."

She shook her head again. "I hear what you're saying, but Dr. Davidson is not a killer, or a thief."

Barone looked at her with interest, then nodded. "Let's move on. In the message Dr. Gordon left you, he said he was stopping at his condominium, then leaving to check things out. What do you think he was going to check out?"

Was Sam still on Barone's list of possible suspects? "The other clinics in the area, to find out which one Chelsea visited." Lisa stood and went over to her bookcase, where she'd put the printed listing of California fertility clinics. She returned to the sofa and handed the list to Barone. "I found this in Matthew's kitchen on

Wednesday night. I didn't mention it to you because I didn't think it was significant." She sat down.

He examined the list, then placed it next to the "Notes" file on the coffee table. "Why didn't Dr. Gordon go to the police?" Cocking his head. "Why didn't he call me if he had information about Ms. Wright's murder?"

She'd asked herself the same questions. "He'd just discovered that someone forged her signature. He was probably afraid the police would suspect him of her murder." She'd already explained to Barone about Chelsea's having been underage when she donated the eggs. She hadn't mentioned the mix-up with Naomi Hoffman. There was no point involving her, subjecting her and her husband to a police interrogation.

"I suppose that makes sense." Barone nodded. "All right. The guard saw Dr. Gordon at the clinic at six o'clock Wednesday morning. Dr. Gordon left a message on your home machine at six forty-five. What time did his nurse first try to reach him?"

"Around nine. That's when we were bombarded with patients and the media about the clinic allegations. Grace tried him at home and paged him all morning."

"But he never called back." Barone frowned. "That would indicate that by nine he'd been kidnapped, or killed. I think he was assaulted in the parking structure. There's no evidence of a struggle in his condo, and the assailant would have had difficulty moving him to the BMW. I'm sorry," he said, seeing the pained expression on Lisa's face. "Do you need a minute?"

"No, that's okay." She'd been so annoyed that Matthew hadn't called, that he'd left her to deal with the media and patients. When all the while he'd already been dead. She stilled her lips with her hand and was grateful when Barone bent his head and busied himself with his notepad.

"Who knew that Dr. Gordon was at his condominium?" he finally asked.

She dropped her hand to her lap. "Anyone who asked Grace that morning about his whereabouts. It wasn't confidential information."

"What exactly did she tell you?"

Lisa tried to remember accurately. "He phoned her from the condo at seven. He told her he'd be there for half an hour or so, that he had something important to take care of after that."

"So whoever assaulted him didn't necessarily follow him from the clinic." Barone pulled at his mustache again. "This person could have phoned the nurse from anywhere, learned that Dr. Gordon would be leaving his place at around seven-thirty, gained access to the parking lot, and waited there for Dr. Gordon."

"It's a security lot. I have an access key—it's a plastic card, actually. But I guess a person could enter the lobby when a tenant is leaving and take the elevator to the parking structure. At seven-thirty in the morning, people are always going to work or walking their dogs." She pictured a sinister figure stealing into the lot, lurking behind a car, waiting to pounce. She shivered and hugged her arms. "If the assailant drove Matthew's car out of the lot, what did he do with his own car?"

Barone thought for a moment, his brow furrowed in concentration. "If I were the assailant, I'd park near the condo, drive the BMW out of the parking area, dispose of the body where no one would find it, then drive home. Then I'd take a bus or ride a bike to the condo and retrieve my car. Late at night, when it's dark, I'd drive the BMW to Lot C at the airport and take a shuttle home."

She'd flinched hearing Barone refer to Matthew as "the body"—it was so cold, so dehumanizing—but she forced herself to focus on what he was saying. "Actually, if the assailant was at the clinic when he talked to Grace, he could have *walked* to the condo—it's only ten minutes by foot. Later, he could've taken a bus back from his apartment to the clinic."

"You're right." Barone looked at her with interest. "Even if he called from outside the clinic, he could have driven there, parked his car, and walked to the condo. In the clinic's lot he wouldn't run the risk of being ticketed, and his car would be inconspicuous."

"Especially on Wednesday morning, when the media and all those patients were there." She narrowed her eyes. "Maybe he phoned the media with these allegations to create a smoke screen and confusion." She had difficulty accepting the coincidence that the charges had aired on the same day Matthew disappeared.

"You'd make a good detective, Doctor." He smiled lightly. "All right, let's assume that the kidnapping or murder took place between seven-thirty and nine o'clock. Where was the lab director during that time?"

She felt instantly uncomfortable again. "Charlie said he arrived at seven, as usual. I didn't see him then, but I had no reason to. I went down to the lab about eight forty-five to watch a procedure he was doing."

"But he could have been out until then?"

"Yes."

"Do clinic staff sign in or out?"

"Not unless we're there outside of regular hours, which are seven in the morning until five in the afternoon."

"So Mr. McCallister could have arrived at the clinic at seven, left, and returned?"

"Yes." She spoke grudgingly; she hated doing this.

"Okay. What about the lab techs?"

"Again, I didn't see anyone until eight forty-five. Margaret was there when I arrived to watch the procedure. So was John. Norman arrived at the end, around nine o'clock."

Barone flipped back a few pages in his pad. "What about Dr. Cantrell? When did you see him?"

"Selena told me Ted was in early in the morning and left to do surgery at another hospital. He came back around ten-thirty, I think. That's the first time I saw him that day."

"And Dr. Davidson?"

She was about to argue again, but realized there was no point. Barone was simply doing his job. "He had a flat tire, so he arrived around ten. He missed his nine o'clock appointment."

"Which doctor is 'Sam'?" he asked, his tone too casual.

She tensed. She knew he was thinking about Matthew's comment in the "Notes" printout. "That would be Dr. Davidson."

"What's your relationship with him?"

"Please don't jump to the wrong conclusion, Detective. Sam and I have been close for years, long before I came here. Matthew may have thought Sam was jealous of our relationship, but he wasn't. Sam's indebted to Matthew for hiring him. They're good friends. Sam even threw us an engagement party at the clinic." I'm belaboring the point, she thought, watching Barone's face.

"Very thoughtful," he said in a bland voice that told her she was right. "You said you and Dr. Davidson have been close for years. Has your relationship ever been intimate? I apologize if I've offended you, Dr. Brockman, but I think you can understand why this is important."

"Never." She was blushing—because of the question, because of the image of Sam kissing her that flashed through her mind.

"Do you think he's romantically interested in you?"

"I can't speak for Dr. Davidson," she said, forcing herself to look Barone in the eye. "Detective, if you read the 'Notes' file carefully, I'm sure you noticed that Ted—that's Dr. Cantrell—was defensive when Matthew asked him whether his nurse could have admitted Chelsea to the donor program."

"I *did* notice that. But thank you for reminding me."

She could see from the smile that pulled briefly at his lips that he knew what she was doing—offering Ted in lieu of Sam. "Dr. Davidson told me Ted has been disappearing lately. He's kept patients waiting or missed appointments altogether. Maybe he's been meeting with someone at another clinic."

"I'll certainly investigate his alibi, along with everyone else's. What time did *you* arrive at the clinic?"

"Me?" She stared at him, incredulous. She felt a flutter of anxiety, then reminded herself that his job was to suspect everyone. "I arrived at the clinic at seven, as always." Somehow, she managed to sound cool. "I did an egg retrieval. Then I went to the lab to observe a procedure, as I told you. Then Selena informed me that the media and a slew of patients had arrived and things were in chaos."

"Thank you. That's very concise." He smiled briefly.

"I should have told you this earlier, but I'm pretty sure someone followed me from Matthew's condo Wednesday night." She expected to see a knowing look—she was telling him this so that he'd eliminate her as a suspect—but he was frowning.

"Why *didn't* you tell me, Dr. Brockman?"

"I convinced myself it was just my imagination. But after someone followed me to Paula Rhodes's, I realized it wasn't. Dr. Davidson thinks I'm in danger," she added.

"I don't want to alarm you, but whoever killed Dr. Gordon must be worried about what he's told you about the research, about Ms. Wright. I think you should move in with family or a friend for a while, until we find the killer."

"I don't have close friends here, and my family's in New York." She'd spoken to her parents early this morning, told them she was all right, holding up fine, told them about the blood in Matthew's trunk, and held back tears.

"We can't give you police protection. Be careful, Dr. Brockman. Be aware. Don't go anywhere by yourself if you can avoid it, especially at night. And if you think someone's following you, call the police immediately." He rose from the sofa.

At the front door he checked the lock and dead bolt. "These seem fine. I noticed this isn't a security building. Do you use the dead bolt when you leave your apartment?"

"Not always."

"Make sure you do." He opened the door and peered at the

outer lock. He frowned. "It looks like someone's tried to jimmy this lock. See these scratches?"

Tensing, she bent closer and saw faint marks around the keyhole. "Yes."

"You haven't noticed any evidence that someone broke in? Nothing disturbed? Missing?"

"No." Her chest was so tight she could hardly breathe.

"Maybe these are old marks, then." He shut the door. "What other entrances do you have?"

She told him about the sliding door and balcony in her bedroom and was grateful when he offered to check them, too.

"Sliding doors don't provide the best security, but this bar is good." He bent down and moved the bar to make certain it fit tightly, then stood up. "Leave the balcony light on all night—someone's less likely to climb onto your balcony if he knows he's going to be illuminated."

She thanked him and accompanied him back to the front door.

"By the way, how *did* you learn about Mrs. Rhodes?" he asked.

Lisa told him about her talk with the waitress. "Yvonne said my being a doctor triggered her memory, because the woman who hired Chelsea was involved with an organization that raises funds for juvenile diabetes."

"Maybe I should take you along with me next time I'm investigating a case." He smiled but turned serious as he opened the door. "Don't do any more detecting, especially with your colleagues. You may be asking questions of the wrong person—or should I say, the *right* person—and make him more desperate than he already is."

She felt a thrill of alarm. "It's going to be so hard, working with people, wondering who could have killed Matthew."

"I know. Casually mention to as many people as you can that you wish you had some clue to what happened to Dr. Gordon, that you wish he'd confided in you. Words to that effect."

It was smart advice. "I don't exactly have a poker face."

"It might be helpful, Dr. Brockman, if you remind yourself that your life may depend on how convincing you are."

chapter twenty-three

Lisa had brought home a list of her active patients and their phone numbers. After Barone left, she called them, hoping to reassure them and convince them not to switch to another clinic. The conversations were depressing, her attempts unsuccessful. Some of the women vented their anger. Some were apologetic. Most of them were firm in their decision to go elsewhere.

"It's not you, Dr. Brockman," said one woman who was scheduled to have her eggs harvested next week. "I think you're wonderful—that's why Rick and I came to you in the first place. But with what they're saying about the clinic, we can't take any chances. I mean, if you were in my situation, what would you do?"

Lisa wished her good luck.

She spent most of the afternoon cleaning her apartment and vacuuming and doing the laundry. There was something comforting about involving herself in manual tasks and seeing the satisfaction in a job completed. She was standing in the middle of the living room, listening to a Beatles CD while ironing a denim shirt, when Edmond phoned a little after three o'clock.

"I hope you're all right," he began. "This must be a difficult time for you."

She knew immediately from the sadness and contrition in his voice that he'd heard about the blood. "You spoke to the police?" she asked, anchoring the receiver between her ear and shoulder.

"Yesterday. We loved him like a son, Lisa," he said simply. "I don't think there's much hope that he's alive, do you?"

"No, not really." She sprayed starch on the sleeve of the shirt and watched the fine mist settle on the fabric.

"I want to apologize for the things I said the other day. I hope you can forgive me for doubting Matthew."

"You don't have to explain." She felt a flicker of anger, but saw no point in holding on to grievances, and reminded herself that she'd doubted Matthew, too. She ran the iron back and forth across the sleeve and made no move to fill the silence.

"I *need* to explain, Lisa. Everything pointed to Matthew. He was preoccupied. He didn't tell me about the cash thefts, which stopped with his disappearance. His car was found at the airport. And Ms. Wright's signature was forged. Obviously, someone engineered all this to make him look guilty. And I bought it."

She felt a flash of pity. "For a while, I did, too, Edmond."

"Thank you for that," he said softly. He cleared his throat. "Why don't you take a few days off? I'm sure the others won't mind covering for you."

"Thanks, but I'd rather be busy." When she was with patients—examining them, performing procedures, listening to their concerns—she felt she was doing something worthwhile, and she could forget her own troubles, at least for a while.

"You're probably right. If you change your mind, let me know. Jean Elliott phoned me yesterday, by the way. The graphologist she consulted will testify that the handwriting on Chelsea Wright's documents isn't hers. Ms. Elliott has filed a complaint for damages against the clinic, claiming medical malpractice and negligence because we failed to substantiate Chelsea Wright's true age at the time she donated the eggs."

Bad news, but hardly surprising. "So she'll subpoena our files?" Lisa slipped the shirt onto a hanger and laid it carefully on the sofa, next to other ironed shirts.

"She's already issued a subpoena. She's asked the court to

shorten the stay—meaning the time we have to respond to the sub-poena—from the normal twenty-day period because of the emergency of the situation. Judge Gilbert has agreed to hear her argument at eleven o'clock Monday morning at the Santa Monica Courthouse, in chambers. I'm going with counsel. I'd like you to be there, too, since you're the most familiar with this matter."

"I'll have to see what my patient schedule is like." She was reluctant to become involved, more reluctant to meet again with the Wrights and their attorney. She switched off the iron, set it on its heel, and, suddenly hungry, moved to the kitchen pantry.

"Of course. And if necessary, maybe Dr. Davidson or Dr. Cantrell can see your patients. This is very important, Lisa."

"I agree. I'll go in early tomorrow morning and see what I can do." Behind a box of Raisin Bran, she found the granola bar she'd been looking for. It wasn't where she'd expected to find it, but she recalled that Sam had been rummaging through the pantry yesterday. "Edmond, Sam Davidson is worried that if the Wrights get legal permission to find out who received their daughter's eggs, other patients will want to do the same."

Edmond's sigh was audible. "He's right. We may be looking at a class action suit, not to mention a police investigation. Allegations of egg stealing are nebulous and unproved at this point. But if Ms. Elliott proves that someone at the clinic forged patient documents, that's a felony. I suspect we'll have to turn over all our files sooner rather than later." He sounded so dispirited.

"You were going to question all the nurses to find out who admitted Chelsea to the program. Did you find out anything?"

He snorted. "Stunned denials across the board. Grace Fenton burst into tears and offered to quit on the spot. I had to beg her to stay. Everyone else was equally indignant. I suppose I'll have to issue another memo."

I suppose you think I'll write it. Lisa had unwrapped the granola bar but decided she wasn't hungry after all.

"Did you find out who received Chelsea's eggs?" he asked.

"One of the patients is Cora Allen, but she never conceived. The other person who's listed as a recipient is Naomi Hoffman, but that's clearly a mistake." Lisa explained about the *shomer*.

"Then why would the records indicate that she received Chelsea Wright's eggs?" he asked impatiently.

"Whoever forged Chelsea's signature had to make sure she donated eggs after she was eighteen. My guess is the forger chose Naomi Hoffman at random."

"What does Mrs. Hoffman's file indicate?"

"I couldn't locate it." Lisa tensed, anticipating criticism.

"Wonderful." He sighed. "More work by our forger?"

"Probably. I've informed the Hoffmans about this situation. I advised them to get an affidavit from the *shomer*, but he's out of the country at present."

"I hope to hell they reach him soon. I imagine I'll be hearing from the Hoffmans' attorney, too."

"Edmond, I'm convinced no embryos have been switched. Whoever killed Chelsea and Matthew probably leaked these false allegations to create a smoke screen and cover up the real motive for the killings."

"What motive is that?" he asked sharply.

She told him about Matthew's file, about the "data lies?!" notation, about Sam's theory.

"I didn't even know Matthew was involved in this research," Edmond said after a moment's silence. "Now you tell me he was killed because of it, by someone who works at the clinic. Does Barone agree with your theory?"

She didn't blame him for being skeptical. "He didn't say so, but he didn't say it was crazy, either. He questioned me about the lab and medical staff."

"I suppose I should be insulted that he didn't ask any questions about me. Then again, it's highly unlikely that I'd steal research data and sell it to another clinic."

This was the first time she'd heard Edmond attempt humor. "I don't know where Matthew left the data. As far as I can tell, it's not in his home laptop." She'd searched through all the files early this morning, before Barone had come. "So his paperwork has to be in the clinic. Tomorrow morning I'm going to look for it and for Mrs. Hoffman's file. I'm also going to start checking other patient files."

"To what purpose?" Again his voice was sharp.

"To find out who received Chelsea's eggs. Also, I'd like to be able to prove that those allegations are false."

"That's a monumental task, Lisa. The clinic's been open for almost three years. We see approximately five hundred patients a year. You're talking about close to fifteen hundred files. This isn't your responsibility."

"I know that." She didn't understand why he sounded disapproving—it wasn't as if she were asking him to help. She wanted to do this for herself, because she was upset by the allegations. She wanted to do this for Matthew, because the clinic had been his dream. And because she was atoning for having doubted him? "I'll start within a smaller parameter. Selena will help, I'm sure. Sam Davidson will, too."

"The police will check the files, Lisa. If you're right, they'll issue a report exonerating the clinic. Although by that time, all our patients will have transferred elsewhere, and the clinic will be closed. If I were you, I'd look for another job."

As if another clinic would hire her now. "I'm more concerned about our patients. These women don't know whether their eggs have been stolen, whether they're carrying someone else's embryos. It's cruel to leave them with this horrible uncertainty for one second longer than necessary."

"You're right," he said quietly. "Sometimes I forget why I helped build this clinic. Thank you for reminding me." He sounded sincere. "I'll see you in the morning at the courthouse?"

chapter twenty-four

The clinic parking lot was empty when Lisa arrived at eight o'clock. Barone had cautioned her against going out at night, especially by herself, but it wasn't really dark, and throughout the rest of the afternoon as she continued straightening up around the apartment, she'd worried about the authorities confiscating the records. What if they arrived early in the morning, when she was with a patient? Or when she was at the courthouse?

She'd wanted to bring Sam along—for security, and for assistance—but she hadn't reached him. She'd left a message on his machine, telling him where she was going. She wished there were a guard, but Victor wasn't on duty Saturdays or Sundays, since there were no patients and no cash or checks in the clinic safe.

Lisa had a key for the lobby door, another for the alarm. After shutting off the alarm, she unlocked the door and stepped inside the ink-dark lobby, then locked the door and reset the alarm. Her heart was thumping as she groped along the wall to her right and flipped two switches, flooding the large room and hallway with welcome light.

Her footsteps were muffled by the carpet as she walked down the empty hall, switching on lights along the way. She passed Matthew's office, but she didn't have a key. She'd have to wait until morning to check his desk and cabinets for his research data. She wondered what she'd find in Ted's office, then decided that if he had something incriminating, he wouldn't keep it in the clinic. Ted was many things, but he wasn't stupid.

She passed into Reception. Inside the large, square room was Selena's L-shaped, brown Formica desk. Against the right wall was a photocopy machine; against the left, a bank of six open-faced cabinets, each with seven rows of folders. The different colors denoted the first letter of the patient's first name: A-B was red; C, yellow; D-E-F, pink; G-H-I, blue; J, gray; K-L, brown; M-N-O, green; P-Q-R, orange; S-T, purple; and U-V-W-X-Y-Z, mustard.

On Friday, when Lisa had looked for Naomi's file, she'd been rushed and anxious. It was possible she'd missed it. She flipped again through the green files in the section tabbed "N," but the file wasn't where it should have been. She checked the green files in the sections marked "M" and "O." It wasn't there, either.

Edmond was partially right: the clinic *did* have close to fifteen hundred files, but not all of them were active. Files belonging to patients who hadn't been seen in over a year and a half were stored downstairs. Still, a quick scan told her there were probably a thousand files in this room.

She was disheartened but refused to be overwhelmed by numbers. She had to find Naomi's file. There were ten file colors, she told herself, so there were approximately only one hundred green folders. Tedious, but doable.

The air-conditioning was set on low when the building was vacant. The room was warm and musty and unnaturally silent. She wished again that Sam were here with her, but soon she was preoccupied with searching through the files and forgot her nervousness. She was halfway through with the As when she decided to check for evidence to refute the charges of embryo switching. A hundred or so random files should be representative.

Returning to the beginning of the Ns, she took a stack of green folders to the desk. She opened the top file: Nora Ashman, age forty-two. Her H and P—history and physical profile—were there. So were her signed consent forms, lab forms, an IVF flow sheet detailing her hormonal treatment and ultrasound evaluations, and an embryo transfer form. A D, followed by a number on top of the lab and embryo transfer forms, corresponded with the consent Nora had signed to receive donated ova.

Lisa examined the second file: Nadine Amherst, thirty-six. H and P; consent form; lab form; IVF flow sheet, embryo transfer form. Again there was a D, followed by a number and a signed form consenting to the acceptance of donated eggs.

There were so many files to look through, and the stillness in the reception area was beginning to unnerve her. She decided to photocopy them and study them at home. She turned on the machine. While waiting for it to warm up, she took two stacks to the desk and looked through them again. Naomi's file wasn't among them.

The machine was finally ready, humming with expectation. *Feed me.* She photocopied the entire first file, pleased by the machine-gun swiftness of the copier, which had spit out all twelve pages in less than two minutes. She copied another file, and another, removing additional stacks, returning the files she'd already copied, looking all the while for Naomi's green folder.

When she checked her watch, she was surprised to see that two hours had passed, though she realized she shouldn't be: she'd photocopied over eighty files and amassed a dozen towers of papers on both sections of the L-shaped desk. She'd staggered the files neatly to separate them from each other.

The shrill ringing of the phone startled her—she was crouching in front of the file cabinets, pulling out a stack from the "T" section, when she heard it. She jumped up, her heart racing, then reminded herself that it was probably Sam, calling to see if she was still here. She hurried to the desk. After the third ring, she picked up the receiver, said, "Sam?" over the recorded clinic message, and heard the sound of a disconnect.

It could have been a wrong number. It could have been Sam. He might have hung up after hearing the recorded message. She was anxious to leave but had fewer than twenty folders left to copy.

She pulled out the remaining green folders and fed their contents to the machine, which suddenly seemed to be taking forever to churn out each page and was whining at the effort. Her hands were damp. She thought about the phone call and the man who'd followed her from Matthew's condo and later to Paula's, wondering why she hadn't listened to Barone, why she'd come here at night by herself. *Stu*pid, *stu*pid, *stu*pid, the copier groaned, echoing her thoughts with each page.

Ten minutes later she'd photocopied every green file in the room but still hadn't located Naomi's. She printed out a copy of the Jane Doe document that listed egg recipients and the donor code number. She also printed a four-page listing of all the donors and their phone numbers. Chelsea's name was there, at the bottom of the last page.

With her keys in her hand, Lisa grabbed a tall stack of papers and, staggering under the weight, returned to the lobby. She turned off the alarm, unlocked the door, and stepped outside.

Except for her car, the lot was still vacant. She looked around as she walked to her car and deposited the papers in her trunk. She was wary on her way back to the lobby, wary with each successive trip she made to her car, and when she had finished and was back in Reception, her arms and shoulders were aching and she was panting from exertion and anxiety.

She slipped her purse strap on her shoulder, shut the light, and had reached the lobby when she remembered the log she'd shown Gina Franco. The log, which followed the Julian calendar, listed the day of the year, not of the month; entries listed patients in the order in which their procedures had been performed. If Lisa could find the entries for Chelsea and Naomi, she might be able to prove Naomi hadn't received Chelsea's eggs.

She set the alarm and returned to the hallway. Opening the door to the staircase, she switched on the light and descended the stairs. Dead air rose to greet her, and she felt as though she were entering a crypt. The hallway door clicked shut behind her. She started, then clutched the banister and told herself she was being silly.

A minute later she was standing in front of the anteroom. She unlocked the door, switched on the fluorescent light, and stepped inside. The current log was there, on the counter against the wall facing her. She found last year's log on the shallow shelf beneath the upper cabinet.

She'd performed the embryo transfer on Naomi in late September; September would begin with day 244. She was paging backward through the log when the lights suddenly went out and she was engulfed in blackness.

Her heart stopped for a second, then lurched. She could feel the pounding in her chest, and her mouth was dry. It was probably an electrical outage, she told herself, no reason to be alarmed, but she stood absolutely still, straining to hear. Upstairs, her eyes would adjust to whatever reflected light was coming through the windows.

Here in the basement there were no windows, just inky blackness that threatened to smother her.

For a long moment—maybe a minute, maybe more—there was no sound. Then she heard footsteps approaching. She turned toward the door and, in the small, rectangular window, saw a flash of light that illuminated a pair of eyes above a mask.

She muffled a scream with her hand. Though the eyes seemed to be staring directly at her, she realized that whoever was there might not have seen her at all. She dropped silently to the linoleum-tiled floor, grateful that she was wearing her Reeboks. The eyes stared through the window for another moment, then disappeared.

She knew he'd be back when he didn't find her anywhere else. He might still be standing at the door, listening, trying to make her think she was safe. She needed a weapon. The bottom cabinet she was leaning against was filled with beakers, syringes, vials. She held her breath as she opened the cabinet door, praying that a squeak wouldn't betray her. The door opened soundlessly. She was flooded with relief and allowed herself to breathe.

She ran her trembling fingers across the shelf until they touched a glass beaker. Grasping the vessel, she removed it gingerly from the shelf, using her other hand to make sure she didn't topple anything in the beaker's way.

She set the container down. Reaching higher, she locked her fingers around the drawer pull and slid it open. Inside the drawer her fingers located a wrapped syringe. She took it and wished that the lab had lethal fluids, but everything here was organic, life-promoting.

She heard the rattling of the doorknob.

She inhaled sharply. With the beaker in one hand and the syringe between her teeth, she moved, still crouching, toward the door to the lab. With her free hand she groped the wall, feeling for the doorframe. When she found it, she ran her hand along the edge and grabbed the knob. Twisting it as quietly as she could, she eased the door open and was moving into the lab when she bumped into a chair.

The noise thundered in her ears.

She froze. She looked behind her, and though she could see nothing, she could hear the click of a key turning in the lock and knew he'd heard her, too. She was shaking badly now and had tightened her grip on the beaker. Her heart was racing, and she could feel her pulse pounding in her throat and ears and head, but she couldn't allow herself to panic, couldn't allow fear to take over.

Another flash of light.

Move! she ordered herself.

Still crouching, she scurried away before the light flashed again and caught her. When she rounded the corner, she stood upright too quickly, and the blood rushed to her head. She was dizzy and couldn't see, and she knew the lab was crowded with too much equipment here, all bulky, much of it with sharp angles. There was no place to hide.

She heard the squeak of the door to the hall opening, then footsteps in the anteroom.

Moving faster now, she felt her way around the lab, running her hands from one sterile hood to the other as she inched toward the back of the room.

Another flash of light told her he was in the lab.

She was standing in front of one of the incubators now. Next to it, against the wall, were the tall canisters of carbon dioxide. She slipped into the foot-wide gap between the side of the incubator and the canisters and set the beaker on the floor. She removed the syringe from her mouth and ripped off the wrapper, clenching her teeth and wincing at the raspy noise that split the silence. The syringe, plunger, and needle were already assembled. She held the unit in her left hand and picked up the beaker again in her right.

She waited.

A beam of light pierced the gray darkness and illuminated cabinets, a microscope, a chair. She guessed he was five feet away. She thought she could hear his breathing, or maybe it was her own. Her heart was beating so hard, so fast, that her chest felt as though it would explode.

The flashlight's beam was dancing up and down and from side to side. It lit on the canisters. She pressed herself against the wall of the incubator and clutched the syringe just as she was impaled within the cone of light. She could see from the rebounding illumination that the intruder was wearing a surgical mask and gown.

She would have run, but he was blocking her exit. She smashed the beaker's neck on the corner of the incubator. She held both arms tightly at her side.

The flashlight went off, plunging the room into darkness.

She heard a footstep. A moment later a gloved hand grabbed hers and wrested the jagged-edged beaker from her clenched fingers. The beaker dropped to the floor and shattered.

Air injected into a vein could be lethal, but she couldn't even see, let alone pin down his arm. And his face was protected with a mask. She raised her left hand and lunged blindly with the syringe at where she thought his neck would be, hoping to stun him and gain a few seconds, but she was stabbing at air.

His hands circled her neck and squeezed. She tried to scream, but no sound emerged from her constricted throat. Gagging, she raised her hand again and jabbed wildly in front of her with the syringe. This time she punctured something.

He grunted. She pulled her hand back and plunged the syringe. Again she punctured flesh. His grip loosened. She slipped her hands inside the circle of his arms and, with an abrupt movement, shoved upward and sideways, forcing his arms apart and easing the pressure on her neck, which was throbbing madly.

She groped upward, searching for his mask. When she touched it, she clawed at it. His hands pushed hers away, and he stepped backward. She shoved with all her might against his chest and knocked him off balance. She heard the thud of his fall, then an enraged cry.

Trying to slip past him, she stumbled over his legs and fell to her knees. She dropped the syringe and groped for it, but she couldn't waste time searching for it. She jumped up and half ran along the aisle between the equipment. She was using her arms as antennae, trying to visualize with the aid of memory where everything was in the room, but she felt as though she was wading through a sea of darkness. When she slammed her hip into a counter, she cried out but didn't stop.

She didn't hear movement behind her and wondered if he was unconscious. After what seemed like an eternity, she was at the door that exited the anteroom. She jerked it open and ran out to her left, hugging the wall, running her hand along it to find the door to the staircase. Finally, she was there.

Inside the stairwell, she clutched the banister and climbed the stairs. The creaking of the door to the lower floor told her it was being opened. A second later she heard footsteps pounding on the linoleum stairs. She climbed faster, gasping for breath. Her throat was raw, aching.

She was near the top step when a hand grabbed her ankle. She yanked her leg free, then kicked swiftly and viciously behind her and made contact with something. She heard a moan.

She was on the ground floor. There was no electricity here, either, but to Lisa, the pale gray moonlight coming through the glass doors in the lobby shone as bright as daylight. She ran into the nearest room, where the embryo transfers were performed.

Looking around, she eyed the lamp sitting on the nightstand. She yanked the plug out of the socket and hurled the lamp at the window.

The glass splintered.

The alarm blared in her ears.

She ran across the hall to another staircase and climbed to the second floor and the operating rooms. Entering one of them, she tore open a sterile surgical pack, grabbed a scalpel, and crouched under the hospital bed in the middle of the room.

Minutes later the siren was still clanging in her ears. She didn't hear the door opening, didn't see him until he was standing in the doorway, playing the flashlight in the corners of the room. *Come out, come out, wherever you are.* She hugged her knees tightly to her chest and held her breath, as if that would make her invisible.

He was in the center of the room now, shining the light around the bed and under it. He stood there for a moment, then suddenly squatted, but she'd scrambled out from under the bed and was running toward the door.

She was halfway there when he caught her. She twisted free and whirled to face him, ready to plunge the scalpel into his chest. He screamed.

"Don't, Lisa!"

chapter twenty-five

She stared at Sam and dropped her hand to her side.

"I thought you were dead," he said, his voice breaking. "I saw this guy in a surgical gown and mask running in the lobby. I thought—" He took a breath. "You're all right?"

She nodded.

Gently, he loosened her fingers, which were still gripping the scalpel. He set it down on a table, then drew her close, and they stood for a moment without talking. The alarm was assaulting her ears, but when he took her hand and said, "Let's wait outside," she pulled back.

"What if he's still here?" she whispered urgently.

"He's not, I promise. He ran out the door into the street."

She believed him, but she clung to him as he led her down the stairs to the lobby. She waited while he shut off the alarm, then went outside with him.

"I got your message and drove right over here," he said. "Your car was in the lot, and the building was dark, and I heard the alarm—I knew something was wrong."

She couldn't stop shaking.

He tightened his arms around her. "I grabbed a flashlight from my glove compartment and entered the lobby. That's when I saw this guy. I tried to stop him, but he got away." Sam's shirt placket was torn. His hair was disheveled, his cheekbone scratched an angry red. "Thank God you're okay," he murmured.

She *did* thank God. She wondered whether her heartbeat would ever return to normal, whether she would ever stop trembling.

Sam said, "It happened so fast, I couldn't even tell whether he's tall or short, heavy or slim. Nothing. What about you? Do you have any idea who attacked you?"

She shook her head and exclaimed at the pain that stabbed her skull. The back of her head was tender to her touch. She remembered being slammed against the side of the incubator. Her hip was throbbing, too. Her larynx was swollen. She probably had other bruises she wasn't aware of. But she was alive.

"I was in the lab anteroom when all the lights went out. It was pitch black." Her voice emerged like a croak. She could still feel the assailant's hands around her neck, squeezing.

"Don't talk." Sam drew her closer. "Wait till the police come." He winced, then rubbed his neck and looked at his hand. "I guess he roughed me up more than I realized. He stabbed me with something thin and sharp."

She saw blood on his fingers. Rising on tiptoe, she noticed puncture marks on the left side of his neck. "He must have picked up the syringe I dropped," she rasped. "Does it hurt a lot?"

"My ego, more than anything." He smiled wanly, then nodded toward the parking-lot entrance. "The cops are here."

She heard a siren wailing faintly in the distance, then louder. A minute later a black-and-white police vehicle pulled into the lot. Two uniformed male policemen exited the car and, with their hands on their weapons, approached Lisa and Sam.

"I'm Officer Reynaldo," the taller of the two said, sounding cautious. He was slim and muscular and had long, dark sideburns. "This is Officer Morgan. We're responding to an alarm."

Sam introduced himself and Lisa. "We both work here at this clinic," he began and told them what had happened.

She was grateful to have Sam do the talking. She watched as the two policemen, both of whom looked to be in their thirties, listened and took notes. Reynaldo asked for identification. Sam presented his driver's license and a business card. Lisa told him her purse was in the lab. She'd forgotten all about it.

"Do you need medical assistance?" Reynaldo asked her.

She shook her head, setting off splinters of razor-sharp pain, and thanked him for asking.

The circuit breakers were in the basement, Sam told the officer. He led the way. He was using his flashlight, and the two policemen were using their high-powered ones, but Lisa still felt anxious and had to force herself to go down the dark staircase.

In the small control room, the policemen focused their flashlights on the control box while Sam examined the circuit breakers. A minute later, light was restored, and they all walked down the hall to the lab. Sam unlocked the door.

Her purse was where she'd left it, on the floor of the anteroom. She showed the policemen identification, then waited with Sam while they checked inside the lab.

"Not much to see," Reynaldo said when he returned. "Some broken glass at the far end of the room."

"I broke a beaker to make a weapon," Lisa said. "He grabbed it from me."

"If it was dark, how'd he see it?" Morgan asked. It was the first time he'd spoken.

"He had a flashlight. He tried to choke me." Her hand went unconsciously to her neck. "I stabbed him with a syringe until he loosened his grip. Then I broke away." She explained in detail what had taken place.

Reynaldo was nodding. "But neither you nor Dr. Davidson here can identify this guy 'cause he was wearing a mask. Could you tell anything from his voice?" he asked Lisa.

"He never spoke."

"What about his height?"

"I couldn't tell. But he wasn't short, judging from where his face was when I pulled at his mask."

"So it could have been a tall woman or a medium-height man?"

"I guess. Or taller."

The officers looked at Sam. He shrugged and lifted his hands palms up.

Reynaldo turned back to Lisa. "You said you sounded the alarm by breaking a window. Who set the alarm?"

"I did, just before I went downstairs to the lab."

"You're sure? You said you made several trips to the car. Maybe you forgot the last time?"

She shook her head. "I was nervous, being here alone. I definitely set the alarm."

"So whoever attacked you had a key to the building and to the alarm? He must have set it after he entered the building."

She hadn't had time to think about it. "Yes, I suppose so," she said softly.

"So it's someone both of you probably see every day. And neither one of you can identify him or her?" The policeman was frowning at Sam and Lisa. "Why do you think he attacked you, Dr. Brockman?"

She explained about Matthew's disappearance, about the blood in the trunk of his car, about the problems at the clinic, about Chelsea Wright's murder. "It's possible that whoever killed Ms. Wright and my fiancé thinks I'm dangerous." She saw Reynaldo and Morgan exchange glances. "You can talk to Detective John Barone from Hollywood Division. He's investigating Chelsea's murder."

Reynaldo wrote down the name. "But why attack you here? Why not where you live?"

"I don't know." She'd been wondering the same thing herself.

Reynaldo asked more questions, then handed a card to Lisa, another to Sam. "If you remember anything else, call me."

It was almost déjà vu, she thought, watching the officers leave. Last Tuesday, less than a week ago, Barone had handed cards to her and to Matthew and said almost the same words. And now Matthew was dead.

She turned to Sam. "I know what you're thinking—I should never have come here by myself. Barone warned me. *You* warned me."

"I don't always do the smart thing. I'm just grateful that you're okay." He gazed at her for a moment, then stepped back, as if he were suddenly uncomfortable, and slouched against the cabinets, his hands in his pockets. "Why *did* you come?"

"Edmond said the authorities will probably take our files soon. I didn't want to wait for that to happen—I'm hoping to find evidence to disprove the charges of embryo switching."

"A one-woman FBI." He shook his head. "Did you?"

She told him about the files she'd photocopied. "They're all in the trunk of my car. The problem is, if the police take clinic files, they'll come to my place and take whatever files I have, too."

Sam nodded. "We can all expect visits from the police. So where will you take all these papers?"

"To the Presslers? I'll call first to ask if it's okay to leave the papers in their garage. I can't take them to Matthew's—the police are sure to go there. *You're* out. So is everyone else from the clinic." She saw Sam's frown. "You think it's a bad idea? Or is it too late to call them?" It was almost eleven o'clock, she saw when she checked her watch.

"No, they're always up late. The Presslers are a good choice and I'm sure they won't mind." He hesitated. "To be honest, though, I think checking the files is a waste of your time."

"You mean I almost got killed for nothing?" she asked, trying to make light of the situation.

"Basically, yeah." He smiled at her. "I don't believe there was embryo switching at the clinic, but I doubt you'll find proof in the files."

"Maybe you're right. Actually, I was really hoping to find Naomi Hoffman's file. I mentioned her—Orthodox, expecting twins?"

He looked puzzled for a moment, then nodded. "Right. The woman who had the *shomer*. Her file's missing?"

"I can't find it anywhere. The problem is, when I checked the donor code number in the computer for Chelsea's eggs on Friday, Naomi's name came up as the recipient."

"But how's that possible? And why didn't you mention this yesterday?"

"I wasn't thinking about Naomi. I was upset about Matthew, and the blood." She fought a wave of queasiness. "Anyway, I think whoever forged Chelsea's papers randomly chose Naomi as the recipient and gave her a code number. I want to see her file—maybe this person forgot to put a D and a code number on her lab form or embryo transfer form."

"Good idea. When did you last see her file?"

"Wednesday, when she was here. I checked every green file, Sam. It isn't in the central system, or in Billing, or on Selena's desk, or in my office. Someone must've taken it."

"It looks like it," he agreed. "So what were you doing down here in the lab?"

"Checking the log. I'm glad you reminded me." It was still on the ledge, where she'd left it. "I thought if I found entries for Naomi and Chelsea, I might be able to prove that Naomi couldn't have received Chelsea's eggs." Walking over to the counter, she opened the black book and flipped through the pages. She frowned, then flipped through them again.

A moment later she shut the log and looked up at Sam.

"Not good news, huh? The log shows that Chelsea and Naomi had procedures done around the same time?"

"It doesn't show anything," she said quietly. "The pages from days two hundred forty-two through two hundred sixty-six have been removed."

"Forget the garage," Elana said when Lisa and Sam arrived. "Our guest room is empty this week. It has a desk, too, which you may find helpful." She hadn't asked what files Lisa planned to leave there, or why she needed to. Maybe she didn't want to know. She hadn't asked how Sam had gotten his face scratched either, but she'd looked at him curiously.

"This is so nice of you, but I don't want to intrude on your privacy," Lisa said, suddenly feeling awkward. Bringing the files here had seemed a better idea on the phone than it did now, when she was standing in the Presslers' entry.

Sam said, "Actually, Elana, do you think Lisa can stay here for a few days?"

Lisa glanced at him quickly and pursed her lips. "Sam—"

"She's just been assaulted at the clinic, and she's in danger. I don't want her staying alone in her apartment."

"Please ignore him." Lisa was blushing and felt like kicking him. "I'd never dream of imposing on you like that. I'd never risk putting you and your family in danger by coming here."

Elana looked troubled. "I doubt that you'd be putting us at risk. And it's no imposition—we have company all the time. You can stay here as long as you need to."

"You're kind to offer. But I'll be all right," Lisa said, although she wasn't sure at all.

"I hope you change your mind." She put her hand on Lisa's arm. "Sam's right—you shouldn't be by yourself."

She led Lisa and Sam down the center hall to a small room at the back of the house furnished with a sofa bed, a desk, and a chair. "You can put papers on the bed, if you need to, or on the floor. The kids know this room is off limits." She smiled, then turned to Sam. "You have a nasty bruise on your face. I'll get you something for it."

She was back a few minutes later with hydrogen peroxide, cotton balls, and a tube of antibiotic ointment. She put everything on the desk. "Call if you need anything else," she said and left the room.

"I don't really need this stuff," Sam said.

"Coward. You're just afraid it'll sting." Lisa smiled. "You can dish it out, Doctor, but you can't take it, huh? Here, I'll do it."

She doused a cotton ball with peroxide and began to cleanse the bruised areas on his cheek and neck, frowning as he winced. Gently she dabbed on the ointment, telling herself that touching him served a purely medicinal purpose, that the butterflies fluttering in her stomach were the aftermath of her attack.

"Not bad for someone who isn't even a real nurse," he said softly when she was done.

She flushed under the intensity of his gaze and capped the tube of ointment. "We'd better get the files."

"Change your mind and stay here, Lisa," he said, serious again. "That way I'll know you're safe."

She shook her head. "I'll be all right."

He helped her bring the papers inside. Somehow they seemed to take up more space in the guest room than they had in the clinic's reception area. She thanked Elana again and said good night and turned down her invitation to have a late snack—she wanted to go home, take a hot shower, and crawl under her covers.

When Sam insisted on following her home and coming upstairs to make sure everything was all right, she didn't refuse. She waited in the living room while he checked the rest of the rooms, suddenly frightened of being in her apartment alone.

So when he offered to spend the night on the living room sofa, she didn't refuse that, either.

chapter twenty-six

Grace chewed on her bottom lip as she read the article in the *Times'* "Metro" section. She knew that the police had found blood in Matthew's car—the story had been on the TV news yesterday—but her stomach twisted as she read and reread the few details and the request that anyone with information call the police.

"Hey, hon, aren't you going to be late?" her husband, Tony, called, fixing his tie as he entered the breakfast nook. "It's six-forty." He kissed the top of her head and went into the kitchen, where he poured himself a glass of juice.

"I'm leaving soon. Is Suzie up?"

Tony worked at a bank and didn't have to leave until eight-thirty. He dropped the baby off at the sitter's. Grace picked her up on her way home from the clinic.

He returned to the breakfast nook. "I just diapered her. She's waiting to say bye-bye to her mommy. She's planning on wearing your favorite denim overalls today." He smiled and waited for a response. When he got none, he glanced at the newspaper. "You have to face the fact that he's dead," he said gently.

"I know." Her lips trembled. "I just wish I'd done something."

"What could you possibly have done? Grace, what could you have done?" he repeated when she didn't answer.

She folded the newspaper, stood up, and headed for her daughter's bedroom. The fourteen-month-old little girl was sitting in her white crib, playing with a tricolored plastic toy as she sucked contentedly on a pacifier.

"Hi, sweetheart." Grace smoothed her daughter's pale blond hair. "You look so pretty. Are you going to have a good time today with Betty?"

"Tee," the little girl cooed. "Tee."

"That's right. Betty." Grace leaned over and picked her up. She hugged her tightly and twirled her around, then placed her back in the crib.

"More!" Suzie squealed.

"Later, when Mommy comes home."

Grace kissed her again, then went to her own bedroom, where she checked her makeup in the oblong mirror over the dresser. Tony wasn't in the breakfast nook when she returned. She unfolded the newspaper, took it with her to the wall phone extension, and punched the numbers printed at the end of the article.

"Detectives, Hollywood. Jensen speaking."

Her chest began thumping. She cleared her throat.

"Hello? Is someone there?"

Out of the corner of her eye, she saw Tony and hung up.

"Who was that?" he asked.

"No one. Just a wrong number."

chapter twenty-seven

Judge William Gilbert was in his mid-fifties with thick salt-and-pepper hair, piercing blue eyes, and a sharp, hawklike nose. Lisa found him intimidating, especially in his voluminous robe, as she did the austerity of the dark-wood-paneled room.

She was sitting next to Edmond and the clinic's attorney, Brian Thompson, a thin, brown-haired, serious-looking man in his forties. They'd met in the parking lot adjacent to the Santa Monica Courthouse and walked to the judge's chambers together. To Lisa's left were the Wrights and Jean Elliott, who looked all business in a navy suit and a white blouse.

Outside, it was a warm, beautiful day, and the Pacific Ocean was only blocks away. Lisa had an urge to excuse herself, to walk down to the beach and stroll along the shore and stare at the water and forget about lawsuits and potential custody trials and the fact that Matthew was dead, that his killer had tried to kill her, too, last night. She'd phoned the Hollywood police station early this morning and left a detailed message for Barone. She hadn't had a chance to tell Edmond. This morning she'd told Selena and asked her to have someone replace the window she'd shattered. Seeing it in daylight had seemed grotesque, surreal.

"Ms. Elliott," the judge said, "I've read your petition, so you don't need to repeat any background information. Please explain briefly why I should shorten the stay for this subpoena."

"Thank you, Your Honor. My clients need to know the identity of the woman who received their dead daughter's eggs so that we can proceed promptly with our complaint for damages. Given the strong probability that the district attorney's office will confiscate clinic records, we're concerned that we will lose access to those records for an indefinite period of time, thereby indefinitely delaying our suit for medical malpractice and negligence, which we are basing on the fact that the clinic removed eggs from Ms. Wright when she was a legal minor."

"Which you will, of course, have to prove."

"I've submitted the graphologist's report, Your Honor. It's conclusive."

"I've read it." His tone was noncommittal. "You're arguing exigency because you're worried the police will confiscate the clinic's files. I'm sure the clinic can make copies of the file or files in questions."

Lisa said, "Your Honor, we have a copy of Ms. Wright's file."

"But we have no guarantee that copy won't be confiscated as well," Jean said, dismissing Lisa with a quick "You're-a-novice-at-this" glance.

"Maybe so." The judge leaned back in his swivel chair. "Still, I don't see why you need the files altogether. If the clinic admits that one of its patients received your clients' daughter's eggs, you don't need to know the identity of this patient. You're suing the clinic, not the patient."

"My clients plan to sue for shared custody as well."

The judge shook his head. "It's not going to happen, Counselor. California statute reads that a child born to a couple during their marriage is irrefutably believed to be the child of that couple."

"Yes, but the Court can order the recipient to undergo DNA testing for the limited purpose of determining whether the eggs were stolen. And since Ms. Wright was legally underage when her eggs were taken, I believe we can ask for DNA testing."

"But only to ascertain negligence or malpractice for the purpose of claiming damages." He turned to the clinic's attorney.

"Mr. Thompson, is your client prepared to admit that it received eggs from Ms. Wright?"

"We're prepared to say that eggs were retrieved from Ms. Wright. We're not prepared to accept the graphologist's report as conclusive. We intend to retain our own graphologist to examine the documents in question."

A waste of time, Lisa thought, irritated. Everyone knew the documents had been forged. This *meeting* was a waste of time. Matthew's killer was out there somewhere, and these lawyers were playing games. She wondered anxiously where Barone was now, what he was learning.

"And in the meantime," Jean Elliott said, "my clients are forced to wait, to wonder who has their daughter's eggs. My clients want to be involved in their grandchild's life, Your Honor, from the beginning. They don't know whether the recipient has given birth, whether she's giving birth today or tomorrow or the next day."

"Do I have to remind you, Counselor, that we're not here today about custody?" The judge fixed his blue eyes on her. He sounded annoyed. "Mr. Thompson, do you know the identity of the woman who received Ms. Wright's eggs?"

The attorney turned to Edmond, who said, "Your Honor, Dr. Brockman is prepared to answer that question."

Lisa had Chelsea's papers with her, though she didn't need them. "Two patients received Ms. Wright's eggs, Your Honor. One of the patients never conceived." Poor Cora, she thought again. "And there's a problem as to the identity of the other woman."

"Explain that, please." The judge's tone was crisp.

In the parking lot, Brian Thompson had warned her to give as little information as possible. "The other patient identified by code number as the recipient of Ms. Wright's eggs wanted to ascertain that the embryos she received were the product of her eggs and her husband's sperm. She and her husband hired a person who observed every stage of the in vitro process."

Jean Elliott was staring at her. So were the Wrights.

The judge said, "Did she mistrust the clinic procedures?"

"No. She and her husband are devout. They did this for religious reasons at the suggestion of their religious advisor."

"I see. Does this woman have an affidavit to that effect?"

"No. The person they hired is out of the country. They're trying to locate him." Lisa hoped they'd find him soon.

Jean Elliott said, "Your Honor, in regard to our complaint for damages, if the clinic is unclear as to the identity of the recipient of Ms. Wright's eggs, then we will certainly need to have DNA testing done on this woman."

Thompson said, "May I suggest that we wait until we get the affidavit from this person?"

"We're not prepared to wait. And the truth is, Your Honor, an affidavit will only attest to what this person observed and the specific times he was in attendance."

"That's true." The judge faced Lisa. "Dr. Brockman, can you be more specific as to what this person observed, and when?"

Lisa described in detail the times the *shomer* had been there. "He signed the labeled test tubes containing the patient's retrieved eggs. He signed the labeled sperm from her husband, and he signed each of the labeled petri dishes in which the sperm and egg were combined."

The judge turned to Jean Elliott. "Counselor?"

"Ordinarily, Your Honor, I'd be impressed. But this clinic is being charged with embryo switching. It's certainly possible that—"

"Those allegations have been made only by the media," Thompson cut in firmly. "No charges have been filed."

"A member of the district attorney's office advised me that a formal investigation is going to be conducted." She addressed the judge. "Your Honor, if embryo switching *has* taken place at the clinic, I would argue that someone could have tampered with the eggs and/or sperm of this unidentified couple, regardless of the precautions they took."

The judge drummed his fingers on his desk. "Dr. Brockman, is it possible, given the presence of this observer, that your patient received fertilized eggs that weren't hers?"

This time everyone was looking at Lisa. She didn't know why her hands were suddenly clammy. "It would be highly unlikely."

"But not impossible? What amount of time elapses from the point when the eggs are retrieved to the time that they're fertilized with the sperm?" His tone was genial, unhurried.

"Approximately two to three hours."

"Where are the eggs at this time?"

"In an incubator in the lab."

"People are coming and going in this lab?" he asked.

"Only lab and medical staff. The door is locked at all times."

"And the observer was there, too. Is that correct?"

"I didn't personally see him there, but the lab tech did. I *did* see him in the operating room, where he initialed the test tubes with the eggs I retrieved from Mrs.—" Lisa stopped herself in time. "From the patient."

"That's nonresponsive, Your Honor," Jean Elliott said.

The judge glared at her. "And we're not conducting a trial here, Ms. Elliott." He faced Lisa again. "Was the observer in the lab for the entire three hours?"

"I don't know."

"Your Honor, may I say something?" Jean Elliott asked.

"As long as it's *responsive.*" He scowled.

"Thank you, Your Honor." She had colored slightly. "Dr. Brockman explained that the observer was hired to witness every aspect of the in vitro process. That would include egg retrieval, sperm retrieval, fertilization, and embryo transplantation. Did I leave anything out, Doctor?"

Lisa said, "The observer was also present each time a lab technician examined the egg and sperm in the petri dish."

"That would make sense, Doctor, because he would have to testify that no other sperm was mixed with the patient's egg and the husband's sperm. But during the two- to three-hour interval before the egg is mixed with the sperm, and it's just sitting in the incubator, what purpose would there be in having the observer wait and watch an incubator?"

"Are you being facetious, Ms. Elliott?" the judge asked sternly.

"I apologize, Your Honor. The fact is, the observer was there to verify that everything was conducted normally. He wasn't there with the expectation that someone would willfully try to switch eggs. He labeled the test tubes. There was no reason for him to remain in the lab during that two- to three-hour period."

She was right, Lisa thought.

"And as far as the labels are concerned, if someone willfully switched Ms. Wright's eggs for this woman's eggs, that person could have duplicated the witness's signature on the test tube or petri dish. I would argue that the coded information is correct, and that this patient did in fact receive Ms. Wright's eggs. But to be certain, and to proceed with our complaint for damages, we will ask that the child undergo DNA testing."

The silence in the room was almost palpable.

"Mr. Thompson," the judge finally said, "Ms. Elliott's argument is persuasive. Given the fact that this observer is out of the country and unable to be located, and given the alleged charges against the clinic, I'm going to assume that the computer is in fact correct." He made a note on a pad in front of him. "By ten o'clock tomorrow morning, I want your client to release the identity of the patient who received Ms. Wright's eggs."

"My client can't do that, Your Honor. That will constitute a violation of privacy and of patient-doctor privilege. We will file an objection to the production of any files and/or information."

"And we will file a motion to compel you to submit the files and information," Jean Elliott responded calmly.

Round two, Lisa thought.

"So we're looking at a full hearing," the judge said. "You're only buying time, Mr. Thompson."

Jean Elliott said, "I have just a few more questions for Dr. Brockman, if I may, Your Honor." When he nodded, she turned to Lisa. "Dr. Brockman, has your patient given birth yet?"

"No."

"How many eggs did you retrieve from Ms. Wright?"

Thompson had told her she could answer this question. "Sixteen. Eight went to each patient."

"And how many embryos were implanted in your patient?"

Lisa glanced at Thompson. He nodded. "Four," she said.

"Is your patient carrying a single fetus or multiples?"

Thompson said, "I don't see relevance, Your Honor." He was frowning. So was Edmond.

"It's relevant, Your Honor, because the number of fetuses will have a definite impact on the damages we will be seeking."

The judge nodded. "Dr. Brockman, please answer."

"The patient is carrying twins." From the corner of her eye, she could see Enid Wright clutching her husband's hand.

Jean Elliott was smiling.

The woman was waiting outside the courthouse entrance when Lisa walked out of the building with Edmond and Brian Thompson. The Wrights weren't there. Lisa supposed they'd left.

"I thought you should know I've been approached by a number of other patients from your clinic," Jean told Edmond.

"Thank you for the information." His tone, like hers, was cool and businesslike.

"You could save yourself attorney's fees if you gave us the name of the patient who received Chelsea Wright's eggs. I think it's obvious Judge Gilbert will rule in our favor."

"Jean, you know we can't do that," Brian said. "We'd be opening ourselves to a lawsuit for violating patient-doctor confidentiality. You don't need the name of the patient to proceed with your suit for damages."

"We're going to sue for custody, Brian." Her tone was grave. He snorted. "You heard Gilbert. No judge will give the Wrights custody."

"In this case?" She raised her finely penciled brows. "Their only daughter was *murdered*, Brian. Her eggs, which were retrieved when she was underage, are now twin embryos being carried by a woman who *could* have other children. The Wrights have no other possibility of having grandchildren. I think a judge would seriously consider these unique factors in deciding custody."

Lisa said, "We don't know that these embryos resulted from Chelsea's eggs."

"The coded number says they did. I think we've established that although this couple had someone witness the IVF, someone else could have substituted Chelsea's eggs for your patient's."

"All of my patient's eggs were viable." Lisa was trying to stay calm. "She didn't need donor eggs. Why do you want to disrupt her life and put her and her husband through needless turmoil?"

"I sympathize, but my priority is my clients. I don't know why someone would switch eggs. I *do* know that your clinic is accused of embryo switching. If these twins didn't result from Chelsea's eggs, the sooner we conduct DNA testing, the sooner your patient has peace of mind. If they did . . ."

"No judge will take these babies from the birth mother," Brian said again.

"I'm not so sure. The babies haven't been born, so no bonding would be disrupted." Jean switched her briefcase to her other hand. "There are *two* babies and *two* sets of parents who want them. King Solomon had to decide custody over *one* baby."

Brian frowned. "Separating twins is contrary to their best interest. Any psychologist will say as much to the judge hearing the case."

She smiled. "I have another appointment. I'll see you in court." She turned and headed toward the parking lot.

Edmond watched her go, then faced Brian. "What do you think?"

"I can't see a judge separating twins or taking them away from the birth parents—unless Jean proves they're unfit."

"They're wonderful people," Lisa said. "They have a nice home. She's a paralegal. He's studying to be a rabbi."

"That's good." Brian nodded. "On the other hand, the decisions of California judges reflect the feeling that children should be exposed to as many relatives as possible. Not shared custody, but liberal visitation."

"My patient and her husband are Orthodox Jews. The Wrights are Christians. What if they disagree on how to raise these children?" Lisa realized with a sinking feeling that she'd already accepted the possibility that Naomi had received Chelsea's eggs.

"Legally, the custodial parents decide on the education and religious upbringing of their children. The judge can give the Wrights instructions, but will they follow them exactly?" The attorney shrugged.

chapter twenty-eight

"**I** appreciate your taking the time to talk to me again, Dr. Brockman. I won't take long." Gina Franco smiled.

"Five minutes, you said." The reporter had ambushed Lisa in Reception and she hadn't been able to escape talking to her, not with an empty waiting room belying that she was too busy.

"Five minutes," Gina agreed. "I want to tell you how sorry I am about Dr. Gordon. I heard they found his blood in the trunk of his car. I guess you were right about him." She looked at Lisa questioningly, clearly inviting more information.

Every time Lisa thought about Matthew's blood, she felt ill. "You had some more questions about IVF?" she asked pointedly.

"Right." The reporter opened her notepad. "Is it true success rates drop with each subsequent procedure?"

"Statistically, yes. But each patient has individual problems, and we try to find individual solutions."

"Bottom line, though: if I were having my third IVF cycle, would I be more likely or less likely to become pregnant?"

"In general, less likely," Lisa admitted with reluctance. "But again, we don't deal with generalities. We deal with people."

Gina nodded. "So here's my next question: if that's so, how can your clinic and others like it afford to offer money-back guarantees for women under forty who don't conceive after three IVF cycles? Aren't you running the risk of going broke?"

"I hope not." Lisa smiled lightly. "The fact is, we offer the guarantee because we're confident we *can* help women conceive, because we've done it over and over again."

"I see." Gina wrote on her pad, then looked up. "Next question. How extensive is your egg donor program?"

"Rather extensive. There's a shortage of eggs, now that patients are freezing their embryos for later IVF attempts instead of donating them."

"So no patients donate eggs?"

"Some do. Our clinic, like many others, reduces fees for IVF and other infertility treatments to women who donate eggs."

"But a lot of donors are young, college-age women, right?"

Was she referring to Chelsea? "Right. Recipients prefer eggs from young college students because they think that the eggs are healthier. Actually, there's no definitive proof of that."

"*And* that their babies will be bright, since the donor's intelligent enough to be in college?"

Lisa nodded. "Exactly. Other patients, though, prefer eggs from women who have borne children—there's more assurance the eggs are viable. And seeing photos of the donor's offspring gives them some idea of what future children may look like."

"Makes sense. Does your clinic encourage open or closed donation?"

"Some birth parents don't tell their child that he or she was born through IVF." Lisa wondered now, as she sometimes did, whether her parents would have kept her adoption a secret if they'd had it all to do over again. "On the other hand, some parents present the child with the petri dish in which they were 'conceived.' "

"No kidding!" Gina grinned. "I'm surprised Baccarat and Waterford haven't produced designer petri dishes."

"I'm sure that sooner or later someone will do just that. Maybe Lalique." Lisa flashed another quick smile. "Basically, the donor and the patient decide whether they want to communicate or remain anonymous. First of all, if the donor doesn't want her identity known, that's her prerogative."

She'd told Sam the truth when she'd said she had no intention of searching for her birth mother—she didn't want to intrude on the woman's life, didn't want to complicate her own—but she'd been thinking about her more. She supposed it was because of the Wrights' insistence on finding out who had their daughter's eggs. Last night, just before she'd fallen asleep, she'd thought about the fact that if her assailant had been successful, her birth mother wouldn't even have known that she'd died.

Last night, too, for the first time in years, the dream had returned: In it, she was walking around, looking for the house that corresponded to the address on the slip of paper in her hand, the house that belonged to her birth mother. Finally she found it. She knocked on the door, but no one answered. She knocked again and again, then jiggled the knob. The door opened. She stepped inside and was facing another door. She opened it and saw another door, then another, and another. . . .

"Why wouldn't she want her identity known?" Gina asked.

Lisa was startled—the reporter was referring to egg donors, but it was as if she'd read her mind. Lisa focused on the question. "What if the family of one or more of the children resulting from her eggs suffers financial hardships? She may not want to be held responsible for any expenses down the line."

"Okay." Gina nodded. "But what if the child has a congenital illness or a genetic predisposition to an illness? Shouldn't the birth parents know about that?"

"Absolutely. That's why the donor fills out an extensive history and medical profile and undergoes genetic screenings."

"What if she wants contact but the birth mother doesn't?"

"Then there's no contact." Lisa rose abruptly, feeling restless, on edge. "Gina—"

"I know. Time's up." She smiled and stood up. "One last question? I heard that the parents of the murder victim who donated eggs to this clinic want to know the recipient's identity. Even though this was a closed donation, since they'll never have other grandchildren, don't you think they have a right to know who has their daughter's embryos?"

Was this the real purpose of the reporter's return visit? "I can't comment on that, Gina."

"Off the record, Dr. Brockman?"

"Off the record and on the record."

Grace seemed reluctant to leave Lisa alone in Matthew's office. She hovered several feet away as Lisa checked the file cabinet and the desk.

"Maybe if you told me what you're looking for, I could help," she said when Lisa shut the last drawer.

"I'm not sure what I *am* looking for." Lisa felt a surge of pity for the nurse, whose red-rimmed eyes showed she'd been crying. Had she stayed in Matt's office because she wanted to talk? "Grace, you must be devastated about Dr. Gordon. If you want to talk about it . . ."

The nurse's eyes welled with fresh tears. "Everybody's upset about Dr. Gordon, but he wasn't just my boss. Tony and I owe him everything. Without him, we wouldn't have Suzie." She wiped her eyes. "Dr. Brockman, do the police have any idea who killed him?"

"No, they don't," Lisa said gently.

"What about Chelsea Wright? That *was* a mugging, right? Her murder isn't connected to Dr. Gordon's." She was staring intently at Lisa, her lips slightly parted.

"The police aren't sure. Grace, I know Dr. Gordon had a lot on his mind just before he disappeared—the missing money, the problem with Chelsea's egg donation. Did he tell you anything else was troubling him? Maybe his research?"

"His research?" She crinkled her eyes in puzzlement. "You don't mean about the anesthetic, do you? He was considering switching from the one we've been using for egg retrievals, because some patients are agitated when they wake up."

"I know." Matthew had mentioned it the night before he'd disappeared; he'd raised the problem at a staff meeting a while ago. Lisa had forgotten about it.

"Sometimes they have bad dreams," Grace said. "Several weeks ago Felicia Perry, one of Dr. Cantrell's donor patients, was crying in Recovery because she dreamed she was going to be punished for giving up her eggs. The recovery room nurse managed to calm her, poor thing, but I felt so sorry for her."

"You're a wonderful nurse, Grace, because you care about people." Lisa smiled warmly at her. "Did you talk to Chelsea when she came to the clinic a few weeks ago?"

The woman stiffened. "I don't know what you mean."

It was as though a glass wall had come between them. "I just meant, did you chat with her? Did she say anything unusual? Sometimes patients talk more to the nurses than the doctors."

"No. I took her to Dr. Gordon's office and told her he'd be with her shortly." She pushed at the cuticle of her thumb.

"Did you see her after her appointment?"

"I don't know why everyone's asking me all these questions about Chelsea Wright!" Grace's lips were trembling, and she pressed her tightly clenched hands at her sides. "Mr. Fisk thinks that I'm the one who accepted her into the program, that I forged her signature. I *know* he does. I offered to resign."

"No one wants you to resign, Grace," Lisa said quietly. "Mr. Fisk has to find out what happened because the clinic is facing a lawsuit." She could see from the anxious look in the nurse's blue eyes that she'd made things worse. It occurred to her that Grace might be guilty. "*Anyone* could have made a mistake. I saw Chelsea's picture. She looks much older than eighteen."

"You think I did it, don't you? I'd never do *anything* to compromise Dr. Gordon or this clinic! Never!" She started crying and ran out of the office.

Lisa sighed, then went to Reception and told Selena what had happened. "So much for providing comfort."

"I'll talk to her. She's upset because Detective Barone questioned her. He questioned just about everyone here."

That would explain why Grace was so agitated, why she'd said "everybody" had been asking her questions. "When was this?"

"When you were at the courthouse. How did it go, *mi hija*?" Selena's brown eyes were soft with worry.

"Not great. But thanks for asking." Lisa rested her hand on Selena's arm. "Who's next?"

"Actually, you're free for the next two hours."

She grimaced. "More cancellations?" She'd seen only two patients early this morning, both of whom were in the middle of a regimen of fertility shots. There'd been no need to have Sam or Ted cover for her while she was at the courthouse.

Selena nodded, then leaned forward. "Honestly, I don't know what's going to happen," she whispered, even though no one else was within earshot. "Has Mr. Fisk said anything?"

"Not yet."

"Everyone's scared. Alice in Billing quit over the weekend. And Margaret Cho gave only two days' notice—she's taking a position at another hospital starting Wednesday."

Lisa didn't blame her. She nodded wearily. "I'll be in the lab if you need me."

She hadn't been to the lab since last night. She felt a stab of anxiety as she opened the door to the stairwell, and her heart was beating faster as she hurried down the stairs and out the lower-level door.

"Hey," Charlie said when Lisa entered the anteroom. He put down a yellow pad he was holding and came closer. "I'm sorry about Matthew. I don't know what else to say."

Her eyes teared. "I know, Charlie. Thank you."

Everyone had been expressing sympathy—the receptionist, the nurses, the secretaries in Billing, the techs. Selena had hugged her tightly when she'd arrived this morning. She'd seen tears in Victor's eyes. Even Ted had told her how sorry he was, how shocked. Lisa had tried to detect a false note, but he'd sounded sincere. Which didn't mean he was. She'd seen him charm patients and mimic them cruelly behind their backs.

"How are *you* doing, Charlie?"

"Depressed as hell. Worried about my job, like everyone else. You heard Margaret's quitting?" When Lisa nodded, he said, "You know what we've been doing all day? Paperwork. Arranging to have patients' embryos transferred to other clinics. Matthew would hate to see what's happening to his clinic."

"You're right," she said softly. "By the way, I was looking through last year's accession log the other day, and I noticed that most of the pages for September of last year are torn out."

He frowned. "Why the hell would someone tear them out?"

"I don't know." She hated lying to him, hated lying to anyone, but she no longer knew whom she could trust. She hated that, too. "When did you last look at those pages, Charlie?"

He scratched his head, thinking. "A couple of weeks ago," he finally said. "That's the best I can narrow it down."

"What about the other techs? Can you ask them?"

"Sure." His voice and eyes conveyed curiosity. He went into the lab and returned a few minutes later. "Margaret and John said they haven't checked last year's log in over a month. Norman isn't here. I'll ask him when I see him. Is it important?"

"I'm not sure."

"A detective was here. He wanted to know when's the last time I saw Matthew, whether he seemed nervous, upset—that kind of stuff. Then he asked me about the other techs and the medical staff. It made me uncomfortable." The lab director looked at Lisa questioningly.

"I know. He talked to me, too, Charlie."

"He talked to John and Margaret and Norman. I suppose he asked them about me." He shook his head. "He asked about you, too. I told them you weren't to be trusted." He laughed at his own joke.

"Funny, I told Detective Barone the same thing about *you*, Charlie." She punched his arm lightly, then went back upstairs.

Sam was in her office, standing near her desk.

"I left a file on your desk." He pointed to a manila folder and smiled. "I knocked this time, but you weren't in."

"You're learning." She hadn't seen him alone since last night. It had felt odd going to sleep, knowing he was in the next room. Odd, and wonderfully comforting. When she woke up this morning and found his note—he'd gone home to shower and change his clothes—she'd been disappointed not to see him. "Thanks again for staying with me last night."

"Any time," he said softly. "So how'd it go with the judge?" He sat on one of the chairs and crossed his ankles.

"Terrible." She told him what had happened. "It's possible someone substituted Chelsea's eggs for Naomi's." She paused. "I heard that Detective Barone was here, questioning the staff. Did he talk to you?"

"You could say that." He grimaced. "I think I'm high on his list of suspects."

"Don't be ridiculous!" She felt a prickling of alarm. "He knows you were attacked last night by the same person who attacked me. I phoned him this morning at the station and left a message."

"He made me go over the details five times and couldn't understand why I had a hard time describing the attacker. To say he was skeptical is an understatement. I can't blame him—he knows I have a thing for you. He asked me whether I arranged for you to get the job here so I could pursue a romantic relationship with you. He asked me if I'd slept with you. I said only in my dreams. Just joking," he added quickly. "I think we need a little comic relief."

Her cheeks were burning. "I'm sorry, Sam. I *had* to show him the printout of Matthew's file."

He nodded. "Of course you did. Don't worry about it."

"Do you know if Barone questioned Ted?"

"*Oh*, yeah." Sam rolled his eyes. "Right after he spoke to me. Ted came storming into my office after he left—what the hell did I think I was doing, telling a detective he was often late for appointments or missed them altogether? Who the hell did I think I was?" Sam expelled a breath. "I let him rant."

"But *you* didn't tell Barone. *I* did."

"No difference. Ted's mad. He'll get over it—unless he has reason to be scared." Sam checked his watch and stood up. "Gotta go. I actually have a patient to see—can you believe it?"

She walked him to the door. "Charlie says most of our patients are having their embryos transferred."

"Who can blame them?" He sighed. "By the way, are you planning to look at those files tonight?"

"I haven't decided yet. Why?"

"I still think it's a waste of time, but if you want, I can help. It'll have to be after nine-thirty, though. I coach a junior basketball league, and I can't let my kids down. I'll call when I'm done. Do you want me to stay over again tonight?" He put his hand to his chest. "My God, can you imagine how that sounds? It's a good thing Barone isn't eavesdropping." He laughed.

She laughed, too. "Actually, you'll be proud of me. I accepted Elana's offer to stay there for a few days." She wondered what would happen if Barone didn't find the killer. Would she be a hostage to fear forever?

"Great decision, although I kind of like your sofa." He grinned, then in a serious voice said, "Joking aside, I don't have to tell you how important your safety is to me."

"I know, Sam." She rested her hand on his arm. "I care a great deal about you, too."

He gazed at her tenderly, then leaned closer. His breath was warm on her face, and her stomach tightened because she knew he was going to kiss her and she wanted him to. Suddenly he pulled away.

"I gotta tell you, keeping kosher and Shabbos is a hell of a lot easier than not touching you," he said with forced lightness. "I haven't always been careful about following this *halacha*, and you're not making it any easier." He smiled. "Benjie's been working on me, giving me pep talks. I think I need another one."

"Probably." Sam was thinking about religion; she'd been thinking about Matthew. Her face was flushed, tingling with desire and guilt. "You said you have a patient?"

He cleared his throat. "Right. You need help taking your stuff to the Presslers?"

"I'm not taking much. I plan on going to my place every day to check my mail." She went back her desk.

"Okay, then." He lingered a moment, then left.

She sat for a few minutes, thinking about what had happened, what hadn't, then tried working on her files but couldn't concentrate. She went to Reception.

"Your three o'clock just canceled," Selena told her. "Why don't you go home?"

"I think I will. When did these come?" She pointed to a stack of glossy brochures on Selena's desk.

"Half an hour ago. They look beautiful, don't they?" Selena sounded wistful. "Dr. Gordon worked so hard on them."

And now his clinic was on the verge of closing down. Lisa took a few brochures. They were less an advertisement, she thought sadly, than a memorial.

She was returning to her office when she saw Ted Cantrell and Grace standing in the hall, twenty feet away. His hand was on her shoulder, and he was talking quietly. He had an urgent expression on his face. Grace shook her head and walked away.

He caught up with her and stopped her. She turned toward him. Lisa couldn't see Ted's face, but she could tell that Grace was listening attentively.

She felt a hand on her shoulder and almost jumped. Turning around, she saw Norman Weld staring at her.

"I'm sorry if I startled you," he said. "I called your name, but you didn't hear me." He was wearing a white turtleneck cotton shirt that bleached his already pale face.

"That's all right, Norman. I'm just a little nervous lately." She tried a smile. "How can I help you?"

"Mr. McCallister asked me whether I remembered when I last looked at last year's accession log." His words were studied, slow. "I'm sure it was several months ago."

"Thank you, Norman. That's very helpful."

"You're welcome. Dr. Brockman, I know this is a trying time for you, even more so than it is for all of us. It's hard to understand God's will. If you want, we can pray together for Dr. Gordon's soul." His tone was solemn.

"That's very kind of you, Norman," she said softly. "But I feel more comfortable praying by myself."

His face turned red, as if she'd slapped him. "Of course. I didn't mean to intrude on your grief."

"You didn't intrude at all, Norman. It's nothing personal. I hope you understand."

He made a little bow, then moved away.

Lisa turned around. Ted and Grace had disappeared.

chapter twenty-nine

"**I**'m so glad you changed your mind," Elana said. "Benjie and I worried about your being alone in your apartment after what happened in the clinic. Were you nervous last night?"

"Everything was all right, but I decided not to take any more chances." Lisa wasn't about to tell the rabbi's wife that Sam had spent the night on her living room sofa.

"You didn't bring much with you." Elana was looking at the small satchel Lisa had placed at the side of the bed.

"I plan to go home every day to check my mail." She'd stopped at the apartment on the way here and packed a few toiletries and a change of clothing. She'd left a message for Barone, telling him where he could reach her. She knew he'd be relieved. Her parents had been relieved; they must have been surprised that she was staying with a rabbi, but they'd made no comment.

"Dinner is at five-thirty, more or less, so that Benjie can eat before he goes back to shul for *mincha-maariv*," Elana said, referring to the daily afternoon and evening services.

"Thanks, but I'd planned to eat out." Whatever was in the oven smelled good, but Lisa didn't want to take advantage of the Presslers' hospitality.

"Don't be silly. Tonight we're having meat loaf, mashed potatoes, and a salad—the kids will be disappointed if you don't join us. Feel free to use the phone. And don't work too hard." She smiled and left the room, pulling the door shut behind her.

Sam was skeptical that Lisa would find anything in the files. She wasn't so sure. Minutes later, when she was sitting on the peach carpeted floor, surrounded by dozens of files, she wondered whether he hadn't been right, whether she wasn't being ambitious, especially since she didn't even know what she was looking for.

One file at a time, she told herself. With a box of paper clips at her side, a pen in her hand, and a yellow legal pad on her lap, she picked up the file closest to her.

Across the length of the pad, she'd created columns: PATIENT'S NAME & AGE; ATTENDING PHYSICIAN; TREATMENT; PATIENT'S OVA/DONOR OVA; DONOR CODE #; DOCUMENTATION/RELEASES; CLINICAL PREGNANCY: YES/NO. Since she was searching for evidence to refute the charge that the clinic had been switching embryos or stealing eggs, she was interested only in patients who had undergone IVF or other fertility procedures that utilized eggs.

She developed a simple routine: After paper-clipping together the pages of each file, she wrote the patient's name and age and the name of the attending physician on her pad. Then she checked the lab and embryo forms. If there was a D for "donor" on the lab form, she looked for a release authorizing the receipt of donor eggs. She also cross-checked each file against the list of donors and the Jane Doe list of recipients.

Forty minutes later she was frowning. In the twenty-one files she'd examined, three patients had Ds on their lab forms and corresponding releases; four, no Ds and no releases. Six had no Ds on their lab forms and no release forms, but their names appeared on the Jane Doe list.

Holding the six problem files in her hand, she got up and went over to the desk. She hesitated, then picked up the phone receiver and, looking at the top file, dialed the number for thirty-nine-year-old Nicole Bellows. When a woman answered, Lisa had a flash of nervousness but quickly identified herself.

"Why are you calling?" There was definite hostility in the woman's voice, and fear.

"We're doing a follow-up on all our IVF patients, Nicole, and

I had a question or two to ask." No response. "According to your file, you had two IVF cycles. Is that correct?"

"Yes." Nicole still sounded guarded.

"I don't see a consent form indicating that you received eggs from a donor."

"I *didn't* receive eggs from a donor. For both IVF cycles Dr. Gordon used my own eggs and my husband's sperm. Are you saying there's a problem?" She sounded tense.

"No, no problem at all."

"If you're suggesting that this isn't my baby—"

"Of course not, Nicole. I don't mean to upset you."

"Well, you *have* upset me! First these allegations about embryo switching, then you call about donor eggs!"

"I'm sorry. Please don't—" Lisa was listening to a dial tone. She put the file aside, glanced at the top page of the next one, and dialed the number for Nessa Williams, age thirty-six.

Again she introduced herself, but before she had a chance to ask any questions, the woman snapped, "I have no intention of speaking to anyone from your clinic!" and hung up.

The next patient, thirty-eight-year-old Nettie Lipman, was hesitant, but finally agreed to talk. Like Nicole Bellows, she'd undergone two IVF cycles. Like Nicole, she'd never received donor eggs.

The next three patients Lisa phoned told her the same thing.

She returned to the files and spent another hour checking them. Again she'd amassed a number of files with no Ds on the lab form and no release forms, but the patients' names appeared on the Jane Doe list.

She phoned the patients. One hung up as soon as she learned Lisa was with the clinic. Two of the numbers Lisa called were no longer in service. She wondered whether these women had changed their numbers to protect their privacy. Those patients willing to talk to Lisa insisted they'd never received donor eggs.

Maybe they were lying—maybe they were afraid to admit they'd received donor eggs because the custody of the fetuses they were carrying might come into question. Lisa could check the donor codes, one by one, on the clinic computer in the morning.

Or she could do it now. In the morning, the computer data might be confiscated, the clinic shut down.

With the exception of Victor and the custodial staff, the building was empty. Lisa hurried to her office and turned on the computer. Using the password, she opened the confidential donor code file.

The document was blank.

She stared at the screen, chewing nervously on her bottom lip, then exited the program and accessed the general directory, where she found the donor code file.

Ten kilobytes.

From the little she knew about computers, that told her that the file was empty. The last time someone had worked on it was last night at 9:53. When she was in the lab's anteroom, checking the log.

She scrolled through the directory and found the listing for the Jane Doe recipient file. Ten kilobytes. 9:56 P.M. She accessed the software program again, opened the Jane Doe recipient file, and typed in the donor code number.

This document was blank, too.

So was the backup file.

Whoever had been here last night—whoever had attacked her— had deleted both files. Or renamed them to hide them until he could delete the questionable entries.

Victor smiled when he saw her return to the lobby. "Find what you came for?" he asked.

"Not exactly. See you tomorrow, Victor."

She wasn't really hungry, but she sat at the table with Elana and Benjie and the children, who were charming and outgoing. Lisa enjoyed listening to their animated chatter about their teachers and classmates. At the same time, she was anxious to return to her files.

She insisted on helping clear the table, and it was six-thirty before she was back in the guest room. An hour and a half later she'd checked the last file and had seventeen patients to call. The file belonging to each one had no D on the lab form and no release form. The patient's name appeared on the Jane Doe list.

She didn't really have to call them—she was convinced from what she'd already learned that someone had been giving patients donor eggs without the patients' consent, though she couldn't figure out why. Still, she was a scientist. She'd taken a random sampling by selecting only the green folders; she was determined to follow through with every problem file.

She dialed the phone number for Noreen Gallagher and heard

distrust enter the woman's voice as soon as Lisa identified herself. But at least she didn't hang up.

Yes, Noreen had undergone two IVF cycles. No, she hadn't received donor eggs. "Dr. Cantrell harvested my eggs."

"I thought you were seeing Dr. Gordon."

"No. Why would you think that?"

"Sorry. My mistake. Thanks for your time." Frowning, Lisa hung up and studied the lab form, which listed Matthew as the attending physician. She peered more closely at the photocopy and inhaled sharply when she saw what could have been an erasure where his name was hand-printed.

Had Ted erased his own name and written in Matthew's? Had he tried to cover up the fact that he'd used donor eggs without a patient's informed consent?

She checked the other files. The first few listed Matthew as the attending physician, but there were no signs of erasures. She was flushed with relief—obviously this was simply a clerical error—and examined the next file. The attending physician was Matthew. Again Lisa was startled to see signs of an erasure.

She examined the remaining files. Two had what looked to be erasures. She phoned one patient and learned that the number had been disconnected. She phoned another, Nicki Sandler, who told her she'd never received donor eggs.

"I don't know why you're bothering me when you can speak to my doctor," Nicki said. "He's the one who retrieved my eggs."

"Dr. Cantrell, you mean?" Lisa was guessing, hoping she was wrong.

"Not Dr. Cantrell. Dr. Davidson. Dr. Sam Davidson."

chapter thirty

Lisa had decided to shower at home early Tuesday morning and was rinsing her hair when she heard the doorbell ring over and over, accompanied by the sound of insistent pounding.

She shut the faucets and, grabbing a towel, ran out of the shower to the front door. "Who is it?" she demanded angrily.

"Police. Open up, please. We have a subpoena."

They were here to confiscate her files. She looked through her privacy window and saw two uniformed policemen and five men in suits. "May I see identification, please?"

One of the policemen held up his badge.

"Who are those other men?" she asked, surprised at how calm she sounded.

"They're with the medical board. Can we come in, please?"

"I'm not dressed. You'll have to give me a minute." She wasn't frightened—she'd been expecting this—but she was nervous anyway.

"Hurry up, then," the male voice said with curt impatience.

Half-running to her bedroom, she dressed as quickly as she could. She wanted to towel her hair dry, but they were pounding on the door again. They probably thought she was stalling so that she could hide something.

With her wet hair plastered to her head, she returned to the front door and opened it, stepping aside as they filed into her home. The officer who had shown her his badge presented her with a subpoena which, she read, granted him and the others the right to search her premises and confiscate any and all property deemed relevant to the investigation of the clinic.

"I don't have any clinic files here," she said, but they'd already starting taking apart her living room.

At first, as they looked under the sofa and its cushions, she felt oddly unmoved, overwhelmed with a sense of unreality, as though what she was observing was happening to someone else. Minutes later they started removing the books from her wall unit, and she felt violated, How *dare* you! she wanted to say, but she was helpless to stop them from taking down the porcelain teacups she'd started collecting, or riffling through the books and tossing them carelessly on the floor.

They moved into her bedroom and she moved with them, even though one of the men in the suits asked her politely to remain in the living room. No one stopped her. They emptied her closets and shoe boxes and looked through her purses. They fingered her panties and bras and nightgowns. They opened packages of pantyhose and removed her bedding. They searched through her desk drawers and thumbed through a brand-new box of stationery. They took the "Notes" printout and her computer and three boxes of diskettes and the journal in which she wrote almost every night.

"That has nothing to do with the clinic," she said calmly. "That's private." There was no response. It was as if she didn't exist in her own apartment.

In the bathroom, from the cabinet under the sink, they took out boxes of tissues and tampons and rolls of toilet paper and spilled the contents of the Estée Lauder gift-with-purchase makeup pouch that she'd bought at Bloomingdale's last month. She wondered who would return everything to its proper place.

From the bathroom they went to the small, narrow kitchen and wreaked their havoc there, emptying her cabinets of pots and pans and searching behind her dishes and glassware. She swore to herself that if they broke anything, she'd sue.

The phone rang. She picked up the wall extension and said hello.

"The police just left my place," Sam said. He sounded depressed. "They took everything except my underwear. What about you?"

"They're here now. I can't talk, Sam." She hung up because she was tense having strangers trash her apartment, and because she hadn't quite figured out what to say to Sam, who might have been lying to her all along.

They were removing everything from her pantry and still hadn't said a word. She was reminded of the silent ritual her father performed every year on the night before Passover eve.

Lisa would hide ten pieces of bread all over the house. Then her father, holding a lit candle in one hand and a long feather in the other, would recite a blessing on the removal of leaven and, walking from room to room, would search everywhere for it—under furniture, on top of the living room mantel, on the kitchen counter. No one would utter a word until he had found every piece of bread and swept each one carefully with the feather into a soft white cloth that Lisa held open for him and which he would burn in the morning in their back yard.

Her father, well aware that her mother had been cleaning the house for weeks, never expected to find any leavened products on the day before Passover. That was the purpose of the ten pieces of bread, he'd explained to Lisa—to ensure that the blessing wasn't in vain. But one year he *did* find leaven—some Cheerios had rolled under the drapes. Lisa could still remember the prickly sensation she'd felt at his discovery. "I don't know how that could have gotten there," her mother had said, flustered.

Lisa had the same prickly feeling now as one of the uniformed officers pulled out a two-inch-thick stack of money and placed it on the kitchen counter and called over the other men.

She moved farther into the kitchen, but no one noticed. They were all staring at the bills, which she could see were fifties. At least the top one was.

"I don't know how that got there," she said.

Three black-and-white police cars were parked in the clinic lot when Lisa arrived at eight-thirty. Entering the lobby, she passed four uniformed officers. Each one was carrying a box filled with multicolored files. She saw more uniformed police and other men in suits walking up and down the halls, robots on parade.

Sam was standing in the waiting room next to Selena, who was looking through the window into Reception. She was grabbing her arms, and her lips were grimly pursed as she watched her office being dismantled.

Lisa approached her and put an arm around her.

"I don't know what the hell they think they're going to find," Sam said. "I phoned Ted—he said they took everything, including his computer and diskettes. Yours, too?"

Lisa nodded. She found it difficult to look him in the eye. "Did you call Mr. Fisk?" she asked Selena.

"He's on his way. We had only a few patients scheduled for this morning, *gracias a Dios*. I called and canceled."

"Did they go to my office?"

"I tried to stop them. 'At least wait until Dr. Brockman gets here,' I said. They just waved that damn paper in my face and told me to step out of the way. I called the people where you're staying, but you'd left. The police took stuff from Dr. Cantrell's office, too. And from the lab."

Poor Charlie. Lisa could imagine his angry reaction to the full-scale invasion of his kingdom.

"I don't know why they didn't just ask to see some of the records," Sam said.

"I can't watch anymore." Selena said. She turned abruptly and left the waiting room.

Lisa wondered what Selena would do now, what the others would do.

"You told me this would happen, but I didn't really believe it." Sam took a sip of water from the paper cup he was holding. "Talk about denial. Did you look through the files last night?"

"No, I decided you were right. It's a waste of time." She kept her eyes on the window and hoped he couldn't see her face.

"Maybe not. I was wrong to discourage you, Lisa. Maybe there *is* proof in those files that there was no embryo switching. Or maybe there's proof that there was—more denial on my part, I guess. I can come over and help you look. Hell, it's not like I have anything better to do." He grunted and took another sip.

"Thanks, but I'm not up to it." Her head had been pounding ever since the officer had removed the money from her pantry.

" 'Not tonight, I have a headache,' huh?" He smiled wryly. "I phoned you last night after the game—my kids won, by the way. Elana said you were sleeping."

"I was exhausted." And she hadn't wanted to talk to him.

She'd lain in bed for hours, staring at the ceiling, her mind in turmoil.

"Probably a delayed reaction from Sunday night."

"Probably." She watched him carefully and said, "The police found a large sum of cash in my pantry." She saw surprise in the lift of his brows.

"How much?"

"Twenty thousand." The officer had counted the bills twice and had made her count them and sign for the money before he'd placed it in an envelope, which he'd sealed and signed.

"Twenty thousand?" Sam's eyes widened. "Where the hell did *that* come from?"

"Obviously it's the cash stolen from the clinic safe." That would be easy to verify—the police could check the serial numbers against the numbers on the photocopies of the cash payments patients had made.

"Who put it there? And why would someone do that to you?"

"That's obvious, too, isn't it?" she said wearily. "Whoever killed Matthew and set him up wanted to implicate me, too." She wondered what Edmond would think, but that wasn't her main concern. "I'm going to my office, to take a last look around."

"You'll only depress yourself, Lisa."

"I'm already depressed."

He touched her arm. "What's going on, Lisa? Aside from the money, I mean. You're keeping something from me, aren't you?"

"No. What makes you think that?"

He stared at her for a moment. "Nothing."

"It's been a horrible morning. Don't pay attention to my mood."

Her office looked pathetically barren now that all the files had been removed. Her drawers were empty. So was her file cabinet. Aside from the medical textbooks and furniture, the only things remaining were the photos of "her" babies and the two charts hanging on the wall—failed sentinels.

She called home for messages. Barone had called. She phoned him at the station and caught him as he was about to leave.

"I didn't have a chance to return your call yesterday," he told her. "I'm glad you weren't hurt Sunday night."

Again she felt hands around her neck, squeezing. She shook her head to clear the image and told him what had happened. "He was wearing a mask and a surgical gown, so I couldn't see his face."

"That's what Officer Reynaldo said. He phoned this morning.

He said this same person attacked Dr. Davidson when he arrived. I'm confused. Didn't Dr. Davidson go *with* you to the clinic?"

Was he checking up on Sam's story? "No. He wasn't home, so I left a message on his machine, telling him where I was going. He came later to make sure I was all right. Something else has happened," she said, anxious to change the subject from Sam and to forestall a rebuke from Barone, who'd warned her not to go out alone. "The police raided my apartment." She told him about the money they'd found in her pantry. "I never saw it before. I hope you believe me."

"How do you think it got there?"

"Obviously someone broke into my apartment. You saw the scratches around the outer lock."

"Who's been there since Dr. Gordon's disappearance?"

She hesitated. "No one." Sam had been over on Thursday night. Sam had helped himself to snacks from the pantry. Sam might have erased his name on the lab form and written in Matthew's. The thought had kept her up most of the night.

"I thought you said Dr. Davidson was with you on Saturday."

"Yes, he was." She was grateful Barone couldn't see her guilty tint. "But he didn't have money with him, or anything else. We're not allowed to carry anything when we're out of our homes on the Sabbath. We can't even touch money, since it has no relevance to the Sabbath." She gripped the edge of her desk. "Detective, I just remembered: when I returned from synagogue, the key wasn't exactly where I'd left it, on top of the door molding. I had to look for it."

"So you think someone used your key and planted the money while you were at the synagogue?"

"It's possible." But was it likely? "Did you find out anything about Chelsea?"

"I spent yesterday checking with all the fertility clinics in the area—as far north as Santa Barbara and south to Orange County. No one at any of those clinics ever met her."

Lisa frowned, puzzled. "Maybe she used another name."

"I went to each of the clinics and showed her picture. No one recognized her. Which explains why no one phoned in after they saw her face in the papers and on the television news."

Barone was right. "So why did she lie to Matthew?"

"That's a good question. There's something else I thought you should know. I spoke to each of the clinic directors. None of them knows anything about new research on freezing eggs."

She was disappointed and confused. "So she wasn't killed because she could identify the person who stole Matthew's research?"

"I'm not discounting Dr. Davidson's theory. One of those directors could be lying. In my line of work, I've learned that people lie more often than not. Out of fear of becoming involved, out of loyalty. And, of course, out of guilt."

chapter thirty-one

Lisa restored her living room first, crying softly now and then as thoughts of Matthew overpowered Elton John, who was keeping her company as she dusted the books and teacups before returning them to their shelves. She tackled the kitchen next. She'd placed the last box back into the pantry and was about to start in her bedroom, then decided she'd finish later, or tomorrow. No difference, really, since she wasn't staying at home. And the files and the information she'd gleaned from them were like a magnet. She was anxious to know what was going on.

It was eleven o'clock. After eating an English muffin smothered with blackberry jam and drinking two cups of coffee, she drove to the Presslers, where she let herself in with the key Elana had given her. She sat at the desk and scanned the ten yellow sheets she'd filled with data.

She'd identified thirty-one problem files. Excluding four hangups and three disconnected numbers, she'd talked with twenty-four women who insisted they hadn't received donor eggs, even though the computer data indicated otherwise. She agreed with Barone that many people lied—in this case, probably out of fear—but she couldn't believe that *all* these women had lied to her.

She forced herself not to think of why someone would have stealthily substituted donor eggs for a patient's own eggs, not to think of who that person or persons could be, and told herself to look at the data and focus on what she *did* know.

Like the fact that all these women were under forty.

And that they'd all completed at least two IVF cycles.

Which meant what?

She studied the data again, focusing only on the "donor problem" patients, and noticed that of the thirty-one women, twelve had sustained a clinical pregnancy.

She did the math on a sheet of paper—that was almost thirty-nine percent.

She counted the women under thirty-five who'd sustained pregnancies. There were nine. Four were pregnant. Forty-four percent. Of the twenty-two women over thirty-five, eight were pregnant. Thirty-six percent.

She was familiar with the statistics published by a rival clinic: a thirty-two percent chance for women under forty to become pregnant; a forty percent chance for women under thirty-five. Matthew had often scoffed and labeled the statistics advertising hype. Now his own clinic was surpassing those numbers.

Lisa realized she was dealing with a specific segment of a random sampling of one hundred and two files. She returned to the yellow pad. This time she counted all patients over forty and noted the number of pregnancies: nineteen patients; four pregnancies. An impressive twenty-one percent for that age group. In the thirty-five-to-forty age group, there was a total of forty-six patients and seventeen pregnancies: thirty-seven percent. There were thirty-seven patients under the age of thirty-five. Seventeen were pregnant: almost forty-six percent.

The numbers were staggering.

It was possible that if she collated the data of all the clinic files (something she couldn't do, now that they'd been confiscated), the numbers would be less impressive.

Or not.

Matthew had known the statistics. He'd used them for the new brochure. She found her purse at the side of the bed and took one out. The third page featured a table showing the clinic's rate of success by age group:

Twenty percent for women over forty.

Thirty-six percent for women between thirty-five and forty.

Forty-four percent for women under thirty-five.

She wondered again whether what she'd suggested to Gina Franco was possible: that a rival clinic had leaked false rumors to ruin the reputation of Matthew's clinic and attract its patients and their dollars. But a rival clinic hadn't substituted donor eggs for a patient's eggs. Unless it had hired someone at the clinic to do it.

Had someone substituted Chelsea's eggs for Naomi's? Two days ago Lisa would have said it was impossible. Now she had a sinking feeling that it had probably happened.

The "why" still eluded her.

She didn't have Naomi's file, but she did have her copy of Chelsea's—thank goodness she hadn't left it at the clinic yesterday, or at her apartment. She found it among the stack of files on the floor and read it again.

It contained nothing she hadn't already known. She was about to close it when she noted the name of Chelsea's gynecologist— Howard Melman. She wondered whether Chelsea had said something revealing to him, whether she'd confided in him about her problems, her need for money.

She dialed Melman's number, identified herself to the female receptionist, and asked to speak to the doctor.

"He's with a patient, Dr. Brockman. May I have a number so he can return your call?"

"Actually, would it be possible for me to see Dr. Melman today? It's rather important." Lisa looked at her watch—it was a quarter to twelve. She felt as if she'd been staring at numbers for hours.

"Let me see." A short pause. "He's really booked, because he's just returned from vacation, but I'll squeeze you in at one, before he sees his first afternoon patient."

Melman shared an office with another OB-GYN on the fifth floor of a medical building on Century Park East. The waiting room, small and cozy, was furnished with two benches and three armchairs, all upholstered in a soft rose-and-blue tiny floral print, all occupied by women in various stages of pregnancy. On the dark wood coffee table, next to a potted plant, lay a fanned assortment of pregnancy and parenting magazines. Currier and Ives prints hung on the texture-papered ecru walls.

Melman's office, paneled in cherry wood, was cozy, too.

"How can I help you?" the doctor asked Lisa when they were both seated. He was in his fifties; he had graying hair and a matching beard, a paunch, and a cherubic face. Santa Claus without the costume.

"I wanted to ask you a few questions about Chelsea Wright."

"I delivered Chelsea, and she was my patient." He sighed heavily. "My wife and I came back Sunday from a two-week trip to Europe I'd been promising her for ten years. I was looking through the *Times* and saw that poor girl's face. A beautiful young girl, killed like that." His eyes misted.

"It's a terrible tragedy," Lisa said quietly.

Melman nodded. "I called her parents. They're heart-broken, devastated. And now they found out she donated eggs to this clinic that's been in the news, and the clinic won't tell them who received the eggs." He shook his head. "Sorry. Why are *you* here? My secretary didn't say."

He would probably throw Lisa out as soon as she explained. She braced herself and said, "Actually, I'm with the clinic."

His body stiffened.

She flinched under the malevolence of his icy stare. "You may have heard that Dr. Gordon, the clinic director, is missing. The police think he's been killed, and that his murder may be connected to Chelsea's. Dr. Gordon is my fiancé." No sign of sympathy from the doctor. "I was hoping Chelsea may have said something to you that would provide a clue to what happened."

"She wasn't even eighteen when she donated those eggs," he said with quiet anger. "How could you people let her do it?"

Her face colored. "Dr. Melman, I understand why you're upset, but the fact is, she said she *was* eighteen. I've never met Chelsea, but from her picture, she looks older than eighteen."

"And you didn't bother to check it out, did you?" He leaned forward and pointed an accusing finger at Lisa. "You didn't care if she knew what she was doing because you needed her eggs, because you have patients willing to pay big money to get them."

She didn't respond. She wasn't about to defend herself and tell him that she wasn't the one who had let Chelsea slip through; that, like Sam, she'd had reservations for some time about having young, childless women donate eggs. But had she done anything about it?

"So why are you here, *Doctor*?" He accented the last word with sarcasm. "I know the Wrights are planning to sue your clinic. Did you come here hoping I'd tell you that Chelsea was a liar, that she was a manipulative girl who'd do anything to get her way? If that's why you're here, you can leave right now."

"I'm not here to discredit Chelsea, Dr. Melman. I'm trying to find out what happened to my fiancé. I hope you believe me." No answer from Melman. "When was the last time you saw her?" It was a safe, nonthreatening question.

He leaned against his armchair. "She had an appointment three weeks ago, the week before I left on my vacation. She brought me a trip journal. 'Make sure you write everything down so you can tell me all about it,' she said." His eyes misted.

"She came to the clinic two weeks before she was killed. She told Dr. Gordon she wanted to donate eggs again because she needed the money. Did she mention that to you?"

"She didn't say anything about donating eggs—I didn't even know until recently that she'd done it the first time. I would have talked her out of it, you can be sure of that." He scowled at Lisa. "I'm not surprised she needed money. She was saving to go to a private college, and her parents are short on funds. Always have been. But they always pay their bills—on time, too." He narrowed his eyes. "I *am* surprised Chelsea wanted to donate eggs again. You're sure about that?"

Lisa nodded. "Why are you surprised?" She felt a prickling sensation at the back of her neck.

He shook his head. "I can't tell you that, Dr. Brockman. That's between me and Chelsea."

And Chelsea was dead. Lisa tried to restrain her frustration. "It's possible that what she told you might have a bearing on her murder, and on Dr. Gordon's."

He shook his head again. "Sorry. There are ethics in our profession, Doctor. Some of us follow them."

She ignored his insinuation. "Dr. Gordon said Chelsea was agitated and depressed when she came to the clinic. Was she like that when you saw her?"

He hesitated. "Yes, she was." His tone was grudging.

"Can you tell me why?"

"I can, but I won't. It's none of your damn business." His tight smile was smug.

She clenched her hands. "You're angry at the clinic, you want to punish me—fine. But aren't you angry at Chelsea's killer? Don't you want to make sure he's caught and punished?"

Melman's smile disappeared. He stood up. "I have patients to see. I imagine you have a lot of free time, now that the clinic's under investigation.''

The doctor would probably be thrilled when he heard that the police had confiscated the files and the clinic was about to be shut down. "Thanks for your time." She took a business card from her purse and wrote down her home number before putting the card on his desk. "If you change your mind, Dr. Melman, please call me."

He grunted. "Don't hold your breath."

She left Melman's office depressed and frustrated and had exited the parking lot when she realized she was only blocks away from the Brentano's where Chelsea's boyfriend worked.

She drove to the Century City mall, parked her car, and took the escalator to the mall level. She'd been here countless times with Matthew—looking at china and crystal and flatware patterns at Bloomingdale's and Macy's, eating ice cream at Häagen-Dazs, going to the movies. She and Matthew had often browsed in the bookstore, which was close to the theaters.

She didn't remember the boyfriend's last name, but she remembered his first name: Dennis. She was prepared to hear that she'd come at the wrong time and was pleasantly surprised when the manager told her Dennis was in the back of the store, restocking the shelves. She found him in the "Psychology" section and watched him work for a moment. He was tall and thin and lanky, with shoulder-length, dark-blond hair and a boyish face.

She walked up to him. "Dennis?"

He looked at Lisa, holding a book in his slender hands. "Yeah?"

"I'm Dr. Lisa Brockman from the Westwood clinic. I wonder if I could talk to you for a few minutes."

He had frozen at the mention of the clinic. Now he took a deep breath. "About what?" Wary now.

"I want to tell you how sorry I am about your loss." She felt inept again, as she had with the Wrights. How did Barone handle the grief of the bereaved? "I've heard wonderful things about Chelsea from everyone, including Dr. Gordon, my fiancé. I'm sure you've heard that the police think he's been killed, too."

"I don't mean to be rude," Dennis said in a soft, pain-filled voice, "but I've told the police everything I know, which isn't much. You can ask them to fill you in." He turned his back toward her and slipped the book into the racks.

"I've already spoken with Detective Barone. Please, Dennis, just a few questions?"

He faced her again and sighed. "What do you want to know?" He sounded tired, resigned, a little angry, too.

Lisa hated intruding on his grief, poking at fresh wounds. "The bartender Chelsea worked with said she was depressed for a while. I just spoke with her gynecologist. He said the same thing. Do you know why?"

He shook his head. "I asked and asked her. She said, 'It's something I have to work out myself.' Then one day she's all smiles, like the weight of the world was lifted off her shoulders. And a week later, she's dead." His voice broke. He looked down and studied his shoes.

Lisa waited until he was composed. "Chelsea said she wanted to donate eggs because she needed money. Do you know why?"

He glanced up at her. "It doesn't make sense. She wanted to pay her parents back for the tuition, I know that. But they weren't asking for it. She could've taken her time."

"I know she was happy about the job with Mrs. Rhodes."

"She was *thrilled*." A ghost of a smile flitted across his young face. "Not just because of the money. Chelsea loved kids. She wanted to have half a dozen of her own." He averted his head and wiped his tear-filled eyes.

She wanted badly to place a comforting hand on his shoulder. She waited a moment, then said, "Dennis, Detective Barone said you had no idea Chelsea came to the clinic three weeks ago to donate eggs again. Why do you think she didn't tell you?"

"That's been bothering me." He frowned. "Chelsea and I, we told each other everything. The only thing I can figure is that she knew I would've tried to talk her out of it."

That was what Melman had said, too. And Chelsea's parents.

"The first time, when she donated her eggs? That was before we met. She told me about it after we started dating seriously, said how rough it was."

"Because of the hyperstimulation of her ovaries?"

Dennis nodded. "That was no picnic. Plus she had this awful dream when they removed the eggs. The nurse told her it was from the anesthesia."

Lisa felt her chest tighten. "What was the dream about?" she asked, trying to sound casual.

"She's lying on this bed with her eyes closed. She hears this male voice from behind her. He starts quoting from the Bible, telling her she's a terrible person because she gave up her eggs.''

Lisa's heart was beating faster. "Do you remember what part of the Bible?''

His eyes took on a distant look. "I don't remember exactly. It had to do with a woman who took her kid to the desert and left him to die. But then God told her to go back to him.''

"Hagar,'' Lisa said quietly.

Dennis gazed at her in surprise. "Yeah, that's it. Hagar. Anyway, the voice tells Chelsea she's going to be punished because she gave up her babies.'' He picked up a book from the trolley and ran his hand along the spine. "She knew it was just a dream, but it freaked her out. So I don't get why she'd want to do it again. Unless she figured they'd use a different kind of anesthesia. What do you think?''

chapter thirty-two

"Sam left a number of messages for you on the machine," Elana reported when Lisa returned to the Pressler house a little after two. "He told me what happened at the clinic. It must have been a terrible experience."

"Not my best day." Lisa smiled lightly.

"What will you do now?" She peeled a cucumber and placed it on a wood cutting board on the kitchen counter.

"I don't know. I can't look for a position at another clinic until this is all cleared up—no one in his right mind would hire me." She hadn't talked with the medical board representatives, all of whom had avoided making eye contact with her and Sam and the others, but Edmond had told her the board was considering suspending the licenses of all the staff doctors until the allegations were cleared. He'd also asked her about the money found in her pantry. She'd told him she had no idea who had hidden the money there; she thought he believed her.

"How will you manage, Lisa?" Elana's eyes were dark with concern.

"I have enough in the bank to tide me over for four or five months." She'd had twenty thousand dollars in her pantry, she thought wryly. And she could always sell the diamond Matthew had given her—Sam's suggestion, she remembered with a pang.

"Sam didn't say, but I can tell he's worried." She sliced the cucumber. "You probably don't know this, but he basically supports his sister and her husband and children."

"Sam never mentioned it." Why not? she wondered uneasily.

"It's not his way." Elana cut open a red pepper. "His brother-in-law lost his job six months ago and hasn't found another one. His sister is pregnant, and one of the children—the youngest boy, I think—has cystic fibrosis. They don't have good medical insurance, so Sam's been taking care of those bills, too."

"Sam is very special," Lisa said softly.

She phoned him from the guest room. After four rings, she heard the answering machine click on and was relieved that she wouldn't have to talk to him, but as soon as she said, "Sam, this is Lisa," he interrupted.

"I was on my way out when I heard the phone," he said. "I'm glad you called. I'm worried about you, Lisa. I phoned at least three times—I tried your place, too."

"I was there for a while, straightening up. Then I went window-shopping. I needed to clear my head." It was getting easier to lie, especially since she was talking into the receiver, not to his face.

"You'll have plenty of time for that now, but you won't have a paycheck. If you need a loan—"

"I'm fine. Thanks for offering, though."

"How about joining me for dinner tonight? We can commiserate about our dismal futures."

"Thanks, but I don't think so, Sam."

There was an uncomfortable silence. He said, "It's because of yesterday. I'm rushing you, right?"

That wasn't it at all, but she was happy to latch onto the reason he'd offered. "I'm confused about a lot of things."

"I don't blame you. And I'm sorry I made you uncomfortable. It won't happen again. Friends?"

"Friends," she said, and hoped that was true.

She hung up, then located the list of egg donors she'd printed out. On the third page she found the name she wanted. She dialed the phone number, and when a young woman answered, Lisa identified herself and asked to speak to Felicia Perry.

"I'm Felicia. How can I help you?"

Lisa heard curiosity and wariness in the woman's voice. "We're doing a follow-up on women who've donated eggs at our clinic during the past year. We want to know whether the experience was pleasant, and whether you had any comments."

"It was fine, I guess. I was happy to help couples who needed the eggs."

"How did you feel after the surgery?"

"Actually, I was kind of weepy because of a dream I had, but the nurse explained that was because of the anesthesia."

"What kind of dream?" Lisa asked, though she already knew. She felt as though a hand were twisting her insides.

"I donated two weeks ago, so I remember this clearly. A man said that Hagar, Abraham's handmaiden, didn't abandon her child, and why was I abandoning mine? He said he was the voice of my babies, that my babies were crying and that I'd be punished." Felicia expelled a breath. "I know it was just a dream, but it was creepy. I don't know who Hagar is, or how she popped into my dream. Maybe it's from some TV show I saw. Or from a Bible class when I was a kid."

"Did you see what this man looked like?" Unconsciously she tightened her grip on the phone receiver.

"I couldn't open my eyes. When I did, no one was there. That's how I knew it was a dream. I hope I've been helpful," she added.

"Very helpful." Lisa thanked her and hung up, her heart hammering.

This couldn't be coincidence—both Chelsea and Felicia Perry dreaming about Hagar, both of them being threatened with punishment for abandoning their "babies." She was alarmed by what she'd heard, convinced that someone from the clinic had approached these women in the recovery room and threatened them.

You're going to be punished, he'd told them. Had he taken on the role of angry prophet, warning them that a divine being would demand retribution? Or had he taken on the role of avenger?

Chelsea had been murdered. Was Felicia in danger, too? Were other donors in danger? But if the man had been angry at Chelsea, why had he waited all these months to "punish" her?

"Because she didn't heed his warning," Lisa said aloud. Because he'd seen her at the clinic when she came to donate again.

Lisa had four pages of donor names. If this man had approached some of the other donors, maybe one of them remembered something that could help identify him.

She called the first donor on the list, but the woman wasn't in. Neither were the next four donors she phoned. The sixth woman answered the phone. Lisa told her the same thing she'd told Felicia Perry, and asked her about her experience donating eggs.

"It was fine," the woman said in a cheerful, game-contestant's voice. "Perfectly fine."

"Did you have any aftereffects from the anesthesia?"

"Nope. I never do. Is that it? Because I'm on my way out."

Lisa was disappointed, but of course this man wouldn't have accosted every patient. She continued making calls and dialed numbers for five patients before she reached one who was at home.

Her name was Bonnie York, and she'd had the same "dream."

"Did you tell a nurse about it?" Lisa asked.

"No. I felt silly and uncomfortable." A shy laugh. "I've thought about it, and I realized I must have had ambivalent feelings about donating the eggs—that's why the dream. I don't think I'd do it again."

"Can you describe the man in your dream?"

"No. At one point I opened my eyes and saw a man wearing a surgical mask. I thought he was real, but of course he wasn't. In my dream, I was confusing this man with a doctor. That's why he was wearing a mask. But I'm not sure what that means. Why would a doctor be warning me not to donate eggs?"

Lisa thought about that after she hung up. She phoned Barone and left another message. "Please tell him it's urgent," she said to the receptionist and gave the Presslers' phone number.

She would have liked to get some fresh air, to clear her head, but she didn't want to miss the detective's call. She had an urge to phone Sam, but she didn't know if she could trust him. The thought filled her with sadness.

She hadn't done her exercises in days. Lying on the floor doing stomach curls, she thought about the masked man accosting donors in the recovery room and wondered whether this was what Chelsea had told Dr. Melman, what he'd refused to share with Lisa. But that didn't make sense; the fact that Chelsea had had an upsetting dream was hardly confidential. And why had she been depressed about it nine months later?

Lisa still hadn't figured out what the files had to reveal—she knew *something* was there. It might be connected to this unidentified man who'd accosted Chelsea and the others. It might be totally separate.

She looked again at the statistics for women under thirty-five: a forty-six percent pregnancy rate. Amazing. Of the thirty-seven patients in this age group, only nine were in her "donor problem" subgroup. She decided to examine the files of the other twenty-eight women.

Three of them had recently undergone corrective surgery. Four were taking oral fertility drugs. Five had completed one IVF cycle. Thirteen of the twenty-eight were pregnant.

Skimming the medical profiles and histories, she found nothing unusual but noticed that more than one patient had been referred by the same physician—Dr. Jerome Nestle. She'd seen the name on other referrals. It wasn't uncommon to have one doctor refer several patients, but she was certain she'd heard his name in a different context.

"Jerome Nestle," she said aloud.

She put aside the twenty-eight files and returned to her original group of "donor problem" files, but the name was teasing her memory. She phoned the clinic and spoke to Selena—Edmond had asked her to stay in the office and field all questions—but the office manager knew Nestle only as a referring physician.

"Is it important?" she asked.

"I have no idea. Just fishing."

Sam might know, but Lisa didn't want to ask him. Or Ted. It was three forty-five. She considered asking Edmond and phoned him at home on the chance that he was there. When she'd spoken to him at the clinic, after the police had left, he'd been angry, depressed. She doubted that his mood had improved.

Georgia answered the phone. "Edmond's not here, dear," she told Lisa. "I'll have him phone you as soon as I hear from him. This has been a terrible day, just terrible—although I don't have to tell you that. Is there something I can help you with?"

"Do you know a Dr. Jerome Nestle? He's an OB-GYN, and he sounds familiar."

"He should—he's a partner in the clinic and one of Edmond's friends."

Lisa frowned. "Really? I've never met him."

"Well, he's a *silent* partner. You would have met him at the engagement party we gave for you and Matthew." She sighed. "But he and Helen, his wife, were out of town at the time. Cancún, I think. Do you still want me to have Edmond call you?"

That was where Lisa had seen his name—on the list of investors attached to the prospectus Matthew had shown her. "No, that's all right. You don't even have to mention that I called. Thanks again, Georgia."

She sat on the bed and reexamined the files, setting aside the ones that listed Nestle as the referring physician. There were four: one patient had just started an IVF cycle; three had recently completed IVF. All three were pregnant.

Three for three. Great odds.

Maybe too great.

She called the first woman and tried not to sound nervous when she identified herself and asked for Nancy Bartholomew.

"*I'm* Nancy Bartholomew," the woman said, her voice guarded. "Why are you calling?"

"Actually, I was looking at your file and was pleased to see that you conceived on the first IVF cycle."

"Larry and I couldn't believe it." Mrs. Bartholomew's tone had lost its edge. "We'd been trying for over a year and were getting discouraged. Then Dr. Nestle suggested the clinic, and here I am, pregnant."

Lisa could tell that the woman was smiling. "You were Dr. Nestle's patient for some time?"

"For years. He's *wonderful*. When Larry and I decided we wanted to start a family a little over a year ago, Dr. Nestle gave me a thorough exam and a Pap smear, to make sure everything was 'baby-ready,' as he put it."

"What kind of birth control were you using until then?"

"The sponge. I have a history of migraines, so the pill was out. And I didn't want an IUD. Anyway, two months later I went back to him, because my periods were longer and heavier and I was having mid-cycle staining."

"Did he do any tests to see what was wrong?"

"No. He wasn't alarmed—he said this happens often to women once they're in their thirties."

Lisa frowned. She'd never heard that it happened "often."

"He *did* give me oral fertility pills after some diagnostic tests, to help me get pregnant."

"Clomid?"

"No. I don't know the name, but unlike Clomid, these pills don't increase the odds of having multiple births. Dr. Nestle keeps a supply in his office, so I never needed a prescription."

Lisa was puzzled. What kind of fertility pill didn't increase the odds of multiple births? And why was Nestle dispensing them from his office?

"A year later, when I still hadn't conceived, he gave me another exam and referred us to the clinic. I phoned him the minute I found out I was pregnant. He was *so* excited."

"So when did the staining and the other symptoms stop?"

"Actually, right around the time of that second exam."

"Before or after the exam?" Alarm bells were going off in Lisa's head. She held her breath.

"Mmm . . . *after*. Because when I went to the clinic the following month, I no longer had the problem. Of course, I mentioned it to the nurse who took my history."

"And you had a Pap smear during this second exam, too?"

"Yes. I don't understand why you're asking all these questions." The wariness was back in her voice.

"Just medical curiosity." She forced herself to laugh. "Sorry. I didn't mean to make you anxious. Did you—"

"I'm sorry. I really have to go."

Lisa heard the dial tone. She hung up, pensive, and phoned the second of Nestle's patients, Nedda Flom. She was friendlier than Nancy Bartholomew, less reluctant to talk to Lisa, even though she'd heard the news about the clinic.

"I've had the *best* care at the clinic. I don't believe for a moment that embryos have been switched." Her voice dropped. "I feel terrible about Dr. Gordon. You're his fiancée, aren't you? My heart goes out to you."

"Thank you," she said quietly. She paused. "You must be excited about the pregnancy."

"Delirious." The woman laughed. "Honestly, I was beginning to think it wouldn't happen."

A little over a year ago, she told Lisa, she and her husband decided they wanted to have a baby. She went to Nestle, who gave her an exam and told her she was in excellent shape.

"Did he give you a Pap smear, too?"

"Uh-huh. Not what I was used to. I had cramping, something I've never had with a Pap smear. Nestle said that's because he took tissue from a little higher up than normal. Sadist." She laughed again. "I had a little spotting afterward, too."

"What kind of birth control were you using before?"

"A diaphragm. I don't like IUDs or pills."

Subsequent to the exam, she'd had the same problems Nancy Bartholomew had described. The symptoms didn't disappear until a year later, after she had another Pap smear. Nestle gave her oral fertility drugs, which he dispensed from his office.

"Do you have any of those pills left? I'm curious to see what they are." That was an understatement.

"I do. God knows why I kept them, since they didn't help me get pregnant." She laughed again. "But why don't you call Dr. Nestle and ask him?"

Lisa thought quickly. "This is awkward, but Dr. Nestle and I had a disagreement, and I'm not comfortable contacting him."

"I understand. Dr. Nestle's okay, but he can be stubborn. To tell you the truth, my husband and I were planning to go to a different clinic, but Nestle practically strong-armed us into going to yours."

Lisa wasn't surprised. "Can I stop by and pick up the pills?"

"Sure, why not?" She gave Lisa an address in Beverlywood, not far from the Presslers. "I'm going to the market. I'll leave the pills in an envelope at the side door, okay?"

"More than okay. Thanks so much. Good luck with the baby."

"Thank you. I hope everything is cleared up about the clinic. If you patch things up with Dr. Nestle and see him before I do, give him my regards."

Lisa had one more of Nestle's patients to call. She dialed the woman's phone number but heard a recorded message. She didn't really need to talk to her. She knew she'd hear the same sequence of events, and she thought she knew what Nestle, who was a silent partner in the clinic, was doing:

Nestle chose patients who told him they'd just decided to start a family. Women in their late twenties or early thirties. Women who should have no difficulty becoming pregnant. He did a thorough exam, probably ordered a blood panel and other chemical screens to make certain these women were good candidates for pregnancy.

And then he inserted IUDs. He blamed the accompanying cramping on the Pap smear. He lied about the change in their cycles, the staining. If the blood tests revealed potential problems, he removed the IUDs. If not, he removed them a year later, when the patients were anxious about not being pregnant. He referred them to the clinic, where they had IVF and quickly became pregnant. No surprise, since they'd never had infertility problems.

And with just two or three more pregnancies, the clinic's success statistics went up dramatically.

And the numbers were advertised in glossy brochures.

And more patients came and paid large sums because the odds were better there than elsewhere that they would walk out the door with a baby.

And the clinic profited.

And so did Nestle.

She realized that she was making this up out of whole cloth, that she had no proof. That she could be wrong. She checked her watch; it was five after four. She hesitated, then picked up the phone again and dialed.

"Dr. Nestle's office," a woman said. "How can I help you?"

Lisa almost lost her nerve and hung up. She cleared her throat and said, "My name is Elysse Landes." Her mother's maiden name. "I'd like to make an appointment with the doctor."

"Have you seen Dr. Nestle before?"

"No. My New York gynecologist referred him. My husband and I are new in town, and we're eager to have a baby as soon as possible. I want to have a gynecological check up before we start." Her heart thumped noisily in protest.

"I have an appointment open next Thursday."

"If you could get me in sooner, I'd be grateful. Now that we've decided, I'm anxious to get going. A day or two shouldn't matter, but somehow they do." She laughed shyly and wiped the sweat off her upper lip. "I know I'm being silly."

"The doctor has a very busy practice, Mrs. Landes."

"I know. I heard he's *wonderful*. Is there anything available sooner? Anything at all? I can come in very early or very late." That was one advantage of not having a job—her time was her own.

A pause. "Dr. Nestle usually isn't in on Wednesdays, but he'll be in tomorrow. Hold on a minute, and I'll check with him."

Lisa tapped her foot while she waited.

"Nine o'clock?" the woman asked a moment later. "You'll need to pay for tomorrow's visit when you're here."

"Oh, that's no problem. I really appreciate this." She hung up, excited and nervous about what she'd done. Her hands were shaking. She sat on the bed to compose herself and heard the phone ring. A moment later Elana knocked on the door and told her Barone was calling. She'd been consumed with her suspicions about Nestle and couldn't remember for a moment why she'd phoned the detective.

"You said it was urgent?" Barone said when Lisa got on the line.

"Yes." She told him about the "dream" Chelsea and the other

women had had. "But neither of the women can identify this man because he was wearing a mask. Obviously he works at the clinic. I can't believe it's one of the doctors. They're the ones who harvest the donors' eggs."

"So this man killed Chelsea to punish her for donating eggs? Why not nine months ago, when she donated the eggs?"

"The first time was a warning. He must have seen her when she came to the clinic recently. He either assumed or heard that she'd come to donate again. That sent him over the edge."

"Interesting."

She couldn't tell what he thought. Even if he were in front of her, she was sure his face would be impassive.

"But why did he kill Dr. Gordon?" Barone asked.

"I'm not sure. Matthew was trying to find out who was responsible for admitting Chelsea. Maybe this man panicked."

"But his investigation would have centered on her admission to the donor program. He wouldn't have referred to the harvesting of her eggs or to her murder—remember, he learned about her death just a day before he himself disappeared."

"You're right." She played with the phone cord. "Maybe the murders aren't connected. Maybe there are two separate killers."

"That's a grand coincidence, Dr. Brockman. I don't buy it."

Lisa didn't, either.

"I ran a check on the clinic staff," Barone said. "You'll be relieved to know that Dr. Davidson has no criminal record. Neither does Dr. Cantrell, although he *does* like to gamble. He's heavily into the stock market and flies to Vegas all the time. He's lost quite a bit over the last year at local casinos, too. Have you found out anything more about Dr. Gordon's research?"

"I checked his office but didn't find anything related to research on freezing eggs. I'm beginning to think I jumped to the wrong conclusions." Or Sam had. This was his theory.

"Then what about the 'data lies' notation you found?"

"Maybe Matthew was referring to Chelsea's age, nothing more. I'm sorry I wasted your time, making you check the other clinics. Now you probably think I'm jumping to conclusions about this dream Chelsea and the others had."

"Not at all. And it wasn't a waste of time. Sometimes what you can't corroborate is as interesting as what you can. By the way, did you know Norman Weld was arrested for harassing a doctor who worked at an abortion clinic?"

Her stomach tightened. "No. No, I didn't," she said softly.

chapter thirty-three

Nedda Flom had left an envelope, just as she'd promised. Lisa opened it in her car and took out one of the four orange-and-white capsules. It was a quarter of an inch long, and there was no lettering to indicate the manufacturer's name. She'd never seen a pill like this. It wasn't something she remembered any of her colleagues having prescribed.

She drove to a local pharmacy and asked the young Asian woman behind the counter to identify the capsule for her.

"My daughter had it in her lunch box," Lisa said, marveling at how adept she'd become at lying. "I think she swallowed one, and I want to know what it is, to make sure it isn't harmful."

The woman walked over to a white-coated pharmacist standing toward the rear. A moment later he approached the counter.

"Is your daughter diabetic?" he asked Lisa.

"No."

"Then you're okay. This is a placebo, a sugar pill. That's why the concern if there's a blood-sugar problem like diabetes. The capsule has a milk base, so it can also cause minor discomfort for someone who's lactose-intolerant, but one capsule shouldn't do any harm." He smiled pleasantly.

"I'm relieved to hear that. Thank you so much." She felt giddy, knowing that her suspicions about Nestle were valid.

From the pharmacy she drove to her apartment and emptied her mailbox before she went upstairs. Mostly bills, a medical journal, some department-store advertising brochures. She'd been checking her phone messages periodically from the Presslers'. She looked at her answering machine and saw that she had two new messages.

The first one was from a clearly agitated Baruch Hoffman. He'd heard on the news that authorities had confiscated the clinic's files. Did this mean the police had the file of the dead woman and the information that would lead them to Naomi? Had Lisa found Naomi's file?

Lisa dreaded returning his call, dreaded informing him that his wife might have received Chelsea's eggs. She told herself she wanted to learn more before she spoke to the Hoffmans but knew that in great part she was procrastinating.

The second message was from Edmond.

"I'm glad you phoned," he told her when she returned his call. "I was so distraught this morning about the clinic that I didn't ask how *you* are. Selena said you were assaulted at the clinic Sunday night. Are you all right? Why didn't you tell me?"

"I'm shaken, but okay." If "okay" included having nightmares that left her in a cold sweat, of panicking at sudden noises. "On Monday we were meeting with Judge Gilbert—I didn't want to bother you then. After that I didn't see you until this morning, and with everything going on, I forgot to mention it."

"What were you doing there on Sunday night anyway, Lisa?" He sounded annoyed.

"I was afraid if I waited till Monday, the police might confiscate the files."

"So did you find anything before this man attacked you?"

There was something in Edmond's tone she didn't like—or maybe she was just being paranoid. She considered the fact that he was the chairman of the board of the clinic. And that Nestle, a silent partner, was his friend.

"I didn't find the Hoffman file. And you were right, Edmond. There are far too many files to look through." She hoped Sam hadn't told him she'd photocopied over a hundred files. She was suddenly anxious to get off the phone.

"By the way, Georgia said you asked about Jerome Nestle. Was there something in particular you wanted to know?"

"No." She wet her lips. "His name came up in a conversation and it sounded familiar. I wondered where I'd heard it."

"He's a fine doctor and a good friend. Georgia said she told you he's a silent partner in the clinic. That's something he doesn't like advertised, so please keep it to yourself."

"Of course. I'm glad you told me." Was this a warning?

In a lighter tone, he said, "I'm confident the police will see that these allegations are unfounded. When that happens—and I hope it's soon—I intend to reopen the clinic. I'll want you to be there."

"I hope to be, Edmond."

"How will you manage in the meantime? If you need some money to tide you over—"

"That's extremely kind of you, Edmond, but I'm fine."

"Let me know if you have any problems. I know Matthew would expect me to watch over you. I won't let him down."

"I appreciate that, Edmond," she said, though the idea of Edmond watching over her filled her with unease.

Her bedroom and bathroom were still a mess from the police search. She put on a Barbra Streisand CD, turning up the volume on her player, and began with the bathroom. The white-tiled floor was a sea of toiletries. She felt again the helplessness, the sense of being violated. Shaking her head to dislodge her anger, she set to work.

Her mind was overloaded with information: The masked man who'd accosted Chelsea; the thirty-one patients who'd apparently received donor eggs without their consent or knowledge; Jerome Nestle and his scheme to inflate the clinic's statistics and increase his profits.

There were definitely profits, she thought as she returned the last few items and shut the bathroom cabinet doors. Matthew had told her that the clinic had been doing extremely well, that Edmond and the board of directors were pleased. There *had* been a period over a year ago, she remembered, when Matthew had been alarmed. That was when the media had blasted the low success rates of fertility clinics. New patient enrollment had dropped.

Then Edmond had instituted the refund policy for women under forty, and the clinic statistics had risen, and the numbers of patients had increased dramatically.

The refund policy.

Gina Franco had asked about it yesterday, wanting to know how clinics could afford to offer refund policies and not go broke, since with each IVF cycle, the odds of getting pregnant decreased. And Lisa had answered that they could afford to offer the refund because they had great success helping these women conceive.

Had someone shared Gina's concern? Had someone tried to ensure that women on the refund policy would conceive, so that the clinic wouldn't have to repay thousands and thousands of dollars?

The thirty-one "donor problem" women were all under forty. All of them had undergone a second IVF cycle. According to the Jane Doe list, they'd all received donor eggs.

Because they'd failed to conceive after the first IVF cycle, using their own eggs? Because the odds decreased with each IVF cycle? Because the probability of their conceiving would be higher with eggs from young donors?

The clinic didn't have to repay the money. The statistics would improve. More patients, more money.

Naomi Hoffman, Lisa remembered with a jolt, was on the refund plan. She'd had one unsuccessful IVF cycle before she came to the clinic. Was that why someone had given her Chelsea's eggs? To ensure that she'd become pregnant?

Maybe this was all a product of Lisa's imagination, of exhaustion. She didn't know for a fact that these thirty-one women were on the refund plan.

The files would tell her.

Sam opened the Presslers' door. "Elana invited me for dinner," he told Lisa as she entered the house. "Don't look so thrilled."

"Sorry. I have a lot on my mind." With an effort, she erased her frown and walked with him to the dining room. Elana was putting a glass salad bowl in the middle of the table and talking to Benjie, who was setting out the forks.

"I was getting worried," Elana said. "Are you all right?"

"I was at my place, putting things back in order, and lost track of the time." She smiled contritely. "I hope you haven't been waiting for me."

"We're just sitting down. The kids ate earlier, so it's adults only—a rarity around here." Elana laughed. "Do you want to freshen up?"

Lisa didn't know how she'd get through a meal with Sam and

considered saying she was too tired to eat, but that would be rude. "Yes, thanks. I'll be right back."

In the bathroom off the hall, she looked in the mirror and could see why Elana had asked if she wanted to freshen up. Her hair was a mess. She was pale. She found a brush in her purse, removed her banana clip, and brushed her hair. Then she put on fresh lipstick and blush.

She went to the guest room and put her purse on the bed. The stack of problem files lay on the desk. She picked up the first stapled file and fanned through the pages. There it was—the fee contract. And there, in bold lettering, was the refund policy.

Her chest felt hollow. She picked up the next file and was searching for the contract when she heard a knock on the door.

"Are you okay, Lisa?" Sam called. "You looked kind of pale."

"I'm fine. I was just coming out." She dropped the file and prepared her face to greet him as she opened the door. "So what did *you* do today?" she asked as they headed toward the dining room.

"Brooded, mostly. I spoke to Edmond. He feels confident that we'll be open again soon. What do you think?"

"I don't know. I hope he's right."

Dinner was roast chicken and baked potatoes, Italian green beans, and salad. Everything was delicious, but Lisa had little appetite and might as well have been eating paper. At one point Sam asked Elana about her therapy practice; though Lisa tried to focus on the conversation, her mind was with the stack of files in the guest room.

"On Shabbos you mentioned a patient who hired a *shomer*," Benjie said to Lisa. "I hope the police won't be interfering, now that they've confiscated the clinic files."

"Benjie, don't bother Lisa with clinic business," Elana said. "She probably wants to forget all about it." She turned to Lisa with an apologetic smile.

"I don't mind. Actually, this couple may be facing a big problem. It's possible that they received someone else's eggs."

"But they had the *shomer*." The rabbi was frowning.

"Right. But the attorney representing the rights of the donor argued convincingly that someone could have switched the eggs when the *shomer* wasn't there."

"Do *you* think it's possible?" Elana asked, her voice filled with concern.

"Unfortunately, I do." Lisa turned to Sam. "How about you, Sam? Do you think someone could have switched eggs?"

"I have no idea." He was looking at her strangely. "Have you learned something that you aren't telling me?"

"No, of course not. But I checked the Jane Doe file and the donor code file at the clinic. They're both blank." She watched him to see his reaction.

He scowled and put down his fork, accidentally clanging it against his plate. "How can they be blank?"

"Someone deleted all the data. Maybe it was the person who attacked me." Still watching him; hating the fact that she was doing it.

"You're right." He sounded pensive. "And you don't have a copy?"

"No." She turned quickly to the rabbi, before her face could betray her lie. "If someone *did* switch eggs, where does that leave my patient? In terms of *Halacha*, I mean."

The rabbi sighed. "The whole issue of donor eggs or sperm is complicated. Few Orthodox rabbis would sanction, a priori, the use of donor sperm. Most experts feel that it violates the basic *Halachic* values that stress genealogy and family integrity."

"But it's been allowed," Sam said. "I was involved with a case where an Orthodox couple had to use donor sperm."

"Yes, but there's no blanket authorization. And I'm sure in your case the use of donor sperm was done in close consultation with a rabbi, and that only gentile sperm were used."

"Why is that?" Lisa asked, surprised.

"Because the child will never unknowingly marry his *Halachic* half siblings. For that same reason, we encourage parents to adopt non-Jewish children."

"I didn't know that." She sensed that Sam was looking at her. "But then the child isn't really Jewish."

"Of course he is. And when he or she reaches maturity—at thirteen or twelve, respectively—the child reaffirms his willingness to be Jewish. There's no problem."

"Maybe not in terms of *Halacha*, but isn't there a stigma when it comes to marriage?" It was hard for Lisa to keep her tone casual.

"I'd be lying if I said it never poses a problem. We Orthodox Jews often obsess about *yichus*—genealogy—when it comes to whom our children marry. And the convert, after all, comes with a blank genealogical Jewish slate." The rabbi smiled. "But Jewish history shows the true status of the convert. Ruth, King David's ancestor, was a convert when she married Boaz. Unkelos, the nephew of the infamous Titus and one of our greatest biblical commentators, converted to Judaism. Rabbi Akiva, one of our greatest sages, was the son of a convert. And we follow his teachings daily."

Lisa took a sip of water. "I remember learning that Rabbi Akiva's father-in-law threw his daughter out of the house when she told him she wanted to marry Rabbi Akiva."

"At the time, Rabbi Akiva was a simple, uneducated shepherd. The father-in-law felt tremendous remorse later. And Boaz, a renowned judge, had no hesitation in marrying Ruth. In fact, even before he courted her, he ordered his employees to leave wheat in the field for her to gather, because he admired her so much. King David and King Solomon both had a special throne for her. And the Messiah will be her descendant, through King David. How's that for *yichus*?" He smiled again and reached for the water carafe.

"What if your son wanted to marry a convert?" She told herself that his answer shouldn't matter to her, but her heart beat a little faster.

"A fair question." He nodded. "I hope I'll have enough wisdom to look at the person, not the pedigree." He glanced at his wife.

Elana smiled at him. "You will," she said softly.

How different would her life have been, Lisa wondered, if she'd met the Presslers, or someone like them, years ago? Then again, years ago she might not have been willing to listen, to believe what they were saying. She nibbled on a cookie, lost in her thoughts. Then Sam said, "About the donor sperm and eggs, Benjie. What about after the fact?" and she looked at the rabbi.

"Post-factum, virtually all rabbinic experts agree that the child is legitimate. But there are other problems. Inheritance, for one. The child born of donor sperm has no relationship to the infertile husband and can't inherit according to Jewish law unless a proper will is drawn up."

"What about donor eggs?" Lisa asked, tensing. What about Naomi Hoffman?

"Again, there's no question of illegitimacy. But who is the mother? What's the religion of the child?"

"Who *is* the mother?" Sam leaned forward and rested his chin in his palm.

"Most experts agree that the person who gives birth is the *Halachic* mother. Some say the donor is the mother. Others say that in terms of *Halacha*, the child is motherless." Benjie turned to Lisa. "Is the donor in your case Jewish or non-Jewish?"

"Non-Jewish."

He nodded slowly. "In that case, my understanding is that the child would probably have to be converted."

If what she feared was true about Chelsea's eggs, she didn't know how she would explain this to Baruch, who was expected to carry on his family's rabbinic dynasty.

chapter thirty-four

Sam offered to take Lisa to a movie, but she pleaded exhaustion and said good night. Back in her room, she returned to the files. Twenty minutes later she put down the last one.

All thirty-one women—thirty-two, with Naomi—were on the refund plan. Lisa tried to think of another explanation for what she'd discovered, but couldn't.

She was horrified, and frightened, too.

Was Nestle involved in this scheme, too? As a partner in the clinic, had he suggested this to Edmond?

But who was switching the eggs? Obviously not Edmond. And not Nestle—he'd kept his distance from the clinic.

Ted Cantrell? According to Barone, he'd lost a lot of money gambling and playing the market. Did he get a bonus for switching eggs?

And what about Sam, who was supporting his sister's family, paying their medical bills? He was the doctor for at least one of those women. Someone had erased his name and written in Matthew's instead. Had Sam done that? Had someone else done it to make him look suspect?

Or Charlie—dear, sweet, Charlie. He was in a perfect position to switch the eggs.

And what about Matthew? He liked luxuries. Had he feared that the clinic would lose so many patients that Edmond would close it? Had he looked away, unwilling to know what was going on? Or had he participated, too?

Maybe Matthew hadn't known. Someone had written his name over an erasure—to make him look guilty? Maybe he was killed because he'd been about to discover everything—because he'd been asking questions, trying to find out who had admitted Chelsea to the program. And then she was murdered. And her parents were certain to demand an investigation into the clinic records.

So this someone had needed a scapegoat. He'd killed Matthew and hidden his body to make it look as if he'd fled, and put money in Lisa's pantry. And if not for the blood in his trunk, everyone would have believed Matthew was guilty.

Just as Lisa had.

Barone wasn't at the station when she phoned, but he called back within minutes. "I haven't found out anything new," he told her before she could ask.

"*I* have," she said with excitement and dread.

She told him about the thirty-one patients, about the blank Jane Doe and donor code files, about her theory. "The police and medical-board people who raided the clinic files this morning didn't have access to those two confidential files. They didn't know about them or ask about them. Based on the patient files, they won't find anything suspicious."

Barone was silent for a moment. "But what does this have to do with Chelsea's murder or the man you think killed her?"

"Chelsea was murdered because she had to be 'punished' by the man in her 'dream.' " When she was murdered, the person responsible for switching the eggs panicked. He knew the police would examine the files, so he set Matthew up and killed him."

A pause. "Is this your theory or Dr. Davidson's?"

She couldn't tell from his voice, but assumed he was being sarcastic. "I haven't discussed this with Dr. Davidson or anyone else." She paused. "I don't know who I can trust."

"That's a wise, though painful, realization, Dr. Brockman," he said kindly.

"I think whoever attacked me Sunday night wanted to stop me from examining the files, especially the two confidential ones. He must have deleted them."

"Who knew you were going to the clinic to check the files?"

"I told Edmond I planned to look at them on Monday. I went Sunday night because I was afraid they'd be confiscated." She hesitated. "As I told you, Dr. Davidson came to the clinic after he got my message."

"Right. And according to him, that's when he was accosted by this masked assailant."

"Are you implying that he's lying?" she said, her voice tight. "That *he's* the one who attacked me?" She was angry at Barone, she knew, because he was voicing the suspicion that had been gnawing at her.

"I'm implying nothing, Dr. Brockman. But as a detective, I can't take something as fact just because one person says it's so. I need corroboration."

"He offered to help me examine the files. Why would he do that if he was afraid of what I'd discover?"

"To *control* what you discovered? That's just a possibility. I'm not suggesting he's guilty. It's possible your attacker had no idea you were planning to examine the files Monday morning. I think you're right—his goal was to delete the protected files. When he found you there, he didn't know how much you'd learned. So he panicked."

"Do you also agree that Matthew was probably killed because the egg switching was about to be exposed? That he was set up?"

Barone didn't answer immediately. "To be frank, I'm not sure the motivation to kill him is strong enough."

"Whoever switched eggs would lose his license, his reputation. He'd be open to numerous lawsuits and could end up impoverished—and in jail, now that stealing eggs is a felony."

"He hasn't stolen eggs—he's switched them."

"He's done both. He's stolen eggs from infertile patients and probably disposed of them. Or used them for research."

"Dr. Brockman, I'd like to look at the lists and the files. Can you come to the station in the morning? If that's not convenient, I can come to where you're staying now or to your apartment."

"Eleven o'clock, at the station? I have to be somewhere at nine." She considered telling him about Nestle, but knew he'd try to discourage her from going there.

*   *   *

Naomi answered the door wearing a rose-and-white floral cotton robe and a navy snood. "Baruch isn't here. He's teaching his nine-o'clock class," she told Lisa as she led her to the dining room and eased herself into one of the armchairs. "We've been waiting for your call."

The simplicity of the statement—there was no hint of impatience, of irritation—made Lisa feel worse. She sat next to her patient. "I'm sorry I've come so late, without calling first. I wanted to get as much information as I could before I spoke to you. Naomi, I'm afraid—"

"Oh, God!" the woman whispered. She started rocking back and forth, whimpering.

"I'm so sorry, Naomi, but there's a strong possibility someone switched Chelsea Wright's eggs with yours. I'm sorry," she said again. Her own eyes filled with tears.

"How long have you known?" Naomi asked dully.

Lisa couldn't reveal what she suspected because she had no real proof; because, as an employee of the clinic, she had to be circumspect. "I had a suspicion on Monday. Something I just learned confirmed it. I could be wrong," she said, wondering if she was cruel to offer hope.

"Do you know what it's like to go through nine years of agony, month after month, hoping to become pregnant?" Naomi whispered. "To have a mother-in-law look at you with pity? Not pity for *you*, pity for her precious son, because he had the misfortune to marry an *akara*—someone who can't have children."

"But you *are* pregnant, Naomi," Lisa said softly. She'd never heard her talk like this. "You're having twins."

"Someone else's twins, not mine. Baruch's twins, not mine. Who's to stop this girl's parents from claiming them?" Her lips trembled.

"Our attorney said the courts won't take the babies away from you."

"Will he swear to that?" With a heavy movement, she pulled herself up and lumbered across the room. "You came here Friday and told us we had nothing to worry about. You *promised* us."

There are two babies, Jean Elliott had said. *Two sets of parents who want them.* "I was telling the truth, Naomi. I hope you believe me. But you have every right to be angry."

"Will anger make this nightmare go away? We can sue the clinic, but will that change the fact that I'm carrying a dead girl's babies? *Will* it?" Tears streamed down her face. Suddenly she winced and, moving forward, grabbed onto the back of a chair.

"What's wrong?" Lisa hurried over to her, pulled out the chair, and helped her sit down.

"Just Braxton-Hicks," Naomi said, referring to the laborlike pains many women felt in the weeks before delivery.

"Naomi, I'm concerned. I don't want—"

"You don't want me to go into labor. Maybe Chelsea Wright's parents haven't prepared a nursery yet." She smiled bitterly and winced again, then massaged her abdomen.

"Don't do this to yourself." She stroked Naomi's arm. "You have to concentrate on staying strong for your babies. You have to stay calm," she urged softly and thought about her own mother. How calm would she have been if Lisa's birth mother had appeared and demanded that Esther Brockman give up her baby?

Naomi took several deep breaths, exhaling slowly between each one. "She wasn't Jewish, was she?" she asked a moment later, her voice suddenly quiet. "The donor, I mean."

"No. But a rabbi told me most *Halachic* experts agree that if the birth mother is Jewish, the child is considered Jewish."

She sighed. "Yes, but what if these people don't want their grandchildren raised as Jews? *Orthodox* Jews?"

"I've met them, Naomi. They seem like very nice, caring people. And the attorney said the parents who have custody determine the child's religious orientation."

"And do these nice, caring people want custody?" she whispered.

It was painful to see the anxiety in Naomi's eyes. "Yes. I won't lie to you. But as I said, I don't think they'll get it."

She studied her wedding band. "Did this rabbi tell you whether the babies will have to be converted?" she finally asked, looking up at Lisa.

"Probably. It's not a big deal," she said, thinking how ironic it was for her to be making this statement.

"I don't want them to know. I don't want *anyone* to know."

"Naomi—"

"You don't understand." Her voice, though still quiet, had a desperate undertone. "Baruch's mother was against our having IVF, even though it was our last hope. 'It's unnatural,' she kept saying. She wanted him to divorce me and marry someone else."

Lisa stared at her. "She told you that?"

Naomi shook her head. "I knew from the way she'd look at

me." She lowered her eyes. "Baruch and I were going through a rough time just before we met you." Her voice was barely audible. "I know his mother was putting pressure on him to leave me. For a while I thought he would. I'd wake up in the morning and say, 'Today's he's going to tell me.' And then I got pregnant, and everything was all right. We've been so happy." She lifted her head. "You could see that, couldn't you?"

"Yes." Lisa felt overwhelming pity for her.

"He loves me so much," Naomi said, her voice suddenly soft, shy. Her eyes were dreamy. "He's the most wonderful, caring husband in the world. And now everything is ruined, and in his mother's eyes this will be my fault, because I'm the one who pressed for the IVF."

"Maybe she'll surprise you. When she sees the babies, I'm sure she'll be thrilled. All grandmothers are."

"If we moved somewhere else," she continued, as if she hadn't heard what Lisa had said, "the Wrights wouldn't be in our lives, and no one would have to know."

My parents moved to New York so that no one would know, Lisa wanted to tell her. "Eventually, you'll have to tell your children the truth, Naomi."

"I can deal with 'eventually.' I don't know if I can deal with having the Wrights standing outside the delivery room, waiting to see their grandchildren, to hold them."

"They won't be there, Naomi." *Or would they*? Would Jean Elliott convince a judge to allow that invasion of the Hoffmans' privacy?

"Why not? Even if they don't get custody, it's a free country. They can stand outside the delivery room. They can stare at the babies in the hospital nursery all day and all night if they want to. They'll get generous visitation rights, won't they?"

"I don't know," Lisa lied.

"Yes, you do. I can see it in your face." She rose slowly. "I'm going to lie down. I know this wasn't easy for you, coming here to tell me. Thank you for not doing it over the phone."

"Do you want me to stay and tell Baruch? I don't mind."

"No. I'll tell him myself."

Like the last time Lisa had been here, both sides of the street were crowded with parked cars. Her Altima was halfway down the block from the Hoffmans, across the street.

It was dark outside and chilly. She hugged her arms as she

walked, lost in thought, reviewing her conversation with Naomi, wishing she'd been more reassuring, wondering if there were something she could have said.

She looked both ways, then stepped off the curb and moved sideways between two cars. She was in the middle of the street when she heard the revving of an engine. Startled, she whipped her head to her left.

A car, its headlights off, was speeding toward her.

She screamed. For a second she was frozen with fear, and her legs felt nailed to the asphalt. Then she ran toward the opposite curb, which was lined with cars separated only by inches.

The car swerved to find her. Now it was only a few feet away.

Taking a running leap, she hurled herself onto the hood of a car and slammed onto the metal. She grabbed the windshield wiper for support and scrambled forward, jerking her legs out of the way just as the car raced by and disappeared.

chapter thirty-five

Jerome Nestle was tall, trim, and good-looking, with short salt-and-pepper hair and tortoiseshell-framed glasses. He stood at Lisa's entrance and waved her into one of the two navy upholstered armchairs in front of his desk, then spent a few minutes studying the medical history form Lisa had filled out in the waiting room.

He looked up. "So you and your husband have decided to have a baby. It's an exciting time in your lives, a *wonderful* time."

His smile, which reached his brown eyes, seemed so warm, so genuine, that she wondered if she was wrong about him. "Jeff and I are *very* excited." She was nervous being here, nervous because of her near death last night, which she hadn't reported to the police. She hadn't seen a license plate, hadn't seen the driver. She didn't know what to do with her hands, which felt like encumbrances. She placed them on her lap.

"You're originally from Long Island, I see. Great Neck."

"Yes. We moved here about six months ago, when Jeff's firm asked him to open a new office. He's an investment counselor. I design computer systems for corporations, so it was easy for both of us to relocate."

She'd realized that one of the prerequisites for Nestle would be a patient who could afford to pay a fertility clinic's substantial fees. She'd decided not to "be" an attorney—Nestle might shy away from anyone connected with the law. Or medicine. "A broker found us a beautiful house in Brentwood," she added.

"Not on Bundy, I hope." He smiled.

She smiled, too. "No." He was referring to the condominium Nicole Simpson had lived in before she was brutally murdered.

"I see your New York gynecologist is Mark Harris. A fine doctor."

"Yes." Harris was chief of obstetrics at the hospital where Lisa had done her residency. She wasn't worried. By the time Nestle had someone phone for her records, this would all be over. "He referred me to you. He said you're the best."

"He's very kind." He smiled again. "May I call you Elysse?" When she nodded, he said, "You seem a bit nervous. Am I right?"

"I feel so silly." She laughed lightly. She'd been so nervous taking the elevator to Nestle's eighth-floor office in the Third Street medical towers that she'd almost changed her mind. "I've never worried about getting pregnant. Now that Jeff and I have decided to have a baby, I want to make sure everything's okay so we can begin trying."

"I'm certain you have nothing to be nervous about, Elysse. And coming here was wise. You'd be surprised how many women— *educated* women—don't realize the importance of making sure their bodies are *prepared* for pregnancy."

"I've been taking vitamins and folic acid."

"Excellent. You're doing your part. Now I'll do mine." Another smile. "We'll do a full exam, draw some blood so the lab can do a full panel, including making sure your hormone levels are right." He scanned her file again. "You've never had any gynecological problems—no surgeries, no condition that required medication, no physiological abnormalities, correct?"

She nodded, thinking how strange it was to be on this side of the desk.

"Your cycle is regular?"

"Yes." She crossed her legs.

"Good. Have you tried to get pregnant before, Elysse?"

"No. Jeff and I wanted to wait until both our careers were established."

"What kind of birth control have you been using?"

"A diaphragm." Nestle probably didn't choose women who were using IUDs—they might wonder why they were experiencing the same symptoms they'd had with the IUD after it had supposedly been removed.

"That's good." Nestle nodded. "For patients on the pill, I recommend a three-month interval after they stop taking the pill before they try to conceive."

Lisa expelled a breath. "Then I'm glad I'm not on the pill. Jeff and I hope I'll get pregnant right away."

"I hope so, too, Elysse. And there's no reason to think you won't." He smiled encouragingly. "But I should tell you that not everyone conceives easily—although high school students certainly seem to, don't they?"

"Yes." She forced another, larger smile for his joke. "I'm thirty-one. I know that can be a problem in terms of fertility."

"I wouldn't call it a *problem*. It's certainly a factor you and your husband should be aware of. But I don't want you to worry. Chances are, you'll conceive within the next few months."

"And if I don't?" She brought her fingers to her lips, flashing her large diamond ring. She'd been overcome with sadness when she'd put it on this morning.

"We'll show you how to chart your ovulation to make sure you take advantage of the right time every month. We can teach you relaxation techniques."

"And if I still don't conceive?" She made her voice urgent.

"After a year, if you're still not pregnant, I'd recommend diagnostic evaluations, including a procedure to see if your tubes are open and another that would allow us to see your pelvic organs. Your husband would have a semen analysis, of course. Assuming that he's fine and that you don't need surgery to correct any physiological problems, I'd start you on an oral fertility drug."

"Clomid, you mean. A friend of mine was on that. She's expecting twins."

"I've been using another fertility drug with excellent results that reduces the incidence of multiple births."

The placebo. "And if that doesn't work?" She saw a frown forming on the doctor's face. "I know I sound neurotic. Jeff says I'm compulsive in the way I need to know everything in advance." She half laughed and shook her head and saw Nestle relax.

"I'd refer you to a clinic that specializes in assisted reproduction, including in vitro fertilization. Unfortunately, that can run into tens of thousands of dollars."

Lisa leaned forward. "Money, thank goodness, isn't a problem. But we're concerned about fertility clinics after what we've heard in the news."

"I'm sure you know that you can't believe everything you hear in the news." He smiled yet again. "I happen to know the chairman of the board of directors and the doctors at the clinic under investigation. It's a wonderful clinic, and the doctors and lab staff are all excellent, all above reproach."

She frowned. "But the head director is missing, isn't he? They say there's evidence that he was killed. And I heard that the police confiscated the clinic's files and shut it down."

"It's terrible about Dr. Gordon—I'll bet we find out that his disappearance had nothing to do with the clinic. And I have every confidence that the police will determine that no embryo switching took place. I hope they do it quickly so that the clinic can reopen and help couples who are trying to conceive."

"And if the police find something illegal?" She knew she was pressing—she could see it on Nestle's face.

"I have connections with other excellent clinics. But you're worrying prematurely." He picked up his phone receiver. "Let's have that exam so I can reassure you that you're baby-ready."

An auburn-haired nurse took Lisa to a small open area off the hall, where she weighed Lisa and took her temperature, blood pressure, and pulse. After Lisa left a urine sample, the nurse led her to a pleasant examining room wallpapered in a soft beige-and-burgundy paisley pattern.

"You can hang your clothes over there," she said, pointing to a cubicle curtained in the same paisley. She handed her a white paper gown. "This goes on top and opens in the front. Doctor will be with you shortly."

The nurse left, and Lisa started to undress. She was in her bra and panties when she was suddenly frozen with indecision. What was she doing here, about to be examined by the man who might have attacked her, the man who might have killed Matthew? She heard a knock on the door.

"May I come in?" Nestle asked.

"Just a moment." With shaking hands she slipped off the rest of her clothes, put on the paper gown, and lay down on the examining table, covering herself with the paper sheet the nurse had left for her.

Nestle stepped inside and shut the door. "The nurse will be here in a moment. Still nervous?"

"A little." She smiled shyly.

"This will be over before you know it. Move down for me, Elysse, and put your feet in the stirrups. There's a good girl."

She hated being called "good girl," hated being called "sweetie" by doctors and assistants she hardly knew. She'd hated the thirtysomething gynecologist who, before examining her, had said, "Drop your pants, honey, I'll be right back," while she'd shrunk, mortified, within herself. And she hated Nestle, though he hadn't said or done one wrong thing, because she knew he was evil. She moved down obediently and placed her feet in the cold metal stirrups, watching as he slipped on latex gloves. She tried not to think about her assailant, who had worn gloves, too; tried not to shiver as she felt his hands around her neck, squeezing.

The nurse knocked and entered the room. Nestle nodded at her and began the examination.

"You're very tense, Elysse," he said softly as he probed. "Try to relax."

She took a deep breath and wondered how he would insert the IUD with the nurse present.

"Your right ovary is fine. So is your left. I don't feel any masses." He closed his eyes. "Your uterus is sound, the size of a large walnut. Perfect. Everything seems excellent, Elysse." He smiled warmly and lifted a speculum from the counter. "Now I'm going to take a cervical sample for a Pap smear. I'm inserting the speculum. It'll feel cold. Try to relax," he said again a moment later, gently pushing her knees apart.

"Okay." Her lips were dry. She licked them.

He turned to the counter again, then faced the nurse. He was frowning. "Denise, we're low on swabs." He sounded disapproving. "Would you get some? And bring a box of mounting slides, too."

"Yes, Doctor." She left the room.

This was it, Lisa thought. Nestle had his back to her. She lifted her head and craned her neck and saw him tear off the sterile plastic cover of an intrauterine device attached to the insertion tube. Her heart beat faster.

"You'll feel a little pinching, Elysse, and possibly a slight cramping sensation, but it shouldn't last long."

"I've never had cramping before with a Pap smear," she said, injecting into her voice just a hint of anxiety. She grabbed the edges of the examining table to steady her shaking hands.

He turned around. "Well, it's nothing to worry about. I like to take a sample higher up than some physicians do. You get a more accurate reading. You may experience a little spotting, too. That's normal."

She knew he was holding the IUD, but she couldn't see it. She pressed her feet against the stirrups.

There was a knock on the door. She turned her head and saw a different nurse enter the room.

"Dr. Nestle, I'm sorry to interrupt, but Nancy Bartholomew is on the line. She says she has to talk with you immediately."

Lisa felt faint, nauseated. Nancy Bartholomew was one of the patients she'd spoken to yesterday, who had been referred by Nestle.

Nestle frowned. "I'm in the middle of a procedure here, Patty. Tell her I'll call her back later."

"I told her you were with a patient. She said she left a message with your service yesterday. She says it's urgent."

Lisa's hands were clammy. She took another deep breath. If a nurse took her blood pressure now, she'd be shocked.

"Have Dr. Jorgen talk to her," Nestle said.

"She insists on talking only to you."

"Tell her I'll be with her in five minutes," he said brusquely. After the nurse left the room, he smiled at Lisa. "Sorry about that. This won't take long."

She felt as if a fist were blocking her air pipes.

"You're shaking, Elysse. Really, this won't hurt." He worked silently, then said, "There, that's it. I should have the results of the Pap smear in a week."

She started to move back on the table when a menstrual-like cramp seized her. She winced.

"Lie still for a moment until the cramping stops. I have to take this call—I won't be more than a few minutes. Then I'll complete your exam." He patted her knee, peeled off his gloves, which he discarded in a round trash can, and left.

She had a minute, maybe two, before he returned to confront her. She was still cramping. Removing her legs from the stirrups, she hurried off the bed and tore off the paper gown, which she threw on the floor. She yanked open the curtain to the cubicle and, her hands shaking, put on her navy straight skirt and pumps. She pulled her cream lace camisole over her head, slipped on her blazer, and stuffed her bra, panties, and pantyhose into her purse. She was about to leave when she spotted the folder with her file on top of a cabinet. Opening the folder, she found the page with Nestle's handwritten notes and put it in her purse.

She opened the door an inch and looked to the right and left. Nestle wasn't in sight. With her heart hammering wildly in her chest, she exited the room and was heading quickly for the waiting room when she came face-to-face with Denise. The nurse was holding a box of slides and another box of swabs.

"Oh, you're all done, Mrs. Landes. I know that Dr. Nestle will want to talk to you before you leave."

"I have to put money in the parking meter," she managed to say. Her chest was tight. Her legs were blocks of wood.

"You definitely don't want to get a ticket." The nurse smiled and walked on.

Lisa entered the waiting room and half ran through it, ignoring the stares of the women sitting on the upholstered chairs.

"Mrs. Landes, you forgot to make a payment!" called the brown-haired receptionist, who had been nice enough to get Lisa this last-minute appointment.

"I'll be right back," Lisa said without turning around. "I'm going to feed the meter."

She raced down the long, wide hall and turned left to the bank of elevators. She pressed the down button and tapped her foot and darted anxious glances to the left every few seconds, expecting to see Nestle's handsome face glaring at her.

The elevator pinged its arrival. The doors glided open. It was vacant. She stepped inside, pressed herself against the wall of the elevator, and, clutching her abdomen, breathed again.

chapter thirty-six

"Please don't worry about a thing, Nancy. You were absolutely right to call me." Jerome Nestle placed the receiver in its cradle.

He left his office, stopping to observe himself in a mirror halfway down the hall. He was proud of the fact that his face didn't reveal the rage and fear threatening to consume him. He walked back to the examining room and forced a smile as he opened the door.

She was gone.

She'd obviously recognized the name the nurse had announced. Stupid cow.

Although what would he have done if the woman were here?

He clenched his hands and returned to his office, ignoring the call of one of the other nurses. He shut the door and went over to his desk and picked up the phone. He was upset to see that his hand was shaking.

He dialed a number and waited.

Finally someone answered. "Hello?"

"I believe that Dr. Lisa Brockman was just here," Nestle said. "She knows."

chapter thirty-seven

Lisa was sitting at Barone's desk in the large, partitioned detectives' room at Hollywood Division. It was ten-fifteen, forty-five minutes earlier than they'd agreed to meet. She'd used her cell phone to make certain he was at the station. She barely recalled driving here and didn't remember that she wasn't wearing underwear until she arrived. In one of the rest-room stalls, she put on her bra and panties and hose and told herself that one day she'd be laughing about this. Right now she didn't feel like laughing.

First she told him about the car. "It wasn't an accident, Detective. The driver was definitely trying to kill me. He had his headlights off." She'd relived the incident in her dreams and woken up several times, bathed in sweat, trembling. She wasn't sure, but she might have screamed aloud. "I didn't call the police because I didn't have a license plate or anything to tell them."

"Could you tell what kind of car it was?"

"Something low and sporty. I'm sorry." She smiled lightly.

"I'm not good about cars, and it happened so fast." Ted Cantrell drove a Porsche, she remembered suddenly.

"What about the color?"

"Not light. It could've been red or black or dark green or blue. Sorry," she said again. "I brought the donor problem files and the protected lists. They're in my trunk."

"I'll get someone to help me bring them in."

"Before you do, there's something else you should know."

He listened impassively, as he always did, while she explained her suspicions about Nestle. With every word she uttered, she realized her story sounded impossibly melodramatic. "I know it sounds crazy, but that's what he did." She wished Barone would react. Even skepticism would be preferable to his blank, controlled expression.

Barone was tapping his pencil on his desk, staring into space. "Explain again why he's doing this."

"As a partner in the clinic, he wants it to turn a large profit. There are more and more clinics, Detective. What draws patients to a specific one isn't the doctor's bedside manner. It's the success rate."

Barone nodded. "You said you spoke to two of his patients. How many files did you examine?"

"A little over a hundred. There are two more Nestle patients in that random sample—one just started an IVF cycle. The other is pregnant, but I couldn't reach her."

"Would three pregnancies alter the statistics enough to justify the risk of what he's doing?"

"He probably doesn't think there *is* a risk. One of our rival clinics claims forty percent success rates for women under thirty-five. Our new brochure says we have a forty-four percent success rate. In my random sample, seventeen of thirty-seven patients under thirty-five are pregnant. That's forty-six percent. If you remove Nestle's three pregnant referrals, that's fourteen pregnancies. Thirty-eight percent."

"An enormous difference. I see what you mean."

"I'm positive that if we examined all one thousand files, we'd find more of Nestle's patients who didn't need assisted reproduction. I'm sure he's involved with this refund-donor egg scam, too."

Barone pulled on his mustache. "But you have no proof."

"Not about the donor eggs. But I *can* prove what's he's doing with the IUDs. I just came from his office. I told him I wanted to get pregnant. He inserted an IUD." She delivered this last information with a triumphant toss of her head, then shivered again at the memory.

"You went to Nestle's office?" The detective's stare was incredulous. "If you're right about him, do you have any idea how *reckless* that was?" His voice was uncharacteristically loud.

Finally she'd elicited a reaction. "I was terrified, but how else could I get proof?" She leaned forward. "Nestle has to be working with someone at the clinic on the refund scam. I think he'll probably invest in another clinic that has a refund policy and work the same scam—he assured me that if the Westwood clinic closes, he's well connected with other clinics. Don't you agree that this gives him a motive for murdering Matthew?"

"He could have been working *with* Dr. Gordon," Barone said, looking at her intently.

"He could have. Maybe Matthew worried too much about the clinic losing patients." The admission was painful, but she didn't flinch. "When Chelsea was murdered, Nestle must have panicked—he knew the clinic would be investigated. I think he killed Matthew to keep him from telling the police about his involvement and set Matthew up to deflect suspicion from himself." She sighed. "Or maybe Matthew *didn't* know."

Barone didn't respond right away. Finally he said, "You're sure Nestle inserted an IUD?" He was avoiding looking at her now, clearly uncomfortable discussing this with her.

"I saw him tear off the packaging on the IUD insertion tube. I saw him hold it. And I had cramping afterward, which I expected. Can you get a warrant for his arrest?"

Another silence. Barone was tweaking his mustache again. "Nestle will say you had the IUD when you came to see him."

"I went to my own gynecologist early this morning—I convinced her I had an emergency. She did an exam and can testify that I didn't have an IUD as of eight-thirty this morning."

Barone chuckled. "You amaze me, Dr. Brockman. Are you sure you haven't chosen the wrong profession?"

She smiled. "I have the placebos Nestle gave one of his patients. If we contact all his referrals, I'm sure we'll find corroboration about the pills, about everything. Maybe he's the one who attacked me Sunday night." She frowned. "Although I don't know how he got into the building. I'm sure I set the alarm."

"If Nestle killed Dr. Gordon, he'd have his keys." Barone rose. "Let me talk to my lieutenant."

★   ★   ★

She felt infinitely better sitting in Nestle's handsomely furnished office with Barone next to her than she had this morning, alone. She was impressed with the doctor's outward calm. If he was worried, he wasn't showing it.

"I don't understand, Detective," Nestle said with an air of sincere bewilderment after Barone had introduced himself. "If anyone should be pressing charges, *I* should. Mrs. Landes rushed out of here without paying for her examination and for the procedure I performed. She wrote a false phone number on the medical form she filled out—my secretary tried to contact her about her bill. She probably gave a false name, too." He stared icily at Lisa.

"My name is Dr. Lisa Brockman. I think Nancy Bartholomew told you that when she phoned this morning." Lisa looked at him coolly. It felt wonderfully satisfying, after so many days of hazy confusion, to be confronting the enemy.

He furrowed his forehead. "Should I know your name?"

"I'm on the staff at the clinic of which you're a silent partner, the same clinic to which you refer patients for fertility treatments after you prevent them from becoming pregnant by inserting IUDs."

"You're Dr. Gordon's fiancée." His voice was suddenly soft with compassion. Sighing, he turned to Barone. "I had no idea until this minute who this woman was. Mrs. Bartholomew phoned because she heard the clinic was shut down, and she was concerned about being drawn into an investigation of embryo switching." He faced Lisa again. "Dr. Brockman, naturally you're distraught over your fiancé's disappearance. That explains why you're not thinking or acting rationally. Under the circumstances, I'll waive my fee and forgive the confusion and embarrassment you've caused me."

He was good, Lisa thought. She wanted to retort but knew she'd be playing his game.

"You mentioned that you performed a procedure," Barone said.

"Yes." Nestle tented his hands. "I inserted an IUD, as per Mrs. Landes's request. Sorry, I mean Dr. Brockman's."

She stared at him, openmouthed. He was so clever, she wanted to strangle him.

"She didn't tell you she wanted to have a baby?" Barone asked in the same polite voice. "That she came here for an exam to make sure she was in good health?"

Nestle nodded his head vigorously. "Yes, she did. She said the same thing to my receptionist yesterday when she begged her for an immediate appointment. This morning she sat in this same chair"—he pointed to Lisa—"and told me she and her husband were anxious to have a baby right away. Of course I believed her. Why wouldn't I?" He regarded Lisa with sad accusation.

"So why did you insert an IUD, Doctor?"

"She changed her mind. She was extremely nervous on the examining table. Ask my nurse—she'll tell you I had to calm Dr. Brockman down several times. You can't deny that, can you?" he asked Lisa.

She didn't respond but forced herself to look at him.

Nestle addressed Barone again. "When I completed the Pap smear, she started crying. She said that her husband was pushing her to have a baby, that she wasn't ready."

"That's a lie," she said calmly, though she was filled with a leadlike dread.

"That's when she asked me for an IUD. She didn't want to tell her husband she'd changed her mind. She wanted to use birth control he wouldn't be aware of. I asked her if she wanted time to think. She said no. So I complied with her wishes."

Everything she'd done was useless—coming here this morning, subjecting herself to his examination, letting him insert an IUD, taking the sheet with his notes. She thought she'd been clever, going to her own gynecologist earlier, but Nestle was having the last laugh. She had no proof now. She clenched her hands and bit the inside of her cheek, choking with anger and frustration. Barone was avoiding looking at her. She wondered if he was angry at her for wasting his time.

"And will your nurse testify to all this?" Barone asked.

Nestle sighed. "Unfortunately, I had just sent Denise for some specimen slides and swabs. You'd think, with all our inventory on the computer, I wouldn't have to deal with this problem." He smiled. "Anyway, after inserting the IUD, I told Dr. Brockman to lie down until the cramping stopped, and left to speak with Mrs. Bartholomew. When I returned, Dr. Brockman was gone. I felt duped."

He turned to Lisa. "I should be angry at you for trying to trick me, but I pity you. Obviously you need to blame someone for what happened to the clinic, to Dr. Gordon." He was trying not to look smug, but Lisa saw the pull at the corners of his lips.

"How can you refer fertile women for assisted reproduction?"

Lisa asked, knowing she was probably giving him satisfaction, that she'd lost. "How can you live with yourself?"

"Dr. Brockman, every patient I've referred to the clinic has tried unsuccessfully for at least a year to conceive."

"It's hard getting pregnant when you're using birth control. The patients I spoke to described symptoms consistent with having an IUD. And those fertility pills you gave them?" She opened her purse and took out a plastic bag with the orange-and-white capsules. "A pharmacist told me this is a placebo. It doesn't do much to promote conception."

Nestle leaned back. "For your information, *Doctor*, I gave certain patients placebos because, in my estimation, after diagnostic tests ruled out any abnormalities, their anxiety about conceiving was preventing conception. I wanted them to relax so that their Fallopian tubes wouldn't contract and prevent the passage of the egg."

"You have an answer for everything, don't you?"

The doctor pushed back his chair. "I think that's all cleared up, Detective. I'm sorry you had to waste your time."

Barone was rising. Lisa couldn't believe it was all over. She was about to stand, too, when she had a sudden thought.

"What about your inventory, Dr. Nestle?" she asked.

He frowned. "My inventory?"

"I'm sure you keep an accurate record of supplies so that you don't run low. Swabs, for example. Specimen slides. Gloves. And, of course, intrauterine devices. I bet that if we checked your inventory records, we'd find a discrepancy between the number of IUDs inserted in and charged to patients and the number ordered and still in stock."

Barone was sitting again. He gave her a quick smile and studied Nestle.

The doctor glared at Lisa. "I've been more than patient, Dr. Brockman, but I won't subject myself to any more of this."

Barone said, "I think it *would* be interesting to examine your inventory records." He turned to Lisa. "How many patients are we talking about, Dr. Brockman?"

"From my random sample, two confirmed, one probable. If we checked all the files, I think we'd find about twenty-five to thirty patients within a year's period. Maybe more."

"This is ridiculous!" Nestle's voice was shaking with anger, but he was sitting down and his face had paled.

"So an inventory check would show thirty or so IUDs unaccounted for?" Barone said, ignoring him.

"Yes."

He addressed Nestle. "There's an easy way to prove Dr. Brockman wrong. Can I look at your inventory?"

"No, you may not! This is a medical practice, not a warehouse."

Barone smiled. "I'm not asking to see patient files, Doctor. Just an inventory analysis—which you said is on the computer."

"I'm sorry. I'd like to cooperate, but I have no intention of inconveniencing my staff and patients to humor Dr. Brockman."

"Humor *me*, then, Doctor," Barone said quietly.

Nestle shook his head. "Dr. Brockman has fabricated this entire scenario. Why would I *do* such a crazy thing?"

"Because you're a partner in the clinic, and negative press about fertility clinics caused a drop in new patients," Lisa said. "And there were more and more clinics. So you inflated the Westwood clinic's success rate by referring fertile women. And you encouraged the use of donor eggs, without the recipient's knowledge or consent, for clinic patients on the refund policy."

He stared at her. "You're emotionally disturbed, you know. You should seek professional help."

"I have." She smiled. "That's why Detective Barone is here."

"Who's your contact at the clinic?" Barone asked.

Nestle frowned. "I don't know what you're talking about."

"Is it Dr. Cantrell? Dr. Davidson? The lab director? It would be better for you if you cooperated with us."

The gynecologist pressed his palms against the edge of his desk and leaned forward. "Don't you understand? I have no knowledge of donor eggs being used without the recipient's consent. I'm a silent partner—I know nothing about the clinic operations. I invested money. I'm pleased when I get a decent return, but I'm hardly dependent on the clinic for my livelihood. I have a thriving practice that allows me to live quite comfortably."

"Or maybe you worked with Dr. Gordon," Barone said as if Nestle hadn't spoken. "Is that why you killed him? Is that why you engineered his disappearance—to make him look guilty?"

Nestle slumped back against his chair. "You can't seriously believe I killed Matthew!" His voice shook. His face, sagging and drained of color, resembled raw dough.

Barone raised his brows in exaggerated surprise. "I didn't know you and Dr. Gordon were on a first-name basis. What happened?

Did you panic? Did he threaten to tell the police of your involvement? Good-bye thriving practice, hello jail."

"I'm not going to answer any more questions." Beads of perspiration lined his upper lip.

"Why not, Dr. Nestle? Unless you're hiding something." The detective stood. "I'm taking you in for questioning."

"I don't have to go, not unless you arrest me. I know my rights."

"If you prefer, I can arrest you." Barone nodded. "I can show probable cause for fraud and subpoena your inventory files. I can probably convince the D.A. to charge you with murder, or accessory to."

Barone's musical voice sounded like a sonata to Lisa.

"I didn't kill Matthew! I have nothing to tell you!" Nestle was blinking furiously. His eyes were darting back and forth.

"I can arrest you and read you your rights and handcuff you," Barone said. "Or you can come in voluntarily for questioning. It's your choice."

The doctor seemed to be cemented to his seat. Barone had to repeat his name sternly before he rose, unsteadily, to his feet. "I have appointments scheduled outside the office."

"Have your receptionist cancel them."

"And say what? That I've been taken in for questioning by the police for something I didn't do?" A little of his bluster had returned.

"You can say you're assisting us in our investigation."

The brown-haired receptionist was on the phone when Nestle, followed by Barone and Lisa, approached her counter.

"Next Tuesday at three is fine," she said and hung up. She fixed her eyes on her employer and avoided looking at Lisa.

"Detective Barone needs my help, so I'll be gone for a while, Katherine," he told her. "Please cancel my afternoon appointments. Check my desk calendar."

"Yes, of course, Doctor." The phone rang. She lifted the receiver and said, "Dr. Nestle's office. Can you hold a minute, please? I see." She put the caller on hold. "It's Paula Rhodes. She sounds anxious. Do you want to talk to her?"

Barone and Lisa exchanged surprised looks.

Nestle took the receiver and pressed the hold button. "Paula? Dr. Nestle. What's wrong, dear?" He started to frown. "You're sure it's not your period?" He listened for a moment. "Well, don't be alarmed. This isn't uncommon postpartum. If the bleeding continues, come in tomorrow morning and I'll take a look. We may have to do a D and C. All right. Yes. Please don't worry." He handed the receiver to the receptionist. "Pencil in a half-hour appointment for Mrs. Rhodes at ten tomorrow morning."

Lisa wondered if the doctor was being optimistic, scheduling appointments. She was even more curious about the fact that Paula Rhodes was his patient.

"Is that the Mrs. Rhodes whose husband died recently?" she asked Nestle as they were waiting for the elevator.

"I don't gossip about my patients, Dr. Brockman," he snapped. "But yes, her husband died five months ago, when she was pregnant. She's a brave, wonderful woman who's been through hell, so before you add her to your list of patients to harass, let me tell you she conceived without any problem and never stepped foot in that damn clinic." He glared at her. "Any *more* questions?"

She had many more questions, but she wasn't even sure what they all were.

chapter thirty-eight

"There's good news and bad news," Barone told Lisa when he phoned her at the Presslers three hours later. "I convinced a judge to issue a subpoena immediately so that we can examine Nestle's inventory. I'm heading to his office right now."

"And the bad news?" She'd been sitting around doing nothing, waiting for the detective's call. She would have loved to have been in the room when Nestle was interrogated.

"Technically, we can hold him for forty-eight hours without charging him, but his lawyer is demanding an immediate OR release."

"What's 'OR'?"

" 'Own recognizance.' He's arguing that Nestle's a highly respected physician and member of the community, that we have no proof of wrongdoing. The D.A. is leaning toward releasing him until we get evidence."

She frowned. "What about the fact that he inserted the IUDs? That's fraudulent medicine, isn't it?"

"We have to prove it first. And we have to get at least one patient to file a complaint. I went to see Nancy Bartholomew and Nedda Flom. Neither one is ready to file."

Lisa was dumbfounded. "Why not?"

"Mrs. Bartholomew refuses to believe that Nestle gave her an IUD. She's furious with you, with me, with everyone who's trying to railroad him, as she puts it. I sensed that Mrs. Flom *believes* it's possible but doesn't want to get involved."

"Isn't she angry at Nestle for what he did?"

"She's having a baby—that's all she cares about. She doesn't want to get dragged into a trial. Maybe in a few days or weeks she'll think about it, get furious, and give me a call. As for Mrs. Bartholomew, she's had a long relationship with Nestle. He helped her get pregnant. She believed he was her savior and doesn't want to think she's been deceived."

"But what he did is grasping and unethical! And he may be a murderer." Lisa couldn't believe this was happening. She had an urge to confront both women and shake them until they saw reason.

"You don't have to convince me. I ran a DMV check on him, by the way. He drives a black Lamborghini."

She was going stir crazy, sitting around doing nothing. She remembered that she still hadn't straightened up her bedroom. She drove to her apartment and checked her mail, then put a load of laundry in the washing machine in the basement. Back upstairs she listened to her phone messages—Sam, Edmond. Sam again.

She finished the bedroom, then decided to call Paula Rhodes. Nestle said she'd conceived without difficulty, that she'd never gone to the clinic—but what if he was lying? What if Paula was another of his "IUD" referrals? What if, unlike Nancy Bartholomew and Nedda Flom, she'd be willing to file a complaint?

She phoned the house, and the maid answered. A minute later Paula came on the line.

"I'm glad you called, Dr. Brockman. I've been thinking about you. Did Detective Barone find the man who impersonated him?"

"No." Could that have been Nestle? "I was wondering whether you'd remembered anything else about him."

"No, sorry. I hope you're being careful."

"I am. How are you? And how's Andy?" She remembered that Paula had been anxious about her baby.

She sighed. "I'm having women troubles—my OB said it's normal post-baby bleeding. Andy's okay, I guess."

"You sound unsure."

"The pediatrician said he's fine. He said there's nothing unusual about a baby not breathing for a few seconds. But he said to watch for any more episodes, and if Andy becomes limp or turns a different color, to call immediately. He didn't say, but I know what he's worried about—SIDS. My cousin's daughter died of that. Lorraine put her to sleep. In the morning she was gone. Just like that. I guess that's why I'm neurotic."

Sudden infant death syndrome. There were usually no symptoms for this heartbreaking killer. But there *were* risk factors, chief among which were premature birth and other incidents of SIDS in the family. Andy was a preemie, Lisa recalled. "Have you been putting Andy to sleep on his back?"

"Oh, yes. And I've been sleeping on the day bed in his room. If you can call it sleep." She laughed lightly. "I'm up most of the night, checking him. The pediatrician thinks I'm a worrier. What if he's wrong? What if I should be doing something?"

"Do you smoke?"

"No, why?"

"Smoking contributes to SIDS. Also, don't leave stuffed animals in his crib. By the way, you mentioned that Andy was born premature. Did you have a difficult pregnancy?" She hated asking for information under false pretenses, but she had to know.

"Not at all. I conceived almost right away, and I didn't worry about a thing because I have the most wonderful OB. Jerome Nestle. Andrew found him—I think one of his cousins used him. Do you know Dr. Nestle?"

"We met just recently." She filled a glass with water and noticed that her hand was shaking.

"I'm going to see him tomorrow, about the bleeding. He's the one who got me through Andrew's death, by the way. He said I had to stay healthy for the baby. So you don't think I have to worry about Andy?" The anxiety was back in her voice.

Lisa was disappointed about Nestle, though she was pleased, for Paula's sake, that the woman wasn't one of his victims. "If you're that anxious, you can buy a special monitor. You can get one at any medical-supply store."

"How do they work?"

"You strap it around the baby's chest. The machine monitors the baby's breathing pattern and heart rate. You can set the alarm to go off if he stops breathing for longer than fifteen seconds, or if his heartbeat drops below a certain rate."

"If Andy has another episode, I'll get one. Thanks, Dr. Brockman. I feel better just knowing there's something I can do."

"I'm glad. And Paula, if you remember anything about this man who impersonated Detective Barone, call me?"

"Of course I will. Right away."

In her dream, she was on an examination table. A masked figure was looming over her, holding a scalpel. "Hagar didn't abandon her child," he said. She sat up and reached forward to tear off his mask, but he shoved her down and shook her and whispered her name, over and over.

"Lisa, wake up."

She forced her eyes open and saw Elana. She pulled herself up quickly. "What's wrong? What time is it?"

"It's a little after two," Elana said in a low voice. "Sam's on the phone. He says it's urgent, or I wouldn't have woken you."

They found Matthew. Her heart lurched. She flipped back the blanket and stood up, then moved to the desk. "I'm sorry he woke you. I hope he didn't wake the kids."

"Don't worry about it." Elana slipped quietly out of the room.

Picking up the receiver, Lisa said, "Sam?" in a tight voice and held her breath.

"Ted Cantrell's dead." Sam's voice shook. "He killed himself."

chapter thirty-nine

"The police notified Edmond," Sam said. "Edmond phoned me. They're not sure whether it was planned or accidental. Apparently Ted took quite a few tranquilizers and was drinking."

This made no sense. "He's a doctor," she said impatiently. "He knows that's lethal."

"That's why they're not sure. His ex-wife found him. It seems she came to collect some alimony checks he owed her." Sam sighed. "Poor Ted. I didn't like him much, but this . . ."

"Why would he kill himself, Sam? Did they find a note?"

"Edmond didn't say." He paused. "Lisa, the police found Matthew's wallet and a Raymond Weil watch in Ted's bedroom. The watch was inscribed to him."

Matthew—I love you. Lisa. She'd given him the watch when they became engaged. "You think *Ted* killed Matthew?" she whispered. She didn't know why she was shocked—it wasn't as though the possibility had never crossed her mind. Had Ted tried to run her down in his Porsche? But what about Nestle? Did that mean he wasn't involved with Matthew's murder? With the egg switching?

"It looks like it. Edmond says the guilt probably weighed on him, so he took the drugs and drank. A painless way to go. I guess Ted's the one who attacked us the other night at the clinic. Maybe he thought you were looking for evidence that he stole Matthew's research. Did Barone ever follow up on that?"

She'd given up on the research theft as a motive some time ago and realized she'd never told Sam. "Barone checked with all the fertility clinics Chelsea could have gone to. He showed her picture—no one recognized her. And no one approached anyone about research on freezing eggs."

"Really? There goes that theory. Barone must be thrilled with me for wasting his time." He grunted.

She almost told Sam about the egg switching and Nestle; something kept her back. She wanted to talk to Barone first. "Actually, I found out something weird about Chelsea." She told him about her talk with Chelsea's boyfriend, about her call to Felicia Perry. "Can you imagine, Sam? Someone's been harassing these donors when they're in Recovery."

"I can believe the harassing. But you think this guy *murdered* Chelsea?" He sounded skeptical.

" 'Punished.' Think about his warning, Sam. It makes sense."

"Where did you get Felicia Perry's name?"

From the donor list. But she couldn't tell Sam; he didn't know she had a copy. She wet her lips and thought quickly. "I found it when I checked the computer for Chelsea's recipient."

"Why would you do that?"

"I don't remember what I was thinking at the time. Why are you interrogating me?"

"I'm not." He sounded surprised, aggrieved. "Look, it's late, and we're both upset about Ted. I'll talk to you in the morning, okay?"

"Okay." She hung up the phone and wondered suddenly whether Nestle was still being held when Ted had killed himself.

"They let Nestle out at five-thirty," Barone told her when she arrived at the station at ten o'clock in the morning. "Dr. Cantrell's ex-wife found his body at nine-thirty. They haven't done an autopsy yet, but from other signs—rigor, the color of the body—the medical examiner thinks Cantrell died around eight."

"Do you think Ted killed Matthew?" Barone had asked her to come down here, and she wasn't sure why.

"I don't know. I'm in touch with the detectives on his case—West L.A. is handling the investigation. They promised to keep me informed. You know they found Dr. Gordon's wallet and watch?" he asked gently.

"Yes. But the police searched his apartment on Tuesday, when they confiscated his files, the same day they confiscated my things. Wouldn't they have found them then?"

Barone shook his head. "They weren't homicide detectives searching for Dr. Gordon's murderer, Dr. Brockman. They were looking for evidence of medical malpractice."

"You're right." She played with the clasp on her purse. "So what about Nestle?"

"I have copies of the inventory files. I'm going through them today."

"I think he killed Ted. Either Ted was his accomplice, or he made him a scapegoat, just like he did with Matthew."

"It's possible." Barone sounded guarded.

"You don't think he did it?"

"There's been an interesting development. That's why I asked you to come to the station. My partner and I went to Norman Weld's apartment this morning. He was reluctant to let us in, but in the end he did. Right in front of us, on his dinette table, he had a stack of pamphlets warning against the use of donor eggs." Barone pulled over a sheet of cream-colored parchment paper and handed it to Lisa.

She read the flowery text full of biblical references, including one to the passage from Genesis. "Hagar, Sarah's handmaid, abandoned Ishmael and left him to die in the desert when she was cast out of the house of Abraham, for she could not bear to hear him cry. God called to Hagar and promised that if she took care of her son, he would grow to be a mighty nation. And Hagar listened to the Almighty. And He spared the child and the mother. Beware, daughters of Israel and of Christ our Lord. If you continue to abandon your babies, if you leave them to cry, the wrath of the Lord will be visited upon you . . ."

"Weld admitted to us that he'd authored the text himself," Barone said. "He seemed pleased, actually. Lucky for us the pamphlets were in plain view. We didn't have a search warrant."

"Did you ask him if he harassed Chelsea and the others?"

Barone nodded. "He denied it at first, but then he broke down and cried. He said he was responsible for Chelsea's death, and he was sorry."

She inhaled sharply. Her breath whistled through her teeth. "He admitted he killed her?"

"He wouldn't elaborate, and then he refused to talk. So we brought him in. He wants to talk to you, Dr. Brockman."

She was taken aback. "Why me?"

"He wouldn't say. Maybe he'll tell you what happened. He's here, in the jail. You'll be perfectly safe."

She hesitated, then said, "All right," in a voice so low the detective could barely hear her.

Norman was sitting cross-legged on the narrow cot in his cell. He was hugging his arms and rocking back and forth, keening.

Barone said, "Mr. Weld, Dr. Brockman is here to see you."

He was still rocking, still moaning.

Barone rattled the bars of the cell and called Weld's name louder. Norman turned around. When he saw Lisa, he shut his eyes.

"I knew you'd come," he said. "God answered my prayers."

"Let me go inside to talk to him," Lisa told Barone. She watched him signal to the guard, who unlocked the cell door. It clanged shut behind her.

"I can't talk if *he's* there." Norman pointed at Barone.

"Pretend he's not there," Lisa said softly. "Pretend we're alone." She sat on a hard chair three feet from the cot and Norman. His face was haggard and tear-streaked. His eyes were owlish.

"I'm so sorry about Dr. Gordon," he said. "You believe me, don't you?"

"Yes. You prayed for him, Norman. That was very kind."

"I *had* to pray for him! I prayed for that girl, too. Chelsea Wright. And for Dr. Cantrell. I'm responsible."

She was chilled to the bone. "What do you mean, Norman?"

"I have the gift of prophecy. I hear the Lord's commands, and I follow them."

Her tongue seemed frozen to her palate. "What does God tell you to do, Norman?" she asked gently.

"To warn those who do evil. To warn those who don't heed His bidding. To tell them He will strike them down and wreak His vengeance!" His eyes had a wild, feverish glint.

"And does God ask you to carry out His vengeance for Him?" Lisa asked, careful to keep her intonation bland.

"Sometimes," he whispered, nodding. "Sometimes."

"Did God ask you to punish Chelsea Wright?"

"I told her she would be punished, and she was." He was rocking again. "So I was right. I'm responsible."

"Because she donated eggs a second time? Is that why, Norman? Because she didn't listen to the first warning?"

His eyes became unfocused. "What?"

She repeated the question.

"I warned her, and she was punished. I'm responsible."

"What about Dr. Gordon? Did you warn him, too?"

"I prayed he would stop what the clinic was doing. And he stopped, didn't he?"

"Did you punish him, Norman?" she whispered. Her heart was racing, thumping against her chest.

"They didn't listen, so I had to put a stop to it. You see that, don't you?"

"You mean Dr. Gordon and Dr. Cantrell? Is that who you mean, Norman? Did you punish Dr. Cantrell?"

"I don't know." He frowned. "I prayed it would stop, so it did."

"Where is Dr. Gordon, Norman?"

"He's dead, isn't he? So is Dr. Cantrell. I'm responsible." He was weeping now, his face scrunched up in pain.

"Did you kill them, Norman?"

"I don't know!" he moaned. "I prayed it would stop, and it did! I didn't want them to die, but they did, so I'm responsible. I am my brother's keeper!"

She flinched at his anger and grabbed onto the sides of her chair. "Why did you want to talk to me, Norman?" she asked when she saw that he was more composed.

"To tell you I'm sorry," he murmured. "To tell you I'm responsible. I don't want you to die, too." He gazed at her lovingly.

She was paralyzed with fear. "Did God tell you to punish me, too, Norman?"

"He said to warn you. He said it had to stop. I offered to pray with you, but you refused. I knew then that I had sinned. I tried to stop it, but Dr. Gordon died anyway. And now Dr. Cantrell is dead, too."

"How did you try to stop it, Norman?"

He smiled. "I called the purveyors of smut because I knew there was no other way, because she was dead. I told them about the evil."

Norman had started the rumors? "You told the media we were switching embryos?"

"God bade me to stop the evil, so I did." Rocking again.

"Did God bid you to kill Chelsea Wright?"

"I'm responsible."

"Did God bid you to kill Dr. Gordon?"

"I'm responsible." Rocking faster, harder.

"Norman—"

Suddenly he stopped. "I'm tired now." He lay on his side and assumed a fetal position, his knees tucked into his chest. He shut his eyes.

chapter forty

"I appreciate your coming," Howard Melman said. "After our last conversation, I wasn't sure you would."

"You said it was urgent." Lisa had called her machine from the police station and heard Melman's message and wondered.

He nodded. "I thought about what you said, about my letting my anger prevent me from helping catch Chelsea's killer. And now I hear that another clinic doctor was killed. Ted Cantrell." He tightened his lips.

"Did you know him?"

"No. That's not the point." He leaned forward. "Tell me again what Chelsea told Dr. Gordon."

"She said she wanted to donate eggs again. He told her that because her ovaries were hyperstimulated last time, he couldn't allow her to do it."

"Something's wrong. Very wrong." Melman's brow was furrowed with worry. "Chelsea *couldn't* have donated eggs. She'd stopped ovulating after she donated the eggs—that's almost a year ago."

Lisa frowned. "Are you sure?"

"They told her at the clinic that after she stopped taking the fertility drugs, it might take a few months before she started ovulating again. Six months later she still wasn't ovulating. So she came to me."

This explained Melman's anger at the clinic and its doctors.

"I took a few tests and told her not to worry, that it takes longer with some women for their natural cycle to kick in, and that stress would only make it worse. She tried to be patient, but when she came here just before I left for my vacation, she still hadn't ovulated, and she was depressed, like I told you. Cried and cried like her heart was broken." Melman shook his head.

"What happened?"

"She'd been reading up on egg donation and learned there could be complications later, fertility problems. Maybe ovarian cancer. So she was worried that she and Dennis—that's her boyfriend—wouldn't be able to have kids."

Lisa felt a wave of pity for Chelsea. "She didn't tell him?"

"She was afraid to. She was afraid to tell her parents, too. She was walking around with the weight of the world on her shoulders, poor thing." He flashed an angry look at Lisa. "I tried to reassure her. Just because she wasn't ovulating now didn't mean she'd never ovulate again. But I could tell she didn't believe me."

Lisa thought for a moment. "Do you think she went to the clinic for fertility drugs that would make her ovulate?"

"No. We'd talked about that. I told her the best thing would be to let her body rest and resume its natural cycle. The worst would be to fiddle around with more drugs. She was only eighteen. If we had to, we could have tried some hormone therapy later."

"Then why did she go to the clinic?"

"I have absolutely no idea." He was staring at her. "But I can tell you for sure that it wasn't to donate eggs."

Checking in with Barone had become a twice-a-day habit. Lisa phoned him again from her apartment and learned that she'd been right about the IUDs—Nestle's inventory showed a discrepancy between the number of IUDs stocked over a period of a year and the number billed to patients. Thirty-three intrauterine devices were unaccounted for.

"We still need someone to file a complaint before we can arrest him," Barone said.

She was so frustrated she could scream. She was frightened, too. She wanted Nestle behind bars. "What about Ted Cantrell? Do the West L.A. police think he killed himself?"

"Let's just say they're skeptical. They spoke to his ex-wife—according to her, he was excited yesterday afternoon. He told her he was expecting big money and planned to pay her all the back alimony he owed her. That's why she went to his place."

"Maybe he was cashing in some stocks."

"That's what his ex-wife thought, but he said no. So why would he kill himself? I spoke with Cantrell on Monday—he didn't strike me as the remorseful type."

"So you *do* think Nestle killed Ted?"

"Norman Weld has practically confessed to all three murders. West L.A. likes Weld. So does the D.A. He's having a court-appointed psychiatrist evaluate Weld to determine whether he's fit to stand trial. Weld has refused to retain counsel or allow us to appoint a public defender. He said God will be at his side."

She couldn't believe this was happening. "Can you explain to the D.A. and the other detectives about the donor-egg switching?"

"I did. I showed them the files, the donor sheets, the statistics you worked up. It's all very interesting, Dr. Brockman, and it looks like unethical medicine, but it's not conclusive. And it doesn't necessarily add up to murder. Weld admits he's responsible for the deaths, and his motive is clear: he had to punish everyone involved with the process of donating eggs. You're the one who figured that out."

"But now I'm not sure. I spoke with Chelsea's gynecologist today." She repeated what she'd learned. "I don't understand why she went to the clinic, why she lied to Matthew. Doesn't it make you wonder?"

"Again, it's interesting, but it doesn't change the fact that Weld had motive and opportunity and has admitted guilt."

"Just because he says he's responsible for their deaths doesn't mean he killed them. I think he means he's afraid of the power of his prayers. He doesn't strike me as someone who would commit a murder."

"Even if God told him to? Murderers don't look like murderers. They're not walking around these days with the mark of Cain on their foreheads. My job would be simpler if they were."

"What about Ted Cantrell's money? Will you try to find out what that was all about?"

"To be very honest, we can't run off in a hundred directions. Right now we're focusing on Weld. If there are any developments, I'll let you know."

She said good-bye and hung up, so frustrated that she had to restrain herself from slamming down the phone.

What kind of deal had Ted been referring to? Sam wouldn't have known—he and Ted had never been close. And Ted wouldn't have confided in his nurse—he'd never kept one long enough.

Grace, she remembered, had been talking to him on Monday. The conversation had seemed intense.

She wondered what they'd been discussing.

Selena had found out about Ted Cantrell. "It's a terrible thing," she said softly when Lisa called her at home. "Terrible."

"Yes, it is," Lisa agreed. She heard in the office manager's voice the same awkward guilt she was feeling. Both of them had disliked Cantrell. Both of them had wished him gone. And now he was dead. *I'm responsible*, Norman Weld had said. *I prayed it would stop.* "You know about Norman, Selena?"

"No." Her tone was guarded.

"They arrested him for Chelsea Wright's murder."

"*Madre de Dios!*" Selena gasped. "You think he did it?"

"I'm not sure." Lisa summarized her conversation with the lab technician.

"He's always been a little strange, a little intense, but I never for a moment thought he was dangerous. So he's the one who called the newspapers?"

"That's what he said." A clever way of putting an end to the egg donations he reviled. "How are you managing, Selena?"

"Mr. Fisk called—he asked me to wait a few weeks until the clinic reopens. He said he'll pay me in the meantime. I said I would, but first that girl is murdered, and then Dr. Gordon's gone, and now Dr. Cantrell." She sighed. "The place is cursed, *mi hija*. I'm glad I'm out of there. You should be, too."

"By the way, Selena, I want to get in touch with Grace. Do you have her phone number and address?"

Selena gave her the information, and they talked for a while longer about the rest of the clinic staff, what they were doing. Lisa had been phoning her every day, ostensibly to find out if any of her patients had called; really, she knew she was trying to hang on to a life that had disintegrated in a matter of days. She said good-bye, let's stay in touch, and wondered sadly whether they would.

The phone number Selena had given her for Grace had been disconnected. Lisa checked with the office manager—there was no mistake. Maybe she'd dialed wrong. She tried the number again. Again a recording informed her that the number had been disconnected. From Directory Assistance she learned that there was no new listing.

Grace lived in a small pink stucco house on Whitsett in Van Nuys, in the San Fernando Valley. The driveway was empty and the shades were all drawn. Lisa rang the bell anyway—maybe Grace was home with Suzie.

A moment later she rang it again, reluctant to admit she'd made the trip for nothing. Still no answer.

"They've gone," a young voice said behind her.

Lisa turned around and saw a towheaded boy straddling a red bike. She guessed he was eight or nine. "You know the Fentons?" she asked, taking a few steps toward him.

"I live two houses away." He pointed beyond Lisa.

"Do you know when Mrs. Fenton will be back?"

"Nope." He shifted his weight to the other leg. "They left early this morning. I saw them putting suitcases in the trunk of their car when I was waiting for the bus to pick me up for school. Then they put the baby into the car seat." He leaned forward and in an important voice said, "She was *cry*ing."

"The baby was crying?"

"Nope. Mrs. Fenton. She kept saying, 'Hurry up, hurry up, hurry up.' It made Mr. Fenton nervous."

Lisa frowned. "Do you know where they went?" Had Grace and her husband taken a vacation since she was out of a job?

"Uh-uh." He shook his head with exaggerated slowness.

"Does your mother know?"

He swung his tongue back and forth like a metronome gone wild. "Maybe."

"Do you think I could talk to her?"

He turned his bike around and walked it up the block. Lisa followed and waited on the sidewalk while he disappeared behind the black wrought-iron gate to the driveway.

A few minutes later a heavyset woman in too-tight jeans and a black sweatshirt opened the gate and approached Lisa. "Can I help you?"

No friendliness there. "I'm Lisa Brockman. Grace Fenton and I work together. I need to talk to her, but her phone's been disconnected."

"Is that right?" Her face was a blank slate, but her eyes were studying Lisa.

"Your son says the Fentons left early this morning. He told me you may know where I can reach Grace."

"He's wrong," the woman said, turning to scowl at the boy, who had walked past the gate and was standing on the lawn. "I don't mind other people's business." She made as if to leave.

"Please," Lisa said.

The woman stopped. "I don't know where they are. They left, is all I know. I don't think they're coming back."

Had Grace been crying because of Ted's death? Had it frightened her? "I have to talk to Grace. I know you have no reason to trust me." She fumbled in her purse and found a business card. "Look, here's my card. I'm a doctor at the clinic where Grace was a nurse. She worked for my fiancé, Dr. Matthew Gordon. He's the one who disappeared. I'm sure she told you about him."

The woman studied the card.

"You can call Detective Barone at the Hollywood station. He'll vouch for me." No response from the woman. "I need to talk to Grace. Please help me."

The woman turned to her son. "Get in the house, Kevin."

"Mommy—"

"I said *now*." Her tone was sharp. She waited until he had obeyed, then faced Lisa. "Anybody can have a business card," she said.

Lisa took her wallet out of her purse and showed the woman her driver's license. The woman glanced at the photo, then at Lisa, then at the photo again.

"She talked about you," the woman said, handing the wallet back to Lisa. "She said you're real nice. She felt terrible about Dr. Gordon. Cried every time she talked about him."

"Where is she, Mrs. . . . ?"

"Eggars. Peggy Eggars. She's gone, left this morning with Tony and the baby. She's afraid they're going to kill her."

The sun was hot and bright and Lisa was shivering. "Who does she think is going to kill her?"

"She wouldn't say. She said they killed Dr. Gordon and that girl. And this morning she read in the paper about that other clinic doctor. That's when she decided she had to leave."

Who was "they"—Nestle, and who else? And why did Grace fear that she was in danger? "Do you know where she is?"

"Nope." Peggy Eggars folded her arms across her full chest and avoided looking at Lisa.

She's lying, Lisa thought. The boy had said his mother might know. "She must be terrified that these people will find her. But if she's in danger, Mrs. Eggars, I'm in danger, too. So are all the other people she worked with."

"I told you, I don't know." An edge of anger in her voice.

But she was still standing there. She could have turned around and gone into her house. "I admire your loyalty, Peggy," Lisa said softly. "Grace was right to trust you." She waited a moment. "I know she wouldn't want any of us to get hurt. Grace would feel terrible if that happened."

Indecision played across the woman's face.

A mild breeze ruffled Lisa's hair. "If Grace knows something that will help the police put these killers away, she'll be safer. So will Suzie."

Peggy unfolded her arms and stuffed her hands into her jeans pockets. "They're staying with her mother in Whittier," she mumbled. "Her name is Mary Rick."

Lisa sighed with relief. "Can you give me the address?"

"Wait here." She walked with heavy strides up the concrete path to her front door. A few minutes later she was back and handed Lisa a small piece of paper with an address on it. "Tell her I hope she's okay."

chapter forty-one

The only thing Lisa knew about Whittier was that it had been the epicenter of a major earthquake—hardly a comforting thought. In her car, she studied a Los Angeles County map. Sam would be proud, she thought wistfully, missing him; he was always telling her to learn to read maps. The freeway system was a tangle of red arteries. She found her location, traced the route with her finger, then refolded the map and headed for the Ventura Freeway.

Twenty minutes later she was on the 101 heading south, approaching a maze of intersecting freeways near downtown. Her pager went off. Had Barone arrested Nestle? she wondered with a beat of excitement.

It was her answering service. Using her cellular phone, she contacted the service and learned that Baruch had called. She almost missed the transition to the Santa Ana Freeway as she punched the Hoffmans' number. She wasn't surprised when he answered on the first ring.

"This is Dr. Brockman. Is Naomi in labor?"

"I don't know." He sounded terse. "She's been having contractions all night and all morning, ever since you were here. She insists they're Braxton-Hicks. I'm not so sure."

It was hard to miss the accusation in his voice. "How far apart are they, Baruch?"

"Sometimes one or two an hour. Sometimes none."

"Did her water break?"

"No."

"Baruch, Naomi's probably right, but just to be sure, and so that you'll be less anxious, meet me at Cedars in twenty minutes." Speaking with Grace would have to wait.

"I'll talk to her. Please hold on."

She checked her rearview mirror and looked quickly behind her before she moved into the right lane so that she could exit the freeway and reverse direction.

"Dr. Brockman, she won't go," Baruch said wearily when he was back on the line. "She says she's not in labor."

"Let me talk to her." Half a minute passed before she heard Naomi's muted greeting. "Naomi, how are you feeling?"

"I'm okay. I don't know why Baruch called you." Her voice sounded dead, leaden.

"He's concerned about you, Naomi. So am I. Do you think you could be in labor?" Patients generally rushed to the hospital prematurely, but this case was different.

"No. I haven't had any contractions in the past hour."

"Yes, you have, Naomi." Baruch had picked up the extension.

"That wasn't a contraction."

"Naomi—"

"Leave me alone, Baruch!"

The van in front of Lisa abruptly crossed two lanes, eliciting a chorus of angry honking. "You'll let me know immediately if you have any consistent contractions, Naomi? Or if you have any other signs of labor?"

"Yes. Thanks for calling, Dr. Brockman."

Naomi was always polite, Lisa thought sadly and heard the faint click of a hang-up. "Baruch, are you still there?" When he answered, she said, "I'm going to give you the number of my cellular phone and pager so you won't have to call the service. Do you have a pencil and paper?"

The woman who answered the door of the small gray house was an older version of Grace. Same light brown hair, same watery, pale-blue eyes. Same petite frame. Same aura of anxiety.

"Grace isn't here," she said after Lisa introduced herself. "I have no idea where she is, but if and when she calls, I'll tell her you're looking for her."

"Her neighbor Peggy Eggars said she and Suzie came here because she's afraid for her life, so I understand your being careful." Lisa extended her driver's license.

The woman pushed it away. "I don't need to see that. I don't know where Grace is. And her neighbor must have been drinking to come up with a story like that." She started to shut the door.

"Isn't that Grace's car in the driveway?" Lisa pointed toward a white Honda Civic.

"No, that's ours—my husband's and mine."

"With an infant's car seat in the back?"

"We bought one for when we take Suzie in the car. If you must know," she added a second later with an attempt at indignation. Her eyes were flickering.

"Tell her Norman Weld's been arrested for murdering Dr. Gordon and Chelsea Wright. Tell her if the police think he did it, they won't look for the real killers. Then Grace and Suzie and Tony will have to hide forever."

"When I see her, I'll tell her." She slammed the door shut.

Lisa crossed the street and sat in her car. A minute or so later she saw the drapes at the large front window being pulled back an inch, then quickly released.

She had plenty of time. It was hot in the car, and sweat was trickling down her back. She turned on the ignition to open the electronic front windows, then shut the engine and sat for over half an hour watching the house. The front drapes were pulled back three or four times. She thought about Chelsea and Matthew and Ted—she didn't believe he'd killed himself—and wondered what grim common denominator had made it necessary for them to be murdered.

She phoned Barone on her cellular and learned that the detective wasn't in. She didn't leave a message.

Another half hour passed. Mary Rick came out the front door and right up to Lisa's car.

"You can't harass me like this!" she hissed, leaning into the open window, her palms pressed against the car door. Her voice shook with anger. "I told you, I don't know where Grace is. You can believe me or not, but if you don't leave, I'm calling the police."

The woman was bluffing. If Grace was here with her family, the last thing she wanted was police cars and attention drawn to her mother's house. "Go ahead, then," Lisa said with a calm she didn't feel. She wondered sadly at what point she had turned into someone who could so easily intimidate, manipulate, lie.

"Why won't you go away?" The mother's eyes were filled with hate.

"I have to talk to Grace. I promise I won't stay long."

Mary Rick spun around and walked back into her house. Lisa got out of her car and followed her. She rang the bell.

"You can't do this!" Mary whined when she jerked open the door.

"The longer you keep me out here, the more people are going to notice and talk."

Fear pinched the woman's face. "Fine," she said between clenched teeth. She opened the door to let Lisa enter a small, square living room, then shut it quickly behind her. "Wait here."

The room was tidy and smelled of lemon furniture polish. The yellow-and-rose cotton print sofa and love seat were covered in plastic. The plush rose carpet showed the parallel lines of recent vacuuming, unmarred except for the traffic to the door. Against the far wall, to the left of a small fireplace, was a reddish-brown spinet. On the piano ledge, on top of a lace doily, stood a large silver-framed wedding photo of Grace and Tony and several smaller photos of Suzie.

"Is it true about Norman?"

Lisa turned and saw Grace standing in the adjoining dining room. Her mother was right behind her. "Yes." Grace looked so different out of uniform—smaller, somehow. Lisa approached her, conscious that she was making footprints on the carpet. "I'm sorry I upset your mother, but I have to talk to you. Can I sit down?"

"I don't know anything." Grace set her lips in a stubborn line. "You've come here for nothing."

"Someone tried to kill me. Twice." She saw the nurse's eyes widen. "Once at the clinic, on Sunday night. You know that broken window in the operating room I asked Selena to have fixed? I shattered it to set off the alarm so the police would come."

Grace looked at her uncertainly. "Selena said it was vandals."

"That's what I told her to tell everyone. I didn't want people to panic. Last night someone tried to run me over." She paused to let that sink in. Grace, she noted, was blinking rapidly. "Peggy Eggars told me you're afraid that the people who killed Dr. Gordon and Chelsea and Dr. Cantrell are going to kill you, too. Who *are* they, Grace?" she asked softly.

"I don't know. I'm just scared. Someone's killing people who work at the clinic. You just said they tried to kill you, too. Why wouldn't I be scared?" Her tone was impatient, defiant. Her chin was quivering.

"On Monday you were talking to Dr. Cantrell. You walked away, and he went after you. What did he tell you, Grace?"

"Nothing." The nurse's face was flushed. She avoided Lisa's eyes.

"You're lying, Grace," Lisa said quietly.

"Don't talk like that to my daughter!" Mary Rick snapped, taking a step closer.

Grace faced her mother. "Would you leave us alone, please, Mom?"

"She called you a liar!"

"Please, Mom. I can handle this, okay?"

"You're sure?" Mary glared at Lisa.

Grace nodded. The mother hesitated, then left the room, casting a backward, hate-filled glance at Lisa before she shut the door. Grace pulled out a chair and sat down.

Lisa did the same. "What did Ted tell you?" she asked.

"He *didn't* tell me anything! That's the truth. Do the police believe that Norman killed Dr. Gordon and Chelsea?" Grace was pulling at the crocheted lace cloth on the pecan dining table.

"Norman told them he's responsible. He admitted to me that he harassed patients when they were in Recovery. Do you know anything about his involvement with the murders?"

"No. I—no, I don't." Grace sounded confused.

"I spoke to Chelsea's gynecologist. He told me she wouldn't have gone to the clinic three weeks ago to donate eggs. She wasn't ovulating. She was afraid she wouldn't have any children." Lisa was watching the nurse carefully. Grace had tensed, but didn't seem surprised. Why not? In a casual voice, Lisa said, "You knew about that, didn't you?"

No answer from Grace. Her eyes were darting back and forth, like goldfish in a bowl.

Lisa thought quickly, then said, "Chelsea told Dr. Melman you knew." Telling a lie to pry loose the truth.

The nurse bowed her head and whispered, "Yes, I knew."

"Why didn't you tell someone?" Lisa asked gently, careful to strip impatience from her voice. The last thing she wanted to do was intimidate her.

"I was afraid. I wasn't sure . . ." She was still looking down.

"Sure about what?" No response. "Grace, do you know who killed her?"

She started to cry. "Oh, God, I'm so scared!" she whispered. "I don't want to die!"

"Tell me who killed her, Grace." Lisa moved closer so that her knees were almost touching the other woman's. "Is it the same person who killed Dr. Gordon?"

"I wasn't sure!" Grace looked up. "That's why I didn't say anything. You know how much I loved Dr. Gordon, but I wasn't sure! You can understand that, can't you?" Tears were streaming down her cheeks.

"Of course I do. What happened, Grace?"

"Chelsea came to me after she met with Dr. Gordon. She was very upset." The nurse wiped her eyes with her hand. "She wanted to see her file. I told her I couldn't show it to her, only Dr. Gordon could. She told me she wasn't ovulating, that she was afraid she wouldn't be able to have children of her own. She wanted—" Grace started crying again. She bit her lower lip before she continued. "She wanted to know who received her eggs."

Lisa's heart thumped. "Did you tell her?"

"She forced me to!" Grace wailed. "I said I'd lose my job if I told her. That's when she told me she wasn't eighteen when she donated the eggs last July! She said she'd file charges if I didn't tell her who received her eggs!" Grace was sobbing, barely able to talk. "I didn't know she wasn't eighteen! She looked so much older. I had no idea! I'd *never* do anything to cause one second of trouble for Dr. Gordon! Never!"

"I believe you, Grace." Lisa patted her arm. "You're being too hard on yourself. Everyone makes mistakes. I have. Dr. Gordon would have understood."

"I couldn't tell him! It wasn't just that I was afraid for my job— I couldn't bear to see the look on his face when he found out I let him down. So I checked the Jane Doe file and told Chelsea who received her eggs. She was disappointed when I said that one of the recipients didn't conceive."

"Cora Allen."

Grace nodded. "But the other patient *did* conceive, with twins. I gave Chelsea her name. I had no choice. You can see that, can't you?" She looked desperately at Lisa for confirmation and grabbed her hand.

Lisa nodded, but her head was spinning. She was thinking

about Naomi Hoffman, how she must have felt when Chelsea appeared at her door. *You're carrying my babies, Mrs. Hoffman.*

Or had Chelsea spoken to Baruch? Had he listened, dumbfounded, as she told him that his wife's twins weren't really hers? Had he torn out the pages from the Julian calendar log when he had Charlie show him and Naomi their frozen embryos? Had he somehow managed to steal Naomi's file?

How far had he gone to prevent his world from crumbling?

"And I did all that for *nothing*!" Grace cried. "Later that day Dr. Gordon said Chelsea *admitted* she was underage when she donated. I've never seen him so angry, so when he asked me how I could have let her slip through, I told him it wasn't me."

"Did he explain why Chelsea told him?" Lisa was reluctant to interrupt Grace, but Matthew hadn't written any of this in his "Notes" file.

"No. He said she came to donate eggs, and she slipped and told him. Maybe she thought the recipient's name would be in her file. Maybe she thought she'd have a chance to look at the file without Dr. Gordon knowing."

Lisa nodded. "Maybe."

Grace took a deep breath. "And then she was *murdered*. I knew there'd be an investigation, so I forged her signature on the waiver and the application. I didn't want her parents to sue the clinic and Dr. Gordon. You think I'm horrible, don't you?"

"No, I don't, Grace. I can see how you felt trapped." Had the Hoffmans felt trapped, too?

"I *was*." She nodded vigorously. "I couldn't tell the police—I was afraid I'd go to jail. And I didn't think any of this was connected to Chelsea's murder, because Dr. Gordon told me the detective said it was a mugging. That same day he found out about the forgeries. And the next morning he disappeared. I thought he ran away because he knew there'd be an investigation and he'd be sued."

"You were very nervous that morning," Lisa said softly. "You were crying."

"Because I *knew*," Grace whispered. "Deep down I knew." She tapped her chest and looked at Lisa.

Lisa sensed that the nurse wasn't telling her everything. "*What* did you know, Grace?"

"Dr. Gordon and Chelsea were killed because they knew who received her eggs," she whispered. "Dr. Gordon must have told the recipient that Chelsea was asking about her, that there could be a problem because she was underage when she donated." She took a breath. "If I'd told the police, Dr. Cantrell would be alive. I know he didn't kill himself. Someone murdered him."

"Why, Grace?"

She pressed her fingers against her scalp. "He wouldn't leave me alone! I *begged* him to stop asking me questions, but he came after me again and again, until I told him who received Chelsea's eggs."

"That was on Monday, when I saw you talking to him?"

"Yes." She shut her eyes briefly. "He figured out right away that this patient killed Chelsea and Dr. Gordon. He asked me if I'd told the police what I knew, and I said no, I was terrified. So he said he'd help me. He'd tell them *he* gave Chelsea the recipient's name. But he must have blackmailed her instead."

Greed, Lisa thought, was certainly more typical of Ted than heroism. This explained the serious money Ted's ex-wife had told the police he'd been expecting.

"I keep telling myself that it was his own fault he was killed, that he was stupid for blackmailing someone who killed two other people. And now he's dead. And what if he told her I gave him her name? She'll kill me, too." Grace started to shake.

Lisa heard muted ringing; it took her a second to realize it was her cell phone. Bending down, she grabbed her phone from her purse, flipped it open, and said, "Yes?" as Grace mouthed, "I'll be back," and half ran out of the room.

"You have to help me!" Baruch cried.

Lisa found it unbearable to speak to him. "What's happened?"

"She admitted she's been having regular contractions. They're strong now. She's been in labor for hours, Dr. Brockman!"

The urgency in his voice helped remind her that she was a physician, not a judge or a detective, that Naomi Hoffman was her patient. That Baruch was her patient's husband. She cleared her throat. "How close are they?"

"Five minutes."

She checked her watch. It was just after three o'clock. "Drive Naomi to Cedars. I'll phone ahead and tell them to expect you. I should be there in thirty minutes." Later she'd think about what Grace had told her and decide what to do.

"She won't go to the hospital, Dr. Brockman. She said the dead girl's parents will be there, and the media."

Lisa pursed her lips. "No one outside the clinic knows who received their daughter's eggs, Baruch." She tried not to sound impatient.

"They know it's someone having twins! They know the babies are due soon, that you're her doctor. It was on the radio news about an hour ago, a special report. Didn't you hear it?" he demanded angrily, as if Lisa were responsible for this, too.

"No. No, I didn't." Damn Jean Elliott for releasing the information. Or had the Wrights done it?

"Naomi says the media will be camped out at the hospitals, waiting for anyone having twins to check in. They have scouts, you know. And they know who *you* are, Dr. Brockman. They'll be watching for you, and when they see you, they'll know."

"Baruch, I don't give a damn about the media or the Wrights. Neither should Naomi. My first concern is your wife and your babies. You have to convince her to go to the hospital."

"I agree with you! But she says she wants a home delivery."

"Absolutely not. I won't do it. What if she needs a cesarean? You know that's a possibility. What if there are complications?" She heard a moan in the background.

"I have to go to her," Baruch said.

"Is she doing her breathing exercises?"

"She was trying, but she's too agitated, because of the news report."

"Make her do the breathing," Lisa said firmly. "Do it with her. And get her to the hospital. That's your job, do you understand me?"

"She won't go!" He sounded frantic.

"Put her on the phone. Right now!" She paced across the dining room while she waited.

"You don't understand, Dr. Brockman," Naomi cried when she got on the line a minute later. "The media—"

"Listen to me, Naomi. I'm not about to jeopardize your health or the health of your babies. Baruch is going to take you to the hospital right now. I'll meet you there."

"I *can't*, Dr. Brockman! The Wrights will be there, I know it! Other people have home deliveries. Why can't I?"

"Because twins are a high risk. You know that." She softened her voice. "Naomi, you've tried for all these years to have a baby. Are you willing to risk the life of one or both of your babies because you're a coward?"

"No, of course not. I'd die before I let that happen," Naomi whispered fiercely.

Give me children—otherwise I am dead. That was what Rachel had told Jacob, Lisa remembered. Was that what Naomi had told Baruch?

chapter forty-two

Traffic was heavier on her way back, or maybe it just seemed so because Lisa was rushing. She was changing lanes more often than she liked to, driving faster than she normally did, praying that a cop wouldn't stop her. At the downtown freeway maze she hesitated—the Santa Monica or the Hollywood?—and by the time she decided to take the Hollywood, it was too late, and she was westbound on the Santa Monica.

She'd already alerted Cedars. She hoped no one from the hospital staff had called the media, but she couldn't worry about that now. She phoned the Hoffmans and was relieved when no one answered. That meant Naomi hadn't changed her mind.

A few minutes later she passed Vermont, then Western. She found it hard not to think about Grace, about what she'd said. There were questions she still wanted to ask her. She switched the radio on and turned the volume up high to drown out her thoughts and push them into a recess of her mind where she could examine them later, after the Hoffman babies were born.

She phoned the hospital and learned that Naomi had been admitted and taken to one of the third-floor labor rooms. Lisa waited while a nurse checked on Naomi's status.

"Her water broke, Dr. Brockman," the nurse reported a few minutes later. "She's five centimeters and completely effaced. She wants to know when you'll be here."

If there were media lurking in the hospital corridors, Lisa didn't see them. She took the elevator to the third floor and stopped at the nurses' station for an update on Naomi's condition. She was relieved to hear that an ultrasound had shown that both babies were still head down.

Baruch was sitting on a chair at his wife's bedside. He sprang up when Lisa entered and hurried over to her. She avoided looking at him directly, but he didn't seem to notice.

"The contractions are three minutes apart," he said in a low, tired voice. His face glistened. "They're really bad, Dr. Brockman, but she doesn't want an epidural. Can't you help her?" He ran a hand across his mouth, wiping away the sweat.

"It shouldn't be much longer, Baruch." She went over to Naomi's bed, took her hand, and smiled warmly at her. "How are you doing? Ready to have some babies?"

"I'm so glad you're here!" Naomi exclaimed softly, squeezing Lisa's hand. She looked pale and exhausted, and the skin beneath her eyes had a bluish cast. She attempted a smile. A second later she placed her hands on her abdomen and started breathing in short, staccato bursts, exhaling on every fifth breath.

"You're doing fine." Lisa checked her watch and scanned the printout from the fetal monitor. The babies' heartbeats were steady.

Naomi's face had reddened and was pinched in concentration; she was only exhaling now in rapid pants. When the contraction was over, she moaned and leaned back against her pillows. "That was a hard one," she whispered.

"Almost ninety seconds. Looks like you're in transition." Lisa smiled encouragingly and moistened Naomi's lips with a wet washcloth, then walked over to the cabinet against the wall, took a pair of latex gloves, and slipped them on. "I want to examine you during your next contraction, Naomi. Okay?" From the corner of her eye she could see that Baruch had turned away.

"How am I doing?" Naomi asked anxiously a few moments later.

"Great." Lisa peeled off the gloves and tossed them in a waste basket. "You're at ten centimeters, and the baby's head is crowning. We're going to move you into a delivery room." Ordinarily, patients stayed in the labor-delivery suite, but with twins there was always the possibility of complications, especially with the second birth. A nurse had attached an IV to Naomi's hand for the same reason.

"Now?" Baruch looked stunned.

"Now." Lisa smiled again and paged the nurses' station.

She had always loved the drama of birth, the finely choreographed movements in the delivery room. This time was no different. Surrounded by two nurses, the anesthesiologist, a pediatrics resident, and Baruch, she felt a heady excitement as she coached Naomi, telling her when to bear down, when to stop; she'd forgotten all about Grace and Chelsea and murder and custody.

She eased the baby's head out and suctioned mucous from its nose and mouth. Pushing down gently, she cleared the anterior shoulder; she pulled gently and eased out the posterior shoulder.

The baby slipped out.

"It's a boy!" Baruch cried.

"Is he all right?" Naomi whispered, craning her neck to see.

"He's perfect." Lisa smiled broadly. She clamped the cord and cut it, then placed the baby on his mother's abdomen.

She would have left him there longer, but she had to deliver Baby B. She did the one-minute APGAR, observing the newborn's heart rate, respiratory effort, reflex irritability, color, and muscle tone. Then she signaled to one of the nurses, who took the newborn and placed him in a warmer, where she dried him and wrapped him in a blanket.

Lisa checked Baby B's fetal monitor—the heartbeat was steady at 145. Good variability. No decelerations. She did an ultrasound and a manual exam to make sure the head was still in the vertex position. Then she carefully broke the amniotic sac. The baby's head settled into the birth canal.

Five pushes later, the head was out, and Lisa repeated the dance of birth.

A girl.

Baruch was weeping and thanking God and saying "It's a miracle, isn't it?" and "I love you" and "You're so beautiful" to Naomi. Her dark brown hair was matted; her face was gleaming with sweat. She was crying and smiling and shaking involuntarily from the aftermath of labor.

Lisa placed another blanket on top of Naomi to warm her, then checked the babies. She did the one-minute APGAR on the newborn Hoffman girl and a second, five-minute APGAR on her brother.

"Do you want to breast-feed your babies?" one of the nurses asked Naomi. "They're both so beautiful. I think they both look just like you, Mrs. Hoffman."

Turning quickly, Lisa cast an anxious look at Naomi, but the new mother was in her own world, oblivious to worry. So was Baruch. She spoke with the pediatrician, did the five-minute APGAR on the Hoffman girl, then discarded her cap and gown. She checked the babies again, marveling at their perfection, overwhelmed with sudden, stinging sadness as she wondered how long Naomi would be able to hold on to this fragile happiness.

She was about to open the delivery room doors when Baruch called her name. She tensed instantly but pulled her lips into a smile before she faced him.

"My parents and Naomi's parents may be waiting right outside," he said in a low, anxious voice. "They don't know that Naomi may have received donor eggs."

What else didn't they know? "I won't say anything," Lisa assured him. Turning quickly before he could read from her face the turmoil she was feeling, she pushed open the doors and stepped into the hall.

She searched to her left, then to her right. No grandparents in sight. She sighed, enormously relieved, because she wasn't a very good actress, and was heading down the hall toward the waiting area when she was accosted by a barrage of popping flashlights.

"Dr. Brockman! Can you tell us . . . ?"

The male reporter who had been at the clinic on that first terrible day was here now, accompanied by the ponytailed minicam operator.

"Are these Chelsea Wright's babies?"

"Is it true Chelsea's parents will get custody of one of the babies?"

Gina Franco was here, too. She smiled at Lisa, almost apologetically. Lisa ignored her and the rest of the reporters and, turning around, walked quickly to the doctors' lounge.

*   *   *

She didn't realize how exhausted she was until she was in the delicious privacy of her apartment, lying in her tub. The tension, and with it all her energy, had started seeping out of her as soon as she sank into the steaming water. She felt listless, weighted down with the heaviness of her bones; she wanted to stay here forever, in the womblike comfort of the silky, rose-scented waters that glided over her.

She didn't want to think about anything. Not Matthew. Not Sam or Norman or Nestle. Not even the Hoffman babies, though she was thrilled and relieved that they were fine. With her eyes shut, she took long, deep, evenly-spaced breaths and tried to focus on the soothing sounds of the Beethoven sonata tinkling from her radio, but her mind betrayed her, and she was back in the small dining room in Mary Rick's house, heard again the nurse's abject cries.

"I couldn't bear to see the look on Dr. Gordon's face when he found out I let him down!"

"Dr. Cantrell was stupid for blackmailing someone who killed two people."

"She told me she wasn't eighteen when she donated the eggs last July!"

The ringing of the front doorbell jarred her. She considered ignoring it, then wondered if it was Barone. Maybe he had more information about Ted or Nestle. But if it *was* Barone, should she repeat what Grace had told her? Should she tell him she suspected that Chelsea had confronted Baruch Hoffman about the eggs she'd donated, the eggs Naomi had received? What if she was wrong?

What if she was right?

The bell rang again. With an effort, she pushed herself up, away from the clinging embrace of the water, and stepped out of the tub. Grabbing the white terry-cloth robe from the hook on the bathroom door, she called, "I'll be right there!" and hurried to the front door.

It was Sam. She stared at him through the privacy window.

"Can I come in?"

"Of course. Sorry." She unlocked the door and opened it, her face still flushed from the heat of the bath.

"The way you've been acting lately, I wasn't sure I'd be welcome." He stepped inside and shut the door, then walked ahead of her into the living room and sat down on the sofa. "I've been calling you all day, leaving messages. You weren't at Elana's, so I figured I'd take a chance and see if you were here."

"I've been out since the morning, Sam. I just came home a while ago."

Sam nodded. "Some day, huh? First Ted is found dead—maybe a suicide, maybe killed. Then Norman's arrested for murder." He shook his head in disbelief, then glanced at her. "I guess you won't be sleeping at the Presslers' tonight, or over Shabbos, now that the police have Norman in custody."

Sam sounded on edge, angry. "I guess," she said, sitting at the other end of the sofa. The Presslers were sure to invite him for both Sabbath meals. She wasn't looking forward to facing him; still, she was afraid of being in her apartment alone. Norman was in jail. Nestle wasn't. And she still didn't know which person at the clinic was the obstetrician's accomplice. Ted, who was now dead? Or someone else . . .

"I have to tell you, I'm blown away about Norman," Sam said. "I called you as soon as I heard, here and at the Presslers. Where were you?"

Not a casual question, she decided. More of a challenge. "Barone called me to the station in the morning—Norman wanted to talk to me." She saw Sam's brows rise in surprise. Quickly, she summarized her bizarre visit with the lab technician. "I'm not sure he killed anyone, Sam. He's lost in his own world."

"What does Barone think?"

"He says the investigation is focusing on Norman, but I don't know what he really believes." She was more certain than ever that there were two killers with separate motives: the person who had murdered Chelsea (Lisa refused to name him, even in her thoughts), and panicked the other person, either Nestle or his accomplice, who had then killed Matthew, and probably Ted. And had tried to kill her.

"Barone doesn't confide in you? I thought you were buddies."

She looked at Sam, uncertain what to make of his tone. She decided to ignore it.

"So what did you do the rest of the day?" he asked.

"Naomi Hoffman went into labor. I delivered the babies at Cedars a little over an hour ago—a boy and a girl. Both healthy." Lisa couldn't help smiling.

"That's great." Sam smiled, too, then frowned. "What about Chelsea Wright's parents? Do they know the babies were born?"

"I'm sure they do. The media was at the hospital."

"I'm not surprised. You think Mrs. Hoffman received Chelsea's eggs?"

Lisa hesitated, then nodded. "I spoke to Grace today. She confirmed it." She repeated what she'd learned from the nurse.

"*Grace* doctored the documents, huh?" Sam whistled, then was silent for a moment. "So you think Chelsea went to the Hoffmans to demand shared custody or something, is that it?"

"It's possible."

"Did you tell Barone?"

"Not yet." Lisa tightened the belt on her robe.

"But you suspect that Baruch Hoffman panicked and killed her?" Sam's eyes narrowed. "But then who killed Matt? And why?"

"I'm not a detective, Sam. And I don't want to jump to conclusions about Baruch Hoffman."

"Absolutely not. That would be *terribly* unfair." Cocking his head, he looked at her thoughtfully. "So whom *do* you suspect?"

"Sam, I've had a long, exhausting day." She rose. "Let's talk later, all right?"

He made no move to leave the sofa. "I was at Elana's earlier, thinking I'd find you there. I lied and told her you wanted me to look through the files in the guest room."

Her stomach muscles knotted. "You had no right, Sam."

"You're absolutely correct. '*Chotosi*,' " he said, using the refrain from the Yom Kippur liturgy of confession. *I sinned.* He pounded his chest. "But what was I supposed to do? You've been acting like I have leprosy or something. I thought at first that you were nervous because of the other day in your office, but that's silly. So I figured it had something to do with the files."

She just stood there, looking at him.

"I said to myself, 'Lisa spent hours photocopying the damn stuff, almost got killed doing it. No way is she not going to look at it.' So I decided to see what you found. You made it easy, charting all that info. Did you tell Barone about it?"

She cleared her throat. "Yes."

"But you didn't tell me. Which means you couldn't trust me. How'm I doing so far, Lisa?" he asked softly.

"Sam, I'm sorry. It's hard to explain."

"Explain what?" His eyes were flashing with anger. "That you thought I was screwing around with donor eggs, giving them to patients without their knowledge or consent?"

"*Someone* was doing it. It's not my imagination!"

"Well, it wasn't me! How could you believe for one second I'd do something like that?"

"Why did you erase your name as attending physician from a

recipient's file?'' she demanded angrily. "Why did you write in Matthew's name?"

He stared at her. "What the hell are you talking about?"

"Nicki Sandler. Remember her?" The name was emblazoned on her mind.

"Nicki's my patient. She just had her second IVF. She was on that list of yours, right? According to you, she received donor eggs."

"She didn't?"

"If she did, it was done without my knowledge. Why?"

"Matthew is listed as attending physician. I spoke to Nicki. She said *you* were her doctor. What was I supposed to think?"

"You weren't supposed to *think*! You were supposed to *ask* me. And I would've told you that she was my patient, and that I had no idea who's doing this stuff, but it sure as hell isn't me."

"You kept nagging at me not to look at the files, Sam," she said quietly.

He groaned. "Because I thought it was a waste of time! I offered to go through the stuff with you, didn't I? I was attacked too, wasn't I? Or maybe you thought I made that up, that I bruised myself after I attacked you."

She glanced away.

"I was being sarcastic, but I guess you *did* think that, huh?" His voice was so soft. "Did I put the money in your pantry too? Dumb of me if I did, 'cause I could use twenty grand now that I'm out of a job."

She was hot with embarrassment. "I'm sorry. I was frightened and confused, and Barone kept hammering at me not to trust anyone, not even you. I'm so sorry, Sam," she said again, sitting down next to him. She put her hand out to touch him, then drew it back.

"What really hurts is that you could believe for one second that I would harm you, Lisa."

"I didn't really believe it. I just crawled into a shell and stopped thinking. Can you understand that, Sam?"

"I don't know." He sat for a while, brooding in silence, then pushed himself off the sofa.

"Please don't go, Sam."

"I need to think about all this, okay?"

She bit her upper lip and nodded. "Okay."

After he left, she went into her bedroom and sat on the bed. In their last few phone calls, her parents had hinted that she should come home. There were fertility clinics in New York, too, her father had told her. Why stay in Los Angeles?

Why, indeed?

She listened to "Bridge Over Troubled Waters" and dusted the bookcases, which needed no dusting. She wondered when she'd get her computer and disks back. She didn't even know whom to call to find out. In the bathroom, she watched the water drain out of the tub, leaving snowy caps of bubble-bath foam.

The doorbell rang. She went to the entry and looked through the peephole, then opened the door.

"I thought you had to think about all this," she said lightly. Her heart was pounding as she stepped aside to let him enter.

"I sat in the car and tried putting myself in your shoes," he said. "I tried to imagine what I would've thought, what I would've done."

"And what did you decide?" she asked quietly.

"That I don't want to lose you."

Her heat beat faster. They stood in the entry, staring at each other, suddenly shy with awkwardness.

He put his hands into his pockets. "You have no idea how much I want to kiss you," he said, his voice husky.

"The rules are the rules." She smiled and saw his shoulders relax.

He smiled, too. "Yeah, the rules are the rules." After a few second's silence, he asked, "Do you feel guilty because of Matthew?"

She hesitated, then said, "Yes."

Sam sighed. "Me, too."

Long after Sam dropped her off at the Presslers', Lisa lay in bed, thinking about the Hoffman babies, about Naomi. Something about her conversation with Grace was nibbling at her subconscious. She'd almost had it, and then Sam had rung the bell. The more she tried to remember now, the more it eluded her. Finally she fell into a restless sleep.

In the middle of the night, she remembered. She sat up with a start and checked the time. Four-thirty.

She couldn't call Grace now. She paced around the room, lay down again, and willed the hours to pass. At six-thirty, after washing up and doing a half hour of exercises, she decided she couldn't wait any longer. She dialed Mary Rick's number and apologized immediately for calling so early.

"I have to talk to Grace right away," Lisa told the woman.

The woman's hostility crackled through the receiver. "She

hasn't stopped crying since you left." Frosty accusation in her voice.

"I have one or two more questions. Please tell her it's urgent."

"I don't want you bothering her anymore!"

"If you don't put her on the phone, Mrs. Rick, I'll have to drive to your house again." She was so tired, she didn't have the energy to sound threatening, but she heard Mary say, "All right," in a tight, angry voice, and a minute later Grace was on the line. Sullen, scared.

Lisa apologized again for calling so early. "Grace, you said Chelsea told you she wasn't eighteen when she donated the eggs in July. You meant that's when she signed up, right? But when did she actually donate the eggs?"

"In *July*." An edge of impatience. "That's when she started the fertility drugs and went through the egg retrieval. She signed up for the program in May." Her voice dropped. "I changed the dates on the application and the waiver to August, a week after her eighteenth birthday."

Lisa dug her nails into the receiver. "You're sure?"

"Of *course* I'm sure. That's why I panicked—because the retrieval was done a month before her eighteenth birthday."

Lisa was rigid with excitement. Unless Chelsea's eggs had been fertilized, they couldn't have been frozen until September, when Naomi had completed her IVF cycle.

But what if they *had* been fertilized and frozen? she wondered with fresh alarm. What if Nestle's accomplice at the clinic had used donor sperm as well? "Do you know when Chelsea's eggs were implanted?" She held her breath.

"Dr. Gordon implanted them three days later. Two of the embryos took, but the patient had a selective reduction. I didn't tell Chelsea—I thought she'd feel worse."

Lisa's relief was so acute she felt light-headed. She couldn't wait to get off the phone and tell the Hoffmans.

"It was all very hush-hush," Grace said. "The woman was there under an assumed name. That's happened before—movie stars do it all the time."

"The recipient is an actress?" Lisa didn't care who she was, as long as she wasn't Naomi Hoffman.

"No. High society, very wealthy. Dr. Gordon didn't tell me who she was, but I thought I recognized her when she came in for the embryo transplant—I read the society pages all the time. I didn't let on to Dr. Gordon that I knew—he wouldn't have approved. And then I saw her picture in the papers about half a year later when her husband died, and I knew I was right."

My God! Lisa thought. *My God.* The blood rushed to her head, and she felt faint. "He died when she was pregnant?"

"A heart attack. I felt so sorry for her at the time, can you believe it? I felt sorry for a *murderer.*" When Lisa didn't respond, Grace asked, "Dr. Brockman, are you still there?"

"What's her name?" Lisa whispered hoarsely, although she knew. She needed confirmation before she went to Barone.

"If I tell you, you'll tell the police, and she'll find out and have me killed so I can't testify." The tension was back in the nurse's voice. "I know she will. She has millions. She can hire someone to do it."

"Tell me her name, Grace."

"I can't! I have to think of Suzie!"

"You wouldn't have Suzie if Dr. Gordon hadn't helped you. You owe it to him to help put his killer away. Don't you owe him, Grace?"

The nurse was silent.

"You said you loved him," Lisa said softly.

"It's Paula," Grace whispered. "Paula Rhodes."

chapter forty-three

Baruch was standing in front of the third-floor nursery. On either side of him were two middle-aged couples. All five faces were pressed against the window.

The grandparents. Lisa watched for a moment, not wanting to interrupt, then came closer and called Baruch's name.

They all turned around.

"This is Dr. Brockman," Baruch said. "She delivered the babies." He was smiling as he performed the introductions, but his eyes signaled a plea to Lisa: *Don't tell.*

Rabbi Hoffman was a stately, bearded man wearing a black felt hat and a black suit. Baruch's mother, wearing a short brown wig, was a little stout in a too-tight navy suit with white trim. Naomi's father was clean-shaven and shorter than Rabbi Hoffman. Her mother was petite and delicate, with hair almost as dark as Naomi's. Lisa couldn't decide whether or not it was a wig.

"*Mazel tov.*" Lisa smiled warmly. She was eager to pull Baruch aside, to allay his fears.

"*Mazel tov, mazel tov!*" they all echoed. Rabbi Hoffman, beaming, pulled his son to his chest and clapped him soundly on the back.

"Naomi tells me you're wonderful," her mother said. "We can't thank you enough. It's a miracle, isn't it?"

"Definitely a miracle." In more ways than one, Lisa thought. She wondered what Baruch would think if he knew that for several hours she'd pondered the possibility that he was a murderer.

She turned to him. "Can I talk to you a minute? Everything's fine," she added quickly, but his face clouded anyway. She could hardly blame him—she'd stood at his doorstep last Friday and told him not to worry then, too.

With an effort, he put on a smile and joined Lisa, who had walked down the corridor. "Is Naomi—"

"She's fine. I just came from seeing her. She looks great and told me she feels wonderful." She smiled again. "Baruch—"

"It's the Wrights, isn't it?" His hands had formed fists.

"Baruch, Naomi didn't receive Chelsea Wright's eggs."

He stared. "How can you be sure? I thought you told her—"

"I just found out Chelsea donated eggs in July. I spoke to the nurse who processed her application." If only Grace hadn't been terrified. If only she'd told the truth right away, the Hoffmans wouldn't have undergone this agony. And Ted Cantrell might still be alive. And Matthew?

"She's sure?"

Lisa nodded.

"*Baruch Hashem,*" he whispered. Blessed be God. "And this nurse will testify to that?"

"I think so."

"But who made the mistake in the first place? How did Naomi's name come up as a recipient?" There was more than a hint of anger mixed in with the curiosity in his voice.

"I don't know. The police are investigating."

Grace had denied altering the donor codes to coincide with the changes she'd made in Chelsea's file. She'd also insisted she hadn't deleted Paula's alias from the Jane Doe program or torn the September pages from the log. Grace might be lying, but why? She'd already admitted she'd forged Chelsea's signature.

"This is a special time for you and Naomi, Baruch," Lisa said. "Don't let this ruin your pleasure, or hers."

He opened his mouth to say something, then nodded instead.

★　　★　　★

Twenty minutes later Lisa was back home. She was exhilarated for the Hoffmans, fearful whenever she thought about Nestle. Which was all the time.

Sam had called an hour ago, at nine-thirty. "Just checking in," he'd said. She smiled at the sound of his voice. Edmond had left a message: he wanted her to call him as soon as possible.

Barone had phoned, too—the D.A. insisted they didn't have enough evidence to charge Nestle. Barone was still optimistic. Lisa phoned the station, but the detective was out. She told the receptionist she'd call back.

She put up a pot of coffee and fixed herself a tuna sandwich on toast. She wished fervently that Nestle were behind bars. She'd feel so much safer. Of course, his accomplice could still be out there. (Charlie? she wondered guiltily. Someone else connected with the lab? Not Sam, she insisted to herself. Definitely not Sam.) Unless his accomplice was Ted.

Or Matthew. More and more, she'd forced herself to face the possibility that Matthew, desperate to ensure the clinic's success, had gone along with Nestle's schemes. And now she knew he'd implanted Nestle's patient, Paula Rhodes, with Chelsea's eggs.

Because of Grace, Chelsea had known, too. What had Paula done when Matthew told her that Chelsea wanted to find the woman who'd received her eggs, that Chelsea had been underage when she donated? Had Paula called Nestle in a panic? Had she called him again, even more frantic, when Chelsea appeared on her doorstep and asked to see the two-month-old infant boy she claimed was the product of her ovum?

Nestle must have panicked, too. He would have realized immediately that if Chelsea filed a lawsuit, the truth about the donor egg manipulations would come out. Killing Chelsea wasn't the answer. Her murder would instigate the investigation of the clinic, which Nestle feared.

Killing Chelsea *and* Matthew solved everything. The police, believing that Matthew was a fugitive, would suspect him of her murder. The medical authorities would blame him for the donor-egg switching. As far as Nestle knew, Matthew was the only one, aside from himself and Paula, who could identify the recipient of Chelsea's eggs. So Paula and her son were safe.

How much did Paula Rhodes know about what had happened? Obviously she'd lied to Lisa about putting an ad on a college bulletin board for a mother's helper. Chelsea had sought *her*.

Had Nestle told Paula to string the girl along until he figured out what to do? *Hire her as a nanny, Paula. Make her think she'll play an important role in little Andy's life.* Was that what he'd advised her?

Or had that been Paula's idea?

And how had she felt when she learned Chelsea had been murdered? *I'd like to help pay for her funeral,* she'd told Lisa. Had that been an expression of guilt because she'd realized what Nestle had done? Or had she been trying to impress Lisa with her compassion?

The coffee was ready. Lisa filled a mug and took a sip—too hot. From her hall closet, she brought the phone directory to the kitchen counter. Taking another sip of coffee, she searched for and found the number for the Rhodes Foundation in Beverly Hills.

A woman answered the phone. Lisa identified herself and said she'd like to speak to the head of the foundation.

"Would that be Mr. James Rhodes or Mr. Curtis Rhodes?"

She had no idea. She wasn't sure what she expected to learn from Andrew Rhodes's family, didn't know whether any of them would talk to her about Paula. She *did* remember Paula saying that Andrew's cousins disapproved of her. She hoped that wasn't another lie. "Mr. James Rhodes."

"I'm sorry, he's not in."

"Is Mr. Curtis Rhodes in?" Lisa asked, more amused than annoyed. She felt like laughing for the first time today.

"Yes, he is. May I tell him what this is about?"

"It's personal."

"I see." A note of polite caution. "Hold on, please."

On the counter, next to her beige ceramic canister set, Lisa noticed yesterday's mail, still unopened. She took a bite of her sandwich, drank more coffee, and slit open the envelopes. More bills. An invitation to speak at a seminar on infertility treatment—obviously issued when her life had been normal.

"Dr. Brockman? Curtis Rhodes. How can I help you?" The man had a pleasant, well-modulated announcer's voice.

"This is a little awkward over the phone. I wonder if I could meet with you this morning."

"I have a full schedule today. Monday would be better."

"It's very important, or I wouldn't be bothering you. It's about Paula Rhodes."

A beat of silence. "I see." His voice was ten degrees cooler. "Are you representing her in some capacity?"

"Not at all. But I need to speak with you. I can be at your office in fifteen minutes."

"Why don't you make it an hour from now, at my home?"

The address he gave her was in the Flats, on Palm near Elevado, just a few blocks from Paula.

A uniformed maid ushered Lisa into a formal living room that was three times the size of her apartment. The furniture was ornate—curved wooden-framed sofas with Queen Anne legs, upholstered in a heavy burgundy floral brocade. Swagged drapes cascading onto the dark, polished hardwood floor. Crystal sconces at either end of the black-marbled fireplace.

"I'm Curtis Rhodes," a tall, gray-haired man said when she entered the room. "This is my wife, Celeste. My brother, James. My sister-in-law, Eleanor."

They were all in their mid-fifties, Lisa guessed. All casually elegant, to the manor born. Celeste's blond hair had been swept into an artfully simple French twist. Eleanor's hair, naturally gray, was cut short and matched the shade of her silk suit. Both women were wearing short strands of pearls.

Feeling as though she was facing a tribunal, Lisa accepted Curtis Rhodes's offer to sit on one of the needlepoint chairs. "I appreciate your talking to me," she began.

"I hope you won't consider me too rude if I ask you to get to the point," James said. His voice was thicker than his brother's. "How do you know Paula? Are you her physician?"

"No. I met her while trying to get information about my fiancé, Dr. Matthew Gordon. He headed the Westwood fertility clinic that's under investigation. He's disappeared, and the police think he's dead." She wondered tiredly how many more times she'd have to recite this explanation.

"I heard about that," Celeste said. "I'm very sorry, Dr. Brockman."

Murmurs of assent from the others. All four Rhodeses, she sensed, were suddenly more relaxed.

"Didn't Andrew invest in that clinic?" James asked his brother.

Curtis nodded. "Paula convinced him to—or should I say her half brother, Jerome, did. He's a silent partner in the clinic. Is that why you met with Paula, Dr. Brockman? Because of Andrew's connection with the clinic?"

Jerome Nestle was Paula's half brother? "Not exactly. You probably know that a young woman who donated eggs to the clinic, Chelsea Wright, was murdered." She saw nods and continued.

"Chelsea was Dr. Gordon's patient. I found out Paula hired her to be a mother's helper for her son, Andy."

A snort from James. "I'm not surprised. I can't see Paula taking care of a child herself."

Lisa felt a prickling of excitement. She'd been right to come here. "Really? She seemed very devoted when I was with her."

"Paula's a wonderful actress," Celeste said with quiet sarcasm. "No doubt you're wondering why we're talking so openly about her." She smiled. "It's no secret that we dislike her. She'll be the first to tell you, although she'll make us sound like snobs who disapproved of her background. Am I right?"

"Something like that." Lisa nodded.

"Don't let her drawl and her beauty fool you the way she fooled Andrew," Celeste said. "She's a terrible, terrible person. She can be very cruel," she added quietly.

Curtis patted his wife's hand tenderly. Lisa wondered what painful episode they were remembering. Though she'd come here with suspicions about Paula, it was hard to reconcile what she was hearing with the lovely, caring, sensitive woman she'd met.

"Why are you here?" James demanded.

"I have reason to believe Paula may be involved with Chelsea Wright's murder, and with my fiancé's as well." She flushed under their stares, suddenly alarmed that she'd made a mistake by revealing what she knew. Or maybe they thought she was crazy—a grief-stricken fiancée. Wasn't that what Nestle had charged? Would they call Paula the minute she left?

"When you phoned me at the office," Curtis said quietly, "I thought you were her therapist. Paula has been sending out feelers indicating that she's under a great deal of stress because of Andrew's death, and because she's wondering whether we're going to contest the will."

Lisa relaxed against her chairback. "Why would you do that?"

James said, "Because she killed Andrew. Is that a good enough reason?"

"James, we don't know that." Curtis glanced at him reprovingly.

Now it was Lisa's turn to stare. "She told me he died of a heart attack."

"He did," Curtis said. "He was only forty-six, but he'd been taking medication for his high blood pressure and arrhythmia for years. We've spoken to his cardiologist. He was shocked by Andrew's death. In his opinion, Andrew's medical problems were under control. But that doesn't mean anything."

"She did it," James insisted. "Doctored his medicine somehow."

"Doctors don't always know what's going to happen," Eleanor put in softly. "Younger people have died from heart attacks without having had any previous symptoms."

Lisa guessed she was the peacemaker in the family. "Why would Paula kill him? Weren't they happy?"

"I know for a fact that Andrew was miserable," Curtis sighed. "He was staying in the marriage because he wanted to have a child, but a year ago he hinted he was planning to divorce her. Then, miracle of miracles, Paula got pregnant."

"She knew about the terms of the will," Celeste said. "She understood that he wouldn't divorce her if she could produce an heir."

Lisa frowned. "Why did he want to have a child with her if he was miserable?"

They exchanged glances.

Curtis cleared his throat. "Andrew was wealthy in his own right, but he stood to inherit over a hundred million dollars that his parents had put in a trust. The money would go to him only when he had a natural child—boy or girl."

"But he would have divorced Paula right after the baby was born!" James exclaimed. "I'm convinced of that."

"I'm not so certain," Celeste said. "He would have had to give her a great deal of money, since she's the child's mother. And he wouldn't have wanted to give up custody."

"Not to that witch," James snarled.

It was as though they'd forgotten about her, Lisa thought. They'd obviously had this conversation before.

"The thought of Paula as a mother gives me the chills." Celeste touched her throat. "Poor Andrew. He must be rolling in his grave when he thinks that his son is in that woman's hands."

"What if it *isn't* his son?" From James. "I still say it's possible she fooled him. I know they were barely having sex in the months before she got pregnant."

"All it takes is one time." Celeste coughed.

"The paternity tests showed that Andrew is the father," Eleanor said patiently. "You know that, James."

"Well, she did *something*," he grumbled.

"She arranged to have Chelsea's eggs implanted in her," Lisa

said. They turned toward her and stared at her again. "Chelsea
found out that Paula received her eggs. I don't know what actually
happened after that, but I believe that Chelsea approached Paula."
Had Paula been trying to conceive for a long time? Or had she
known when she married Andrew that she had a condition that
would present problems?

"I told you!" James's face was mottled with triumph.

"Assuming she got this girl's eggs, how did she manage to get
Andrew's sperm?" Curtis asked.

Lisa chewed on her bottom lip. "You said Andrew was trying
to have a child. Did he ever undergo any tests?"

"Yes, he did. He was concerned when Paula didn't get pregnant right away. She had tests, which indicated she was fine. He
took tests, too. Paula's brother handled everything."

Lisa nodded. "He probably froze Andrew's sperm when Andrew gave a specimen to be tested."

James grunted. "Clever bastard."

They sat in silence for a while. Lisa heard the muted ticking of
the ornate, glass-encased gold clock sitting on the fireplace mantel.

Curtis spoke first. "Maybe James is right. Maybe she *did* kill
Andrew. Maybe she worried he'd find out about the egg donation."

"How?" Celeste asked. "How would he find out?"

"I'm sure there are tests to determine who the mother is."
Curtis looked at Lisa.

"There are," she told him.

"So we've got her!" James rose. "I'm going to call Russell. This
should break the will."

"Not necessarily," Curtis said. "Since Andrew is the father and
Paula is the birth mother, a judge will probably decide that little
Andrew is, as the will stipulates, a 'natural heir.' What do you think,
Dr. Brockman?"

"You're probably right."

"So she gets it all—millions of dollars." James shook his head
and slumped down into his chair. "Disgusting."

"Not if the police prove that Paula was involved with Chelsea's
murder," Lisa said. "They're planning to arrest her half brother
for medical fraud." She explained briefly what she thought Nestle
had done. "I believe he killed Chelsea and Matthew."

"What do the police think?" Curtis asked.

"They have someone else in custody right now." She told them
about Norman Weld. "I don't think he killed anyone. I'm going to
tell the detective in charge of Chelsea's investigation what I found

out today—that Paula received her eggs. I hope that will convince them that Nestle is involved with the murders. If they arrest him and interrogate him, maybe he'll implicate Paula."

"Implicate, my foot," James said. "Paula's the killer, not her brother. He'd be better off in jail, where she can't get at him, too."

"Do you have proof of all this?" Curtis asked Lisa.

"One of the nurses can identify Paula—she recognized her when she had the embryo transplant done at the clinic. She knows Paula received Chelsea's eggs."

James snorted. "Let's hope Paula doesn't find out about *her*."

chapter forty-four

Lisa couldn't stop thinking about Paula.

After leaving Curtis Rhodes and his family, she stopped at a kosher deli on Pico and ordered a hamburger and fries. Not a great idea, since she'd be having a full Shabbos meal tonight at the Presslers, but she was suddenly very hungry.

Sitting in the elegant Rhodes living room, she'd been convinced by the family's condemnation of Paula. She wondered now if James and the others weren't prejudiced against their late cousin's wife because she wasn't one of them. Because she was from Alabama and had a drawl. Because instead of having the good taste to be born into wealth, she'd married into it.

Ten minutes ago Lisa had been willing to believe that Paula was a cold-blooded manipulator who'd conceived a child and killed her husband for millions of dollars. What if she were simply a woman who had been desperate to conceive because she'd wanted to hold on to her marriage? And now that her husband had died, she was desperate to hold on to their child?

Then why had she told so many lies? Why hadn't she gone to the police when she heard Chelsea was murdered? Even if she'd thought that was a bizarre coincidence, why hadn't she gone when she heard Matthew had disappeared?

Maybe she was afraid to turn against her half brother, Lisa thought. Maybe she couldn't bring herself to believe he was a killer.

Or was *she* the killer?

She'd seemed genuinely devoted to her infant son. *If anything happened to Andy,* Paula had told Lisa, *I'd kill myself.* She was concerned about his breathing to the point that—

Lisa dropped the burger onto her plate. Grabbing her cell phone from her purse, she hunted in one of the side pockets for the card on which she'd written Curtis Rhodes's home number.

She found the card and dialed, praying he was still in. He answered on the second ring.

"This is Lisa Brockman. I forgot to ask you before—now that there's an heir, who inherits Andrew's parents' estate?"

"The baby. Paula inherits part of Andrew's personal estate, according to his own will."

"And if the baby dies, who inherits then?"

"Paula gets everything. Why? You don't think she would harm Andy, do you?" He sounded shaken.

"She told me she's worried because Andy stopped breathing once or twice. She said she took him to the pediatrician. She said she's neurotic because her cousin's child died of SIDS."

"My God!" Curtis whispered.

"I think she's laying the groundwork for SIDS. The pediatrician will say she was worried about it, that she was a conscientious mother. He'll explain that Andy was at a higher risk because he was born premature, that there's SIDS in the family." Lisa took a breath. "I think she's going to smother him in his sleep." And take the money and run.

She said the same thing to Barone in her apartment an hour later. She hadn't been sure he would come, even though she'd left an urgent message at the station. He was polite as always when he stepped into her living room, but she sensed he was tired of responding to her calls. She watched his impassive face when she told him about Grace and Paula and the millions Paula stood to inherit, and knew before he spoke that she'd presented too many theories, that she'd lost credibility.

She told him so. "I know what you're thinking—'Dr. Brockman's theory of the day.' I don't blame you for being skeptical. Talk to Grace. She'll tell you Paula Rhodes received Chelsea's eggs. And Andrew Rhodes's cousins will tell you that he was about to divorce his wife before she conceived."

"So what was the motive for the murders, Dr. Brockman?" Barone asked in a bland voice. "The money Mrs. Rhodes hopes to inherit, or Nestle's fear that his role in the donor-egg switching and his other misconduct would be discovered?"

Was he being sarcastic? "The money."

Barone nodded. "I'll talk to the Rhodes family. I'll contact Grace Fenton, too."

She felt a wave of relief. "What about the baby? I'm convinced Paula plans to kill him. She won't get the money if he's alive, and SIDS is a perfect camouflage. No symptoms. No warning signs."

"She told you she's getting a monitor, didn't she?"

"She said she'll get one if Andy has another episode. So he won't have one for a while, and when he does, it'll be the fatal one. Can you take her in for questioning? That would scare her. She won't kill Andy if she knows the police are watching her."

"I have no cause to arrest her or even question her. Let me talk to Mrs. Fenton."

An hour and a half later, Barone phoned Lisa. "Grace Fenton and her family are gone," he told her. "I drove out to Whittier and spoke to her mother. They skipped. The mother swears she doesn't know where she is."

And now there was no witness. "Her husband just left his job?"

"Apparently. I contacted the bank where he works—he showed up this morning but left around ten, saying he was coming down with the flu. Before he left, he cleaned out a savings account."

"Grace is afraid Paula will have her killed if she testifies. Paula's going to kill her baby, Detective Barone. You have to arrest her." Lisa's voice sounded shrill to her ears.

"On what grounds? That she's going to inherit millions? It's not exactly a crime. Ostensibly, she's a loving mother. You thought so. I'm putting out an APB on Mrs. Fenton. I'll bring her in as a material witness."

"What if you don't find her in time?"

Barone sighed. "I'm doing the best I can, Dr. Brockman."

She phoned Curtis Rhodes and told him the bad news. "Detective Barone is trying to find the nurse. In the meantime, I think you should advise Paula that you're contesting the will and are demanding that DNA testing be done on Andy to determine who his mother is."

"She can refuse, and a judge will support her. After all, she's the birth mother. The will says nothing about not using donor eggs."

"Yes, but this way, you'll be putting her on notice, and she'll think twice before harming Andy." When he didn't respond, she said, "Mr. Rhodes?"

"I'll talk to the family, and we'll decide what to do."

"Don't take too long to decide, Mr. Rhodes. I don't know how long Paula will wait."

chapter forty-five

Berta eyed Lisa through the privacy window and admitted her into the grand entry hall.

"*Momento, por favor,*" she said and disappeared.

Lisa took a few steps to her right and looked into an enormous sunken living room. Two oversized cream-colored chenille sofas sat in the middle of the room on an area rug with muted shades of mint green and gray. In the far corner of the room was a black grand piano. Above the fireplace was a lithograph that, even from a distance, she recognized as a Chagall. There was something familiar about the feel of the room—the quiet, elegant beauty, the artwork. She'd probably seen it photographed in *Architectural Digest.*

"What brings you here this Sunday morning, Dr. Brockman?" Paula asked. "No bad news, I hope?"

Lisa turned around. "Thank goodness, no. Please call me Lisa, by the way." She smiled. "I hope this isn't a bad time."

"Not at all. I've been packing and could use a break. I'm taking Andy to Alabama tonight to see his grandparents."

"How long will you be gone?" Lisa asked, trying to sound casual. Was Paula running away because she was anxious about Nestle implicating her? Would Andy have a fatal episode and succumb to SIDS in Alabama?

"I'm not sure. To tell you the truth, with my husband gone, there's nothing to keep me here. I don't have many friends, and Andrew's family hasn't exactly welcomed me. What's that?" She pointed to the wrapped, oblong box Lisa was holding.

"I came to bring you something. Actually, it's for Andy." She handed Paula the box.

"A present?" Paula smiled. "That's so sweet. Let's go in here."

Lisa followed her into the living room and sat next to her on one of the sofas. She watched as Paula tore off the paper, opened the box, and stared at the contents beneath the white tissue paper.

"It's the monitor," Lisa said. "You sounded so anxious about Andy on the phone the other day. I was near a medical supply house and picked one up for you."

She'd done so on Friday, before going to the Presslers to spend the Sabbath. The weekend would have been perfect—Sam had been there; the Presslers, as always, had made her feel welcome; she'd enjoyed playing with the children and getting to know Elana. But Lisa hadn't been able to stop worrying about Andy, and wondering about Grace. As of this morning, Barone still hadn't located the nurse.

"This must be expensive," Paula said, looking up. "I can't allow you to pay for it."

Lisa wished she could read the woman's mind. "It isn't a big deal. And I'm happy to do it. Frankly, since we last talked, I've been anxious about Andy, just as you are. So I thought, why should you worry about SIDS? Why take even the smallest risk when there are monitors to prevent it, right?"

"Right."

"It's very easy to use. Here, I'll show you." Lisa demonstrated how the straps should be wrapped around the baby's chest, how to read the dial. "The alarm is loud enough to wake you, so you can finally get a good night's sleep."

"I'm touched." Paula's voice was soft, her drawl pronounced. "I honestly don't know what to say, how to thank you. You hardly know us." Her dark eyes were bright with tears.

"Knowing Andy's safe is thanks enough." Had Paula been

convincingly teary when she told Chelsea how happy she was to meet her? How had she persuaded Chelsea not to tell her parents or her boyfriend? Had she promised to take care of Chelsea's tuition? To pay her off? To let her help raise Andy? *We can both be his mother, Chelsea, but only you and I can know.*

Lisa lowered her voice. "We've only met once and talked a few times, but now that Matthew's gone, I understand all too well the pain you've been going through since your husband's death. And I thought about what you said—how there are no coincidences, how you and Chelsea were destined to meet. Maybe you and I were destined to meet, too. I'd like to think so, anyway."

She smiled again and stood, proud of the fact that for once, her face hadn't betrayed her. She slipped her purse strap onto her shoulder. "Good luck with your interior decorating." At the arched living room entrance, she turned. "Oh, I almost forgot to tell you! You'll be happy to know they nabbed that man."

Paula looked blank. "Which man?"

"The one who called you and pretended to be Detective Barone. The one who was following me."

There was a moment of silence. Then Paula said, "Really? That's wonderful." She cocked her head and gazed at Lisa. "Who is he?"

"Just a reporter. Can you believe it?" She laughed. "And here I was *terrified* that he was going to kill me."

"I'm so glad, Lisa. You must be enormously relieved."

She nodded. "I am. Nothing will change the fact that Matthew's dead, but it's gratifying to know that the police have the murderer in custody. He was a lab technician at the clinic. I saw him every day." She shuddered. "Apparently he killed Dr. Cantrell, too."

Paula frowned. "I heard on the news that Dr. Cantrell killed himself."

Lisa shook her head. "The police think he was murdered. To tell you the truth, I was shocked when the lab tech was arrested. I had this wild scenario in my head. I thought, What if Chelsea was killed because she tracked down the woman who received her eggs? What if Matthew was killed because *he* knew the identity of the woman? Crazy, isn't it?"

"I have to say it sounds bizarre." Paula's smile revealed a hint of condescension. "Why would she kill Chelsea?"

"She panicked. Maybe she was afraid Chelsea would want her

child back. Maybe there's money involved." Lisa shrugged. "I didn't think it through. I *did* mention it to Barone."

"*Did* you?" Paula nodded. "And what did he say?"

It was eerie, Lisa thought, looking evil in the face. "That I'd need proof, a witness who would testify as to who received Chelsea's eggs. I think he was humoring me."

"But you don't have a witness?"

She wondered where Grace was. Had Barone found her? "No. It was just a theory, anyway." She shrugged again. "And the police have their suspect in custody. I never would have believed him capable of murder. It's funny, isn't it, how people can fool you?"

"Very," Paula said.

"Take good care of Andy."

"You know I will," she said softly.

"Don't forget to take the monitor with you to Alabama."

"I wouldn't dream of it."

chapter forty-six

Lisa was fine until she was sitting in her car. When she turned on the ignition, she started shaking uncontrollably and had to wait a few minutes before she was calm enough to drive to a Judaica store on Pico, where she bought a silver match box and tray for Elana and story books for the children.

She'd told Elana this morning that she'd be going home today. "Spend next Shabbos with us," Elana had said, and Lisa had happily accepted.

The Pressler house was empty when she returned from Paula's. Lisa packed her few things and took the files, stack by heavy stack, to the trunk of her car. She wasn't sure what she'd do with them when she got home—cart them upstairs or dump them in the trash. All that paper, all those trees. She smoothed the bedspread, gave a last look around the guest room, then slipped a note under the ribbon of one of the wrapped gifts on the desk, next to the spare key. She remembered to kiss the mezuzah on the front doorpost on her way out.

Back at home, she phoned Sam and he came right over. She couldn't believe she'd ever doubted him. On Friday night they'd taken a long walk, and she'd told him everything about Paula, about Nestle. Now she described her visit to Paula.

"I still think you're crazy for going there." There was admiration in his voice and in the way he looked at her.

She loved the way he looked at her. She loved his smile, loved the way he was constantly adjusting his glasses and his skullcap, loved being around him. It seemed so natural and easy, eating sandwiches together at the dinette table, sitting on the couch afterward and laughing morosely about their career options while Rosie O'Donnell chatted happily with one of her celebrity guests. His arm was almost touching her, and she leaned close to him and wondered if, like her, he was thinking about Matthew. She was resigned to the possibility that the police might never find his body, that she would never have the closure she needed. There were worse things in life.

Sam left to do some errands. She was used to long days crowded with patients and reports and didn't know how to cope with idleness. There was nothing to do in her apartment—no dusting, no laundry to wash—and though she loved to read, she hadn't been able to concentrate lately.

She was working on the daily crossword, listening to "Candle in the Wind," when the phone rang. She ran to answer it, but it wasn't Barone. It was Edmond. She apologized for not returning his call.

"I had a busy few days," she said, and told him about the Hoffman delivery, wondering as she was talking whether he knew she'd gone to Nestle, whether he was aware of what Nestle had been doing. Edmond told her he was shocked about Norman Weld. She said she was, too—not really a lie.

"At least it's over, Lisa. If there's anything Georgia or I can do . . ." he said, and she promised to call if she needed help.

She went for a brisk walk. When she returned she learned that Curtis Rhodes had called. She phoned him back; he told her the attorney had advised Paula that the family was contesting the will and would ask that DNA testing be done on Andy.

More bad news for Paula. "How did she react?" Lisa asked.

"He said she was very calm, very polite. Then again, she's a good actress. She told him that although she couldn't stop us from contesting the will, she has no intention of subjecting Andy to any maternity tests, since it's a matter of record that she gave birth to him."

"At least you put her on notice. I stopped by late this morning and dropped off a monitor. She knows that I know."

"That's good. Then the baby's safe."

"I'm not sure. She's leaving tonight with Andy to visit her parents. She's staying indefinitely—she says there's nothing to keep her here now that her husband is gone."

In Alabama, would the monitor malfunction? Or would Andy have a fatal accident? Apprehension gnawed at her. She said goodbye to Curtis and phoned the police station. Miraculously, Barone was there.

"There's nothing I can do," he said after she informed him Paula was leaving town. "Let's hope we locate Mrs. Fenton soon."

"Paula's leaving *tonight*."

"I'm not happy about that, either." He sounded annoyed. "If we find Mrs. Fenton after Mrs. Rhodes leaves, and she verifies what you've told me, I'll personally fly to Alabama and bring Mrs. Rhodes and the child back. All right?"

"All right." She hung up the phone and paced around the apartment. Fifteen minutes later she called the station again and waited impatiently for Barone to get on the line.

"I'm sorry to bother you, Detective, but—"

"Dr. Brockman, I know you're concerned, but I can't get much done if you call every five minutes." His tone was clipped, terse.

"What if she's leaving the country? She *has* to be worried that her brother's going to be arrested any day. If he implicates her in the murders, she can kiss the money good-bye, in which case she doesn't need the baby. She'll disappear, and no one will ever find her." If she was leaving the country, she wouldn't take Andy—he'd be an encumbrance, a risk.

"Dr. Brockman—"

"Can you check with the airlines to see where she's going?" Lisa had heard the weary impatience in his voice. "You must be angry with me. I'd resent anyone who tried to tell *me* how to do my job. But I feel so *frustrated*, Detective."

"I was trying to say I've already phoned two airlines. It occurred to me, too, that she might not be going to Alabama."

"I'm sorry." Her face was hot with embarrassment.

"I'll call *you* if I hear anything."

Sam phoned. He had a Talmud class to attend at eight but offered to take her out for a quick pizza dinner—"A cheap first

date, but what do you want from an unemployed fertility specialist?" She wanted to go. She wanted to wait for Barone's call. She
said no to the pizza but invited him to come over after the Talmud
class, and fixed herself a salad and an English muffin, which she
ate while she worked on the crossword puzzle.

She couldn't stay in the apartment, willing the phone to ring.
She drove to the Ralphs on Overland to buy groceries she didn't
really need and was standing in the checkout line when her pager
beeped.

It was Barone.

Feeling conspicuously showy, she called him on her cellular
phone, but of course no one paid attention, because L.A., and
probably the whole country, was filled with people who used cell
phones. She was so nervous while she waited for the detective to
come on the line that she didn't hear what the young man bagging
her groceries said, and had to ask him to repeat his question.

"Paper or plastic, ma'am?"

"Plastic," she said and heard Barone's voice, low and musical:
"She's booked on a flight to Alabama at ten-forty tonight."

"Oh." One part disappointment, two parts relief.

"She's also booked in first class on a United Airlines eleven
forty-five P.M. nonstop flight to Mexico City."

Lisa held her breath. "With the baby?"

"Just one ticket, in her name. One way. She doesn't have to
buy the baby a ticket—airlines block seats for children under two,
unless the flight is sold out. Which it isn't. But she hasn't informed
the airline that she's bringing an infant."

Lisa checked her watch. It was almost nine-thirty. "How will
you stop her?"

chapter forty-seven

A limo was parked behind the Jaguar. From across the street Lisa watched the uniformed driver place two suitcases in the trunk.

A few minutes later she saw Paula coming out the front door. She was wearing dark slacks and a blazer; a large satchel was slung over her shoulder.

The driver opened the left passenger door and helped Paula in, then shut the door and got behind the wheel. In a moment he backed out of the driveway and, facing Santa Monica Boulevard, pulled away from the house.

When the limo was halfway down the block, Lisa heard a siren and saw a car with a flashing domed red light cut the limo off. Barone's unmarked car.

Almost simultaneously, a patrol car arrived and parked in front of Paula's house; two uniformed police—one male, one female—walked to the front door and rang the bell.

Berta answered. Lisa could see that the maid was talking to the police but had no idea what Berta was saying. After several minutes she saw the limo turn around, followed by Barone. The limo pulled into the driveway. Barone blocked it with his car.

Barone and another plainclothes male detective got out of the car. While Barone went over to the passenger door of the limo, the other detective approached the driver. The limo's rear lights turned off.

Lisa knew that Barone would probably kill her, but she found it impossible to remain in her Altima. As quietly as she could, she got out of her car, crossed the street, and stood to the right side of the house, where she hoped she'd be inconspicuous.

The two uniformed police disappeared into the house. A few minutes later the male returned and approached Barone. Lisa could hear them talking but was too far away to make out what they were saying. She moved closer.

". . . infant is upstairs, asleep, Detective."

"Aside from the maid, is there anyone else in the house?"

"No."

Barone turned and leaned toward the open passenger window. "Mrs. Rhodes, leave your purse on the seat and get out of the car slowly. Have your hands where I can see them."

Paula must have responded, but Lisa couldn't hear.

Barone repeated his instructions. The door opened and Paula emerged.

"Would you care to explain what the hell is going on?" she demanded coolly. "Why are you treating me as if I'm a criminal?"

"Mrs. Rhodes, where were you going when I detained you?"

"I don't see why that's any of your business, Detective."

"Mrs. Rhodes, you can cooperate or not." Quiet, unhurried. "If you don't, the limo driver can provide us with the answer. So I'll ask you again, where were you going? And I hope you won't say to the market."

"To the airport." She was almost spitting the words.

"What was your planned destination?"

She hesitated, then said, "Alabama. I'm visiting my parents."

"How long are you planning to be away?"

"I'm not sure. A few days, maybe longer."

"When we spoke a few days ago, you mentioned you have an infant son. Who's taking care of him while you're away?"

Even from where Lisa was standing she could see Paula's suddenly tense expression.

"I have a nanny coming in the morning to take care of him. In the meantime, my housekeeper is watching him."

"Are you referring to Berta Gonzalez?"

"Yes. She's wonderful with him."

"She doesn't speak any English, isn't that true?"

Another hesitation. "No, but she doesn't need to speak English to diaper or feed or bathe him."

"What if there were an emergency? You mentioned to Dr. Lisa Brockman that you're concerned about your baby's breathing, about the possibility that he might die from SIDS. I find it extremely strange that, under those circumstances, you'd leave him in the care of a woman who doesn't speak English."

"Andy's been better the past few days. And Dr. Brockman was kind enough to drop off a monitor to protect him."

"Yes, but it's not attached to him. Officer Volansky checked. Your son is sleeping without the monitor, which is downstairs in the living room."

She pursed her lips.

Barone reached into the limo and pulled out her purse. He opened it and removed a slim envelope. The airline ticket, Lisa guessed.

He said, "This is a one-way ticket to Mexico City, Mrs. Rhodes. I guess your travel agent goofed."

She cleared her throat. "Look, I lied about Alabama because this isn't really any of your business. I'm just going to Mexico for two days to relax. I've been under a great deal of stress lately. My doctor recommended a break."

"This ticket is one-way."

"That's because I'm not exactly sure when I'm returning." She reached for the ticket.

He moved it away. "Very extravagant, Mrs. Rhodes. Buying two one-way tickets is far more expensive than buying a round-trip and making a change."

Her smile was patronizing, aloof. "Money isn't one of my concerns, Detective. My husband left me well provided for."

"I'm pleased to hear it. What's the name and phone number of the nanny you hired?"

Her smile froze. "She's with an agency, but I don't know the number offhand. I'd have to look it up."

"I'll have Officer Volansky bring the phone directory."

"I don't know that it's listed. I got the number from a friend who happens to be out of town now."

"Didn't you write the number down for your housekeeper?

Didn't you write it down for yourself?" When she didn't respond, he said, "Mrs. Rhodes, where's Dr. Gordon's body?"

"I don't know what you're talking about." She was standing very straight now.

"You remember Dr. Gordon. He fertilized a number of Chelsea Wright's eggs with your late husband's sperm and transferred the embryos into your body. That's how you conceived your son."

Paula shook her head. "You've been talking to Dr. Brockman, haven't you? I feel terribly sorry for her, but she's delusional. I have no idea how she came up with this outrageous story."

"She came up with it from the person who will testify that Chelsea forced her to reveal your identity. The same person who revealed your identity to Dr. Cantrell and made him a threat to you."

Lisa's breathing quickened. Had Barone located Grace? Or was he bluffing?

"What person?" Paula asked.

"I'm not at liberty to say."

Paula's voice hardened. "You don't have a witness, because this never happened. Detective, I'm not answering any more questions. I'm going to ask you to leave now."

"I'm afraid I can't do that. Mrs. Rhodes, you're under arrest for child abandonment and child endangerment. Please turn around and place your hands behind your back."

She laughed. "Has the whole world gone insane? This is a trumped-up charge. My attorney will have me out in five minutes."

"We *do* have a witness. By the way, did I mention that your brother is being arrested at this very moment? He'll be charged with murder, or accessory to—the D.A. will decide after Jerome talks to us. He was extremely nervous the last time we spoke. I have the feeling he'll be eager to tell his story. At which point I'm confident that we'll add murder to the charges against you. Turn around, please."

She stared at him for a long moment, then obeyed.

He snapped handcuffs on her wrists, then continued speaking. "The female officer who talked with your housekeeper will stay with your son until someone from social services arrives. I'm going to read you your rights now, Mrs. Rhodes. You have the right to remain silent. You have the right to an attorney . . ."

Less than a minute later Barone was done. Paula walked down the driveway, ahead of him. As they neared the street, Lisa tried to flatten herself against the wall of the neighboring house, but Paula spotted her and stopped.

They stared at each other.

Paula continued walking to the patrol car. Officer Volansky opened the rear door. She turned toward Lisa.

"By the way, I wouldn't grieve too long for your fiancé if I were you. He told me you were pathetically boring, and lousy in bed." She smiled and got into the car.

chapter forty-eight

The hotel room was large but old-fashioned, and the ceiling fan was making the warm temperature comfortable.

The bellboy hung up Lisa's garment bag and set her suitcase on a webbed tray at the foot of the bed. She tipped him and locked the door after he left, then walked into the bathroom and splashed cool water on her face.

She looked tired and disheveled from the flight. She put on a blusher and lipstick and brushed her hair, then sprayed Giorgio in the hollow of her neck and on her wrists. She'd never used this perfume before; she was aware of the strong fragrance minutes later as she turned down the bedspread and changed into a silk print nightgown and matching robe.

She took two scented candles from her suitcase and placed them on the round table in the corner of the room. She lit them and switched off the overhead fixture, then decided the room was too dark. She turned on the lamp on one of the nightstands.

The room had a small balcony. She parted the drapes and

looked outside at the darkened city. She hadn't been nervous when she'd decided to come—it had been her suggestion, in fact—but she was trembling now with nervousness and excitement. She wanted everything to be perfect. She wondered if Sam was nervous, too, and twisted the ring on her finger.

She heard the sound of a key in the lock. The door opened and she knew without turning that he was here.

Her heart fluttered, then beat rapidly. She wondered idly what effect a rapid pulse would have on the perfume, which was making her a little queasy.

"I like the candles," he said. "I brought champagne, to celebrate."

The room had carpeting, but she could hear his footsteps. A moment later she felt his hands on her waist. He ran them up and down over her hips, then moved her long hair aside and kissed the back of her neck.

"You have no idea how much I've wanted to do that, how much I want you," he whispered.

"Me, too," she whispered back.

"You're shivering. No second thoughts, I hope?" He caressed her shoulders.

"It's Andy," she said in a voice she could barely hear herself.

He tightened his grip. "You're not going to back out now, are you?"

She didn't answer. She placed her hands on top of his.

"You have to do it, Paula. Otherwise everything was for nothing. Chelsea, Ted." He sounded anxious and a little angry.

She still didn't respond.

"It's the only way you'll get the money. We talked about this, Paula. It didn't bother you at the time."

"I'm not the woman I was then," she drawled, and she could tell from the quick intake of his breath that he recognized her voice. A thrill of fear mixed with satisfaction coursed through her.

She turned slowly. He stared at her, then stepped back.

"Hello, Matthew." She smiled. "You're looking handsome as always. A little pale, though."

He swallowed hard. "Your hair," he managed to say.

"It's a wig." She pulled it off and walked to the bed, where she put it down. She shook her blond hair. "I borrowed it from Naomi Hoffman. You know Naomi—she's the one you chose to be the recipient of Chelsea's eggs. Why did you choose her, by the way?

Because I mentioned that she inspired me to become Orthodox
again? Having a little fun, were you?"

He ran his fingers through his hair. "How did you find me?"

"Paula told the police. They're coming down here tomorrow
to arrest you, but I had to see you first, alone. They'll be very angry
when they find out, but I don't care."

"Lisa—"

"I didn't believe Paula when she said you were alive. The police
didn't believe her, either, at first. Can you imagine how I felt, Matthew? *Can* you?" It was hard to keep from yelling, but she did.

"I couldn't tell you. You don't understand."

"I borrowed this nightgown and robe from Paula—she said it's
your favorite set. And the Giorgio. She says you like that, too. Do
you like the new me, Matthew? Paula said you found the old me
pathetically boring and lousy in bed. I have to tell you, that hurt."
She'd thought over and over about every time she'd been with Matthew, searching for some sign, some clue. She'd found none, but
she'd still felt naive, stupid. Knowing that he'd fooled everyone
else—Sam, Selena, Edmond—offered little consolation.

"I love you, Lisa," he said, his voice husky with urgency.
"Paula's a liar. You have to believe me."

"That's what I thought at first, too. Not Matthew, I told her.
He'd never cheat on me. I thought she was just trying to get back
at me for having her arrested. Did I mention she's in jail? She's
being indicted for murder."

"Thank God!" He expelled a breath. "Paula is evil, Lisa. She
killed Chelsea and threatened to kill *you* unless I did everything she
said. She killed Ted, too, when he blackmailed her."

Lisa frowned. "You weren't involved in any of this?"

"Of course not! She's obsessed with me, Lisa. She planned
everything! She said I had to leave the country, and she booked my
tickets in her dead husband's name. She gave me his driver's license
for identification. She made me put the money in your pantry. She
told me where to leave the car. She made me cut myself so she
could put blood in the trunk. I've been living in fear for my life,
and for yours." He took a tentative step closer.

Lisa tilted her head and gazed at him, her forehead furrowed.
"The police found a gun packed in a tin inside her suitcase," she
said quietly.

"You see? She was planning to come here and kill me, because
I could expose her. She almost killed *you* twice. She hates you because she knows I love you. She attacked you in the clinic. The

other time she tried running you down. She gloated when she told me about it. She's ruthless, Lisa."

"You brought champagne, Matthew. To celebrate, you said." Her lips quivered.

He lifted his hands. "I wanted her to think I was on her side. I was *acting*, Lisa."

"What about her baby? A minute ago you were encouraging her to kill him. 'It's the only way you'll get the money.' Those were your words. Were you acting then, too?"

"I thought she was testing me." He sighed. "She's done it before. She's always playing games. I wanted to find out the details so I could notify the police anonymously, so they could save Andy. I've dedicated my life to helping women conceive—do you honestly think I'd condone taking a child's life?"

Her eyes filled with tears. "I don't know what to think. I'm confused, Matthew. I came here so angry. I loved you so much," she whispered. "When I thought you were dead . . ."

"Of *course* you were angry," he said softly. "I hated putting you through that. But now you know the truth." He took another step closer. "Thank God you're all right, Lisa. That's all I care about. I never thought I'd see you again." He pulled her close and stroked her hair.

She rested her head against his chest. "You hoped I'd find the paper in your trash, right? You wanted me to read the 'Notes' file. You knew I'd figure out the password. But you didn't write the truth in it."

"Paula dictated what to write. She knew you'd try to find me. She wanted to lead you and the police in the wrong direction. It was *her* idea to write about the research, about Chelsea going to another clinic."

"So you lied to me?" Lisa asked quietly.

"I told you—she said she'd kill you if I didn't do everything exactly the way she wanted it."

"Why didn't you go to the police, Matthew?"

"I couldn't! Her brother, Jerome, convinced me to give patients donor eggs without their knowledge to boost the IVF success rates. I was desperate to keep the clinic going, so I went along with it. Paula said if I went to the police, Jerome would talk. I panicked—I couldn't face going to jail. I'm not proud of what I did, Lisa. I hope you can forgive me."

She searched his face for a moment, then drew her hand back and smacked him hard across the cheek. "That's for letting me think you were dead and making my life hell for the past few weeks."

He blinked. "Lisa, for God's sake—"

"You and Paula must've had a good laugh when you wrote the 'Notes' file. Little Lisa is smart, but not smart enough—is that what you figured? Jerome is in custody, Matthew. And Grace talked to the police. She told them everything."

The nurse, Barone had informed Lisa, hadn't been completely truthful with her. When Chelsea was killed, Matthew had confronted Grace and told her he knew she'd revealed Paula's identity to Chelsea. He'd said that he feared for his life, that she should be afraid, too, because Paula had millions of dollars and endless resources and would stop at nothing to protect herself. And Grace had believed him, especially after he disappeared and the police found blood in his car.

"I was trying to protect Grace! Paula kept wanting to know how Chelsea found her—I knew if I told her about Grace, she'd kill her. So I frightened Grace and told Paula that Chelsea probably accessed the computer file. You *have* to believe me." He grabbed Lisa's shoulders.

She took pleasure from the fact that his face was bright red where she'd slapped him. "No, I don't, Matthew. You can tell your story to the police when they come tomorrow. But you won't be here tomorrow, will you?" She sighed. "You'll disappear and no one will find you."

He studied her face. "That's why you came here alone, before the police. To warn me. You still love me, don't you, Lisa? Admit it," he said softly. Smiling, he leaned forward to kiss her.

She stepped back and turned, facing the balcony.

"I'd leave the champagne, but it isn't kosher," he said.

She folded her arms across her chest and watched his reflection in the sparkling glass of the French door as he crossed the room and opened the door to the hall.

Barone was waiting, just as they'd planned.

chapter forty-nine

The social hall was crowded with round tables, many of them already occupied. Sam made his way across the room to the men's side while Lisa looked around, trying to decide where to sit. She heard her name and turned.

"I'm so glad you could make it," Naomi said, coming closer. She looked slim in a two-piece teal cotton piqué suit. "I'd love to have you sit with me and the family."

"That's not necessary, Naomi. I can find a seat."

"I insist." She smiled warmly and touched Lisa's arm. "If it weren't for you, we might not be having this *simcha*," she said, using the Hebrew word for "joyous occasion."

"All right." Lisa smiled shyly in return. "You look wonderful, by the way. I see you've lost all your weight."

"Just about. I can hardly believe Reuben and Aliza are a month old, that three weeks have passed since his bris."

Even though Reuben was premature, his circumcision had taken place on time, when he was eight days old, on a Thursday morning. Lisa had attended the ceremony in Rabbi Hoffman's small storefront shul on Beverly Boulevard and Ogden. That same morning Baruch had celebrated the twins' arrival with a large breakfast prepared by Baruch and Naomi's family and friends. "We named our daughter for you," he'd told Lisa.

Lisa had been touched then; she was touched again now. "Where are the babies?"

"In the stroller. My mom's watching them and whispering to Reuben, getting him ready for the big event."

Today was the *pidyon haben*, the redemption of the firstborn male child that took place when the infant was thirty-one days old. Lisa had been to a *pidyon haben* before—two of her high school classmates had given birth to firstborn males—but that had been long ago, and she'd forgotten the details of the ritual ceremony. She remembered that the baby's father redeemed his infant son by paying the equivalent of five pieces of silver to a Kohen, a direct descendant of the priestly family that began with Aaron, the brother of Moses. And that, following the ceremony, everyone present rejoiced in a festive meal.

Naomi introduced Lisa to the family—her two grandmothers, a younger sister, several cousins. Naomi's mother-in-law and mother welcomed Lisa warmly.

"So nice to see you again, Dr. Brockman," Naomi's mother said. "God willing, we'll meet only at *simchas*." She pointed proudly at her granddaughter and grandson, who were half dozing in a double stroller. Both infants were dressed in beautiful white knit outfits with embroidered collars.

Baruch came to the table. He greeted Lisa warmly, too, and she wished him mazel tov, feeling a kernel of residual embarrassment at the fact that she'd suspected him of murder.

"We're ready," he told Naomi, his voice filled with tenderness. He was beaming.

In the center of the table, on a silver tray, lay a white Battenberg-lace-covered pillow. Naomi carefully lifted Reuben from the stroller and placed him on the pillow. He whimpered; she inserted a pacifier in his mouth and stroked his cheek.

Naomi's mother removed her cocktail ring and a strand of pearls and placed both on the pillow, next to Reuben. The grandmothers, sister, and cousins followed suit, adding rings, brooches, a necklace of onyx-and-silver beads, a gold watch. Women from the other tables joined in the ritual, and within minutes Reuben was laden with jewels.

The reason behind bedecking the infant with jewelry, Lisa's father had explained to her a long time ago, was to show love for the mitzvah, the biblical commandment. Her mother had added that the jewels enhanced the value of the child in the father's eyes. Not that Baruch needed any help to realize the value of his tiny son or daughter.

Lisa watched as Naomi, flanked by her mother-in-law and by her mother, who was holding her granddaughter, carried the tray with Reuben and his finery to her father, who then passed it to her father-in-law. Rabbi Hoffman set the tray on a table in front of Baruch and a clean-shaven man Lisa assumed was the Kohen. Lisa, with the other women, followed along; soon they were all crowded around the new father and the priest, who were now standing.

Baruch was holding his son. "This is my firstborn son," he declared, his voice husky with emotion. "He is the first issue of his mother's womb, and the Holy One, Blessed is He, has commanded to redeem him. . . ."

From across the room Sam caught Lisa's eye and smiled. She smiled back. If she married him and their first child was a boy, he'd told her on the way here, they would have a *pidyon haben,* too. "Even though I'm a convert?" She'd asked. "Even though," he'd said softly, and she'd felt a flutter of joy.

The Kohen asked, "Which do you prefer: to give away your firstborn son, who is the first issue of his mother's womb, or do you prefer to redeem him for five shekels as you are required to do by the Torah?"

What if the father chose not to redeem his son? she remembered asking her own father. She remembered his answer: that redeeming the son wasn't really optional; that even if the father didn't pay the five shekels, the child didn't belong to the Kohen. So why did the Kohen ask the question? she'd pressed. To increase the father's love for his son and the mitzvah of redeeming him, Lisa's father had explained.

Ever since she'd returned from Mexico, Lisa felt as though she, too, had been redeemed. Barone had refused at first to let her go, but she'd worn him out with her arguments—that it wouldn't be dangerous, that she'd earned the right to confront Matthew, that she needed to reclaim her dignity, her pride.

Baruch said, "I wish to redeem my son. I present you with the cost of his redemption as I am required to do by the Torah." Holding five silver dollars, he recited the blessing for the redemption, then another, more general blessing. There were tears in his eyes.

Lisa joined the others and said, "Amen." This evening she'd read in an ArtScroll prayer book the teaching behind this ritual: "Though firstborn children are the culmination of much yearning, labor, and sacrifice, and it is human nature to want them for oneself, the Torah wants man to recognize that the child is a gift from God."

She thought about Naomi and Baruch and the countless other couples she'd treated who had incurred enormous debts and suffered great emotional distress to have a child. She thought about Paula Rhodes and could not comprehend that a mother would kill her child for money.

Paula was in jail, waiting to be tried for murder. So was Matthew. Both had accused each other of carrying out the murders.

Jerome had turned state's evidence in exchange for total immunity. He'd admitted implanting the IUDs and convincing Matthew to substitute donor ova for patients' eggs. Because of the worrisome lack of donor eggs, he'd also referred women who wanted tubal ligations to Matthew. And Matthew, telling the women that he was preparing them for contraceptive surgery, would give them drugs to stimulate ovulation, then remove their eggs during the surgery. Lisa wanted Nestle punished but understood how valuable his testimony would be. There was no perfect justice, she knew.

Norman was still under psychiatric observation; Lisa had visited him at the hospital. She knew from Barone that Matthew wanted to talk to her. She had many questions to ask him but had no intention of seeing him again and listening to his lies.

Some questions were minor: When had he put the money in her pantry? Whose idea had it been to erase his name and write it in again on the patient files—Matthew's or Paula's? Why had he erased Sam's name to implicate him? Why had he kept accurate data regarding donors and egg recipients, data that had led Lisa to discover what he and Nestle were scheming? Because as a scientist, he'd wanted to document the success of his procedures? Because he'd been driven by his ego?

When had he ripped the September pages from the lab log, and the July page that contained Chelsea's name and Paula's alias? When had he begun his affair with Paula—long before he helped her conceive? Paula had told Barone she'd decorated Matthew's apartment—that was why her living room had seemed so familiar to Lisa. Was that when they had become close? Had they schemed while looking at fabric swatches?

Some questions were more important:

Why had he chosen Lisa as his "fiancée"—because she was naive, trusting, lonely? (She would like to think that at some point he'd loved her, but she suspected that it had always been about greed.) Had he felt even the smallest qualms about letting her believe he'd been murdered, knowing that she would be racked with guilt and confusion about a marriage he knew would never take place?

Where had he learned to be so cruel?

When had he become a killer?

The Kohen accepted the money and, swinging it in a circular fashion over the baby's head, recited the ritual blessing of redemption: "This instead of that . . . this is pardoned because of that. . . ."

Edmond was committed to reopening the clinic when the negative press died down. Lisa didn't think the press would *ever* die down—new lawsuits were being filed daily against the clinic. And she wasn't sure she wanted to work for Edmond. Unlike Barone, she wasn't convinced that he hadn't known about the donor-egg scheme. Or that he'd wanted to know. She blamed herself, too—she'd had reservations about the ethics of the refund policy but had done nothing. She should have spoken up.

She wasn't worried about her career. She'd get another position. In the meantime, she could use the money she'd received from selling her engagement ring. She felt not an iota of guilt.

The Kohen placed his right hand on the infant's head and blessed him: ". . . *Hashem* will protect you from every evil. He will guard your soul."

"Amen," Lisa said fervently, not only for Reuben and his sister, both of whom had almost been victims of Matthew and Paula, but also for Andy, who had certainly been redeemed from evil. She was confident that he'd be in good hands with Chelsea's parents, who were officially adopting him. Curtis Rhodes had told her a few days ago that his family approved of the adoption. He wasn't certain as to the disposition of the trust, but he'd guaranteed that the boy wouldn't lack for anything.

The Kohen handed the infant to Baruch and filled a cup of wine.

Out of the corner of her eye, Lisa saw Sam appear at her side. Her heart swelled with happiness.

Elana had gone with her to meet with a board of three rabbis who handled conversions. Though Lisa had been converted as a child, the rabbis had explained sympathetically, she would have to convert again because she had rejected the observance of Judaism. She'd felt a flicker of the old resentment—at the rabbis, at her parents—but she was over that now.

In every phone call with her parents, she could hear how happy they were about her return to observance, how pleased they were about Sam. And she was deriving immense pleasure from studying Judaism with Elana. The process might take a while, she'd warned Sam. The rabbis wanted to be sure this was what she wanted.

I'm a patient guy, he'd said. I've been waiting years for the right person.

He leaned close to her now. "My parents are coming next week," he whispered. "They can't wait to meet you."

"I want to meet them, too." She felt a spasm of normal anxiety, but not the numbing fear that would have overwhelmed her two months ago. Another redemption, from the pain of her past.

"They're going to love you," Sam said.

"You think so, huh? I guess we're a match made in Heaven," she said lightly.

"No question about it." His gray eyes were serious. "You know what Benjie told me? Forty days before a child's conception, a heavenly voice decrees who his or her mate will be."

Not Asher, she thought. Not Matthew. "I like that," she said quietly, nodding.

"I thought you would." His smile was a caress.

The Kohen took the cup of wine and recited a blessing, and the crowd said, "Amen."